HANNAH'S HEART

KLAUDEN'S RING SAGA

HANNAH'S HEART

AWARD-WINNING AUTHOR
JM PAQUETTE

DEDICATION

To the 9pm Club, without whom this book would have taken
another two years to finish.

TRIGGER WARNING

This book contains violence, gore, a lot of blood spatter, and steamy sexual content.

TABLE OF CONTENTS

I

Hannah Tallerin, once Hannah van Kreeosk, stood at the end of an alley. She didn't recognize the place, but the buildings on either side were pale, probably white stone in the sunlight, though it was dark now, the only light from the half-moon drifting through the scuttling clouds. It was windy, Hannah's red hair blowing first back from her face, then swirling around before her eyes, the faint tinge of the ocean in the air. She quickly tucked her curls behind her ears, peering through the dim light, keen vampire eyes picking up the details of stone and dirt as she expected, but she couldn't see anything obviously out of place. Still, something wasn't right. She could feel it.

There were two people at the other end of the alley, the taller form embracing the other like a lover, a head bent into the other's neck. Hannah recognized the pose, having held her share of victims just like that, and she stayed where she was, allowing the vampire to finish. Time was strange, and Hannah waited for her mind to fill in the missing pieces.

When she saw the body of the victim slowly slump to the ground, gently drifting in a motion defying normal laws of gravity, Hannah understood.

This is a dream.

But that wasn't completely accurate. This didn't feel like her own dream. She had enough experience with other people's dreams to know the difference. This didn't feel like one of Solyn's memories, either. Since she had reclaimed her body, she hadn't had a dream like this.

That left another possibility.

The person at the end of the alley had abandoned the body and was now walking toward her. She knew it was Rory by the gait of his stride, recognizing her husband even before she could see the moonlight gleaming off his dark hair, the glint of silver hoops on the tips of his long elf ears. Those were something he hadn't had when she'd last seen him, when he had run from the inn in Severin, when he had learned Solyn was with child.

When he'd realized that she'd betrayed him.

"Rory..." she breathed, the sight of him stirring her heart despite the distance between them, but he didn't seem to notice her standing there, his form striding right through her. Her hand dropped to the necklace at her neck automatically, seeking the ring she'd worn there for so long, wondering if the artifact's magic allowed her to see the *real* Rory. She tugged Klauden's ring off her neck and held it out, staring as it spun on the end of the chain, the metal glinting in the moonlight. The ring allowed *Klauden* to see the wearer, though—it wouldn't connect her to Rory. She wondered if maybe she was seeing one of Klauden's dreams, though dreamwalking wasn't normally her ability. That didn't make sense either.

She tried to imagine why Rory would be dreaming about killing someone, but then she turned to follow him, and abruptly, she was standing in a different place, a room this time, a much fancier space than Hannah had ever seen Rory in. She took in the fabric on the walls, the fine carpeting, the well-crafted furniture. It wasn't her father's castle, but the sense of luxury was familiar.

Hannah thought it might be the Elven city of Firene—but that didn't make any more sense than Rory killing someone vampire-style. He couldn't possibly be in Firene yet. She could have gotten there with her vampiric speed, but Rory was just an elf. An amazing elf, but an elf all the same, reliant on fresh horses at towns along the way. He would still be a few weeks away.

She took in the scene, seeking affirmation that this couldn't be an actual Rory dream.

Her husband sprawled on his back in a large four-poster bed, sleeping the way she'd seen him countless times, his hair in disarray, a hand flung above his head, and—Hannah noted with a start—a topless blonde elf wrapped in the sheet beside him. Her heart began to pound, an odd feeling of strong fingers clutching at her chest, and she realized she'd stopped breathing for a moment. It didn't matter; she didn't need to breathe like a mortal, but it was still jarring. As she watched, Rory rolled onto his side, the moonlight glinting on the scars on his neck and shoulders, an arm reaching out to the strange woman and tugging her closer to him, tucking her into his embrace the way he had when he shared a small bed in Severin with Hannah.

I don't want to see this, Hannah thought as she backed away from the bed, necklace and ring falling from her hand, then bouncing on the plush carpet. *I don't belong here.*

She closed her eyes, willing herself out of the dream, away from the scene.

It's just a dream, she told herself. *This isn't real.*

II

"What?" she mumbled, aware of a hand on her shoulder. "Lemmego."

"Wake up," a voice said.

Hannah opened her eyes, staring up at the pale face and blue eyes of her childhood companion. "Klauden," she murmured, the dream of Rory still heavy in her mind. "What?" She brushed a languid hand over her face, tucking wisps of red curls behind her ears.

The vivid red welt across her palm swam into focus, a grim reminder of her encounter with Kelvin Malbrek, her former teacher, as well as the realities of life inside this body. She had started wearing the long-sleeved jacket to cover it in case they met anyone who might recognize the meaning of the divine sigil. Not that they'd met many people on the road who would ask questions.

"You were talking in your sleep," the vampire explained.

"Was I?" She sat up in her bedroll, stiff limbs popping as she moved. *Gods, I miss sleeping in a bed*. Weeks on the road were wearing on her. An image of the bed she had shared with Rory crossed her mind, quickly doubled by the image of Klauden's bedroom at her father's castle, and she rubbed her eyes. Any bed would do, but she would prefer one without memories.

"You kept saying 'no' over and over again. It disturbed me."

She took in the vampire as he settled himself atop his blanket, tugging a book back onto his lap, eyes squinting to read in the light of the setting sun. "You were sleeping?"

"Alright, fine. It distracted me from my book." He gave her a pointed look. "It *annoyed* me."

"Good," Hannah said, flopping back down. "Anything that annoys you sounds great to me."

"Don't snap at me," he snapped, closing his book in a huff as he rose in a flurry of black robes. "Get up."

She sat up, her limbs protesting violently. "Where's the Sleeping Damsel?"

Klauden gestured to Solyn's still prone form huddled in her bedroll, coils of short blonde hair massing around her face. The girl was a fledgling, but her nature wasn't what kept them traveling at night. Made vampires could travel by day just as easily as born vampires. Stories about vampires only being allowed to come out at night were rumors carefully crafted by Hannah's people generations ago to keep the Houses of the Vanya Mountains safe from mortals bent on destruction.

Solyn had very few restrictions on her abilities now. Stronger and faster than mortals, she was now frozen in her appearance and subject to blood tears. Her only true need was for blood, and because she was a fairly new fledgling, barely three months old, her need was stronger than Hannah's or Klauden's ever was. Hannah could go several days between feedings due to her distant human heritage, and Klauden nearly two days as a normal vampire, but Solyn required blood daily.

Klauden had his fledgling well under his control, a commanding presence Hannah could feel. It wasn't the same as when she had been inside Solyn—then, she had felt what he felt, known what he wanted, been unable to deny his wishes.

Now that she had returned to her old body, her connection to the vampire was more complicated. It was kevna, the ancient magical bond between mates. Hannah had hoped she would escape it when she returned to her own body, but she had been wrong. Now not only could she feel everything Solyn felt through her fledgling bond to Klauden, she also felt everything else her oldest friend tried to hide from her. She only needed to look, and she could see it all.

Hannah tried not to look as much as possible, though she could feel the warmth of the fire on his face as Klauden moved the logs closer to the center, could feel the sharp zing on his skin as one of the sparks touched his hand. He didn't look at her, but Hannah could feel him everywhere. It was easy to lose herself in it, to forget everything else existed and just breathe him in. She rallied, pulling away, trying not to indulge the magic any more than she had to. There were things in Klauden she knew he didn't want her to see. She tried to respect those boundaries as often as possible.

She knew she was just as transparent when he looked at her, and she tried not to think about it. Traveling together on the road north to find Rory hadn't made this easier, but Klauden refused to let Hannah out of his sight until he had a better understanding of their bond, and Solyn went wherever her master went.

Now that the girl was pregnant with his child, Solyn would never leave his side.

Not that Klauden would've let her.

Hannah understood his reasoning. They needed to know how far the connection went. And there was still the question of the army heading to the north, the fledglings that may or may not be bound to Hannah's body, not to mention the Elven healer at its head. Hannah understood her connection to Herrick: she would feel her fledgling Elven leader's pain as he felt hers. She had to figure out how to break the bond without dying, and, if Klauden was right, without dragging him and Solyn down with her into oblivion.

When she told Klauden she wanted a simple life with Rory almost two years ago, Hannah couldn't imagine how far she'd go or how much things would change. She never thought Rory would abandon her, though she understood why he had left and really couldn't blame him, nor had she ever hoped to see Klauden again, never mind the bond of kevna, and she certainly hadn't expected Solyn. Hannah thought she should be used to change by now, to the uncertainty of her life, but it was still a shock to find herself chasing after Rory with both her oldest companion and his fledgling tagging along.

Although when they had all agreed to travel north together, leaving the remains of Severin behind, Hannah didn't think they would spend quite so much time watching the fledgling sleep. She knew pregnant women needed more sleep, but she was starting to wonder how much of their slow progress was legitimate. She wondered if Solyn was slowing them on purpose, dragging out their journey, letting Hannah's frustration build with each passing day, letting Rory get farther and farther away.

Hannah watched Klauden leave the fire and head back to his blanket, collapse in a graceful display of limbs, and tug his book back onto his lap. She glanced at the sleeping Solyn, sighing heavily. They didn't need to sleep the day away and travel at night. She and Klauden could have found enough sustaining fare at high noon in a crowded marketplace. Still, she admitted bringing a fledgling, and a pregnant one at that—even one firmly under her master's control—near a mass of people was probably asking for trouble and delays she couldn't afford, not with the army heading farther north every day. They would have to stick to sneaking through the night like a bunch of demons for a little while longer. It was somewhat degrading, but utterly practical. There were fewer people around at night: less temptation, less chance for problems.

That's what he would say, Hannah thought, crawling out of her bedroll and beginning to wrestle the blanket back into a small roll. She wondered if Rory would approve of the strategy, even if he understood her need to hurry. Her husband had barely approved of her when she had been a vampire anyway, she thought bitterly; it wasn't until Klauden's spell had placed her in a human body—Solyn's body—that she and Rory even had a future.

Hannah had started to wonder what would've happened if her father's magician hadn't captured her so long ago, prompting Rory to rescue her, albeit in a new body. *If I hadn't been mortal, would we have stayed together?*

Probably not.

It was a sobering thought, especially since she'd regained her vampiric body and was on her way to retrieve Rory. *What if my husband doesn't want me?* She thought of the dream again, of Rory with another woman, and her stomach squeezed uncomfortably.

She shook the thought away, shoving violently at the bedroll as it tried to unfold. She grunted at it, twisting the leather strap around and jerking it tight. She groaned as the strength of her pull snapped the leather, the movement propelling the bedroll a few feet away and her body unceremoniously back onto her butt. "Malfek!" she cursed, staring at the leather strap in her hand. She tossed it aside, kicking the bedroll away for good measure as she rose to her feet.

"It seems we're in fine spirits this evening," Klauden observed, casually turning a page in his book.

"Shut up," she snapped.

He looked at her, raising a curious eyebrow.

Hannah closed her eyes and took a deep breath, deliberately ignoring the low stream of thoughts she could hear in his mind, and forcefully looked away from him, eyes slowly taking in the campfire, Solyn's sleeping form, and the distant mountains to the north. Rory was inside those mountains by now. He had returned to Firene, the Elven city far to the northeast on the edge of a different mountain range, to warn his people of Malbrek's army.

Actually, he had gone to Firene to get away from her, but Hannah tried to forget that part. They had intended to tell the elves, but that was before he had learned about the baby, back when everything was looking up.

Wasn't that only a month ago? Maybe he didn't keep his original plan. Maybe he's at an inn somewhere, entertaining himself with wine and women.

The image stung, but Hannah couldn't really believe it, even with the dream. She knew, somehow, she was certain... *He's north of us,* she thought. Not quite at Firene yet, but close enough to remember he'd been banished from that city, probably planning his entry. He wouldn't delay, not with the army heading that way.

"You dreamed of him," Klauden said softly.

Hannah glanced at him. "So?"

"Do you think it was a dream, or was it him?"

Hannah considered. Rory could always dreamwalk to find people in the dream world. He found Klauden that way, to ask for the vampire's help when Solyn had first woken up in Hannah's mind. *Was he really there in my dream, feeding on someone in an alley?* But dreamwalking was Rory and Klauden's ability, not hers.

"Just a dream," she told Klauden, trying to swallow her disappointment. "He wouldn't try to find me now." She reached for her necklace, an old habit rising again, and floundered a little when she felt only bare skin.

"You'd be amazed at what your elf would do for you," Klauden observed.

"Klauden," she began, wanting to ask about the missing necklace, but the vampire had returned to his book. His lips began to move quickly as he read along.

Her fingers left her neck, and though she returned to search her sleeping area, she knew she wouldn't find it there. She remembered dropping it in the dream, the feel of the metal sliding off her fingers.

No, she decided. *It's not possible.* The magic required to somehow send the artifact to Rory through a dream was beyond her skill. She'd talked to Rory before in dreams but never had anything physical in the dream world been real.

And if I somehow dropped the necklace inside a dream, only to discover it's gone now, that means it wasn't a dream, and I was just standing in Rory's room.

Where he's currently sleeping with some random blonde elf.

No, she insisted. *I'm not doing this.*

She looked at Klauden, wondering how much he was gleaning from her frantic thoughts, and she pictured closing a huge iron door in her mind, all thoughts of Rory and the blonde and the ring hidden away behind it. Klauden looked up from his book, frowned at her, then returned to his reading. Hannah didn't know if she had actually succeeded in hiding something from him for once or if he was just humoring her. She decided to pretend her wall was working for the moment.

Hannah considered her spellbook, thinking of memorizing her spells to distract herself, annoyed that Klauden didn't have to bother with such things. The vampire actually chose to read for pleasure. Hannah suffered through her reading, doing it only because she needed her spells to keep herself alive in a fight. She decided against it, knowing that extra spells would probably come in handy but unwilling to frustrate herself now that she had another way of casting more or less reliably. The connection with Klauden helped there, she was sure, and while there were a lot of reasons for her to want to sever the bond, her newfound ability to cast without words was not one of them. She was still figuring out the limits of her new powers, but she knew she could use some of Klauden's strength in her own magic now, and she didn't always need to rely on memorized words.

At first, Hannah had wondered if they could use the teleportation spell to get to Firene instantly, but Klauden had dispelled that notion. They certainly had enough power between them to manage it. Except the spell only worked for places the user had already been, and neither of them had been to Firene. Klauden had spent his days walking south to get to her in Severin, so he could return to anywhere along that route, but he hadn't ventured close to the eastern city.

As she moved to an open space beyond the campground, turned her back to Klauden, and pulled two of her daggers from her belt, preparing to practice the training techniques Rory had taught her, Hannah remembered the vampire explaining that the teleportation spell only worked for him and one other person, which would leave Solyn stranded. Hannah hadn't said the thought that crossed her mind, that she wouldn't mind abandoning the evidence of her mistakes to her own devices. That was her father's daughter speaking, not the person she had become since leaving home two years ago. She had asked why he couldn't just teleport her then return for Solyn, but they would need time between spells for Klauden to recover, and he wasn't willing to leave either of them alone that long until he figured out her connection to Herrick and the fledgling army. Hannah considered suggesting they try the spell together, intentionally combining their magic, but such a spell would only draw them closer, and she wasn't willing to risk it.

I'm a coward, she admitted as she moved into the first few steps of the exercise, *and I know it. I'd rather walk to Firene than chance getting closer to him again.*

That's because you know what will happen the next time you do, her mind snapped back, and she couldn't ignore the rush of sensation flooding her memory, Klauden's lips against hers, his hands on her skin as he moved in her. She mis-stepped but quickly recovered, not looking in Klauden's direction despite knowing he had felt it too.

No, she insisted, placing her feet firmly into the next position, settling her grip on the daggers. *I won't give in to this. It's just magic. I can fight magic.* Her mind calmer, she focused on the movements again, losing herself in the routine.

She remembered to breathe as she twisted first left then right, recalling Rory's hand on her back as he moved her through the technique. The feeling was somewhat comforting, reminiscent of the time she'd spent in Solyn's mortal body, when breathlessness had been a novelty to Hannah's vampiric senses. Though she didn't have to breathe now, doing so was familiar, and she measured her steps according to the rhythm she enforced on her body, dodging an invisible blow from behind, rolling to her right and coming to a graceful crouch facing the would-be foe.

She thought again of Klauden's spell, of being able to instantly travel wherever he wanted. Such power! She had never been so adept with her own magic. That's why she trained with the daggers. Her magic had always been useful, but it alone had never saved her in a fight. Her body had always done most of the work. Now that she was back in it, she just had to remind herself of how to move. Hannah slid both feet forward for the next position, bending to her left this time as she let both blades fly toward a nearby tree, hearing the satisfying thud as they landed in the wood. She was getting more accustomed to her old body each day. By the time they reached Firene, she should be as deadly as she had been before everything, perhaps even more so with the new skills she had learned in the mortal body.

Hannah didn't know if any of her people had been to Firene or, at least, returned from such a journey. She didn't even know if the elves knew of the Houses in the Vanya, never mind what kind of people inhabited them. She frowned, recalling her lessons with Malbrek, most of the history he had shared a droning buzz in her memory. She hadn't paid much attention then, but it didn't take a wise woman to assume that if the elves suspected they were vampires, it wouldn't take long to destroy even their hardy bodies, born vampire or made fledgling. Strong as she was, she couldn't defend herself against an entire city. Hannah hustled the three steps to the tree and her blades, retrieving both with deft hands and using the tree to spin around to face possible attackers. It was foolishness to go to Firene in the first place, but Hannah knew she had to find Rory.

No matter how I find him, she thought. *Or with whom.*

Hannah pushed the thought away. She was breathing hard now, though part of her knew she didn't have to, and she glanced at where the vampire sat with his book, black robes carefully folded around his knees. Klauden had made it clear that he went wherever she did, and Solyn was now his fledgling, so she went where he did, and now the unhappy threesome headed toward a city that wouldn't welcome their true natures revealed.

As she got into position for her next technique, Hannah wondered what they would do about Solyn when they got there. It was one thing to set the new fledgling loose among the mortals in some minor village. It was another to expect her to restrain herself amid the glorious paragons of health and vitality that the elves were to her kind. Elven blood was supposedly a rare elixir, a coveted prize, and though Hannah knew that myth for the falsehood it was, Solyn wouldn't know, and when the fledgling heard the blood calling to her, who could say what she might do, even with Klauden's iron will keeping her in check. Hannah had even taken to doubting her own ability to restrain herself, given the newness of her own vampiric nature all over again.

Still, she had managed to resist the call of Rory's blood, never giving in to the urge to take him. Though, as she thought about those few precious days after she had reclaimed her body and they had been alone in the house in Severin, both recovering from their injuries, she didn't remember wanting the elf as she once had.

Perhaps her body had simply been sated, glutted with blood as Anna preferred. Perhaps she had finally learned to control herself. Rory had still been healing from what happened in the tent, his body ragged with wounds. Hannah thought of his neck, of his refusal to let Klauden heal him, and for a brief moment, she considered the impossible.

No, she decided immediately. Anna hadn't bitten him. She'd been clear about that, gloating as she bragged to Hannah.

But then you died, Hannah told herself. *Who knows what happened after that?* She thought she remembered Rory's neck being unmarked when she arrived at the tent, but her recollection of that time was blurry, partly because she had literally died, but also because she didn't want to remember.

She jumped up into her next series of moves, trying to lose herself in the familiarity of the steps. Though she had learned this pattern in Solyn's body over weeks as Rory trained the slave girl's body how to fight, Hannah was trying to get this new body—her old body—she reminded herself, to obey her mind's newfound instincts. It was unnerving all over again to be so at odds with herself all the time. She had just gotten used to being mortal and slow and easily hurt, *and blonde*, she thought with a sigh, when Solyn's consciousness had returned, turning Hannah's world upside down.

Too focused on her own thoughts, Hannah's foot slipped too far to the right as she spun about, and the move disturbed her center of gravity, causing her to overbalance and tumble ungracefully to the ground. "Oof!" she exploded, using both hands to push herself back to her feet. The fall hadn't lasted more than a second, but when she was back on her feet again, she felt Klauden staring at her with hopeless disapproval.

"You know ... you don't need to fight like them," he told her. "If only you'd try—"

"Don't," she replied. *I'm not in the mood for one of his If-you-would-only-try-you'd-be-a-great-magic-user speeches.* She stalked angrily to the edge of the campsite. "I'm going swimming," she announced. "Come get me when you're finished, and you can go hunting. I'll stay here with her." Hannah hooked a thumb at Solyn's still sleeping form.

Hannah didn't stay to see Klauden's nod; she could feel his acknowledgement. It wasn't like there was anything else they could do.

III

Hannah stood under the water for a long time, trying to let the quiet muffling her ears soak into her soul and calm the raging storm of her thoughts. She didn't want to think of Klauden, knowing the thought would reach him, call him to her even though she wanted to be alone. She didn't want to think of Rory either, the image of him in bed with another galling in her memory, then a heavy pit of self-loathing settled in her gut, and she allowed herself to surface, gulping in air in an attempt to clear the ache in her chest.

It's my fault, she told herself. *What did I expect him to do when he found out about the baby? What would I have done if our roles were reversed?*

This wasn't a new line of thought, but Hannah retraced the familiar steps as she made her way to the water's edge, shaking the water from her hair and settling herself on a nearby stone, letting the night air dry her body.

Could she accept a Rory who was bound to another, who had allowed ancient magic to push him into bed with an old companion? Hannah wanted to swear that she would, that it wouldn't matter, that what she felt for Rory was stronger than anything, but as she sat there, her night-vision capturing the night sky, each detail revealed to her vampiric sight, she wondered if she was just lying to herself. She insisted it was her duty to warn the elves, that the army was partly her fault since she was responsible for Herrick in the first place, but she knew that was a thin excuse. She wanted to see Rory, to say the words in her heart, to hear the words from him. If he no longer wanted her, so be it, but she wouldn't give up without hearing it directly from her husband.

Her hands gripped the stone she sat on as she pondered, and she forgot her strength again, her right hand squeezing suddenly, and a small exposed piece of the stone snapped off, the shards gouging her palm with a sharp explosion of pain. She held her hand up, examining the small wounds in the moonlight. She wasn't worried. She would heal—one of the perks of her vampiric nature. As she stared at the small trickles of red blood, she had a queer doubling of her vision, of another hand held before a face, phantom pain echoing through him.

It was Herrick, she realized suddenly, jerking the palm out of her sightline and scanning the river, as if expecting her Elven fledgling to show himself in the darkness. But Herrick was miles from this place, likely farther north but to the east. She suddenly knew that he was staring at the Wild Waters, the river just south of the Rasa mountain range. He meant to cross through the mountains then, cutting northeast through the Kelsin Deadlands and reaching Firene over land.

Rory was likely already north of the mountains, his skill with horses allowing him to cover far more ground. Alone, she could have caught him, but with Klauden and sleepy Solyn, they were still on the Rasa Road. She had hoped they'd be able to keep up over land, but if Herrick was already so far north, they needed a faster route.

Rasa is a port city, she mused. There would be ships there. Surely, they could get to Firene over the water before Herrick managed to get the army across the mountains, through the deadlands, and over the continent to Firene. Fledglings could be fast, but they were also easily distracted and hungry all the time, not to mention how he would keep any remaining goblins focused. Herrick would struggle to herd them north quickly.

She was concentrating on a new plan, her mind doing the mental calculations of time and distance and the little she knew of ship journeys, so when the thought came, she almost ignored it.

<*Cut my hand, will you?*> The voice was bitter, and she recognized the Elven ex-healer. She ignored him, not wanting to strengthen the bond between them.

She looked at her hand, still streaked with blood but scabbing over. It would be totally healed soon. Unlike the scars on her chest, any wounds her body received would heal easily with new blood. She climbed down from the stone, rinsed her hand in the water, and put on her clothes, the white shirt getting damp around the neck as she pulled it over her hair, the black skirt ending at her calves, a leather belt at the waist holding everything in place, including her daggers. She thought of her new style, recalling how she had worn brown skirts and sweaters after leaving home, but that only reminded her of the new clothes Rory had gotten her in Kalford after hers had been ruined in the fighting, and she abandoned the memory, not wanting to think of that night.

Her new jacket lay on the rock, and she was just pulling on her second boot when pain exploded in her right hand. For a moment, she thought something in the water had attacked her, perhaps bitten off one of her fingers, but a look at her hand reassured her that she was whole.

There was no mark, no blood, and she understood.

Just as her wound had reached Herrick, his wound would reach her. She had a quick vision of a right hand held out in front of her face, the pinky finger dislocated and hanging askew. The pain was violent, throbbing, and then, as she watched, the finger was set, Herrick realigning the joint, and the echoes of pain receded, still present but distant now.

That's not good, Hannah thought, and tucking her jacket under her arm, started to head back to the camp. *If he can hurt himself and I can feel it, what will happen if he hurts one of the fledglings Anna made?*

She had barely finished the thought when agony exploded in her right side, and Hannah staggered, falling to her knees with a cry. Her hand went to cover the wound, knowing there was nothing there but unable to stop herself. She tried to ignore the pain, but she couldn't ignore the image in her head, a brown-haired fledgling standing before her with a sword sticking out of his gut, and she could see the faint outline of a cord attached to him, the cord cutting through time and space to connect ever so faintly to her body.

"N—" she managed to say as the sword was tugged from his body with a spray of blood, and the pain in her stomach doubled. She crawled a few steps, unable to see the world around her, lost to the vision of the fledgling before her.

<*Klauden,*> her mind cried. <*I need you. I need—*>

The sword flashed again, and the fledgling's head thudded to the ground, bouncing a few feet from his body. Hannah's entire body imploded with the pain, and she fell into the darkness.

IV

She felt a hand run down her cheek, smoothing her hair behind her ears. Then, a reassuring voice said, *<Chaivin, come back to me.>*

That's not my name, she thought, mind trying to catch up to what she was feeling. She was back in her body, her actual body, and someone was touching her face, the warmth of skin on skin causing little sparks of desire to run through her nerves, and she was suddenly filled with need, though not the familiar need for blood. This was something else, a need for connection, for more, then she had hands again, and her fingers were twined in something—hair?—and warm lips were touching hers, then she had an entire body again, her form filling with the thrill of physical pleasure.

<Yes.>

She wasn't sure whose thought it was, but it was everywhere, and her fingers tightened in the hair and her mouth moved, and a tongue was pressing against hers.

<Mine. Always mine.>

Of course, she thought, her body flaming with desire, her hands abandoning hair to stroke down a neck, across a collarbone to shoulders, then pulling closer into a tight embrace.

<Chaivin, yes.>

That thought definitely wasn't from her, and she paused. *But I'm not chaivin,* she insisted. *I'm Hannah. Only Klauden calls me that.*

With a start, Hannah realized she was passionately kissing Klauden, and she jerked away, using her hold on his shoulders to push back, but then her shoulders hit the ground, and there was nowhere to go. She opened her eyes to see Klauden's face looking down at her, one hand still pressed against her cheek, the other wrapped around her back. She was laying on the ground, and Klauden leaned over her, his hair falling down to make a cave around his face. Hannah really wanted to touch his hair again, to complete the mad connection in her soul.

"What?" she gasped. *How the hell did I get here?* She recalled the swim, then she touched her hair. *It's still damp.* Not much time had passed. She remembered her hand, then the sword in her gut, and finally, the wrenching pain as the fledgling had been beheaded. Her breath came in short gasps as echoed pain retraced its way through her body, but it was distant now, blocked by Klauden's touch, his presence. "How?" she asked him, knowing she hadn't been anywhere near him when she fell.

"You are not subtle, chaivin," he said, sitting up, and tugging her with him. "I would have heard you across the continent."

She sat up, wiping a hand over her lips, very aware of how she'd jammed her tongue into his mouth. "I hurt my hand," she said, trying to forget the feeling of closeness. She held it up, seeing only a thin series of lines where a mass of scabs had been earlier. "And then I heard him in my head, and he broke his finger." She wiggled her pinky, relieved when it didn't hurt. "Then a few moments later, he stabbed a fledgling. And it hurt. A lot."

His lips pursed in thought. "And that's when you called me?"

She shook her head. "No, it was when he cut off the fledgling's head."

Klauden's mouth dropped open, and he stared at her. "This is a serious problem, chaivin," he said finally.

She nodded in agreement. "What happened? I passed out, I think, when I called you."

"I heard you yelling, and then I found you on the ground near the water."

Hannah looked around. They were sitting only a few feet from where she had crawled away from the water's edge. It was night, but she could see just fine, and so could Klauden, the red tinge of his eyes glowing in the darkness as they spoke.

"And?" she asked, though she didn't know if she wanted to hear the rest.

He sighed. "You were somewhere else." He paused, then added, "Again." Hannah thought of the ragged scars on her chest, the evidence of Anna's last desperate bid to defeat her, and of the darkness she had fallen into then. "I had to call you back."

"Thank you," she said, gratitude welling under her scarred chest. "When he killed the fledgling, I thought I was going to die."

"I think part of you might have died," Klauden said.

Hannah shot him a glare. "What?!"

"The part of you tethered to that fledgling is gone," he reasoned. "Concentrate. Can you still feel the rest of them?"

Hannah frowned. She disliked doing this. Focusing on the tiny cords binding her body to the fledglings made her feel like a bloated spider on a monstrous web. They were still there, though fewer connections now than the first time she'd felt them. She'd been inside the body with Anna then, and her half-sister had sired nearly a hundred fledglings with her body over the year she'd had it. Some of those cords had been severed immediately when Hannah took over. She didn't know if those fledglings had died or not. Some of the connections had gone with Anna's spirit when Hannah pushed her out—those fledglings had probably died with Anna. But a few dozen had remained tethered to Hannah, a crawling sensation on her skin that she tried to ignore. She'd rather spend time in Klauden's thoughts than think about being connected to so many strangers.

She had an image of her body but with Anna's eyes leaning down to bite a strange man, and she shuddered, shaking her head and trying to think of anything else. Klauden helpfully reminded her of their kiss from a few moments ago, pushing the memory into her with ease, and she relaxed instantly before anger filled her.

"This is my body!" she yelled at him. "Can it just be mine for one single moment? Can't I just be myself without crazy magic jerking me around?"

Klauden pulled away, returning her privacy with his mind and body. "You can still feel them, then," he said after a moment.

Hannah frowned and nodded as the anger cooled, and she considered her situation. "How much of myself can I lose? If they keep dying, what happens to me?" She looked at him, realization dawning. "And to you?"

Klauden sighed, shaking his head. "I do not know." He frowned. "I must understand this." He gave her a reassuring look, and something inside Hannah eased, though she knew the look was pure bravado. "And I will. I just need time. I will figure this out." She did believe that.

"But that was close." She paused, sighing. Then a thought struck her. "For me. How was it for you?"

Klauden shrugged, the gesture one he had picked up south of the Vanya while living among the mortals. "I found you." His tone clearly suggested he didn't want to answer her question. Hannah let it go, exploring another angle instead.

"But if he continues to kill them, can you keep finding me?"

Klauden shook his head and rose in a graceful display of movement. He reached a hand out to bring her to her feet as well. "He won't keep killing them. This was an experiment ... and likely petty vengeance. He needs those fledglings if he wants revenge on Firene."

Hannah let him tug her to her feet, enjoying the feel of his hand on hers despite her better judgement. "Thank you," she told him again, "for bringing me back."

"Always, chaivin," he said.

Behind them, a noise came from the woods. Hannah turned first, relaxing when she recognized Solyn, the fledgling awake and staring at them with glowing red eyes. *How long has she been watching us?*

Judging by Solyn's expression, the fledgling had probably seen more than she wanted to.

FIRENE: LIRA

Lira Dinuviel Galadron sat at a table overlooking the ocean, her appreciation for the view diminished by her growing agitation. There was a time when sitting by the ocean would've calmed her instantly. But that was before she had left Firene, before she had forsaken home and calling to accompany her Tallerin gods-knew-where in the lands beyond. It was strange to be back after so many decades of travel. The city seemed foreign to her now, but she knew the change wasn't in Firene. The city hadn't changed—she had.

She took another sip of wine, but the taste didn't soothe her as expected. Her years on the road had spoiled her for fine wines. She found herself longing for an ale, and the desire annoyed her even more.

"Damn," she muttered, another word she wouldn't have used before leaving home, and let the delicate glass hit the stone table with more force than she expected, a few drops of red liquid sloshing out. Lira swiped at them with her hand, shoulders hunching as she considered her options.

I can ignore everything, return to the temple of Valerian, and live out my days as an Elder, having seen the world beyond the walls and returned to mentor the initiates. There can't possibly be so many fools there.

The thought was mechanical, though, a vestige of old desires and habits, and Lira quickly dismissed it. Though her faith was still stronger than ever, she would never belong in the temple again. Besides, she now knew there were fools everywhere.

I can just leave Firene behind, pack a bag and head south, or even north, or perhaps take a ship to the east. She shook her head, swirling the remaining wine in her glass, watching as it caught the sunlight in the fine crystal. Lira knew she didn't do well on boats, so east was out, and she didn't particularly enjoy the cold weather, so heading farther north wasn't appealing either. She had already been south, so that left the west into the mountains. She glanced that way, knowing the Houses of the Kindred were located in the Vanya Mountain valleys, the vampires like Hannah, strongholds she didn't wish to explore. There were also the wolves to consider. Though Lira had discovered she liked meeting new people and experiencing different customs, she wasn't quite ready to face the wild shapeshifters yet.

That left her stuck here in Firene—and facing her Tallerin. It was not going to be a pleasant encounter. She knew Rory well, had traveled with him far and wide, had seen him in nearly every situation, but his recent behavior made her pause. Her old friend had been distraught when he thought Hannah had died, a wreck of rage bent on revenge, but she could deal with that Rory far more easily than the Rory she'd seen return to Firene.

She hadn't been in those early meetings with his brothers, but she had rekindled enough of her connections since her return a few months before to hear what had happened. There was an army to the south, apparently a blend of goblins and fledglings, creatures she hadn't known the elves knew about—but clearly, they did—led by an elf that some had called Herculindarus Canadys. Lira remembered Herrick from years ago. He had been a fool then; apparently, time and vampire blood hadn't changed much. She had learned much of Rory's adventures since he had fled from Kalford, leaving her behind with Gorn to handle what they thought was Hannah's corpse.

But she still hadn't learned what happened to Hannah. Rory had been gone too long to have failed to retrieve her from her father's castle. Lira thought they must've been living somewhere quite contentedly for a time, but then something happened. She didn't quite know what it was, but she would find out.

Lira didn't doubt the Elven fledgling and the approaching army were all connected to Hannah. The girl *excelled* at trouble.

If Rory was here without her, with that haunted betrayed look in his eyes, it meant Hannah was still very much alive, and Rory was running again. Lira had waited, wondering if time would change his behavior, but Rory had only continued to slide down a self-destructive path she had seen before. The last time he had been like this, it had ended with a dead body—and his exile from his homeland.

"Something on your mind, Lira?" As always, Gorn's voice was pleasant. Lira gave the dwarf a rueful grin as her friend took the seat beside her. Gorn Haversont hadn't changed at all despite his months in the Elven city; he still carried his axe with him everywhere, and he was always ready with a welcome drink. With a small flourish, he set a crystal goblet down before her, the glass sloshing with amber liquid. He slid the red wine glass away from her with a scowl and tapped the new glass instead. "Got what you need, lass." Lira smiled, taking a gulp of the ale and letting it settle her as the wine couldn't.

"Still can't find any mugs?" she asked, gesturing at his own delicate glass filled with ale.

The dwarf frowned. "Damn elves. Don't know what's good for them," he mumbled. "But I know what's good for us." He smiled at her and withdrew a silver flask from the pouch at his belt, refilling both of their glasses with more ale. "Talk to me now. What's going on?"

"Something beyond the fact that I'm not a lass," she replied, "or that I'm actually older than you are?"

Her friend smiled as he ran his fingers through his red beard. "I'll never tell," he whispered.

Lira took another gulp of ale, drinking it in earnest, now knowing there was more. "Where did you find that?" she asked, gesturing to the seemingly never-ending flask.

"You'll never guess where I spent my morning," Gorn said, refilling their glasses, then leaning back into the comfortable balcony chair, his axe handle still accessible above one shoulder.

"I'm guessing it wasn't the bar?" Lira offered. The public bar offered the finest wines. Ale wasn't readily available in the city proper of Firene, but Gorn didn't smell like he'd been down by the docks.

"I was just having a lovely chat with our friend Caganasti," Gorn told her. Lira thought of the Elven magician, the topknot of bristling black hair that crowned his shaved head, the lines of power tattooed on his skin, the silver barbells threaded through the tops of his forearms. Occasionally, she let her mind wander when it came to Caganasti, wondering how far the marks went beneath his modest robe, and how many of those bars he had on his body and where. He was a handsome elf beneath everything. And she had known him when she was younger, too, and she remembered the way he had looked at her before she joined the temple.

"And what did Caga say this morning, besides providing us with fine drink?"

Gorn smirked, and Lira thought the dwarf probably knew about her little crush, but her friend said nothing about it. "I found out what happened with Rory ... and wee Hannah."

Lira sat up, draining the remains of her glass in one long gulp, and held out the empty for Gorn to refill. "Tell me everything."

Standing in the disorganized chaos of Rory's palace rooms, Lira stared at her oldest companion, taking in his sleepless bloodshot eyes, the haggard cheeks from too much drink. "You look like crap, Rory," she told him bluntly.

"I'm fine," he slurred, and the reek of alcohol hit her. His shirt was rumpled, half unbuttoned, the glint of a silver necklace visible around his neck, but at least he was wearing pants, his bare feet striking. In their long friendship, Lira had rarely seen the elf without his boots on, pants perfectly smooth, shirt clean and straight, the years in the military having left their mark on his appearance. His hair was long again, nothing new there, but it was messy and unwashed.

There was something else about him now, something foreign, and Lira struggled to acknowledge the signs, not wanting what she feared to be true, but staring at him now, she knew. Despite his ragged looks, he was still oddly appealing, something attractive that Lira noted but didn't respond to. She knew it was the power of her god that protected her, but she also knew the strength of that appeal on others. The moment she saw him, his scarred neck should've told her the truth, but she hadn't wanted to think about it.

She thought Hannah was smarter than to turn Rory into a fledgling, but now that she knew the whole story—Caganasti had been quite thorough—Lira wasn't sure. It might have been Hannah's body that bit him, but Lira wondered if Hannah would've done it eventually anyway. Such things seemed unavoidable when dealing with vampires.

Lira shook her head at her friend, then walked across the room, occupying herself with picking up the discarded clothes on a nearby chair rather than punch him in his stubborn face. "Yeah, you look just fine," she said sarcastically. She folded his shirt and set it aside, then sighed when she grabbed the next garment—a blue silky dress. "Seriously?" she asked, tossing the dress aside in disgust. "This is how you plan to spend your triumphant return home?" She gestured at the messy room; empty wine bottles littered the dresser and dining table as well as the windowsill, and clothes were tossed everywhere.

Rory took another long swig from his current bottle, then sprawled awkwardly on the unmade four-poster bed. "And how should I be spending my time here?" he asked bitterly. "I'm a hero, haven't you heard? Risked life and limb to warn my brother of the approaching army. I can do whatever the hell I want with my time here."

"I see that," she snapped. "Drowning your sorrows and shacking up with the Valrina?" She shook her head, clearly judging him.

Lira hadn't much liked Annilyn Valrina when she knew the elf before leaving Firene with Rory. Decades away hadn't improved her opinion. Though her family name may grant her certain privileges, like rooms overlooking the garden in the center of the palace, Annilyn was still a social climber desperate to improve her standing with Firenian royalty, and the Valrina had latched onto the returning Tallerin as soon as he arrived, sinking her gorgeous blonde hooks into the clearly defenseless elf, taking advantage of his pain.

"I thought you had better sense," Lira said tartly. She wondered for a moment if perhaps the Valrina was there because of Rory's new appeal, unable to resist the pull of a fledgling, but she dismissed the idea. Annilyn would've jumped on Rory at any time. It was only his marriage to Galina that kept her away in the past. Now that he was here alone, the Valrina didn't need any encouragement.

Rory gestured the bottle at Lira, annoyance crossing his face. "You don't know anything about it," he snapped.

Lira raised an eyebrow. "Really? You mean I don't know how you left Hannah with her ex-fiancé and the pregnant fledgling body she inhabited for the past year? Left without actually facing her about the child the fledgling Solyn now carries?"

Rory choked, face reddening as he gasped for air. Lira saw how his skin flushed, but the color was different now, the scars on his neck pale in comparison. He composed himself, then sniffed, frowning at her. "You've been talking to Caga. He really needs to learn to keep his mouth shut."

Lira snorted. *Like Caganasti could ever be accused of being too free with his words.* The elf tried to kill everyone who spoke to him as a matter of course. She caught the angry retort on her lips, swallowed hard and, taking a different angle, said gently, "He's worried about you. We all are."

"I'm fine," Rory repeated, taking a final swig of wine before dropping it on the floor beside the bed with a hollow sound. It tipped and rolled away, and Lira stopped it with her foot.

"You're not fine," she told her old friend, knowing her Tallerin needed her to be blunt when others were circumspect, critical when others looked away. "You're falling apart."

He flopped back onto the bed, staring at the ceiling.

"You know I'm right," she said, sitting on the bed's edge beside him. "This isn't the Rory I know."

There was a long moment where she thought he might shut her out completely, but then he sighed again, the sound tortured, and he turned his head to look at her.

"She betrayed me," he said simply. "After everything, after all this," his hand went to his neck, touching the scars there, "she couldn't even be true to me."

Lira gave him a scathing look, in no mood for his self-pity. "I doubt Hannah had much control over what happened. She seems to be drowning in magic and destiny." She gave him a pointed look. "Don't pretend to be a victim. You knew what you were getting into, even before Kalford."

He frowned, face blanching at first but then calming. "I knew what she was," he agreed. He pulled a necklace out from beneath his shirt, fingering the silver ring on it, Klauden's ring. Lira could feel the power from the artifact from where she sat a few feet away. She wondered how he had ended up with it. If Hannah gave it to him and he was still holding on to it, he must not be as ready to move on as he said. Rory looked at the ring, then at Lira, face hardening. "But she swore to me. It was a simple promise."

"And then something got in the way of that oath," Lira reminded him, shrugging. "Things happen." She glared at him. "You make it seem like she willingly went with him just to spite you."

"She did!" Rory exploded. "You weren't there. You didn't see them together."

"No," Lira admitted. "But I've seen you two together, and *that* was real. More real than any magical bond."

Rory sat up, dragging his legs up so he sat cross legged. "What are you suggesting? That I just forget about it, forgive her, and move on?" He looked down, dropping the necklace beneath his shirt again. "I won't. I can't."

"You seem to have moved on just fine," Lira observed drily, reaching down to tug a silky slip from beneath one of the pillows jammed against the headboard behind where Rory sat.

"That's different," Rory said, snatching it from her and tossing it across the room. "That's just..." he paused, "company."

"Really?" she sneered. "Do tell me what ancient magic compelled you into the bed of the Valrina? Some ancient spell forcing you to seek her company?"

"It's different," he repeated. "I'm here now. Hannah isn't. We're done."

Lira snorted, a hand snaking out to touch the skin of his neck. "You will never be done. You can't be." She pulled away, shaking her head. "I really thought having a fledgling bond with her would've widened your perspective on such things." As Hannah's fledgling, he should be able to sense her feelings, share her emotions. "You should be able to understand."

Lira assumed Hannah could also feel the elf, but if the vampire was indeed drowning in ancient magic like kevna, she might not feel anything outside of that bond. *I wonder if Hannah knows that Rory was turned.* From what Caganasti had said, there was a good chance she didn't, especially since Rory hadn't told her.

Rory shrugged. "I barely notice it."

Lira took in the general mess of the room. "Yeah, you seem to be not noticing extremely well." She gestured at the bottles. "You've been drinking yourself into a stupor so you don't notice it." She paused, then asked quietly, "Where are you finding blood?"

He looked at her, and his eyes reddened, alcohol dulling his senses and bringing his emotions to the surface. A single tear rolled down his cheek, the red tinge a sign of his new status. He shrugged, looking away as he wiped his face.

"I manage," he whispered, and Lira saw what his new desire did to him, the guilt and frustration and pain beneath the numbing alcohol. "It's not like anyone was there to show me."

"So Hannah doesn't know," Lira confirmed, shaking her head. "Why didn't you tell her? She would've gladly shown you."

He shook his head. "I was a little distracted, learning about Solyn's pregnancy—and with *his* child." He spat the word.

Lira nodded. "Fine, but what about before that? You had a few days together recovering before Solyn told you anything. Why didn't you say something then?"

"I couldn't. I couldn't say anything. Not after..." He looked away, remembered pain in his eyes, and he wiped his face again. "She died, Lira." The words burst out of him. "I saw her, and she was dead."

Lira waited for him to continue, relying on their decades of friendship to loosen his restraint. After a moment, he continued. "And then he brought her back. From the dead."

"Kevna is powerful magic," Lira commented neutrally.

"I couldn't bring her back. I couldn't do anything." Lira heard the bitterness in his voice, the guilt, the anger. "I could only lay there, helpless ... and I thought Anna was her..." His voice trailed off, and Lira touched his hand. When he didn't pull away, she reached out for his arm and tugged him to her for a long hug. He collapsed into her, body shuddering as he wept. Lira hugged him for a long moment.

His face was buried in her shoulder, and she became aware of the small shifts in him, the way his body tensed as he sat back from her suddenly, face streaked red by his bloody tears, his mouth puffy from where his teeth had grown long. He turned away from her, swinging to sit on the other side of the bed with his legs hanging off.

After a moment, he said, "I'm sorry. But please don't move." He took a few deep shuddering breaths, trying to calm himself, though Lira knew he didn't have to breathe anymore.

Lira obeyed his request, sitting still, fairly sure she could hold her own in a fight against the Tallerin she had known, but not certain of this new Rory's abilities. Hannah had been a formidable opponent as a vampire. Lira knew she could always use her divine power to stop Rory now that he was one of Cairn's children, but she didn't want to kill him.

A long tense moment passed, then he turned back to her, looking truly sad. "What am I going to do?" he asked in a small voice.

Lira pursed her lips. "That's a great question, Tallerin," she said, watching his face as she used his title. "What do you plan to do?"

He looked around the room. "I suppose I should stop drinking so much first," he admitted. "But it helps dull the ... cravings."

Lira nodded. "That sounds like a start." She gave his rooms a look. "You should probably have someone clean up here—and you need a bath, like immediately." She wrinkled her nose at him. "Honestly, how does the Valrina stand to be near you?" She put up a hand. "Never mind. Don't answer that. I don't want to know."

Rory rose, then bowed to retrieve the slip he had thrown earlier. He ran it through his hands, contemplating. "The Valrina is ... convenient," he said finally.

"I said I don't want to know," Lira repeated. "I don't care about that—though Hannah would probably have an opinion about your taste." She put her hands up again at the darkening look on his face. "But that's between you and her," she said. "You sort it out when she gets here."

"Gets here?" Rory repeated. "Why would Hannah come here?"

Lira gave him a look reserved for idiocy. "Is that a serious question? Why wouldn't Hannah come here? *You* are here."

"But I left her. Left them." He twisted the dress a little more vigorously, the material straining between his hands. "She wouldn't want to see me."

"But you didn't see her," Lira reminded him. "Apparently, you decided to say goodbye to Solyn, trusting the pregnant fledgling and completely avoiding your actual wife."

"My actual wife who had been having sex with her ex-fiancé," Rory quipped.

"To whom she is bound by kevna, a magical blood bond strong enough to resurrect her from the dead," Lira retorted. "Do you really think she can ignore something like that?"

"If she loved me—" Rory began.

"Oh please," Lira interrupted. "You mean to say you expect her love for you to be strong enough to stop magic that literally called her back to life?"

Rory gave a sheepish look, then stuck out his chin. "Yes, actually I do. She swore to me. That kind of thing matters."

"Of course it matters," Lira agreed, "but this isn't Galina."

He gave her a dark look. "I know that."

"Do you?" Lira asked. "Because you're treating Hannah the same way despite the difference in circumstances."

"I didn't kill Klauden," Rory defended. "I wanted to, but I didn't."

"Congratulations?" Lira offered in a thick, sarcastic tone. "Does this mean you're finally growing as a person after all these years?" She turned to address the empty room. "The Tallerin, everyone, who after a hundred years of exile has finally come to grips with his anger problem." She laughed. "You're being ridiculous."

"You don't understand," he told her. "You've never been betrayed by someone you love!" The fabric between his hands ripped, fluttering into two pieces. He shook his hands, letting the pieces fall to the floor.

"Haven't I," Lira said, voice flat, and Rory gave her a sharp glance.

"If you have, you'd understand how I feel."

"If I were you," Lira suggested, standing up, "I would use that bond to figure out what your wife is feeling right now." She gave him another look. "But even more than the wreck that is your relationship, you need to work on a plan to stay here."

Rory gave her a surprised look. "Am I staying here? I planned to get sloppy drunk and forget where I was at all."

"So sloppy drunk that you messed up while feeding and someone had to kill you?" Lira asked, a bite in the question. "I expect more from you."

"Can't I, the Tallerin, wallow in my pain for a moment?"

Lira walked over to him, invading his space, daring his fledgling senses to attack her. "You're not allowed to die, Rorinvalranus Tallerin," she told him, using his full name and title in an echo of his mother. "You are my friend. I've stood by your side for nearly a hundred years, and you're done wallowing, or whatever this is." She backed up. "And for the sake of all the gods, go take a bath! You reek!"

"And what then?" he asked quietly. "Say I get myself together, get a grip on this new ... desire... Then what?"

"What are you talking about? You're the Tallerin. Jasper may be running this city right now, but you know what everyone expects." She glared at him. "You'd better have a plan for after this army situation is taken care of because you're still an exiled prince in dangerous company. They are letting you linger right now because you're still a hero for coming home to warn us, but this warm welcome will only last for so long." She sighed. "Have you even spoken to your brothers?"

Rory peered down at his rumpled shirt, at his bare feet. "They were in the room with me, yes."

"So that's a no." She paced to the window, looking at the sea beyond. "And have you seen the Sarkoza at all?"

Rory reddened at the mention of the foreign dignitary. "Rory!" she shouted at him. "You're in the same palace as a visiting kindred from one of the Houses of the Vanya, and you haven't even had a conversation? What is wrong with you?"

"Maybe I don't want to reveal myself to one of them," Rory hedged. "I don't know if he can sense what I am."

Lira sensed the lie in his words. "But you don't think he can, do you? Hannah must've told you something of fledglings, especially after she became one in Solyn's body."

"She said she normally wouldn't be able to tell unless it was someone of her blood or if she was actively looking," Rory admitted.

"And do you think he's actively looking? Does he know there's a fledgling here?"

Rory considered. "I've been very careful covering my tracks. I don't think anyone knows."

Lira opened her mouth to ask him how he had been surviving, on whom, but closed it instead. She could accept this new Rory, but she didn't need to know the details. There was one question she couldn't avoid asking. "And the Valrina?"

"What about her?"

"How much does she know?"

He shrugged dismissively. "Nothing."

Lira glanced around the room. "She's been staying here, though, right?"

"So?"

Lira sighed, rolling her eyes. "Rory, you talk in your sleep. Let's just hope you haven't said anything she can use against you."

"You make it sound like she's out to get me. Annilyn and I are just … having fun."

Lira snorted. "You couldn't be more male right now if you tried," she judged. "The Valrina is using you for her own ends."

Rory shrugged. "I know that. And I'm using her. It's fine."

"I hope so," Lira said. "She's dangerous. If she knew what you are, she would betray you at the first opportunity."

"I haven't bitten her if that's what you mean," Rory snapped.

"Do you want to?" Lira asked, her words almost palpable in the room.

He rolled his eyes. "Of course I do. It's why I've been drinking myself into a stupor!" he admitted. "I want to bite everyone I see." He braced his hands on the window glass, staring at the night sky. "But I haven't bitten anyone." He turned back to her. "And before you ask, I've been incredibly inventive. Apparently, I can stun people now, make them forget what's happening. I can cut them, bleed them, and let them go. They don't have to die."

"Well, at least that's one thing we don't have to worry about," Lira said, sensing there was more to what he was saying that she didn't want to know.

"We?" he echoed.

"Yes, we, you fool," she snapped. "You don't believe I'd abandon you after all this time, do you?"

He smiled at her. "You're a good friend, Lira. Thank you."

"You don't deserve me," she replied truthfully. "And you know it. But this is not about me or even us. It's about you." She speared him with her stare. "You need to get it together, find out what's going on with the Sarkoza, figure out what to do about Herrick and his army, and decide how you're going to escape this alive." She paused. "See, I'm not even going to mention Hannah right now."

"You make it sound so easy," he said. "But where should I begin?"

"With a bath," she told him, tossing the silver servant bell at him. "Now."

V

"I think we should take a ship from Rasa," Hannah said, watching Klauden's face as he considered the option. They sat on their blankets before the fire, Solyn laying a few feet away, still wrapped in her blanket. Klauden's books still surrounded him where he sat cross-legged, several open to different pages so he could reference things as he went through them. Hannah remembered other times spent sitting beside him while he worked on a project, hours in the library together. Now they sat beneath the stars.

Gods, was that only two years ago? Hannah marveled at how much her life had changed. *No wonder mortals live such a short time,* she thought— *their lives are filled with events.* Hannah could remember years spent with nothing more exciting than finding another passage into the mountains, or even just getting a new dress. She glanced down at the simple shirt and skirt she wore, different from the brown she had favored after leaving home, but a far cry from the elaborate affairs she had worn in the castle. She glanced at Solyn, her back exposed above the blanket, the simple blue dress old but sturdy. She wondered idly if Solyn would want something else to wear when they got to a city again. Hannah had been wearing simple dresses because that's what Solyn had worn when Hannah was placed in her body. Maybe the fledgling wanted something else. Hannah decided she would try to remember to ask when she had time, but time for clothes shopping was in short supply if they wanted to get ahead of the army.

"Herrick is already too far ahead of us," she said, thinking of the elf standing before the Wild Waters to the north. "We need to go around if we're going to make it to Firene before the army."

"And why are we rushing to arrive before the army?" Klauden asked, raising an eyebrow, and Hannah glared at him.

"You know why," she snapped. "I have to find Rory."

"After what you've seen in his dreams," the vampire commented, "it doesn't seem like he wants you to find him." An image of the blonde elf swam through Hannah's mind, the image blurry since Klauden's eyesight wasn't as sharp as hers. It was so easy for him to push things into her, Hannah thought, frowning at him.

<*It could be,*> Klauden thought at her, then he slid another memory into her mind, his body moving above her, inside her, and she shook her head hard.

<*No,*> Hannah thought, retreating to the safety of voices instead of thinking, recalling his last comment about Rory.

"They're not his dreams," Hannah insisted, willing the reminder away. "They are my dreams—nightmares. Nothing in them makes sense. It's just my crazy head." She looked away.

"How can you be sure?" he asked quietly, leaving her to her thoughts at another respectable distance. He was waiting for her to figure something out, to admit something of her fears.

She looked down, and the words burst out of her. "Because in them, Rory is a fledgling, and if he had been bitten by Anna, I would know," she confessed quietly. "I should have known." She said it because it was the biggest thing on her mind, the sight of Rory feeding on someone in an alley, but she didn't say the part that hurt most—seeing him with another woman in his bed. *I deserve it,* she told herself. *But it doesn't matter if he's moved on*, she decided. *I still have to see him, to finish things.*

It couldn't end like this.

She told herself that she could handle seeing him with someone else, but she couldn't handle him as a fledgling, especially if she hadn't even noticed.

"Would you?" Klauden asked, and he glanced at Solyn, the fledgling laying by the fire, her golden hair glinting red and orange as the wind made the flames dance. The weather was still cold, though Hannah rarely noticed unless it snowed. Being wet on the road was uncomfortable. She didn't admit it, but that was partly why she'd suggested the boat. An actual bed in a room with a roof would be glorious, even one on a boat at sea.

Hannah caught a glimpse of something in her companion, a question, a sense of speculation, but then it was gone, Klauden hiding himself in a way that made her jealous. He was very good at blocking her out sometimes. She, on the other hand, couldn't even begin to stop him from invading her thoughts. "Why?" she asked, a bad feeling in her gut. "Do you know something?"

Klauden shrugged, and she was back in his mind a little bit more. *He doesn't know anything specific.* "No," he told her. "But I was very focused on you at the time. To be honest, I'm not even sure how he and Solyn got back to Severin."

"I guess they walked," Hannah suggested. "I should probably ask her about it."

Klauden shrugged again. "You may if you wish."

"I wasn't asking permission," Hannah snapped, disliking the way he sometimes referred to Solyn as a possession.

Klauden gave her a small smile. "Perhaps you should."

"Just because she's your fledgling doesn't mean you own her," Hannah argued, keeping her voice down even though she knew Solyn could hear them if she was awake.

Klauden raised an eyebrow. "It doesn't?"

"No!"

"Why is it so wrong for me to own her?" he prompted. "She's my responsibility, my fledgling, the mother of my child, and the other half of a blood bond. What happens to her concerns me a great deal."

For a split second, Hannah wondered what would happen to Klauden if Solyn died in childbirth, as many women did. Would he die with his fledgling? The idea was too frightening to contemplate. Because of the kevna between her and Klauden, what happened to the vampire concerned her a great deal.

Dear gods, she thought in a small panic, realizing what Klauden had no doubt reasoned a long time ago, *if Solyn gets herself killed somehow or dies in birth, we could all die.* Suddenly, the fledgling's safety took on a whole new meaning.

All moral quandaries of Solyn's free will left her, and she turned to Klauden. "How deep does the bond go? Do we know that?"

He gave her a cool look. "I think we know just how far it goes," he said neutrally, and Hannah caught the memory from his mind—smooth skin beneath torn clothing, sweat and sticky blood on his hands as he moved in her.

"No." She shook her head. "Stop doing that."

"You keep bringing it up," he said, shaking his head. "Would you have me stop thinking?" He reached for his bag, carefully placing the books on his blanket inside. The poor bag was bursting at the seams when he finished.

"You can control it better than that," Hannah said, fascinated by the way his hands touched the covers, curling around the spines. A shiver ran down her spine as she thought of those hands on her skin. "I know you can. I think you just enjoy reminding me."

The vampire turned back to her with a small smile, and the firelight glinted against the red of his nightvision. "No, chaivin," he murmured. "What I enjoy is reminding you that it need not be a memory."

"Don't call me that," she snapped. Every time he called her "chaivin," it reminded her of decades spent together as children. Lately, it seemed he'd only used the pet name when he tried to remind her of that shared past. And she resented it.

"I could just as well call you kevnisha," he quipped. "Not that it matters."

She scoffed at him. They may be bound by kevna, but she wouldn't let him call her his soulmate, no matter how deep their connection was.

"Deny it all you like," he added pointedly. "It still won't go away."

Hannah sighed. "It should have gone away," she told him. "When I returned to this body, the bond should have stayed between you and Solyn's body."

"Certainly, a blood bond should've," he agreed. "But not when kevna is concerned. That ancient magic is a matter of souls, chaivin, not flesh. It transcends all boundaries."

"I know," she said quickly, remembering the pull of his body, the persistent need to be near him, to touch him, to rip open the connection between them. *Gods, will I ever be alone in my mind again?* She shifted her thoughts to the Rory problem instead. At least there, she could do something. "Like I said, if we can get a ship from Rasa, we have a chance to get ahead of them," she suggested.

Klauden considered, allowing her to change the subject. "I've thought about traveling by sea," he admitted, "but how will we feed on board?"

"If we can find a ship sailing up the coast, it will probably stop at the ports along the way," Hannah offered. "It depends on how long between stops. And we can show her how to feed without biting," Hannah suggested, looking over at Solyn. "We can be careful. Besides, it's good practice for when we get to Firene. We can hardly keep feeding as we do in a city filled with elves."

Klauden considered his fledgling, then nodded. "She will not be pleased, but it can be done," he agreed.

"Thank you," Hannah said, "for helping me hurry."

"I do not wish to walk all the way to Firene," he told her. "I already walked here from the Vanya once."

"We could—" Hannah started to suggest the teleportation spell but stopped herself. It would leave one of them alone, and if she tried to combine her magic with Klauden's to allow the spell to bring all of them, it would bring them closer together, and she was having a hard enough time not watching his mouth when he spoke, thinking about the soft skin of his hands, the feel of his hair.

Klauden was staring at her, no doubt knowing what she was thinking. He reached out a hand to touch her, just his fingers covering the back of her hand. Hannah shivered at the contact, willing herself not to move away. She avoided touching Klauden if she could, knowing physical contact made their bond stronger. But still, it was nice to touch someone like her, something that wasn't young, fragile, and mortal. The thought came from deep inside, and she tried not to follow it but couldn't help herself. She remembered his bed, the feel of him, the pure joy of being with someone like her, of not having to hold back for fear of hurting someone else.

His fingers glided up her arm, touching the sensitive skin of her inner wrist, a delicate touch that wasn't threatening. She closed her eyes without thinking, losing herself in the feeling, the magic enveloping her. *I shouldn't be doing this.* What remained of herself fought to ignore the need suddenly building in her, trying to think of anything but how very much she enjoyed the closeness of kevna.

"Stop," she whispered, the word small and pathetic in her mouth. "Please."

His fingers left her skin, and the rush of his desire emptied from her mind. "As you wish, chaivin," he whispered. "But you cannot run from this forever."

Hannah opened her eyes, clearheaded again. "I'm not running from it," she told him. "I'm ignoring it completely." Hannah stood up, stepping away from him.

She glanced at Solyn, still lying by the fire. The girl was Klauden's fledgling—his companion now. Klauden stood up too, standing just behind her, and sent her another thought, a gentle nudge of pleasure, and suddenly, Hannah was furious.

"In case you've forgotten," she snarled, turning around, grabbing the front of his robe into a fist, "we are on our way to find my *husband*." She barked the last word at him, wanting his face to react, wanting that smooth shell to crack. Klauden rarely lost his calm. It was pointless to try, but then again, she could remember seeing the vampire without that control in place, and what she had seen had scared her.

It was too much like what she felt all the time, and to know that they were so alike, so connected, made her even more angry.

"You're bound to her," she told him, pointing to Solyn's form across the campsite. "That body. Not this one. And don't tell me it doesn't matter because we are still bonded." She released Klauden's robes, reaching around to shove him toward his fledgling. "That is your destiny. Accept it."

Klauden fell backward gracefully to his knees, and adjusted his robes calmly, sniffing delicately as he smoothed a rough patch left by Hannah's small grip. "Solyn is mine," he said quietly. "I think we have established that quite clearly now, yes?"

"Yes," Hannah whispered in agreement, hating the way her skin still ached to touch his hand, hating how the bond lessened her.

"And whom, pray tell, is responsible for that little fact?" he asked, carefully folding his hands inside his robe in his customary pose.

Hannah glared at him, recalling his reluctance to make her his fledgling, even in Solyn's body. If she hadn't been dying then, he would never have done it. "Fine," she snapped, hating the deep well of gratitude that she ought to feel toward her childhood betrothed. "So you turned her to save me. What of it?"

"Don't speak to me of destiny, chaivin," he defended, voice growing cold, and she felt something in him, a wave of quiet anger, but it was quickly gone. Hannah wanted to see it again, knowing it was foolish but unable to stop herself. "We are all caught up in this," he added.

"I'm not caught in anything," she insisted, knowing denial was pointless, even childish, but unable to stop the words. "I will get Rory, then we're getting the hell off this continent."

"Where will you go?"

"I don't know. There must be a place without goblin armies and pureblood Houses and stupid blood bonds."

"And you're not running?"

She glared at him, but her real anger had faded as quickly as it came. "There has to be somewhere far enough away to stop ... this," she said, gesturing between the two of them.

"No," the vampire said quietly. "There is not."

"Maybe it could be dampened, then," Hannah tried. "With Rory, I could be..."

"What? Happy again?"

"Yes."

"You seemed content enough with me."

"That's not real," she told him. "All of this is just because of that ridiculous bond."

Klauden stood and moved toward her, his vampiric speed eerie even to her senses. He grabbed both of her hands, pulling them around his back, and kissed her. She wanted to push him away, to stop this, but the power of the connection pulled her closer. She heard Klauden in her mind.

<*This isn't real?*>

<*No,*> she insisted. As far as her body was concerned, there was nothing more real. In fact, she had leaned into him and was wrapping her fingers in his hair, strong hands tugging his head to one side, mouth leaving his to bite his neck, to mark him as she'd marked him twice before.

<*Yes,*> she heard his voice in her mind. <*This is destiny.*>

In the moment while she waited for her teeth to catch up to her instincts, Hannah managed to gain a shred of self-control. She yanked herself away, tugging out some of Klauden's hair as she did so, and shoved herself back, several feet away, her chest heaving as she regained her senses.

Her mind cleared again, and she realized that while she'd been ready to bite the vampire, to begin the slow path toward disaster once more, he hadn't moved. In fact, he hadn't moved at all. He was still kneeling where she had pushed him. The entire scene was in her mind.

She knew he could do that to her, overwhelm her senses with images and actions that didn't really happen. *I forgot.* It had been a long time since he had illustrated that level of power over her.

And while his advance had been largely imaginary, her own response had been quite physical. She had thrown herself at him. The rage was sharp and impotent, uncertain of where to turn. She looked at the ground, seeing small bits of grass and twigs jutting through the muddy edge of the clearing, focusing on tiny details instead of the fury inside. She swallowed hard, twisting her fingers to get rid of the pieces of hair she'd torn from Klauden's head.

"I will get my husband," she said fiercely. "And then, I'm leaving you behind. In fact," she added, "I wish you would go now, and leave me alone."

"You will never be alone," Klauden said, shaking his head. "That is your destiny."

"I'm so tired of that word. I'm going to leave this place and my stupid destiny behind."

"I see." Klauden nodded, giving up for the evening, Hannah hoped. He turned to Solyn, and Hannah wondered if the fledgling could hear what she and Klauden said to one another. She knew Solyn's hearing was sharp, all fledgling senses were incredible, but if she heard, the girl said nothing.

Klauden headed toward Solyn's blanket, but turned his head as he stood, tossing the words quietly over his shoulder. "That's assuming your elf still wants you, of course."

VI

Five days later, Hannah stood in the center of three mortal men, her power easily holding one gently in place while she stared at him. She thought about how nice it would be to feed on him, biting his neck and draining him until he was dead, absorbing his memories with his life's blood, but that wasn't the goal this time. Klauden held the other two men in place with his own magic. The frozen man stared back at Hannah, bewitched by the strange creature he saw.

"Watch," Klauden said to Solyn. Hannah took that as her cue to move forward. She drew her dagger slowly, not wanting to startle the petrified man, his mind recognizing her for the predator she was, but she was using her power to soothe him.

"Come here," she told him, and his body obeyed, seemingly without the agreement of his mind if she judged by the expression on his face. Hannah pushed more power into him, easing his fear. It was so easy now, her magic stronger than it had ever been before. "There's nothing to fear," she assured him. "You're fine."

He took another step toward her, and she reached out for his arm. Pushing up his sleeve, she drew the dagger across his inner lower arm, avoiding the wrist and blood vessels there that would be fatal. She didn't want to kill him, and she didn't want to infect him with her bite.

The blade was sharp, and the blood began to flow. "You're fine," she repeated, lifting the arm above her face and letting the blood drip into her mouth. She swallowed, moving him close but not close enough to touch his skin. There was a flutter of memories, of many nights sleeping by a campfire, of a small terrified child, of men in armor marching by on the road. Hannah distanced herself from the images and the man himself.

She wasn't exactly sure what precise moment created a fledgling, whether it was in her teeth or her saliva or her intention, but she would never make that mistake again. She thought it was probably something in her teeth because she had kissed Rory many times without him changing, so she kept the man's skin away from her mouth, letting the blood fall into her mouth instead. "You're helping me," she told him, feeling a rise of fear in him as his mind tried to rally. After another moment of drinking, she let his arm fall to his side but didn't let him go. She had been practicing the magic of healing humans with Klauden, but she still wasn't very good at it. She tried to heal the slice she had made, but she must've gotten it wrong because the man cried out in pain and jerked away from her.

Surprised by the movement, Hannah lost her control over him, forcing him to stumble back with a yell. She reached for him again, but Solyn was faster, the fledgling leaping before her and latching onto the man's neck, biting him ferociously and knocking him to the ground. She felt Klauden's magic fade for a moment, and one of the seated men tried to stand up.

"What the—?" she started to say, but then Klauden was reaching out with his power, in control again, and the man sat down hard, joining his dazed companion.

"Solyn!" Klauden snapped, and the fledgling jerked away from the man, falling back with an angry expression, the beast denied its prey, blood coating her face and the front of her dress. The man lay on the grass, throat torn out, heart slowly fading to a stop.

"Klauden." Hannah's voice was low and angry. "Please control your fledgling."

"What happened?" Klauden asked Solyn, voice way more controlled than she expected. It wasn't that Klauden often lost his temper, but Hannah would've raged if her fledgling had done that. She was barely holding herself back as it was. She knelt beside the body, lifting both of his arms and resting them across his chest. *Such a waste*, she thought angrily, and after she'd been so careful with him. "<Be well,>" she said in her native tongue.

Normally, Hannah had no qualms with death or with killing people. Drinking blood was fundamental to her survival, and she wouldn't make any fledglings, so if she didn't want to bleed her victims, she killed them to be sure. But she only killed certain people, and only after seeing their memories. Certainly, she had killed her share of innocent people over the years, but she didn't relish it, didn't share Solyn's current expression.

Or if she did, it had been a very long time ago.

She hadn't meant for the man to die tonight, for any of them to die, but now there was no choice. She could have turned the memory of the attack into a dream, and with no evidence of the wound, he wouldn't have known the difference. But now since their companion had been attacked and brutalized—not to mention the man was now dead—Hannah couldn't make them think this was a dream. *They all must die.*

She took a deep breath and looked up at Klauden. <*Is it worth it to still try to teach her? She's sated, mostly, and might be willing to listen.*>

Klauden's face was stern. He disliked that Solyn had disobeyed him, disliked that she wasn't learning the lesson. He really disliked the suggestion that his own fledgling needed to be *willing* to obey him.

<*She will listen to me.*> Hannah was a little shocked by the forcefulness in him. This side of Klauden as a Master was new to her. Maybe it had always been there, but he had never been so to her. Even when she'd been newly turned, and she had given her will to him so he could help her control her cravings, he had been gentle, asking instead of demanding. The Klauden who stood before her now was a different man altogether.

Hannah wondered if being with her these last few months had changed him so much, or if she would've seen this side of him even if they had stayed in her father's castle and married. Hadn't she accused him of that when she was trapped inside the Star of Elgiva? That, one day, he would turn on her. She hadn't really believed it then, saying it only to hurt him in her anger, but seeing him now, she wondered if she'd been right. For all she knew of Klauden, he was still shrouded in mystery, secrets about himself that he hid from her.

She looked at Solyn, and pity replaced her anger. The fledgling was young, still learning, her body no doubt subject to all manner of changes with the baby. Klauden turned to face Solyn and Hannah could feel the tirade building in him.

<*Wait!*>

Klauden paused, turning to look at her, annoyance pooling but not spilling out.

She rose and moved over to sit near Solyn instead. "Solyn, you can't do this," she said gently.

"Why? Because he doesn't want me to?" Solyn's voice was petulant, her own frustration rising.

"Because you must learn control," Hannah told her. "You can't kill people like this or the mortals will find you."

Solyn stuck her chin out, and through the bond with Klauden, Hannah felt the rebellion building in the fledgling's chest along with a newfound sense of pride. "And do what to me? They can't hurt me. I'm strong now."

Hannah felt Klauden readying himself for a lecture, but she stopped him with a thought. "It's not about strength," she told the fledgling. "It's about survival. If you kill like this, it puts the mortals on their guard, making it harder to feed next time." She looked at the other two men sitting on the ground, faces blank under the magic. "We are going to get on a boat," she reminded Solyn. "They will toss you overboard if they suspect anything. Sailors are a notoriously suspicious lot."

"I can swim," Solyn snapped, though Hannah's words had started to get through. Solyn might be angry right now, but she wasn't stupid. After all, she had seen Hannah die despite her vampiric strength.

"And so can many other creatures," Hannah reminded her. "You're strong, no doubt, and fast, but I wouldn't want to test that against those creatures living in the ocean deep."

Solyn's face shifted as she considered the limits of her strength.

"I've never tasted the blood of a shark," Hannah commented, "and I don't ever want to need to. I don't even know if we can swallow blood in water with any effect."

Solyn nodded. "I understand," she said finally. "I must be careful on the boat."

"You need to be careful everywhere!" Klauden snapped, unable to contain himself. "We cannot go to Firene if you behave in such a way!"

As Hannah watched her, the fledgling turned to her master, eyes calculating. "Then perhaps we shouldn't go to Firene," she said in a low voice, fingers rubbing against the smeared front of her dress.

"Not go to Firene," Klauden repeated. "Where would we go, then?" He sounded weary, frustrated, a tone Hannah rarely heard him use. Klauden certainly had his hands full between the two of them, she mused—one ex-betrothed soulmate and one fledgling mother-to-be with violent tendencies.

"Back to the castle," Solyn suggested. "Back home." She looked up at him, face searching. There was a question in her voice, like this was something she had longed to ask him. Hannah could feel how much Solyn wanted his answer. It surprised her—she didn't think Solyn would ever want to return to her father's castle. Too many dark memories lay in that place. What was the fledgling thinking?

Klauden just stared at her. When he spoke, his voice was careful. "Back home to what, Solyn? There's nothing left for me there." He gave her a long look, understanding crossing his face. "If you have some delusion of returning home triumphant on my arm, think again. I will not return there. Think, girl," he snapped. "Kelvin Malbrek still lives. What would make you think I could go anywhere near him after what has happened? He'd have my head before we even got past the outer guard, and even if we did make it," he continued, gesturing at Hannah, "her father would place me in the tournaments before I even had the chance to explain what I was doing anywhere near Severin and the army Hannah's body amassed there," he shook his head, a bit rueful, "not to mention what my mother would do to me if she got her turn." He paused, a bitter smile curling his mouth as he considered. "No, I cannot ever return home, Solyn. Not anymore. I thought you of all people would understand that."

Solyn's face darkened at his words, but she didn't reply. It seemed she had gotten the answer she wanted. When Klauden had finished, she sniffed, tucking blood-streaked hair behind her ears. "Is that all?" she asked finally.

"Is that all?" Klauden repeated, voice rising a little. He took a moment to visibly calm himself. His face turned cold. "When you are starving because you cannot find anyone to feed on, ask me again if *that is all*." He shook his head in disgust, taking in her filthy dress. "And what are you supposed to wear now? That blood will ruin your dress. You cannot just wander about wearing a blood-stained dress." He rolled his eyes, and his gaze took in both of them. "I don't know if it's a female trait or just something you both have in common, but a little forethought would not hurt anyone."

"I have forethought," Solyn said, and her gaze turned to the two men sitting near her. She was moving again, so quickly Hannah worried for a second, but she only knelt down before the closest man. Her hand reached for his arm. "I will not starve." She looked up at her master, the obedient fledgling again, at least for the moment. "Show me, then."

VII

"So the thing to remember is that mortals do not heal through blood as we do, but with time. All the magic does is quicken the process, rewrapping time around the affected area and healing it within seconds instead of a week or a month," Klauden explained. "It's really quite simple when one comes to think of it."

Hannah nodded, understanding the concept. "But isn't it dangerous to mess around with time?"

Klauden shook his head, his long fingers tucking a loose blonde strand behind his ear. "It's only mortal time. We can manipulate it because we stand somewhat outside of time, but even we can only do so much. We cannot undo what has been done. We can only speed up what could already be remedied, but without the dangers of infection or exhaustion."

Hannah considered the vampire, then glanced at Solyn, the fledgling sitting by the fire, face impassive as she studied the flames. They were camped again, but this time, they would leave in the morning light and enter Rasa to find a boat north.

"We aren't exactly beyond time," she said, thinking of the weeks on the road. "Solyn is as a fledgling, a turned vampire, but we still age."

"True, but so slowly as to make no difference."

"Tell that to my father," Hannah remarked, recalling her last memories of her father before she left the castle, even the untouchable Magnus van Kreeosk had started to have small wrinkle lines on his forehead, the perfect skin marred by the five centuries of his lifetime. "He would do anything, I think, to have Solyn's immortality."

Klauden shook his head. "I don't think so. As a fledgling, Solyn is denied many of the characteristics we take for granted. She isn't nearly as strong, though she was when she was first created, nor can she see or hear as well as we can. She is well beyond a mortal, yes, but to us, she is still as a mortal before a god."

Hannah remembered the fight with the fledglings during her attempt to rescue Rory, remembered their steely strength, their blinding speed—unnerved that those creatures were, in Klauden's mind, as mortals before gods. What precisely was her body capable of if that was true? It seemed every day she spent away from the castle and others like herself, she learned more of her own capabilities than she had in decades living at home.

"But she will stay forever as she is, and you and I will age. Shouldn't she be better at time magic than we are?" Hannah asked.

Klauden glanced at the fledgling, then back at Hannah. "Solyn has no magic. It's not in her."

"But when I was in her, controlling that body as a mortal, I could cast magic. It was harder when she woke up because she can't read, and memorizing didn't work anymore, but the magic was still in me, ready for when I needed it. Even now I don't have to memorize the words. Now the magic just comes to me."

Klauden considered, a hand stroking his chin as he thought. "There is some mention in the ancient texts of soul magic. It could be connected to kevna."

"Soul magic? What's that?"

"I think it is the name for the way you now prefer to cast spells," he told her. "The power is connected to the soul, I think, always, hence the reason why Solyn can no longer cast spells. The connection to the power was through you, not the flesh—not her essence, but your own. When you had to find a new way to cast, you awakened another aspect of kevna, thereby deepening the bond between us." He thought for another moment. "Your spells are more powerful now, yes?"

Hannah considered. "Sometimes. Not always."

"I think that is because of me."

"You?"

"I'm a better caster than you."

"And modest too," she commented.

He smirked at her. "You know I speak the truth." He sighed. "I studied much longer and much harder than you ever did. It makes sense that I'm better." He paused. "But now, through kevna, you're somehow tapping into my power when you cast. The magic is still connected to you, your essence, but it's now attached to me too."

"Does it weaken you?"

"I don't know," he replied. "We'll have to see. Maybe we can try a more complicated spell together." Hannah almost said no, that she didn't want to discover what would happen if it meant getting closer to him again. But he shook his head, dismissing the idea, lack of knowledge a particular frustration he couldn't deal with. "There's too much we don't know about kevna." He considered another moment, then gave Hannah a serious look. "We really must get our hands on some of the books in the library."

"The library?" Hannah asked, then understanding dawned. "You mean back at the castle? Are you crazy? We can't return there. Like you said, they'd kill you, not to mention what they'd do to me."

"True, but it's not as if we'd walk right in the front entrance."

"The teleportation spell?" Hannah asked. "But that only works for two." She looked up, seeing Solyn's form outlined by the fire. Was he willing to leave Solyn alone so they could retrieve some ancient texts?

"You know those tunnels beneath the castle better than anyone," Klauden said. "It has to be you."

"She might know them," Hannah suggested, gesturing at Solyn. "She was a slave there for several years. She's probably familiar with every passageway in the complex."

"Yes," Klauden agreed, "from the laundry to the kitchen, then back again." He shook his head. "Be sensible, chaivin. She only knew the upper levels, if anything, where our rooms were. She wouldn't have had access to the dungeons or the library, nor would she have cared."

"What's so important in these books that you'd risk leaving her behind?"

The vampire paused. "I don't know, chaivin. That's why I have to retrieve them. I just don't know and..."

"And it's making you crazy," Hannah finished for him.

"Yes."

"Klauden, eventually you must accept the fact that there're things in this world you will never know. Deal with it."

"I know that," he snapped at her. "But I won't risk the chance that there is something in those books about kevna that we don't know. Anything that would make some of this make more sense."

"Make more sense?" Hannah asked him. "I thought you knew all about it." She raised her hand, tapping off points on her fingers. "It's an ancient bond between soulmates, connecting them in all things—mentally, spiritually, and physically. It connects people beyond life and death." She put her hand down. "You told me all this when the bond first appeared."

He was silent for a time, long enough for Hannah to question it, then he sighed, and she sensed something in him, some long decision finally reached. "When did the bond first appear, Hannah?" Klauden asked, and Hannah gave him a hard look. He never called her by her name unless he was quite serious.

"When you turned me," she answered easily. "When I was in Solyn's body, when I was mortal and the fledgling bit me." Something about Klauden's face was not as it should be. "When I was dying," she added helpfully.

"No." The vampire shook his head slowly. "Hannah, no."

"No what?"

"That is not when kevna appeared," he replied.

"When did it appear, then?" Hannah distrusted the look on his face, a look suggesting bad news was on the horizon. She'd seen that expression before, back when he first admitted to watching her since she left home through the ring—his going away present to her. She tried not to think of the ring now. It hadn't reappeared since she dropped it in Rory's dream. Had Klauden somehow gotten it? Was that what he planned to tell her?

The vampire still hadn't spoken. She stared at him. "Well? When did it appear, then?"

He took a deep breath. "It's always been between us," he told her. "Since we were children. It's why we were promised to begin with." He ran a hand through his hair, smiling a little. "Do you think your father would have given you to me if he'd had a choice?"

"Where else could I have gone?" Hannah considered the options of her father's house. "Vailen van Joosen?" She felt her skin crawl at the mention of the other First Son in the castle. She'd never had much use for him, but after spending time in Solyn's body and inside the slave's memories,

Hannah had a very clear idea of what Vailen van Joosen considered a good time, and now the thought of him carried an urge to vomit.

Klauden laughed. "Not a chance. The van Joosens are Third Family."

"And you're Second."

"Was Second."

"You still are," she told him, "even if it doesn't mean anything anymore to you. You were the only one available. Or…" She thought about it. "Would my father have sent me to another House?"

Klauden shook his head. "Oh no," he said. "Not you, but through you, he could've called a First Son from another House. How better to weaken them than to demand their First Son for his own House?"

"So, you're saying he settled for you because of kevna? That's ridiculous. My father wouldn't have surrendered that kind of political leverage. He wanted you because you were to succeed him," Hannah told him. "You're Second Family. It all makes sense."

"Does it? That your father would've chosen a spellcaster from Second Family as his successor when he already had a fledgling who excelled at magic? Think, chaivin."

"I am thinking," she told him. "My father wouldn't have passed things on to Kelvin Malbrek. He's not a pureblood. My father needed you."

"No, he settled for me. He wanted someone else like himself—a fighter, a strategizer." Klauden paused, then added, "With you, he could have had the Sarkoza under his thumb as First Son." Hannah frowned, thinking of her cousin. Milo van Reegan was First Son to the Second Family in Gerter van Lartner's castle, something that normally would have made him unworthy. But he had a special ability to make others obey him when he spoke, earning him the name Sarkoza—the Voice. Stealing such a powerful vampire from House van Lartner would have been a prized victory. She recalled a visit from Milo and his family when they were children, remembered the fancy dinner parties and the serious conversations, but she had been too young to realize what had been discussed. They had probably come for her, but her father, a vampire who lived for nothing but power and influence, had refused.

Though she didn't want to admit it, Klauden's words were making sense to her. There were so many other choices for her beyond Klauden. Her father would've preferred someone less scholarly as his successor, no doubt. And Klauden did have the same skill set as Kelvin Malbrek, her father's second. *Why didn't I see it before?*

"But what convinced him, then?" she asked. "Why did he give up the chance to have another House indebted to him through me? Why didn't he just ignore kevna?"

Klauden gave her a pointed look. "One cannot ignore kevna." Hannah had a flash of his mind, of hands on skin and paralyzing need to be closer, to touch deeper. She shuddered, trying to separate herself from his thoughts. The bond made it too easy sometimes to get lost in him. She supposed that was what kevna did, though. "It was your mother," he said after a moment.

"My mother?"

"She convinced him to give you to me. He originally wanted to kill me, you know."

"Really?"

Klauden nodded. "He thought it would sever the bond, but then your mother convinced him that it may do that, but it may also kill you in the process. And he'd lose his chance at a precious First Daughter."

Hannah stared at him, the implications of this information far reaching into her childhood. A lot of little things suddenly made sense to her.

"And Anna?" she asked, the name of her half-sister suddenly innocent on her lips, as she thought of the child she'd known and not the enraged spirit she'd had to fight out of her body back in Severin.

"Anna was just in case something should happen to me, inadvertently killing you."

"But ... if it's always been there, why didn't I feel it before?" Hannah watched his face when he didn't reply right away. The magic rushed through her, through them both, and she wanted to touch his skin, to feel him close to her. She knew he was thinking of her hand tangled in his hair, her lips against his. He forced the memory away, looking down at the blanket they both sat on instead of facing her.

"That is," he admitted slowly, and Hannah could feel some big emotion inside of him, something like ... shame, "partly my fault."

"What do you mean?"

Instead of answering out loud, Klauden concentrated, the force of his will shocking despite knowing he was strong. Then suddenly, there was an iron barrier between them, locking him away. She could still feel his presence, an echo of the Klauden she knew, but it was like looking out a window to see a tiny form far away on the ground outside. She stared at him, seeing the handsome face she knew so well, the eyes so guarded. She could sense the magic in him, but it was contained behind that wall. She turned away from it, from him, and suddenly, there was something else out there—dozens of lines from her to others. She was keenly aware of the fledglings connected to this body, many of them moving through a deep forest, but one was somewhere else, much farther away. She got a sense of silken sheets, the sound of the ocean, but then it was gone. The wall Klauden had built disintegrated, and kevna swirled over her again, obliterating everything else.

Klauden took a ragged breath, running a hand through his hair, and frowned. "I can't hold it anymore, chaivin. I am sorry." She could feel his exhaustion, the cost of the magical effort to shield her.

"Wait," she said, speaking instead of thinking to give him space, "you've been doing that … our whole lives?"

He tilted his head, biting his lip, the movement making her want to lean over and kiss him, to feel him so close to her again, and she fisted her hands, curling her fingers so her nails dug into her palms. A huge well of gratitude was growing inside of her. "Not exactly," he said. "It wasn't always like that, like this." He stared at her mouth, seeming unable to stop himself. "Before, I could contain it without much trouble. But not anymore."

"Why?" she asked, though part of her knew what changed. Memory flashed between them, his hands on her skin, his mouth on hers, and that perfect sense of satisfaction.

Klauden shook his head as if to clear the sensations.

"I see." Hannah stayed perfectly still, not trusting herself.

"No, you don't see," he said, bursting to his feet. "We've always had something between us, something powerful, but this is different. It's changed. It's … so much more." He shook his head again, running nervous hands through his hair. "I have to know what it means," he insisted.

"And you need the books for that. You need the library."

"I need the library," he nodded, giving her a suspicious look. "You're taking this very well," he commented.

Hannah looked at her old friend, years of memories slowly shifting into place, the connection between them amplifying her love for him. She knew it was the magic, but it didn't make it feel any less real to her. They would always be bound to one another, no matter what happened. The solidity of the promise reassured her instead of terrified her for once. She sniffed, a slow smile working its way onto her lips as she soaked in the feeling. "I know," she said, wondering at the deep calm within herself. "No worries. I'm sure I'll be angry with you again soon."

VIII

Hannah had been in a handful of large cities since leaving home, so she knew what to expect: the crush of bodies, the deluge of smells, the mismatched jam of hovels and houses and mansions, and the noise of many people doing so many things. They followed the Rasa Road to its end right at the gates, joining a swiftly moving line of travelers entering the city.

The guards didn't comment as they walked through the gates, and Hannah was impressed how both Klauden and Solyn handled their first sight of a true city. Klauden's gaze slid from side to side as they walked into the large marketplace, observing everything from meat pies and juice to fancy kettles and fine bolts of fabric. Hannah was glad to see Solyn's eyes linger on the fabric instead of the people they passed. She wasn't entirely sure how the fledgling would react to the crowded place, but Klauden seemed to have her impulses well controlled.

They had draped Hannah's old cloak over Solyn's ruined blue dress, hiding the bloodstains, but they paused in the market to get her some new clothes. Solyn didn't choose a dress, instead settling on two pairs of pants, one soft black leather, the other a brown cotton, and three shirts in varying styles. She took a long time to decide on a belt, but when she stepped out wearing the outfit, Hannah was impressed. Solyn really was lovely to see. Hannah bought another dark skirt, a pair of leather pants, and a soft shirt for herself, unable to resist the indulgence, though the material of the shirt was slightly sheer. Her jacket was still in good condition, the sleeves long enough to cover part of her hands, so she put it back on over her new clothes. Keeping her scarred palm hidden was more important now that they were in a city.

Klauden left for a few moments to grab a few items in the market, but then he waited patiently for them to complete their shopping, politely declining when the shopkeeper offered him new clothes. His robes were still clean, no doubt kept spotless by the magic he used. Hannah and Solyn had been washing their own clothes in any water they passed as they traveled. Hannah suddenly wondered how Klauden was cleaning his body, and she was rewarded with an image of him standing waist deep in water, blonde hair dripping down his bare chest, and she shoved the image away.

< *You're not the only one who goes swimming, chaivin.* >

They passed through the market into the city center, wooden stalls and tables giving way to formal shop fronts and permanent housing. The street moved progressively downhill, and Hannah assumed they were heading to the docks because the smell of ocean air and gutted fish was growing stronger. They reached another market, this one for seafood, and Hannah could see the dozens of ships in the harbor. Hannah looked at Klauden.

< *You should do the negotiating,* > she thought to him.

Klauden's face was confused. < *Why? I know no more about ships than you do.* >

< *Because you're a man. They will respect you more than us.* >

Klauden rolled his eyes, the idea foreign to him. In his mind, people were respected based on blood status, not gender. Back home, Magnus van Kreeosk may be in charge of the castle, but Keller van Sherinak and Reina van Joosen ran everything else. He deferred to Hannah's knowledge, nodding in agreement. Hannah stepped slightly behind him and Solyn moved to stand beside her.

Klauden and his two women, Hannah thought bitterly, but then regretted it. The vampire was doing his best to help her get to Rory, something she knew he didn't really want to do. He was also managing to keep Solyn's bloodlust in check while people surged around them. The thought of blood made her skin tingle, and she glanced over at Solyn, recognizing the echo of the fledgling's desire.

< *Solyn?* > Inside of replying, Solyn reached out a hand and quickly grabbed Hannah's, seeking calm through touch as the smell and sounds of the people intensified around them. Hannah gave her a reassuring smile, holding her hand tight, and followed Klauden, sending soothing thoughts in Solyn's direction. She remembered the feeling from when she'd been

in Solyn's body, the call of blood sudden and overpowering, but she also knew how to get Solyn through it.

<Soon,> she promised her. <We'll be out of here soon.>

<I know,> Solyn thought, and Hannah heard her clearly in her mind, her bond with Klauden allowing her to connect to his fledgling easily. <I just need a moment of quiet.> Hannah moved a little closer to her, fingers laced together, pushing her control into the fledgling in small waves, letting Solyn regain her own control slowly. Klauden looked back at them over his shoulder.

<Everything alright?>

Hannah nodded. <We're fine.>

They reached the edge of the market where the cobblestone street shifted into wooden platforms, joining a large, interconnected mass of docks. Several people lingered there—a few elves, more humans, and a halfling Hannah had mistaken for a human boy.

Klauden approached a well-dressed man who stood on the dock, looking at the boats. "Excuse me," Klauden began. "I'm looking to book passage north."

The man turned an eager face toward the obvious quality of Klauden's robes, then glanced at Hannah and Solyn. He dismissed them, turning back to Klauden. "Are you now? I know a few ships heading north," he shared. "I might be willing to tell you," he said, "for a price."

"I think you should tell me anyway," Klauden suggested, and Hannah felt the push of his magic, the suggestion strong as the spell enveloped the man. They had plenty of coin and could pay the man, but Hannah knew Klauden had decided not to show any weakness at the start of negotiations. "Which boats are heading north?"

"The *Crystal* and the *Dark Mistress* are heading that way," he said in a dreamy voice. "Captain Simmons and Captain Trudeau." He paused, about to say something else, but he stopped himself. "Either one of them would take you north."

"And who else heads north?" Klauden prompted, not wanting to accept the first suggestions from this man. "Who would you not recommend?"

"The *Volant*," the man sneered. "Captain Red has no respect for any man. Woman needs to learn her place in the world," he added, and Hannah sensed there was a long history of hostility there.

Klauden thanked the man and handed him a silver coin, which he accepted while shaking his head in confusion. They walked away to stand in an empty space on the dock. "The *Volant*, then?" he asked, and both Hannah and Solyn nodded.

"Anyone he hates has to be decent," Hannah said. She stopped a passing young man who was scurrying into the market. "Where can we find the *Volant*?" she asked him, flashing a silver coin and a smile.

The sailor paused at the money and froze at the words, posture suddenly wary. "Who wants to know?" he asked.

"Three paying customers," she told him, "looking to head north."

He cocked his head, considering them, keen eyes skimming their clothes, no doubt judging their wealth. "How far north?"

"Firene," Klauden told him.

"Far," the boy said, nodding his head. "Just the three of you? No cargo?"

Klauden shook his head. "Just us." He paused, then added, "We require cabins. We will not be sleeping on deck."

The boy looked mildly offended. "Captain Red would never make a paying customer sleep on deck," he insisted. "She's got more sense than that." He rolled his eyes. "You'd just get in the way anyway."

"Bring us to your captain, then?"

The boy nodded, then turned and led them down the maze of docks, heading toward a three-masted ship docked on the edge of the harbor. He gestured up at the ship, a modest caravel being loaded with boxes and barrels. Two women stood on the dock beside it, heads together as they watched the men loading the cargo. One was a tall freckle-faced woman wearing a black hat, long red locks down to her chest covering the front of her blue velvet jacket. A leather belt crossed her hips, the loops holding a cutlass on her right hip and a sabre on her left, both weapons clearly from different cultures. Her pants were a fine material, her boots well-made, and Hannah was reminded of Lira, the elf she'd met when she first met Rory, though the woman was human. The other human had dark skin and long hair twisted into braids that sprawled over her shoulders and down her back. She wore a tight-fitted leather shirt and a knee-high skirt with slits up the sides, displaying the blades fastened to both thighs. She was barefoot, but leather straps wrapped around her calves in an intricate design. Hannah felt her bloodlust stir at the sight of the women, of so much vitality in one place, and she took a deep breath to settle herself. She felt Klauden's question, asking if she needed his help to control herself, but she ignored him. She could do this; she was in control.

The young man walked up to them. "Captain, ma'am, these passengers looking to book passage to Firene." He looked back at them, then added, "They'll pay for a cabin."

"Two cabins," Hannah said, needing some space for herself.

The woman in the hat looked them over, then stepped closer. "Firene, huh?" She cocked her head. "That's a long way."

"Longer on land," Klauden said. "Are you heading that way?"

The captain nodded. "Eventually." She gestured to the cargo still being loaded. "Got a few stops along the way though," she told them.

"Where?" Hannah asked, trying to decide how three vampires would feed on such a ship. She estimated maybe a dozen crew in total—not enough if they didn't want to be caught—especially if the ship kept stopping along the way.

"Upsen across the bay," the captain replied, "then Warin, and then Firene."

"How long?" Klauden asked, no doubt doing the same calculations about blood aboard.

The captain considered, then looked to her companion. "How long to Firene, Lady Black?" she asked.

The other woman frowned, then said, "Two weeks to the Elven city, Captain Red."

Hannah nodded. Two weeks was much faster than the six weeks they could manage by land. "Two weeks work for you?" the captain asked.

"It does," Klauden agreed. "And the price?"

"Depends," the captain replied. "You want two cabins?" She sniffed. "You're not getting mine, nor Lady Black's. But I can spare two rooms down on the lower deck. Nothing fancy, but they're clean." She looked again to Lady Black.

"Two cabins for three people for fourteen days," Lady Black said, musing. "Let's call it thirty gold."

Hannah considered. It was expensive, but not unreasonable. They had plenty of coin.

"Up front," the captain added. "It includes two meals a day, plus water and rum rations." Hannah smirked. It wasn't like they would be eating much of the food. Solyn could still eat if she wanted as a fledgling, though it wouldn't sate her need for blood, but Hannah and Klauden could only manage soup or thin liquids. They could survive solely on blood.

Klauden shook his head. "Half up front. The rest when we get to Firene."

The captain frowned, then nodded. "Fine. We leave on the tide." She turned to her first mate. "Tell Mister Bates and Mister Sims to move their things to the crew quarters." She looked back at them. "You coming aboard now?"

"When is the tide?" Klauden asked.

Captain Red smirked at their lack of knowledge. "Indwellers, huh? You ever been on a boat?"

All three of them shook their heads, and the captain laughed. "Let's hope you don't get seasick, then. Be back by sunset."

IX

L ater that evening, they returned to the *Volant* after finding willing participants in the city to feed their needs. Hannah was pleased at Solyn's restraint, all three of them drinking their fill of three young men they spellbound and led to a shadowy alleyway. Hannah managed the healing spell to mend the line of ragged flesh from her dagger, careful not to leave behind any evidence—and certainly not any fledglings.

The *Volant* was not a seemingly large ship in comparison to some of the galleons docked in the harbor, but Hannah was pleasantly surprised to see how big it actually was when they climbed aboard. Captain Red introduced them to the crew, a mishmash of three Elven women who seemed to live in the rigging, two halflings of indeterminate gender who ran the kitchen, and seven humans—four men and three women—who seemed eager to get back to work, though they were polite enough. The captain gestured to her left at the two doors on either side below the quarterdeck.

"Far one is the dining hall. You'll hear the meal bells. Go down to the kitchen to get your food, and then you can come up here to eat if you like company. The other one is mine. I like my sleep and don't like being disturbed. If the door is shut, leave me be, save fire or sinking."

Hannah wanted to ask if either occasion was likely, but the captain was already moving. She led them down the wooden stairs belowdecks and turned to the back of the ship and a short stub hallway with four doors. She pointed to the far doors in the back. "That's Lady Black's cabin and the office. You have no business in there." She gestured to the two doors facing one another at the start of the short corridor, opening both doors into the hallway. "These are your rooms." She held out two brass keys, and Klauden took both awkwardly. He was already wondering how they would sleep three of them in two rooms.

Hannah could tell the rooms were identical—a small berth built into the wall at the back of the small space, and a linen hammock hanging from the ceiling. Bedding and a pillow were neatly folded on the beds, and there was a small wooden locker built into the right of the bed, no doubt for storage, the lid flipped open to reveal the empty space inside. The closed lid would make a small surface to rest things on. The rooms weren't big, but the bed looked softer than the ground she had been sleeping on, and everything was clean and smelled fresh. They must mop the floors on a regular basis.

She turned, surveying the rest of the area. Above her was a metal grate that could open skyward, a way for the ship to load large cargo. Then Hannah realized—the wood platform she stood on could also be opened to move things into the hold below. She had always wondered how tall the inside of a ship was, and though she was short and never risked bumping her head on a ceiling, Klauden was not, but he had plenty of space above him to walk comfortably. Hannah assumed the lower deck had a similar height. On the front of the deck were two openings, one a doorway into what Hannah assumed was a kitchen, based on the smells coming from that way, and the other door closed tight. The captain didn't mention the room, and Hannah didn't ask.

The captain did gesture down the stairs, telling them the hold was fairly packed, but they were welcome to look down there if they got bored. "Be careful of your light, though," she warned. "I would not appreciate it if you set my ship on fire."

Klauden was studying the deck carefully, and Hannah could feel the question in him before he spoke. "May I ask why you have no cannon?"

Captain Red laughed, raising her eyebrows. "You expecting trouble I should know about?"

Klauden shook her head. "No, of course not. I just always thought ships like this had cannons."

The captain shook her head. "Some do, but I found I don't need them."

"Are you not concerned about pirates, then?" he asked.

She laughed again. "Not in these civilized waters," she promised. "Though if it troubles you, rest assured the *Volant* is a fast ship. We can outrun any pursuit far easier than we could blow them out of the water with cannons." She considered, looking up, the last of the fading daylight on her pretty face. "We do have the ballista up top, though I don't know how much good it would do you." She smiled and nodded at them, clearly done with the tour and ready to leave them with some final words. "I don't have many rules aboard," she said, lifting up her hand and pointing with each finger. "Don't bother my crew. Don't rifle though things that aren't yours. Don't set my ship on fire. Don't fall off my ship." At this last command, she paused, looking them over. "Can you swim?"

Hannah nodded confidently. Klauden and Solyn gave a quick and completely unbelievable jerk of the head.

"Right," the captain said. "Maybe just stay down here until we set off, though you should come up after that. Watching the lights fade as we sail away from Rasa is quite lovely."

She turned and headed back up the stairs, leaving the three of them standing before the open doors of their rooms. Hannah was about to say something about wanting the time alone when Solyn walked into the room on the right, turned to face them both, snatched one of the keys from Klauden's outstretched hand, said simply, "Work it out. I'm tired," and slammed the door in their faces.

Hannah walked past Klauden into the other room, setting her bag on the bed. She turned to face Klauden, who followed her after a moment of hesitation. He looked from the bed to the hammock and back again, a question in his eyes. Hannah shrugged. "I fit both places, so it's up to you." She looked at him, then back at the bed, eyeballing the size. "You should fit here." She scooted her bag off the bed and onto the floor, then climbed into the hammock with more ease than she had anticipated. Occasionally, the dexterity of her vampiric body still surprised her. She pushed her body out, adjusting in the strong material. It wasn't soft like the bed probably was, but it hugged her body in a pleasant way. She drifted slightly from side to side, and though the feeling was nice, she hoped she wouldn't regret it once they were out at sea. She thought ships rocked a lot in open water, especially if the weather was rough.

Klauden settled himself on the bed, putting his bag down on the floor beside hers, then stretched out to his full length on the mattress. It was a narrow bunk, but Hannah could feel the contentment slip over him as his body sank into the cushion. It wasn't his bed back in Castle van Kreeosk, but it was a far cry from the ground he had been sleeping on, not to mention the wooden floors before that. He raised his hands and settled them under his head, looking up at the ceiling in the little room.

They could hear the bustling of activity taking place above them on the ship—a heavy step on the deck above, a shouted command, the small creaks of the ship in the water.

Alone, Hannah thought, staring at the ceiling from where her hammock gently swayed. *Finally alone.*

Klauden's voice echoed in her mind. *<We're never alone, chaivin.>*

DREAMING:
KLAUDEN

Klauden recognized the dream immediately, knowing it for what it was. He sat in a comfortable chair before a round table in a large chamber with tapestries and banners decorating the walls, and he knew enough history to recognize the Elven victories depicted. He was in the War Room in Firene, a place he'd heard about but had never seen.

He wasn't alone. Three other men sat around the large wooden table with him, a few empty chairs spread between them. Caganasti sat to Klauden's right, the elf wearing simple black robes decorated with thin silver design work, his hair through his top knot and falling over his shoulders in small black braids, delicate tattoos lining the exposed skin of neck, face, and shaved head, a line of silver barbells through the skin of his forearms disappearing under his sleeves.

Rory sat across from him, the elf shirtless from what Klauden could see, his scarred neck clear even to Klauden's eyesight. Klauden frowned. *Can he not find a shirt even in dreams?*

The elf wore a familiar ring on a silver necklace, and Klauden closed his eyes for a moment, the image of the room and Rory oddly doubling for a moment as his connection with the artifact showed him what was happening, and the view clashed with his own perspective of the room. Klauden knew how to adjust for the complication; he'd done a similar thing back in Severin when he was near Hannah as she wore the ring. He pushed the ring's sight away and down; though he could never quite make it go away—that was the price of being bound to the artifact—he could push it to the back of his mind and focus on the moment from his own experience instead.

The man sitting to Klauden's left was a bit of a surprise, though Klauden was quick to comprehend the situation. He was average looking in many ways, the kind of man who could pass in a crowd without much notice, dark-haired and plain-faced, but his skin was pale, not yet too pale to stop passing for human, but in a few days, if he didn't feed, Klauden knew it would be. The other vampire wore a plain white shirt and a dark jacket with simple designs stitched along the arms.

Klauden had only seen the Sarkoza once before in person, but he had still been Milo van Reegan back then. His cousin had visited Castle van Kreeosk as a child accompanying his parents, Rika and Irfan van Reegan. They had tried to negotiate for Hannah, but Magnus had refused to give up his First Daughter, and the van Reegans had retreated to Castle van Lartner and settled back into being Second Family. Given Milo's ability to compel people with the power of his voice, though, Klauden didn't believe they'd remain Second for much longer. The Sarkoza would mate well.

He considered what the vampire was doing in Firene. But given that his only expectation back home would be to claim the First Daughter of a prominent House, Klauden could guess. He'd only spent a few days with his cousin, but he'd gotten the impression that no one could make Milo do anything against his will. His gift made forcing him impossible.

Klauden wondered if the elves knew what he could do. Certainly, Caganasti must suspect something. The elf wasn't a fool.

Klauden looked down at himself, curious what he would be wearing in a dream, and was not surprised to see his familiar red robes. Red had always been his favorite color. He'd regretted that in his last hasty exit from the castle his mother hadn't given him more red robes, grabbing the black ones on top in her haste to get him to safety. As he sat there, each of the men eyeing the others, none wanting to be the first to speak, Klauden was aware of another presence, Hannah also seeing the dream, though not a part of it, no doubt drawn there by her bond to him.

The silence dragged out, and finally Caganasti leaned forward and pushed up his sleeves, placing his elbows on the smooth surface of the table, silver barbells glinting in the sunlight streaming through the windows. "I assume you're wondering why you're all here," the elf began.

"I can guess why *we're* here," Rory said, looking at Caganasti and the Sarkoza, "but why is *he* here?" He glared at Klauden, but he didn't leap across the table to attack him. The elf was developing a basic sense of self-restraint, Klauden observed, mildly impressed. *No doubt his new appetite has forced him to hold himself back more often.*

"There are matters that concern us all," Caganasti said. "You because you brought the news of the army," he told Rory. "You because you have come for an alliance," he told the Sarkoza, who nodded in agreement. Klauden absorbed the information, adding it to what he already knew about the Sarkoza and the lay of the land in House van Lartner. An Elven alliance would change a great many things, open new doors for everyone involved. Caganasti addressed Klauden, "And you because you bring the key to the army with you to Firene."

"Key?" Klauden echoed, but he already knew what Caganasti meant. "Hannah," he breathed, then watched as a dark shade of red worked its way up Rory's chest. The elf looked away, down at the table, and said nothing.

Caganasti nodded. "She is Master of the fledgling who leads the army, Herrick. She's how we must destroy them."

"We are fighters," Rory declared, shaking his head dismissively. "The Firenian army is strong."

"Fledglings are stronger," Klauden interjected.

"But there aren't many of them," Rory countered. "How many survived what happened? They are strong and fast, but they can't defeat an army of thousands."

"There are about 30 fledglings left," Klauden offered, sharing what he had seen when Hannah nearly died by the river. The time for secrets had passed. He needed answers now. "Plus scores of goblins. The goblins are not a huge threat, but those fledglings can destroy your Elven fighters."

"Elves defending their home are stronger—" Rory began, leaning forward as his pride in the army swelled, though he hadn't been Warmaster in a hundred years.

"The elves don't concern me," Klauden cut him off. "What does concern me is what happens to Hannah if your army starts slaughtering those fledglings."

Rory raised an eyebrow. "What do you mean?"

Klauden sniffed, laying his hands flat on the table. "Herrick beheaded one of the fledglings. I nearly lost Hannah in the maelstrom."

Rory sat back, face blank as he absorbed this knowledge.

"So she's connected to them, then?" Caganasti asked, giving Klauden a curious look.

"Yes?" Klauden replied, the answer more of a question.

"Fascinating. Is the bond spiritual or physical?" Caganasti probed.

Klauden shrugged. "I do not know."

"What do you mean, 'you don't know'?" Rory sneered. "I thought your bond showed you everything."

"It only shows me everything about my connection to Hannah," Klauden told him. "Not her connections to others." He layered his words with enough innuendo to annoy the elf. Before Rory could reply, Klauden continued, "I need to do more research." He turned to Caganasti, knowing the elf would understand his needs. "I have to understand this."

Caganasti nodded, frowning as he contemplated.

"But this is a different matter," Klauden said. He looked at the Sarkoza, who had stayed silent, watching them speak. Klauden knew this was his way; his cousin was careful with his words, mindful of the power he wielded. "How does this concern you?" he asked him.

"He wants to start another House," Rory answered for him. "Near the eastern edge of the Vanya."

Klauden nodded. It made sense, though he doubted Magnus van Kreeosk or Gerter van Lartner would see it. Both men were old, though, and times changed. A House of the Vanya with an Elven alliance would be powerful indeed. "And what does he offer in exchange?"

"I can remove your army problem," the Sarkoza offered. His voice was ordinary, no power behind the words this time.

"How?" Rory asked, though Klauden thought they might have already had this conversation.

"I can be very persuasive," the Sarkoza said quietly, and Klauden smiled at him. So the elves didn't know about his gift.

"Perhaps you can talk Herrick out of his crusade," Klauden suggested. "Convince him to stop his advance."

"But that still leaves fledglings on the loose," Rory complained. "What can you do about them?"

"Fledglings that are connected to Hannah," Klauden reminded him, and Rory sat back, face contemplative. *Though he is angry with her*, Klauden thought, *Rory still cares about Hannah.*

"Tell me more about Hannah," the Sarkoza said, and the room went awkwardly quiet. Rory looked away, his jawline clenching again. "The First Daughter is bound to many fledglings?"

"It's a long story," Klauden offered. "Rory can tell you." Klauden smiled at the elf. "Or perhaps he is too busy these days to focus on the past." He paused, then added, "Or the present."

"I'm here, aren't I?" Rory snapped.

"You're here because Caganasti is controlling this dream," Klauden reminded him. "I doubt you would leave your bed for anything less." He was surprised at the vehemence in his voice and reminded himself to calm down. The elf didn't know that Klauden could see his every move through the ring. Klauden swore that if he ever decided to make another artifact, he would be much more specific in its application. His first attempt was powerful but clumsy—and sometimes awful. He shook the images away, taking a deep breath as his time beyond the mountains had taught him.

"Where I spend my time is hardly your concern," Rory said.

Klauden nodded. "Nor with whom," he agreed, and Rory gave him a sharp look. Klauden ignored it, turning back to the Sarkoza. "Through a series of unfortunate events, Lady van Kreeosk's body was used to make many fledglings while she wasn't in it," he explained. "Upon her return, many of those fledglings died but not all of them."

"And where was she when she wasn't in her body?" the Sarkoza pressed.

"In the body of mortal," he began, watching his cousin's face as he glanced to Rory, then back to Klauden.

"And her body was...?" the Sarkoza prompted.

"We thought Kelvin Malbrek had destroyed it, but it turned out he placed another in it instead," Klauden explained. "It was ... complicated."

"Given Malbrek's involvement, I'm not surprised," the Sarkoza observed in a moment of unguarded honesty. "So if Lady van Kreeosk was in this mortal body, why did she leave it?" He looked to Rory for the answer.

"The owner of the body woke up," Rory answered quickly, seeming unable to contain himself. "And we discovered that Hannah's body still lived. We had to put her back in her own body." Rory's face reddened, recalling how Anna and Herrick had tortured him. His hand slid to his neck, touching the scars there, before he forced it down onto the table where he pressed it flat against the wooden surface, trying to calm himself.

Milo nodded, his face thoughtful. For a brief moment, Klauden thought the look was too perfect, too contrived. He wondered if any of this was new information for the Sarkoza, or if they had merely confirmed what he already knew. Milo van Reegan was clever, even without his gift.

"This mortal still lives?" the Sarkoza asked, face revealing barely concealed shock at the story.

Klauden swallowed, deciding to play along for now. "She is my fledgling," he admitted.

The Sarkoza pressed his hands together and chuckled. "You have indeed been busy since leaving home, Master van Sherinak."

"Things have been ... eventful," Klauden allowed.

"And this bond between you and Lady van Kreeosk?" the Sarkoza prompted.

"Kevna." It was Rory who spoke, practically spitting the word out.

The Sarkoza nodded. "I had heard of such things, whispers mostly, but not confirmed." He paused, gathering his thoughts. "Very well," he said after a moment. "I can handle your army," he told the elves, "but first you have to figure out how to break the bond between Lady van Kreeosk and these fledglings."

"And what of Herrick?" Klauden asked. "I might be able to find something for the fledglings—soul magic is different—but Herrick is her fledgling." He paused. "Well, hers and Malbrek's."

A slow smile crept across the Sarkoza's face. "Kelvin Malbrek has a fledgling," he mused, nodding slowly. "This is good." He looked to Klauden. "You will find a way to free her. Leave Herrick to me." He looked to Rory. "And you, Prince? What will you do?" He gestured to Klauden. "Is he right? Will you return to your bed and your woman?"

Rory frowned. "She's not my woman."

"Thank the gods," Caganasti commented, then raised his hands before his chest defensively when Rory glared at him. "Come, man," the elf continued. "The Valrina is lovely, but she is poison. Your Hannah may be complicated, but she's a far superior choice."

"Are we done here?" Rory snapped. "Or is this meeting about my love life now?"

"You haven't answered me," the Sarkoza said, and this time, there was a small push of power behind the words. "What will you do, Prince? Tell me."

"I will help you," Rory said instantly, unable to stop himself. "I will do what needs to be done."

The Sarkoza nodded. "I am glad to hear it." He looked at Klauden again. "Time is short. The army grows closer every day. You have to break the bond." He sighed, then added, "You know I respect Lady van Kreeosk, but I will not forgo an Elven alliance for her sake, nor will I watch my new allies be struck down in battle. I, too, will do what must be done."

Klauden sensed the meeting was over, the dream starting to fade at the edges. The Sarkoza nodded again, then put a hand first to his shoulder, then to his chin in Klauden's direction, a parting of equals, and was gone.

Rory stood up, mouth open as if to say something to Klauden, but suddenly, a lovely, naked elf was standing slightly next to and behind him, her hands touching him in that familiar and possessive way. She tugged the elf to her chest, and he was gone a moment later. Klauden sat alone with Caganasti, both of them staring at the spot where Rory had been before the Valrina had woken him.

"You'll need to return, then," Caganasti said, turning his attention to the vampire, and Klauden nodded. "And I presume you'll need something to hold all those books," the elf added, and Klauden nodded again. A leather satchel appeared on the table before Klauden, starting as a thin outline filled with smoke and slowly darkening until it was solid. Klauden reached for it, slinging it over his shoulder, pleased to feel the solidity under his hands.

"So," Caganasti began, "whom have you already consulted?"

X

Klauden woke in the small cabin, sitting up in the bed, blanket falling to his waist, mind filled with the authors Caganasti had suggested. Looking down, he saw his bare shoulder and chest were still crossed by the bag given to him in the dream. He tugged it off, examining it carefully to judge the magic, then grabbed one of the books from where he had left it leaning against the wall and placed the book inside. He lifted the bag, clearly pleased with the weight and fit, then began sliding in all of the books currently lining the wall of his bed. They all fit, and the bag didn't get any bigger or heavier. He nodded, then reached inside and removed the books one by one, lining them up again. Distracted by the bag, he didn't realize Hannah was sitting up as well, her eyes glowing red as she stared at him.

She gestured toward the magical bag. "He gave you that. In the dream. Which wasn't a dream at all."

Klauden nodded, setting the valuable new bag inside the built-in chest to his right and closed the lid gently. Hannah was still staring at him in the darkness, eyes a smolder amid the gray planes of his own nightvision. He could feel her anger, a slow boil beneath the surface.

"You knew," she breathed quietly, the betrayal still raw in her voice. "You knew my dream was real."

Klauden nodded again, watching as realizations moved through her quick mind, connecting the details. She would know everything about Rory in Firene—that Klauden had been watching the elf for weeks now.

"Why didn't you say anything?" she whispered.

Klauden sighed. "I know you don't believe me, chaivin, but I do not delight in causing you pain. If you wanted to think it a dream, I thought I should let you."

"But you knew I left the ring there. You knew you could move a physical object in the dream. That's why you reached out to Caganasti, needing to get a special bag for the books because you're still planning to return to the castle." She shook her head. "I don't believe this."

"Your elf is still very angry with you," Klauden said, surprising Hannah. "Pay it no mind. No doubt he will be back to chasing you soon enough."

"I'm not talking about Rory," Hannah snapped, ignoring his words about her husband. "I'm talking about *you*, Klauden."

"What of me?" the vampire asked, confused as he sat up to face her.

"You already knew he was in Firene ... with *her*. You knew he was a fledgling. You knew, but you chose not to tell me."

Klauden shook his head. "It is not my business to tell you these things," he said. Hannah knew he mostly believed what he said—that it was his responsibility to shield her from certain things. But he ignored the small part of him that whispered of his ulterior motives.

"You claim to love me," Hannah told him, voice steady despite the wave of emotion inside of her. "You embrace this bond between us—and yet you withheld this from me." She paused, trying to understand why he wasn't seeing the problem. He didn't see this as betrayal.

She stared at him, his handsome face plain even in the darkness, her eyes picking up the familiar lines and shapes. She knew his face so well, but it was the bond that allowed her to know him, and she still only brushed the surface. She sighed, pursing her lips as she selected her words with more care than she normally used, especially with Klauden. She needed him to understand. "Even with kevna between us, you are hiding things from me." She paused, shaking her head, the words spilling out. "You keep saying you love me, Klauden, but I don't think you know what love means."

"Love does not mean sharing information that will hurt you," Klauden snapped, clearly feeling her anger but not knowing why it was directed at him instead of the elf who was currently bedding another. "I know that much."

"But you didn't do it because of that," Hannah accused, focusing on Klauden and ignoring Rory. It was time to face some truths about the connection between them. "It's more than that. You keep secrets because you don't truly trust me. You build walls between us while insisting I'm the one who needs to embrace the bond. This is not love, Klauden."

"Do not tell me again that this is just magic, chaivin." Klauden's voice was low, dangerous.

"Don't tell me that this is love," she retorted. "You wouldn't hide nearly so much from me if you loved me."

At her words, she sensed a small avalanche starting inside Klauden, walls collapsing under an onslaught of emotion. "Can you feel that?" he whispered.

<*Yes,*> Hannah answered in a thought, adrift in the warm glow of his affection, his loyalty, his devotion to her. <*I feel that.*> She pushed against it, pressing herself away from the center of the maelstrom and sliding to the edges. <*But what of this, Klauden? You still hide so much from me. How can I ever trust you with so many secrets?*>

"You don't want to trust me," he said bitterly, his voice cutting the connection between them as he erected another wall. "It doesn't matter what I do, or what I say, or how I feel."

"You don't *know* how you truly feel!" Hannah shouted at him. "It's always the magic between us!" She looked away, heart pounding so hard she could feel it in her ears. "Everything you show me is an echo of kevna," she told him. "It's what you think is love, but it's not."

"And what is love, then?" he sneered, getting to his feet. "What you feel for your elf?" His eyes narrowed into thin red slits in the darkness as he stood before the hammock. "Tell me, chaivin, how did it feel to see him with another? Knowing he beds that elf every chance he gets, that he distracts himself with another in his anger with you?"

"Stop it," Hannah said, looking away. "You're just being cruel."

"Am I?" Klauden laughed, and there was an ugliness underneath the sound. "You accuse me of keeping secrets, Hannah? You say I do not love you because there are things I won't show you?" He stepped toward her, and his hands cupped her face. "Do you want to see?" he asked, red-tinged eyes dark with fury. "I could show you everything. Every. Single. Time. I can show you how he touches her, how he moves in her, what he says to her as they lay naked together. Shall I *trust* you enough to share that?"

Hannah tried to pull away, but he held her fast. "I have seen so many things," he whispered. Hannah got a glimpse of his mind then, of Rory holding someone up against a wall, but then the image changed, and she could see herself laying on Rory's chest, both of them naked in the small room in Kalford so long ago.

Hannah gasped. She knew Klauden had known she slept with Rory, but she hadn't realized he'd seen them together that first night. "I've seen..." His voice drifted off, and Hannah could feel it then, the burden of the ring, the knowledge it conveyed whether he willed it or not.

The image shifted again, and she saw Solyn, only with Hannah's green eyes, looking down at him, blonde hair a riot around her face. <*This one is mine,*> Klauden whispered in her mind. <*It's all I have. It's all I know. How dare you tell me I do not know how to love?*>

<*That's just sex,*> she retorted. <*That has nothing to do with this.*>

Klauden let out a breath and pulled away from her, clearly frustrated. "Perhaps it is you who does not know what love is, chaivin." He walked away and stood beside the wall, giving them space in the tiny room. Hannah knew he wanted to grab her shoulders and shake her before pinning her against the nearest wall and having his way with her. Hannah could feel the walls of the cabin closing in on them both.

She climbed out of the hammock and left the room without another word, heading up to the deck to clear her head in the ocean air.

XI

Hannah stood on deck, watching the last of the sun sink below the horizon. She was leaning against the railing at the front of the ship, away from the hustle and bustle of the quarterdeck where the captain stood at the wheel, head deep in conversation with her first mate.

They were three days beyond Upsen now, with three more before they would reach Warin. Hannah was not looking forward to the next few days. She was getting hungry, the meal she had secured in the city long faded, her limbs tingling, skin burning with the start of withdrawal. She wondered how much of her hunger was her own and how much was spilling over from Klauden and Solyn.

She'd always been able to go longer than Klauden, one of the few gifts from her human grandfather's blood, but her body seemed different now. Even though she'd been back in it for two months now, she sometimes felt like a stranger in her own skin, the hunger an unexpected burden she hadn't expected so soon. She knew she could keep herself in check, though, not willing to risk a snack on a sailor and finding out just how well she could fare against the sea creatures when they tossed her overboard. She hoped Klauden could keep Solyn's needs under control. Hannah knew they were sharing blood, a temporary solution to their need, the bond able to keep them alive and in control, but Hannah was not willing to join them. The image of Klauden biting Solyn slipped into her mind, and she closed her eyes, trying to unsee it, hating herself for the burn of jealousy she couldn't deny.

She looked out at the ocean instead, focusing on the feeling of the sea breeze against her skin as she leaned against the railing, a moment of peace from the constant turmoil of sharing the cabin with Klauden. They had barely spoken since the night of the dream, only interacting enough to get through the days spent so close together. She knew they would reach another boiling point, that there were still things to be said. *But not yet.* She still had time to consider her options.

And what are my options? She decided to take serious stock, something she rarely did in her life, staring at the blurring line of sky and sea.

I can continue my current path. I can go to Firene and warn the elves ... and face Rory. Even if he's moved on, I need to see him. She thought of her elf, the image of that woman's hands on his bare chest as she dragged him out of Klauden's dream, so familiar with his skin. The rush of jealousy made her skin warm, and she hated herself a little bit more for it. Of course he would move on. She had betrayed him.

And for what?

Her thoughts turned to Klauden, and the way she saw him now, her perspective so shaped by kevna that she had taken to jamming her fingernails into her palms every time she was near him so she didn't reach out to touch him. Even now, she could feel him in the cabin though he was on the other side of the ship. If she focused on him at all, she could dive into his mind, his feelings, the desire for her that never ended, the confusion and hurt growing each time she walked away from him.

And what if I didn't walk away? What if I embraced the bond, and everything that goes with it? She tried to picture her life with Klauden, accepting his love and what it meant, imagining herself lying in bed with him every night. The image was comforting, familiar, expected, everything she should want in life. *But that's just the magic talking.* She tried to expand the image but failed. *Where would we even live? We couldn't return home.* She tried to imagine sharing a small house with him in a village somewhere, her working in a forge, him sitting behind a desk in a library, perhaps even some small children running around, but the fantasy faded quickly.

Where would Solyn fit into our life? No, a future with Klauden wasn't something she could imagine. But knowing that didn't stop her from wanting to abandon the deck, march down to their cabin, and pin him to the bed.

What is my future, then? After this is done, one way or another, where do I end up? Staring at the darkening sea, Hannah didn't know—and the feeling was freeing. No expectations, no demands, no magical destiny forcing her hand. *Yes*, she decided. *That is what I truly want.*

Suddenly, her gut roiled, the sensation of falling at great speed taking over as one of the threads binding her to a fledgling abruptly snapped, shock and surprise rippling through her. She caught a quick glimpse of a distant mountain range, a gorge, her foot slipping, then she was falling into space. There was darkness and silence, her body disappearing as she lost herself.

Hannah came back to herself underwater, the shock of the cold against her skin yanking her back, her hair floating away from her face, her clothes weighing her down, and the voice of Klauden yelling inside her mind. She was back in her body again, no doubt tugged back by the bond of kevna, and she took a moment to look around. There was water everywhere. Not a concern. Hannah didn't need to breathe, and she knew how to swim. Her concern was which direction was up or down. Everything had taken on a hazy blue glow. She shook her arms free of her jacket, watching it float away, but she couldn't tell if it was going up or down either. She concentrated on Klauden instead, starting to swim in the direction he was in, hoping he was still on the boat and hadn't jumped in after her in some foolish heroic rescue.

Her head broke the surface, and she took a deep breath to help stay afloat, paddling her arms and kicking her feet as she circled, looking for the ship. She spotted it a few hundred yards away, the crew a flurry of activity as the sails of the *Volant* first puffed out wildly, then sagged as the ship slid sideways. She could hear shouting, and she could see the dark outline of Klauden standing on the back of the quarterdeck, leaning against the railing while they lowered the rowboat, blonde hair blowing around his face as he shouted and pointed at her. As she watched, he deftly leapt over the rail and joined the four bodies already in the small boat, other crew members moving on the ship to lower it to the water below.

The rowboat drew closer, no doubt propelled by Klauden's magic, and the crew tossed her an oar that was tied to a rope. She caught it easily, fingers tightening on the wood, but then something grabbed hold of Hannah's leg just above her boot and yanked her under the water. More surprised than anything, Hannah let go of the oar, not wanting to drag the rowboat under as she allowed herself to be pulled deeper.

She squinted through the water, trying to see what had her, but when she couldn't make it out, she used her nightvision instead. The dim ocean water suddenly cleared into distinct images in various shades of gray. Hannah stared, mouth opening in her shock, at the pale hand currently gripping her calf, tracing the limb back to a shockingly human arm and shoulder, connecting to a lovely female body with flowing light tresses. Water rushed into her mouth, and Hannah closed her mouth abruptly, spitting out the seawater through tight lips.

She was being tugged deeper underwater by a mermaid. The creature seemed to notice her watching it and smiled, exposing a mouth full of sharp teeth. There was a sound then, some kind of singing, but Hannah ignored it, focusing on the creature.

Not a mermaid, then, Hannah thought. *An actual siren.* She'd heard stories of the creatures, but she had thought them a myth. So did Klauden. They both knew better now.

In the stories, sirens lured men off the safety of their ships with their lovely music, then drowned them under the waves before eating them. Hannah had no plans to be drowned or eaten this day.

Luckily, she too was a creature of myth. She reached down to grab the hand, fairly sure that her vampiric strength was enough to pull the creature close to her. She tugged the hand free from her leg with ease, lifting it to her. The creature shrieked, an odd sound under the water, but Hannah didn't let go, only pulled it in even closer.

She'd never tried to drink underwater, but considering how many days it had been since they left Upsen behind, she was willing to try. There was a splash somewhere above her, and she knew Klauden had joined her.

<*Good,*> she told him. <*Get down here. You want to see this.*>

She reached out with her other hand to grab the creature's free arm, easily catching her from where she flailed in the water. Hannah pulled herself into the siren's embrace, completely ignoring the snatching teeth. They were still sinking, but the environment that would disable a normal human had no effect on her. Nor did the sound she assumed was the famous siren song.

Her own teeth were huge in her mouth, and in another moment, the siren would be unable to attack at all. Hannah nestled her face into the space of the creature's neck, blowing away a tress of silky hair, and bit swiftly, the blood flowing quickly. She made a seal with her mouth, marveling at the sensation of feeding without worry of making a fledgling. It had been so long since she had bitten anyone.

Her thoughts drifted as they often did when she fed, blending with the siren's memories—a kaleidoscope of terrified sailors, a frenzy of flesh and bone—and Hannah was fascinated. She had fed from her share of humanoids—humans, goblins, even elves—but never a creature like this, something more akin to a monster than a person. She wondered idly if she were to let the siren live if the creature could be turned fledgling, if such a transformation was even possible. The siren was still struggling, but weaker now, hands beating uselessly against Hannah's strength. Hannah could still hear the song, likely the siren trying to seduce her into stopping, but it was easily ignored.

New hands found her body then, a familiar grip on her shoulder and another at her waist, Klauden reaching around the siren to touch her. The vampire didn't hesitate, leaning down as if to bite the siren on the other side of her neck, to join in the feast, but then he halted abruptly, body jerking with the force of stopping. His fingers tightened on Hannah, but he didn't move forward and bite the siren, seemingly frozen in place. Hannah could hear that song again, and suddenly, she could hear it through Klauden, feel the undeniable pull, the order in that voice, the command and the desire to please the one singing. Klauden was trapped, completely and utterly under the siren's spell. In a moment, he would obey the command and try to free the creature from Hannah's embrace.

Oh, hell no. He's mine!

A fierce possessiveness took over, and Hannah reached for Klauden through the bond, yanking him to her with her mind, yelling his name and commanding his attention. For a moment, she thought the siren song might be stronger, but then he was with her again, kevna swelling between them. He gave her a look over the creature's shoulder that Hannah would never forget, his normally calm and handsome face filled with predatory gaze of the hunter, a vengeful rage she didn't think him capable of, then he struck, sinking his fangs into the siren's neck, and the two of them continued to drink together, spiraling down deeper into the water, both of them lost in the ecstasy of feeding.

Hannah was aware of very little after that. She was no longer feeding, the siren drifting away, lifeless body sinking into the darker gray beneath them, but Klauden was there, and his mouth was against hers, pledging himself to her again and again.

<*Mine,*> she told him, hands wrapped in his hair, legs wrapped around his waist. <*Mine.*>

<*Yours,*> he promised. <*Always yours.*>

His arms tightened around her, their bodies pressing close together, and Hannah lost herself in the moment, in him, reveling in the idea that he was hers and always would be. No one would ever take him from her. Her mouth drifted to his neck, and she bit him without thinking, claiming him again in another way, and he responded immediately, biting her in return, and Hannah disappeared into the sheer joy of being with him, her mate, her love.

Hannah's mind drifted again, this time lost in the rush of the blood singing through her body, an effect of gorging on blood as she hadn't in a very long time. A hand slid from her back and down her arm to grip her hand, and the lips touching hers faded away. *I lost my skirt in the scuffle*, either with the siren or with Klauden. She still wore her shirt, but she had lost a boot.

She looked down at her arm, at her hand, following the line that lead to Klauden. He'd lost his robe, including his shoes, only wearing a pair of shorts. The soft material waved in the water as he tugged them both gently upward.

She let herself be moved, unwilling to think about what had just happened, just wanting to lose herself in the wonderful sensations still flooding her body.

Together, they broke the surface. Hannah immediately began to tread water, her body reacting without her mind's focus. She heard water splashing against something and turned to face the sound. A rowboat was close to where they had surfaced, the oar still floating only an arm's reach away. She lunged for it, passing it to Klauden first. She could swim. He was managing to stay afloat by doing an odd combination of flailing kicks, but it was a struggle.

<*Go,*> she managed through the haze in her mind. <*I can swim.*>

She watched as he was dragged to the edge of the small boat and heaved inside in a tangle of limbs, then many hands latched onto her, and she let herself be pulled in as well.

She fell on the floor of the small boat in a heap, and one of the men tossed a blanket over her, the material rough against her bare wet skin. She was aware of Klauden kneeling beside her, and she felt the magic as it left him, the spell pushing the boat faster than the sailors ever could with their oars.

She didn't move, not wanting to think about anything, unable to acknowledge what had just happened. The boat glided through the water, the sailors said things that she couldn't hear, then there was an odd sensation of the rowboat being lifted out of the water. After another long moment, strong arms tucked underneath her body and lifted her to a bare chest, still wet with seawater, Klauden carrying her off the rowboat and back on the deck. She opened her eyes long enough to see several sailors tugging hard on ropes, doing something to the mainsail so that it ballooned with wind instead of hanging idly, but the expression on their faces as they passed made her close her eyes again. Klauden carried her down the stairs to their cabin and opened the door.

"She better not leave that room again," Captain Red said in quiet anger, "or I swear I will lock you both in until we get to Firene."

"Of course," Klauden replied in a subdued voice. "We won't disturb your ship again."

Klauden laid her down on the small bunk, rubbing her skin with the blanket to dry her off. He tugged her up so she was sitting, red curls still dripping in her face, and gestured for her to raise her arms. She obeyed, letting him remove the soaked shirt, then she sat there, naked. Klauden stared for a split second at the massive scar between her breasts and looked away, guilt spiking through him. She wondered what he would do, but instead of kissing her as he longed to do, he pulled the blanket from her hammock around her shoulders, covering her up.

Turning his back to her, he eased out of his wet shorts, quickly tugging on a dry pair from his bag, aware of his nakedness and the way she stared at his bare skin for the brief moment. He took a deep settling breath, then bent to retrieve a small glass pot from his bag, filling it with water from the bottle they kept in the locker at the foot of the bed. A moment of concentration had the water boiling instantly, and he added a few herbs to the mixture, letting the tea steep for a moment as he pulled out two battered cups. Hannah recognized them from the kitchens of her father's castle, and she stared at them on the lid of the built-in chest, marveling that Klauden had somehow salvaged this tea set from home. He cast something else, another spell that Hannah didn't recognize, then he poured the tea into the mugs. He pressed one into her hand, gesturing for her to drink.

"What is it?" she asked numbly, taking a sip and enjoying the warm feeling flooding into her body.

"Something we both need," Klauden replied, settling himself on the edge of the bunk. They drank the tea in silence. When Hannah finished hers, leaving the dregs at the bottom, Klauden took the mug and set it on the chest beside his empty one, trusting either that the ship wouldn't rock enough to toss them to the floor or using magic to spell them in place.

Hannah had started to sag to one side, the tea infusing her with satisfaction and ease, the euphoria combining with her bloodstupor to make her body sing with pleasure. Klauden eased her down to her side, climbed in beside her, and tucked her close to his body, but only through the blanket, not allowing any of his skin to touch hers.

They were silent for a long time, Hannah drifting through the remains of the bloodstupor, Klauden contemplating the events of the evening. After a time, Klauden said, "Another fledgling died." It wasn't a question, more of a confirmation.

Hannah nodded, satisfied exhaustion filling her as she lingered on the edge of sleep. "I think he fell," she mumbled, remembering the frantic moment before she had fallen with him. "They must be near the Kelsin Gap."

Klauden nodded against her back. "We must figure this out, chaivin. We cannot have you falling off ships every time a fledgling misses his footing."

Hannah sighed, not wanting to think about it. "I know," she agreed. "And we will. Tomorrow."

"Tomorrow we will return to the library," he told her. "No more waiting."

Hannah nodded, knowing time was running out. Memories of the water flashed through her mind, and she smiled, awe in her voice. "That was a siren, Klauden. An actual siren."

"I know," he marveled, letting her change the subject. "And I nearly lost myself to it."

"But why?" she asked in a weary voice. She'd rather talk about sirens all night if it meant they didn't have to discuss the rest. "It didn't bother me at all."

"You are not a siren's ideal target, chaivin. I am."

Hannah huffed, turning to face him, though something in her said it was a bad idea. Her hair fell in her face, and Klauden gently tucked it behind her ear, careful not to touch her skin.

"You are no one's target," Hannah told him as she shivered at the thought of losing him. "You are mine."

"Always," he agreed.

She looked at him, really looked at him, his face calm, his hair still damp, his eyes bright with his nightvision. "Why did you stop?" she asked suddenly, the words out before she could stop them.

"Stop?" he echoed, and she shoved the memory of their frantic kissing into him the way he liked to do to her, reminding him of the feeling of his skin beneath her hands, his blood on her tongue. He shuddered, a thin tremble running through him, but he took a deep breath instead, putting his hands on his own body, so very careful to stay away.

"You know why," he said finally.

"But you could have had me," she pushed, his blood still singing in her. "You could have me now."

She could feel what her words did to him, and for a moment, she thought he would kiss her, but then he pulled away, just a little bit on the small bed, but enough to give them space. He shook his head, smiling a little. "No," he told her. "I would very much like for both of us to be more aware the next time we make love, chaivin. I tire of these frantic couplings under duress."

Hannah stared at him, unable to find the words.

"Turn around," he ordered her, a gentle hand on her hip pushing her to face the wall, away from him. "Sleep."

Hannah let herself be moved, then settled into the bed, allowing herself to enjoy the moment. The mattress was soft, the blanket was warm, and Klauden's body was a comforting presence tucked behind her, holding her close, but not suggestively.

"I don't deserve you," she mumbled. The small part of her that could still think was grateful for his restraint.

"You don't know what you deserve," he insisted. "Now sleep." The words had a push behind them, a magical command, and Hannah surrendered, letting herself fall into the solace of the magic.

XII

Hannah woke the next morning to find Solyn standing in her cabin, the fledgling's back pressed against the closed door as she peered down at Hannah in the bed. Hannah scrambled, trying to recall the events of the night before. She glanced at her obviously unslept-in hammock, then down at her naked body under the blankets, and back up at Solyn, guilt filling her stomach.

The fledgling raised her eyebrows, then gestured for Hannah to move over so she could sit on the bed. "We need to talk, you and I," Solyn said.

"Okay," Hannah replied, sitting up and tucking her feet beneath her, wrapping the blanket under her arms and around her back to preserve as much modesty as possible. Solyn narrowed her eyes at the motion, clearly judging her. "What?" Hannah asked, running a hand through her hair. "What's that look?" She knew she could find out if she wanted to, follow the bond through Klauden and see what Solyn was thinking, but after last night, she wasn't in a huge hurry to connect to Klauden any time soon.

"You are still a ridiculous person." Solyn sighed, shaking her head. "You've learned nothing."

"What? Why would you say that?" Hannah's guilt faded, replaced by low-level annoyance. "What are you doing here anyway?"

Solyn sighed, rolling her eyes. "You are bound to him, Hannah. All this resisting and holding back is accomplishing nothing but frustrating you both—and me."

Hannah stared at her, recalling the blunt voice inside her head. "But … why would you want me with him?" she asked quietly. It wasn't the most important question, but Hannah couldn't understand why Solyn would urge her into Klauden's arms. The fledgling carried his baby—wouldn't she want him for herself, unattached and devoted only to her?

"You *are* with him," Solyn said. "You just haven't accepted it yet."

Hannah looked around the cabin, gesturing with one hand. "We are on a boat on our way to find Rory," she told the fledgling. "I am not with him."

Solyn nodded. "Of course not," she replied sarcastically. "That's why you're naked in his bed right now."

"That—It—I fell—" Hannah stuttered.

Solyn held up her hand, stopping Hannah's flustered attempts. "If you don't want him, then set him free," she said decisively. "If you do want him, then stop this incessant game and bed him already." She shook her head. "Either way it would be decided, and I'm too tired to keep dealing with your tension." Solyn tapped Hannah's knee, then got to her feet. "Good talk."

Hannah watched the fledgling walk out of the cabin, shutting the door behind her. She stared at the door for a long time, mind swimming with possibilities, before standing up to find some clothes. She had lost her skirt to the water, but she had another in her bag, so she stepped into it and tugged on her dry shirt. She only had one boot, and she had lost her jacket, so she left the cabin, searching for a friendly sailor who could be persuaded to part with some clothing. They were going back to her father's castle today, and she would definitely need shoes.

XIII

The rush of magic was dizzying, but Hannah managed to keep her feet as the spell evaporated around them. She was wrapped in Klauden's arms, his lean muscles taut around her back, but as she oriented herself, she stepped back. His arms resisted at first, still holding her tight, but he released her a second later. She pushed curls behind her ears, trying to see where they were.

The floor wasn't moving beneath her feet anymore, so they had left the *Volant* behind, using Klauden's teleportation spell to get back into the castle and the library. They had also left Solyn behind, something Klauden seemed way more eager to do than he had been the week before, but they all decided they couldn't risk any more fledgling deaths. Even Solyn didn't seem to mind their going, simply nodding her head when Klauden told her to stay inside her cabin. Hannah wondered if she would obey with her Master so far away and unable to physically control her, but she thought of the water, and the creatures there, and she knew Klauden's fledgling understood enough of what happened with the siren to not risk going overboard herself.

Hannah knew the fledgling was irritated with both of them, wanting some time to herself—as much as was possible, at least. If she concentrated, Hannah could still feel Solyn, the fledgling on the edge of Klauden's senses. None of them could be truly alone. There was something else there too now; Hannah could sense it if she tried harder. She wondered if it was the baby, now several months along. *Klauden's child.* The thought made her stop thinking abruptly and focus on her surroundings instead.

It was dark, so she invoked her nightvision to take stock of her surroundings. As the world crystallized into shades of gray and black, she saw

Klauden's eyes glaze over with shine, his own nightvision appearing. They were standing in one of the tunnels in the lower levels of her father's castle. Hannah glanced around to pinpoint a landmark.

"Where did you bring us?" she asked Klauden, stepping over to the walls to find clues.

"Somewhere familiar," he said quietly, adjusting the bag he slung across his chest, straightening his black robe. Hannah knew it was the last one he had left to wear, having lost the other in the ocean the night before.

"I know that," she said. "The spell only transports you to a place you know well. Where is this?" Hannah looked around, pushing up the too-long sleeves of her new jacket. One of the sailors had given her a new jacket, this one grey and more roughly made than her old one but definitely appreciated.

Hannah didn't get cold on the ship, her vampire body rarely got cold at all, but her thin shirt was not enough for her to feel comfortable wearing it alone. She hadn't enjoyed dressing in layers back home, but beyond her father's castle, she rarely left her bed in only one layer of clothing. Her feet were encased in soft leather slippers, another gift from a generous sailor, but she wasn't cold. She did hope she would find another pair of boots while they were in the castle, though.

"You don't remember?"

Hannah looked at him. "Should I remember this tunnel?" She glanced again at the walls. "I would guess third level by the structure, but there's nothing on the walls to tell me if we're even close to the entrance to the library." The first and second levels were the castle proper aboveground, the living space in the castle, but the third level housed the library and vaults built into the mountainside, and the fourth level held the dungeons. Hannah disliked the fourth level, but she knew it well, just like she knew every other inch of the castle. She ran a hand against the rough stone, memories spooling in her mind. "This seems deeper in the mountain." She knew there was a time when she would've known their location immediately, even though she had literally been teleported into the middle of a maze. Now she had only a vague sense of familiarity, but nothing more.

"It is." He took a few steps down the hall. "I can't believe you don't remember." He gestured to her, and she closed the distance between them. Her hand found his automatically in the darkness, an old habit of constant touch as a precaution against getting lost. He moved abruptly to the right, his form disappearing into a small crevice in the wall, and Hannah felt a fresh breeze on her face. The air was cool and suddenly lighter.

"What?" she asked as he led her down a short tunnel. "Why are we—?" Before she could ask the question, they emerged onto a small rock outcropping. A valley lay below them, trees and rocky hills dazzling in the pre-dawn light.

Klauden stood for a moment as his nightvision faded, then turned to her, other hand collecting her free hand. "<You remember this place, yes?>" In the moment, he had relapsed into the tongue of their youth.

Hannah answered him in kind, feeling the syllables almost foreign on her tongue. It had been so long, but she would never forget. "<I remember now.>"

They had been so young then. She barely out of her thirties, he just edging into his sixties, and she had dragged him outside in yet another attempt to get him to continue exploring with her.

"<You wanted to study,>" she said, the memory echoing in their linked minds. "<You were in the library, and I dragged you out here.>"

"<You always tried to drag me outside,>" he said, and for a moment, Hannah saw herself through his eyes—a young girl with red curls loosening from her braid, trouble etched on her face, and a dare perched in her eyes as she tugged his hand. *Come on, Klauden. Come see.* "<You always wanted to explore.>"

"<You were happy to have an excuse to leave,>" she admonished, a hand going to her hair to push it behind her ear, suddenly surprised to find free flowing curls instead of the childhood braid. She was grown now, that memory was of a girl long gone. But Klauden was still here. Some things would never change. There were more complications between them now, obligations and expectations and something that sometimes felt like destiny, but in the end, it was still just the two of them, standing on the cliff where they had spent so much of their childhood.

"<I was happy for an excuse to be with *you*,>" he replied, and suddenly, Hannah was back in the memory again, more completely than before, the restrictions of the moment fading away.

"<You always seemed so annoyed,>" she whispered, seeing Klauden as he'd been then, still taller and lean with that wiry strength, but his eyes were bluer, his hair brighter. His skin held that healthy glow that came from feeding regularly on humans, the same radiance she knew her own face must have.

"<You delighted in annoying me,>" he said.

"<I delighted in annoying everyone,>" she admitted.

"<Especially Malbrek,>" he said, and they both grinned. Of all the shared memories of youth, their mutual disdain for their tutor was the thing that brought them closest, and it was an innocent similarity—one devoid of the awkward implications everything else she recalled now held. Hating their tutor was ordinary, nothing connected to kevna, not remotely involving any of the new and disturbing feelings that threatened daily to resurface. Hannah remembered her father's second berating her, his face growing a dangerous white as his voice rose from serious lecture to angry tirade.

"<I would grin at him,>" Hannah said, "<when he shouted at me. The more he yelled, the more I grinned, and it drove him crazy.>" Her thoughts about Malbrek had grown from dislike to outright hatred since he'd spent some time trying to destroy her in the last year.

Klauden nodded, the cool mountain breeze blowing his blonde hair away from the angular profile Hannah found so appealing. *He looks like Rory*, she thought suddenly. *Almost Elven*. Thoughts of her husband made her feel terribly guilty, and the warm memories she was floating in evaporated.

What am I doing here in this place with Klauden when my husband is leagues away? What kind of wife am I? A terrible one, she answered herself. She saw Rory in her mind, then that flash of a woman standing beside him, hands on his body. Klauden's words echoed in her mind, *Shall I tell you what he says to her when they lay naked together?* Hannah shook her head. Thoughts of Rory wouldn't help her now, not when she was here in her father's castle with Klauden, not with kevna threatening to drown them both. The idea that she even had a husband was somehow foreign, a notion both fantastical and unbelievable. Even the memory of his face was fading a bit in her mind, replaced by blue eyes and bright hair.

No, she told herself then, forcing everything except Rory from her mind. *No Klauden, no kevna, no memories of childhood pranks,* she insisted. *Remember Rory. Remember the reason you're here at all, on this journey.*

As she concentrated, the elf's face swam into focus, his black hair, his brown eyes, the scar on his chin, and that half-teasing grin he always had on just before jumping into a fight. She heard his laugh then, purely masculine as he whispered, "Let go, Hannah. Let go and see what happens."

Her own nervous response, "What then? What happens then?"

His joking tone, "Why don't you find out?" She felt his hands on her shoulders, smelled the sweat on his skin, tasted the juice on his lips as he kissed her. *Where were we?* It was Severin, in summer, one of the days they'd spent lounging by the spring behind their house. Rory had packed a lunch, and Hannah could never separate the taste of juice from her memory of that afternoon again. He'd taught her to swim at long last, and then afterwards, he'd taught her even more.

Gods, how could I forget memories like this? How could I forget for one second how important he is to me? Even if he's with another right now, she thought, *I shouldn't forget him.*

Kevna.

It was the bond, she decided, the damn magical bond somehow warping her memories of the elf, bringing her closer to Klauden every day. *Is that even possible? Is the magic somehow sentient and able to think, to work like that?* She just didn't know.

That's why they were here, after all, she reminded herself. To get the books that might know.

"Hannah." The voice was far and indistinct.

"Hmm?" she answered, still wrapped up in her thoughts.

"Come back to me," the voice suggested.

"What?" Her mind cleared some, and she opened her eyes. She was still standing on the cliff edge, the wind toying with her hair, the valley spread out beneath her feet. She knew Klauden was standing behind her, could almost see her form from behind as he saw her. The queer doubling of her vision made her unsteady for a second, and she closed her eyes again, rubbing them with her fists. "Don't," she whispered. "It makes me dizzy."

The image faded, her connection to Klauden dimming, then Klauden did something else, built a wall in his mind, and suddenly they were alone, Solyn shielded, unable to see them. Hannah wanted to ask him how he did it, but she didn't bother. She could sense how he did it—she just couldn't manage to do it. She had tried. And tried. She thought of Solyn alone in her cabin, the fledgling standing in just her new shirt, her blonde hair curling around her face, her hand pressed against the growing bulge of her belly.

"What will happen to us, Klauden?" she asked, not bothering to hide the fear in her voice.

He didn't pretend to misunderstand and ask what she meant. He knew what she was asking. Hands were holding her from behind then, strength offered and accepted as she leaned back into him. She kept her eyes closed as his arms wrapped around her, relishing in the connection between them. Hannah admitted that she had enjoyed cuddling in bed with Klauden the night before, a newfound comfort in his embrace that should repel her, but now only made her feel safe.

Safe? Since when have you ever wanted safe? The question was a low voice in the back of her mind, a part of her demanding that she let go of Klauden and walk away immediately.

Since I haven't been certain of anything in too long, another part of her answered. *I just want ... what?* She let the question linger.

"What do you want, Hannah?" he asked, his breath brushing the top of her head.

"No," she shook her head, "you're always asking me that. It's my turn now." She folded her hands over his where they held her shoulders. "What do *you* want, Klauden?"

"You know what I want," he replied.

"Do I?" she asked. "I know you want me to embrace the bond, to be with you, but what then?"

"I have a fairly good idea what happens then," he said, and the pure masculinity in his tone surprised her, sending a wave of delightful shivers through her skin.

"I'm serious," she said, focusing. "Say we do this, and I'm with you. Then what?"

He sighed, body lifting and falling behind her. She could feel the uncertainty in him, the lack of knowledge causing constant anxiety, but beyond that, she could sense a larger plan in place. "Why are you asking me this?" he asked her instead. "Are you considering it?"

It was Hannah's turn to sigh, sinking deeper into the safety of his arms. "It doesn't change my plans," she told him quickly. "We still need to help the elves, and I still need to see Rory." She paused. "But..."

"But what?"

"But what if I am considering it, considering you? What does that mean for you?"

He sighed again, his breath warm against her head and tickling her hair. "It means that perhaps you finally believe me when I say I love you," he murmured. "And it also means that I trust you," he added, referring to their argument about trust and walls.

"Do you trust me?" she whispered. "Enough to share your plans with me?"

"I trust you to break my heart," he told her honestly, and she winced, not willing to turn and see the look on his face, though she wanted to. She brought one of his hands to her lips instead, kissing the palm gently.

"I do not always mean to hurt you," she told him.

"What else could this talk of a future possibly do?" he asked, voice raw. "You want to know what a future with me would be like—you as my kevnisha and Solyn as my fledgling and the baby with us all?" He paused, and the words flooded out of him. "After we deal with the army and break your connection to the fledglings, we would start a new House with the Sarkoza near the elves. We would make our own rules. Solyn would be with us, and the child, but as my fledgling and nothing more." Hannah nodded, knowing that many fledglings and Masters had physical relationships as well as emotional and mental connections. "We could be happy together, you and I," he whispered the last part, and Hannah had a vision of them living in a new castle, sitting in a courtyard, him reading a book, her running through her morning exercises, a small blonde child running between them, and Solyn giving chase. It wasn't a bad image.

It wasn't the future she had envisioned when she lived in her father's castle, nor was it one that she had imagined while living south of the mountains. But seeing it in Klauden's mind—it was ... nice. A nice possibility.

Hannah admitted that she had been so focused on getting to Rory that she hadn't allowed herself to properly consider the possibility. She could barely admit it existed, never mind seriously think about what it meant. Everything was tainted by kevna, influenced by the magic.

But what if it doesn't have to be? What if I can give this possibility some room to grow? What if I choose to follow this path on my own, to see where it leads?

She thought of Rory one more time, remembered the woman's hands on his body, and shook him away. He wasn't here with her, standing on the cliff. He was in Firene, doing gods knew what to someone else. He had made a choice. She could choose too.

She could choose Klauden.

"I have to know something," she said suddenly. "Tell me the truth."

She felt Klauden nod behind her, echoes of him steeling himself for whatever she was about to say.

"Was Solyn part of your plan from the start?" she asked. Sensing his confusion, she added, "When you put me in her body, did you plan to turn me into your fledgling and get me pregnant with your child?"

She felt the shock run through him, the hurt that she would think him capable of such plans. "You think I can see the future?" he asked out loud. "How could I have known what would happen?"

"But you came to Severin," she pressed. "Did you come there to claim me, to make me yours again?"

"I practically *walked* to Severin," he said, emphasizing the words, "because you needed my help. I didn't think Solyn would wake." He paused, and she caught a quick glimpse of Solyn's body on the dirty ground in the street, blood on the back of her neck. "I did not think you'd be bitten. I never thought I would make you my fledgling." There was a long silence. "I never dreamed she would have my child."

"No?" she prompted. "You didn't think there was a chance?"

He shrugged. "There's always a chance. But our kind breed so rarely..." He leaned down to kiss her head. "This child is a blessing."

"Are you happy to be a father?"

"I do not think my parents will be pleased," he admitted. "Though if they knew it was you, they would understand."

"But it's not me. It's her."

"Yes, but it's something of you as well."

"How?"

"It may be Solyn's body, chaivin, but it was you," he told her. "You and me." He paused, then asked, "And what if we hadn't put you back in this body, chaivin? If you were still in Solyn's body and pregnant, what then?"

"What do you mean, 'what then'? I guess I'd be having a baby in a few months." The thought was terrifying yet exhilarating at the same time. Hannah didn't know how she would feel.

"But would you be happy?"

It was her turn to shrug in the circle of his arms. "I don't know," she said honestly. "I've never been around babies before." She sensed a thought in Klauden, a possibility, but he dismissed it quickly, the thought gone before it had even formed completely.

"Nor I," he admitted. "But I imagine I will learn."

"I'm sure there are plenty of books on the topic," Hannah quipped, and she felt his warm smile, though she didn't turn around to see it. Another possibility struck her, and she didn't dismiss it as he had. She bit her lip, then let the words out. "And you are sure it's not his?"

Klauden sighed behind her, body tightening, then releasing. "Solyn seems certain. And I can do simple arithmetic." He seemed to think, then added, "I think that's what she told your elf, though—that she was certain. That is why he left."

Hannah stiffened, refusing to think of Rory. She appreciated that Klauden would tell her, though. He was clearly trying not to keep secrets from her. She looked around at the cliff where they stood, so comfortable with one another. The moment stretched out, both of them contemplating the future, something Hannah had never allowed herself to see with him.

"Why?" she mumbled, feeling lips against atop her head, slowly, cautiously working their way down the side of her face. She knew Klauden could feel what she felt, could hear her thoughts. She turned into his touch, wanting to taste him, wanting to feel that same tangy fruit on her tongue like that day by the spring.

But the mouth wasn't the same, and there was no fruit juice, and it wasn't Rory she was kissing, but Klauden. She pulled away for a second, opening her eyes to stare at him, but the circle of his arms didn't loosen, and he didn't let her move very far away. "Why did you bring me here?" she whispered.

"This place," he whispered. She could feel his breath against her lips, could see the tips of his fangs—a sign of how enthralled he was—as he moved toward her, his lips meeting hers in a chaste kiss, "is where I should have done this."

Hannah shivered, memories of so many days spent in this exact spot. She would stand here, staring out into the distance, watching the sun rise or set, and he would come up behind her and hold her in that rare, close way. She recalled now, staring at the same sun rising some fifty years later, that such moments of intimacy between them had been few and far between.

They had never kissed when she lived here, only shared a few lingering hugs like this one, and that first night with Rory had been a long list of firsts for her, but Klauden hadn't had any real experience—beyond what he read in books, of course—until that crazy day when everything had gone to hell in Severin. They'd both been seriously wounded when he used the teleportation spell to save their lives, both delirious with bloodthirst and magic, and what had happened in his rooms had seemed the most natural and logical thing in the world—an inevitable result of the fighting, Hannah knew, and of course, kevna. Like Klauden had said when the bond first became apparent to her, kevna cannot be denied. The bond would keep shoving them toward one another, sometimes subtle in its plotting, sometimes obvious, but always present, always lingering in both of them.

Of all things, Hannah hated to lose control like this. *If I'm going to do something*, she thought fiercely, *then I will do it, and damned if I'll let some magic turn my will.*

She remembered the only other time she'd had sex with Klauden, that morning, in the house she shared with Rory, when they'd planned to invade the goblin camp and rescue her husband. She could picture the vampire as he'd been then, dressed in Rory's clothes because his robes had been ruined in the fighting, nervous yet determined to help her if that's what she wanted. She remembered the feeling of Solyn's fledgling body, so different from her own.

It may have been Solyn who had asked her to do it, making it easy to blame someone else. But standing on the cliff face, feeling Klauden's lips against hers, the wind in her hair, his hands wandering down her back and curving her sides, Hannah knew she was telling herself a terrible lie.

Truthfully? She wanted him, always had. And it didn't matter if it was kevna's influence or not. She'd always been impulsive, had always gone after her wants with a single-minded determination that made Malbrek grunt, Klauden groan, and Rory grin, giving her a conspiratorial wink.

She sighed, allowing herself to come out with the truth; she had always been brutally honest before. It didn't make sense to deceive herself now.

She focused on the bond, using it to draw Klauden closer than lips or hands would allow. <*Yes,*> she told him, her own small-boned hands sliding across the lines of his shoulders, around the smooth skin of his neck, feeling his own hands grow more aggressive in their wanderings, now seeking seams between her skirt and shirt, wanting bare skin instead of this tenuous touch through layers.

<*Yes and yes and yes,*> she told him, her hands wandering down his chest, fussing with the small ties that held his robe closed. He paused as she did that, as if finally realizing her true intentions, marveling how she'd moved beyond intention into action. This wasn't kevna, not a response to one of his mind tricks. It was just Hannah, and she was going to undress him right there on the cliff face.

The ties quickly unraveled, and when she ran her hands up his bare chest, Hannah was struck by how cool his skin was, how different from the heat Rory always carried with him. She knew he hadn't been feeding properly, and though she could be sated by a victim every three or four days, missing a day meant the start of bloodthirst for Klauden. *He must be going crazy,* she thought, taking in the pale complexion, the start of hollows beneath his eyes that she'd managed to ignore. The siren blood had been good, and her own, but he needed more.

<*Oh, Klauden. Come to me.*>

He bit his lip in that slow teasing way, rubbing his tongue along his fangs as he contemplated her. "Hannah," he said, his voice soft yet loud in the silence as he gauged her actions, using her name to show his seriousness. "You... This..."

She shushed him with a kiss, tugging his head to meet her neck. <*You must feed,*> she told him. <*Drink.*>

She felt his hesitation, that need threatening to drag her under.

<*Drink,*> she told him more forcefully, <*or I will lose myself in you. Do it now.*>

<*But we lose ourselves,*> he said in her mind, and she felt his mouth against her skin, lips and tongue tingling. <*That is how it is between us.*>

<*Not this time. Right now, this is just you and me. No magic, no ancient bonds or spells. Just us.*>

<*It's never been just us.*>

<*Well, maybe it should have been.*>

When he bit her, exquisite pleasure flooded Hannah. *Normal sex isn't like this.* Those many afternoons she'd spent in Rory's arms weren't like this. *I am a vampire,* she reminded herself, *and this is how vampires have sex. This is how Klauden should have been having sex, but both times before, I was in Solyn's body, and things were different.*

As she tilted her own head to nip at his neck, Hannah reminded herself to go easy. Klauden hadn't fed and taking any more of his blood than necessary was foolish. He moaned, and she pushed his robe off both shoulders with eager hands. His hands started to tug on her shirt, wanting to touch more skin, and she grabbed both hands before he tore it off.

"I need these clothes," she said, unwilling to lose another article of clothing so soon. She pushed him gently away, watching the way he licked the blood from his lips, seeing the somewhat dazed expression on his face as he stared at her. "Let me take them off." She shrugged the jacket off onto the ground, then lifted the thin shirt over her head, feeling the morning breeze cool against her bare skin. She still wore the skirt—a thin material clinging to her small hips, no shirt or jacket to cover her. Klauden's hands slid the skirt off her waist, lingering on her skin as the material piled around her feet. Klauden stared at her naked body for a long time, taking in something he had never seen before. Hannah realized she was still wearing her new slippers.

Before she could reach down to pull them off, Klauden had pulled her close again, lifting her small frame off the ground, and she wrapped her legs around his waist, hands tangling in his hair as they kissed again. He turned then, taking the few steps to the cliff face they had emerged from, and pressed her back against the stone. She gripped his shoulders to support her weight as his hands abandoned her hips to fumble with his shorts. She felt the material go as he freed himself, then she angled her hips to help him inside.

<*Yes and yes and yes,*> she told him again, her entire being narrowing to the place where their bodies joined.

In a distant part of her mind, she heard his response. <*Yes, chaivin, always yes.*>

XIV

"We should get going," Hannah said, glancing over at Klauden as he sat before her, heart finally steadying into a normal rhythm. "Go?" he asked, blinking up at her in surprise. He was naked, legs still somewhat tangled beneath her, but their bodies were no longer linked. Hannah stood a bit awkwardly, one foot still wearing a shoe catching between his crossed ankles. She flailed for a second, and he caught her other bare foot against his chest, steadying her as he gave her a pointed look. "You seem in an awful hurry." Hannah could feel his heart slowing to a normal rhythm under her foot pressed to his chest. She tried to pull away, but he held her ankle tight.

"We have to find those books," she reminded him, trying to reclaim her foot and failing. Instead, he tugged her closer, tossed the leg over his shoulder, and pressed his face between her thighs. "Klauden!" she shouted, equally surprised by his forcefulness and his forwardness. She tried to wiggle away, but his arms wrapped behind her, holding her close. "I... We..." she gasped, trying to ignore the small streaks of pleasure.

When she made a titanic effort to free herself, he used the movement to topple her off balance, then crawled atop her, pinning her hands over her head. "You didn't think we were leaving yet, did you?"

Hannah wanted to yell at him, wanted to remind him of their purpose here. But instead, she grinned at him, reveling in the physical pull of her body. "What do you have in mind?"

XV

"Now, chaivin," Klauden told her, "we can get going, as you put it."

Hannah was on her stomach, hair a sweat-matted mess around her face. At his words, she rolled over, hand landing on a conveniently nearby shoe, and she picked it up and chucked it at him. He ducked easily, but the supremely male grin on his face didn't vanish.

"In a second," she told him, body still singing with release. "The library isn't going anywhere."

"No," he agreed, "but we need to go. It's after noon."

Hannah squinted at the sun, a hand blocking the worst of the glare. "Really?"

She groaned. "What's the hurry? You can't cast the spell again until this evening anyway."

"Not anymore, chaivin," he told her. "Not with my power joined to yours."

The words made something in Hannah's gut begin to churn. She rolled to a sitting position, blinked a few times, then began to look around for her clothes. She found her shirt first, and tugged it slowly over her head, wiping away the small streaks of blood from her neck where Klauden had bitten her. She tried not to think of it, feeling the tangles in her hair instead, trying to ignore the feeling inside. "I really need a brush," she commented.

"You can brush your hair when we get back," he said, reaching for his own shorts and standing up. "Besides, you look wonderful."

"Shut up," she told him, rolling her eyes, wanting to get angry at the smug tone of his voice but unable to yet. She got to her feet then, reaching down to grab her skirt and step into it. She was tucking the material around her hips when Klauden walked up to her, a shoe in one hand. Hannah finished with the skirt and glared at him, hand held out to receive the shoe. "Thanks." She disliked how she felt—a mixture of relief, satisfaction, and happiness, but underneath it all, a low layer of guilt.

So that's that, she told herself. *Choice made. Now deal with it.*

She watched Klauden as he wandered back to the wall where he had left his robe and shrugged it on. He looked at her, no doubt aware of her whirl of emotions. "You seem out of sorts, chaivin."

"Please," she snapped, awkwardly stepping into her new leather slipper and tying the strap. She had grown accustomed to her body's needs, the desire for more blood always lingering beneath her surface thoughts. But that need was gone now. She remembered the feeling from Klauden's bedroom, when she had felt utterly sated for the first time in her life. Then, she had assumed it was kevna's doing. She'd been right because the feeling had returned—and she hated it.

When she looked up again, Klauden was standing there, holding her other shoe, robes untied and bare chest shining in the sunlight. When she went to reach for it, he pulled it just out of reach. "Did you not enjoy yourself?" he asked. Despite his teasing tone, Hannah knew he was very nervous. It was kevna again, and she wasn't glad to feel it wash through her.

"I did," she told him truthfully, hating herself a little, then reached for the shoe. He pulled it farther out of reach.

"Then why are you acting like this?" he asked.

"Like what?" she snapped. "Give me my shoe."

"Like a child who has been bested at her own game," he replied, handing her the slipper. She reached out to grab it before he dropped it, turning away from him to tighten the strap.

"It's just sex, Klauden. It's not a big deal," she said dismissively.

"Isn't it?"

She stood, finger combing her hair into manageable tangles around her face. "No," she said, facing him. "It's not."

"You seem fairly determined to make it meaningless."

"And?"

"You know, chaivin, your determination to make it mean nothing speaks volumes of its true import."

She glared at him, suddenly wanting to hurt him as she latched onto the first image that came to mind: Solyn—pregnant and *alone* in her room. "Would Solyn think it means something?" she snapped, hating herself as she said the words.

He smiled. "Solyn understands what lies between you and me," he said, and Hannah realized that the two of them had probably already had this conversation. Jealousy burned through her, fast and unbidden, thinking of Klauden's closeness with his fledgling.

"I hope so," Hannah said, though the fire had gone out of her tone. "She's carrying your child." There was a pause, then Hannah's eyes widened, her mouth falling open. She stared at Klauden, a hand pressing to her own belly. "Malfek!" she cursed. "I could be carrying your child." The thought was overwhelming, and Hannah sat down suddenly, the world tilting. She expected Klauden to hurry to her side, but the vampire hung back, watching her carefully.

"And now we know your true feelings about that," he observed. She could hear the hurt in his voice, but he brushed the feeling aside. "Don't trouble yourself, chaivin. There will be no child from our joining—not now anyway."

"How can you be sure?" she asked, the wave of panic receding as she felt the certainty in him.

He frowned, then sighed, clearly deciding to simply tell her. "It's a spell," he admitted, "to prevent conception."

"When the hell did you cast that?" Hannah asked, mind retracing the events of the morning. There had been a lot of feelings and magic, but she thought she would've noticed if he specifically cast something.

He looked down at his feet, then back at her. "Yesterday," he said, unashamed.

Her brows creased. "But ... how could you know what would happen here?"

He raised his eyebrows at her. "I know you, chaivin." A rush of desire flooded her, an echo of his need for her, and he gave her a supremely male look. "It was only a matter of time."

"So you planned this?" Hannah wanted to be angry again. Anger was easier than the hint of baffling disappointment she felt now. *I don't want to have Klauden's children*, she told herself. It's better this way.

"I was prepared for this," he snapped, "because unlike *some* people, I like to think about the future."

Hannah accepted the rebuke without comment. He was right. She was not very good at planning for the future. "I didn't even know there was such a spell," Hannah admitted. "How does it work?"

"It was in the tea," he told her, "after the siren. I knew we would be here eventually. And I know that you're not ready to build a family with me now." He sighed, then added, "I don't plan to have any more surprise children."

"Is that what you want?" she asked suddenly. "A family with me?"

He approached where she still sat on the ground, feeling very young and foolish. He reached out a hand and lifted her to her feet. "I want everything with you, chaivin," he vowed. Hannah opened her mouth to reply, but he cut her off. "Don't tell me it's just the magic," he whispered, suddenly vulnerable. "Don't do that to me again."

Hannah's words died on her lips, trying to abandon the thought so he wouldn't hear it, but she wasn't fast enough.

< *This is just sex, Klauden. This isn't everything.* >

He closed himself off from her, walking away to where her jacket lay in a pile by the passageway back into the tunnels. He picked it up and held it for a moment, considering. He shook his head, giving the jacket a quick flip with his wrist to straighten it out. When Hannah thought he'd make her walk over to collect it, he flung it at her in a swift motion, the ball of material hitting her in the chest. He turned his back to her, heading back into the passageway. Hannah pulled the jacket over her arms and followed him. In the darkness, she heard his voice floating back to her.

"It's always everything with us."

"Klauden, it's—" she started, but then a hand closed around hers in the darkness.

"Enough now," he told her, all business again. "Take us to the library."

Hannah nodded in the darkness, letting him lead her through the tunnel without invoking her nightvision. She wondered just how right he was and if this new technique to regain control of herself was going to work out at all.

XVI

F inding the library was easy, but Hannah didn't relax until the blue glow surrounding the doors faded as Klauden spoke the password. The fact that it hadn't been changed since they left assured her that no one in the castle suspected the books were important, and no one thought that she or Klauden would be interested in the information held there.

It may also mean that no one else had been researching kevna, and that possibility made Hannah feel better.

Still, as Klauden pushed the wooden doors open and Hannah stepped into the vast chamber behind him, she couldn't quell the unsettling feeling that something wasn't right.

She paused. "Wait," she whispered, stopping Klauden with their linked hands.

Klauden turned back to her, his hand pulling out of her grip. "What?"

"I don't know," she whispered. "Something feels ... *wrong.*"

"It's just the wards," he explained, making his way to a sconce on the wall. He turned the wick up with deft fingers, whispered a soft word, and the candle flared to life, illuminating a half-circle into the room. Hannah shivered, unable to shake the nervous feeling, but she had to admit, nothing seemed out of place. The walls were still lined with the more valuable books. Some so ancient, they were archived into tiny cubbies built to accommodate scroll tubes, while the freestanding bookcases were still the same sagging wooden structures Hannah remembered from childhood. Staring at them now, it was hard to believe she had once climbed one of those precarious looking shelves, creeping silently along the length until she stood above the table where Klauden had arranged his books and paper, then leapt out above him, landing amid his research with a spray of pages and a splat of ink, laughing hysterically the whole time. She could still see the surprise on Klauden's face as he stared at her, trying to decide what was more upsetting—his destroyed books or the ink dripping from the tip of his nose.

Those few tables were still scattered across the space, their worn wooden surfaces scarred with ink and scratched from quills, and the over-stuffed chairs looked a little worse for wear, but still very inviting. As much as the place looked lived in, it also looked recently abandoned. It had the slightly neglected feel of a room forgotten, a space unnecessary. With Klauden gone, Hannah realized, the library had been largely unused. She wondered who would come to the castle to take his place, who else would leaf lovingly through these pages of history.

"I forgot about the wards," she said, taking a few steps into the center of the space, the thick rug spongy beneath her feet. "These are yours, no?"

Klauden nodded at her. "Just before I left, I had a feeling someone may be watching me, so I set them for protection." He looked around. "They aren't strong enough for any real damage, just enough to keep out the unwanted." He glanced at her. "I'm surprised you feel them."

"Why?"

"They are aimed at the curious, anyone nosing around where they don't belong. You're here with me, with my permission, as it were. They shouldn't bother you at all."

"Is it kevna?"

He shrugged, but he was still frowning. "Maybe. Maybe you feel them because they are of my magic." He paused, considering, then crossed behind her and lit the other wall sconce. The room was brighter now, but still dim in the far corners. "Though if you know they are my magic, you should know they aren't aimed at you."

Hannah reached out with her senses, trying to get a feel for the ner-vousness in her gut. "No," she told him. "It's more than that. I can feel you here, but there's something else."

He walked over to her, and she could feel him reaching out through the bond, trying to sense what she felt. After a second, he froze, took a sharp breath, then stared at her. "You're right," he said, surprise in his voice. "There is something wrong."

"What is it?"

He glanced around the room, stepping in front of her and using an arm to push her protectively behind him. "Someone has been here," he said, eyes scanning the room. Hannah watched as he called on his night-vision, the magic glazing his eyes red as he searched for the intruders.

"They've gone," Hannah told him, pushing his arm away and stepping forward again. "We're alone."

"Yes," he took in her new position, shook his head with a sigh, then strode purposefully into the stacks. "But what did they take while they were here?"

"Did you leave things here?"

He gave her a meaningful look. "I did leave in a hurry."

"But it wasn't a surprise. You knew things were happening. You knew you weren't going to come back here." She paused, recalling those last desperate days in Severin when everything had gone wrong, and stared hard at him. "Didn't you?" She glanced at the empty tables, at the long rows of shelves. Klauden was walking down the length of the center one, and she hurried after him. "What did you leave here?"

"It's nothing," he snapped at her.

"By the way you're moving, I'd guess it's more than that," Hannah observed, catching up to him at last.

"It's just some notes," he told her, his stride lengthening as they neared the end of the row, and he made an abrupt right turn. Hannah knew this end of the library very well. It was furnished with a large, cushioned couch, covered with several different kinds of blankets ranging from soft fur to woven string, and provided many options for the discriminating pillow connoisseur. Hannah had spent many long afternoons sleeping on that couch, books forgotten in her lap or on her chest. There was also a low table situated before the couch, just the right height, Hannah knew, for resting her feet if she chose to sit correctly on the cushions. She'd once spent an entire day stacking cards on that table, only giving up when she had to stand on the couch to reach the top row of the house of cards she'd built. Klauden had been impressed with her then, but Malbrek's angry commentary when he'd seen it—disapproval accompanied by a well-aimed swat that had brought down the entire structure in a flutter of paper—had stuck with her. She'd intentionally ignored lessons for several weeks afterwards, instead spending each day building a new tower, but she'd never gotten one as high or perfectly formed as that first one.

Klauden stepped beside the enormous couch, slid his hands underneath the overstuffed arm, and pulled the whole thing forward until it touched the low table.

"What are you doing?" Hannah asked, walking forward. "There aren't any passages back there."

"Not passages," he said, kneeling down in the space he'd just made between the couch and wall. His voice was muffled through the thickness of the furniture, then Hannah heard the small scraping of rock on rock. Klauden was moving part of the floor to reveal a secret compartment beneath the couch, similar to the one they had discovered her grandmother's journal in on the other side of the room.

"A stash?" Hannah asked him, incredulity making her voice high-pitched. "Really?" She laughed a little. "What in the nine hells did you hide in there, Klauden? Coded answers to one of Malbrek's little tests?" She had a sudden image of a younger Klauden stealthily moving the couch aside as he stashed extra quills, pots of ink, and paper lined with study notes into the cubby.

"It's still here." Klauden sighed in relief, standing up, a worn leather book in his hand.

"What's that?" Hannah teased. "Your journal?"

"Hardly," he said, sliding the rock cover back into place with his foot. He tucked the book under one arm, then pushed the couch back against the wall with a hip. "These are my notes."

"Great. Now can we find some books on kevna and get out of here?"

He nodded, thought a moment, then headed to the middle of the far-right bookcase. His long fingers ran along the battered spines of texts, located one, and pulled it forward. He put his journal atop the new book and hooked both under one arm, heading purposefully to the other side of the room where the cubbies held scrolls. He started at the left end of the shelf, and Hannah could see he was counting as he paced the length back toward where she stood by the couch. He paused at twenty-seven, fingers tugging free a dusty roll of parchment wrapped around a bronze baton. He brushed a light coating of webbing to the floor, then squinted at the tiny writing on the outside of the roll. Confirming the words, he turned to examine the end of the rod, nodding again as he saw whatever he expected to see. Having finished his inspection, he twisted to allow the bag hung across his body to swing forward and stuffed the book and the roll into the bag.

"That's it?" Hannah asked him. "We came all this way for two books?"

He held the journal up to her. "All that we really need is in here," he said. "It has everything I've learned about kevna so far."

"And the others?"

"I think they may bear re-examination," he said cryptically, then headed off toward the entrance.

"Excellent," Hannah agreed, keeping in step with him and deciding to ask questions later. "Now we can go."

He paused. "Not exactly."

"What do you mean?"

"Well," he began, readjusting the bag against his back before sliding the journal inside one of his wide sleeves, cuffing the bottom to secure it inside, "these are my notes."

"Your notes, as in *you* wrote them?" Hannah paused, shaking her head. "Klauden, why did we need to get your notes? It's not like you're going to be surprised by what you find in there."

"No, but I may find something different if I reread them," he said defensively.

"We had to come all this way for two books and a few notes? That's ridiculous. What's really going on?"

"Well, this has everything I'd learned so far, like I said, but there's one more book about bonds..."

Hannah groaned at him. "And where is it, Klauden? No. Wait. Let me guess. It's with Malbrek, on his desk in his chambers. That's why you really wanted me to come along, isn't it? You know I can get in and out of his rooms easily. I know those passages like I know my own face."

Klauden smiled at her, a *real* smile. "You don't trust me very much, do you, chaivin?"

"We've been over this," she told him, trying not to think of his hands on her body, his lips on her skin. "Why should I?"

"I don't know," he mumbled, toeing the carpet back and forth. And then she knew. *He's thinking about my body against his.* He dismissed the image, focusing on the moment again. "Maybe my repetitive saving of your life could give me some credit." At her look, he added, "Apparently not, but one can hope."

Hannah sighed, changing the subject. "So, where's this book, then?" She glanced at the extensive collection. "It's not one of these?"

Klauden shook his head. "I was studying it the last time I was here. It's probably still on my desk."

"In your room?"

He nodded.

"Klauden, you realize they've probably warded your room by now, right? We'll never get in without notice."

"You think I can't get past a few simple wards?"

"Not Malbrek's wards," Hannah said. "He's too good."

Klauden snorted. "Hardly. The man can make his magic look elegant, but his quality is barely serviceable." He gave her a pointed look. "Like yours sometimes."

She made a face at him, then shook her head. "You're sure you can get by them?"

He nodded. "Besides," he added, "if not, we can just get back with the teleportation spell. Nothing can hold us here."

Hannah nodded as they exited the library. But something in her gut said there were an awful lot of things that might hold her here, least of all warding spells.

XVII

They were creeping down one of the back passageways on the second level, one floor beneath where Klauden's suite of rooms were, when they heard voices. Hannah froze in place, hand pushing Klauden back against the wall as she listened again.

"No one can see us here, Marjorie," a male voice said. "I assure you... We're alone."

"What if I am missed?" a female replied. "Sturagis will not accept another story. If he catches me missing again, he'll send me to another duty."

"He won't miss you," the voice assured, and a deep giggle was followed by a low moan. "Trust me." There were the unmistakable sounds of people kissing.

"I trust you," the female said between a hiss and a deeper breath. "I just don't want to get put on as a nursemaid."

Hannah held Klauden firmly against the wall, trying to make the two of them blend into the side of the passageway. Klauden was obeying her, but she could feel his frustration. Of all times for a tryst, they had to pick this hallway right now?

Hannah echoed his sentiment, but then she realized what the woman had said.

<Nursemaid?> She sent the thought to Klauden, knowing he heard her. <Who had a baby?>

<I don't know.>

<Livenna?> Hannah tried to recall any female in the castle whose child would warrant a nurse and came up blank. Still, she had been gone almost two years now. A lot could have changed.

<Not the last time I saw her,> Klauden answered. *<She was still trying to mate her way up the social scale by lounging around Vailen.>*

<Do you think Father would let them mate? They are the only ones left here.>

She felt Klauden shrug beneath her hand. *<He might have to.>*

"You should be so lucky," the male voice said, and Hannah stopped thinking to Klauden to listen.

There was the sound of someone kissing again, but this time it ended abruptly.

"What?" The woman again, Hannah noted, though this time she sounded annoyed.

"Huh?"

Hannah shook her head. Sometimes the rules of her people didn't make any sense, but in this case, this particular Second Son deserved to be one of the Kargin. He certainly couldn't be very bright, not if he were fooling around with one of the slaves.

"What did you just say?" Hannah heard the distinct tone of a fight about to begin and settled herself back against the wall. Perhaps fighting would take less time than kissing.

"Nothing." He was defensive now, desperately backpedaling.

"I mean it," the woman said. "Did you just say I should be so lucky as to get nursemaid duty?"

Hannah could feel the shrug in the man's reply. "Yes. So?"

"So?" The word was nearly a shout.

"Hush," the man told his woman, then a sound that suggested he must've grabbed her. "Someone will hear."

"Let them hear!" the woman shouted, then more scuffling. "Let go of me," she snapped.

"That's not what you said last time," he tried.

"That was before I knew how mean you could be!"

Hannah stifled a sigh. Perhaps the kissing might have been quicker after all. She could feel Klauden listening intently beside her. He was as intrigued by the fight as if reading a new adventure story.

"I'm not mean," he defended. "Nursemaid duty is an honor!"

"An honor?" the woman replied, and this time there was disgust in her voice. "Do you know what happened to the last wet nurse she had?"

There was silence, and Hannah waited, curious despite herself.

"Well, do you?"

"I heard..."

"Yes, you heard," she snapped again. "I'm sure you heard! She killed her, tore her open with her baby teeth and bled her out all over the floor! And that's the second one this month!"

"There have been some rumors," he tried.

"Not just rumors," she insisted. "I heard it from Joelus, and he's second cousin to Matthias, and she's second assistant to Kelvin Malbrek's tailor, and she heard him say—"

"Joelus?" the man asked, and there was a new note in his voice now. Hannah thought it was jealousy. "What were you doing talking to Joelus?"

"I... Uh... He... Uh..." The woman trailed off, then began again. "It doesn't matter," she insisted. "He said the last two nurses have been killed, and if I'm caught missing again, Sturagis may send me in next."

"You were caught missing already? When?"

"Two days ago," she replied.

"Two days ago," the voice repeated.

"Yes, when I was with you."

There was a long moment, then the man said, "Two nights ago, I was on overnight duty for Magnus."

"Did I say two nights? I meant..." But the voices trailed down the passageway. Hannah heard the woman cry out something that was probably "wait!" but the man said nothing else. She listened another few seconds, waiting for the slide and snap that would signal they had left through the opening into the hallway by the kitchens. Hearing it, she turned to Klauden.

"What's she talking about? Who had a baby that's killing nurses?"

"I don't know," he said. "I've only been gone three months, and no one was expecting when I left."

"Maybe Father brought someone from another House?"

"She wouldn't have brought a child with her. It defeats the purpose of First Sons and Daughters."

Hannah considered but couldn't make anything of the information. She tried to refocus on their purpose here. *Get to Klauden's rooms,* she told herself, *and get the book, then get back to the ship. Simple.*

Still, it seemed like she was surrounded by babies lately, between Solyn's pregnancy and this new infant killer. She grabbed Klauden's hand again in the dark, leading him back down the passageway, making turns as the map in her memory instructed.

XVIII

"You really think they haven't gone through your rooms by now?" Hannah asked. "This book could be anywhere."

Klauden shrugged, the motion running down to tug the hand Hannah still held in the darkness. "Maybe." He sniffed, other hand reaching out to touch the stone wall near Hannah's body. "But Malbrek knows I was researching kevna. That book was more generally about bonds—a long shot, to be honest. But it could be helpful for our current situation." He slid his hand down the wall, seeking the tiny lever that opened the secret door into his bedroom. "He may have dismissed it as irrelevant."

"Maybe," Hannah said, reaching out to guide his hand to the lever, loving the feel of his skin on hers as they reached the metal bar. "Maybe not." They gripped the mechanism together. "You sense anything?" she asked.

Klauden reached out with his magic, feeling the echoes of his old wards, newly covered with Malbrek's spells, but the rooms seemed empty. Before she could ask about the new wards, Klauden pushed with his magic, and another layer of spellwork began to build, a tiny space between the old wards and the new ones, a bridge of sorts. "That should give us enough time to get in and out," he said.

"If you say so," Hannah told him. "Is there anything else you're grabbing while we're here?"

"The book is the most important thing, but I have a few other things in mind if we can." Hannah was about to object but closed her mouth. When she'd left home, she was able to plan, to pack what she wanted. Klauden had left in a hurry, soaked in her blood and desperate. She couldn't begrudge him the chance to grab a few more belongings.

"Okay," she said. "Let's do this." She tugged the lever, the door sliding open soundlessly, the stone moving aside just enough for them to slip inside before closing again. Inside, Hannah paused, waiting to feel Malbrek's magical wards alerting the magician to their presence. But Klauden's spell seemed to work, holding them in a small space for the moment. She nodded, deliberately not looking at his bed and the memories it conjured. He walked past her through the curtain to the front room, sliding the bag on his back around for easy access. She followed quietly, slippers sinking into the soft carpet. She marveled at the feeling of luxury beneath her feet, then paused, a thought striking her. She returned to Klauden's room.

<What are you doing?> Klauden's voice was in her head, both of them preferring silence.

<Getting boots,> she told him. *<You had clothes for Solyn in here before. Did you have shoes too?>*

<Be quick.>

She opened the bureau, eyes scanning the interior. Klauden's clothes remained undisturbed, robes in many colors folded neatly on the shelves. She had a moment of pure jealousy. Klauden's rooms were preserved as they were, his belongings still where he left them. Her own rooms had been given to her father's other daughter, Livenna, not long after Hannah left. She had no place at this castle anymore. She knelt, rifling through the shoes on the bottom shelf. She expected to find at least a handful of shoes in Solyn's size, and while the girl's feet were bigger than Hannah's, it was better than the borrowed sailor shoes she had now. To her surprise, the very back corner had a pair of familiar battered boots in faded red leather. She lifted them carefully, shocked to see her old boots from decades before.

<What in the nine hells, Klauden? Why are my old boots in here?>

<What are you talking about?> Klauden's voice was brusque, clearly distracted with his mission in the other room.

Hannah held the boots out, staring at the well-worn leather. *I haven't seen these in a very long time, not since we were young and exploring.* She flipped them over, examining the soles—still plenty of life in them. She had abandoned them in favor of more fashionable footwear, but these had been good to her. She slid off the sailor slippers, sitting down and sliding on the old boots. They fit perfectly, the well-crafted cut forming to her feet. She stood up, sinking into the comfort. It had been some time since she had worn anything specifically made for her body. It was easy to forget how nice luxury could be. She tossed the sailor shoes into the back of the closet. Standing up, her hand slid along the lines of carefully folded robes, and she tugged out a familiar red one resting on top. This was always one of his favorites. She slid it under her arm and closed the door slowly, careful not to make extra noise.

Hannah was facing the curtain, preparing to walk into the front room when Klauden came back through it, a hand over his lips indicating silence.

<*Did you get it?*> She asked him in her head.

He nodded.

She squinted, tilting her head in surprise. <*It was still there?*>

He nodded again, shrugging and settling the bag around his back again, reaching out to take her hand and lead her to the door.

<*This seems really easy,*> she commented as he opened the latch, pulling her through and back into the hallway. <*Too easy.*>

<*Not everything must be difficult,*> Klauden replied. <*This may come as a shock to you, but we can retrieve a book without engaging an entire army.*>

<*Our lives are very different,*> Hannah told him, taking the lead as they moved away from the doors and headed back down into the lower levels. <*And you make it sound like I seek trouble. Things are never this easy for me.*>

<*Maybe they could be,*> Klauden replied, <*if you would let them.*> He showed her an image then, a possibility, him sitting behind a desk reading, her nursing a child in a comfortable chair, the room quiet and candlelit. <*Life isn't always running and screaming,*> he insisted.

Hannah remembered the house in Severin with Rory, of lazy evenings spent in front of the fireplace, talking or sunbathing by the pond, running though her practice routines with Rory at her side, a hand here or there to adjust her stance. <*I know,*> she replied quietly. <*I know that.*> Hannah realized she was still carrying Klauden's robe tucked under her arm, and she paused, pulling it out and handing it to him. "Here," she whispered, voice loud in the empty hallway. They were far enough away now. No one would hear her.

"What's this?" Klauden asked, eyes glazing as he used his nightvision in the darkness to see what she was giving him. "Clothing?"

Hannah looked down, suddenly embarrassed. "It's your favorite," she said meekly. "I thought you might want it."

Klauden held it out, examining it, then smiled, folding it carefully and moving his hip so the bag on his back slid forward again. He tucked the robe inside gently, then shifted the bag back again. "Thank you, chaivin," he said. "How thoughtful of you."

She could feel his happiness, his joy that she would think of him and something he loved, finally taking him seriously as a partner. He remembered their time on the cliff, his body against hers, and another wave of joy-filled pleasure spilled into her. <*Finally,*> he thought. <*Yes.*>

<*Yes,*> she thought, part of her thrilled at the idea of being with Klauden, of actually doing this for real. She ignored the tiny, protesting voice in the back of her head, pushing it aside.

<*It's done now,*> she thought. <*Just get through the rest.*>

FIRENE: RORY

Rory didn't know how long he had been sitting on the chair facing the open balcony doors, staring into the night with his new eyes, but he did know the moment Hannah appeared on the balcony. He hadn't been sure he was dreaming until then, but something about the quality of the night air, the stillness, the way Annilyn had stopped her little snores in the bed made him think he had fallen asleep in the chair.

He stared at his wife, taking in the familiar red curls, the bright green eyes, the heart-shaped face with the small ridge of freckles across her nose. He had lived with her in Solyn's body for a year, but this was still how he always pictured her: Hannah as she was when they first met on the road from Talperin. Her clothes were different, though. Back then, she had worn brown skirts and sweaters. Now she still wore a dark skirt, but she matched it with a plain white shirt and a jacket that looked like it belonged on a sailor. Her feet were covered in well-worn dark-red leather boots.

He stared at her for a long time, trying to decide if she was part of his dream as she sometimes was, or if she was actually here, dreamwalking into his mind. The ability had always been his, though Klauden and Caganasti could also do it; Rory didn't think Hannah could do it on her own.

"Did I call you to me?" he asked, surprised at his words as they left his mouth. He wondered if it was part of the bond they shared. She was his Maker, after all, her body at least. He wondered how much she could feel of their fledgling bond. He knew that when she had made Herrick, she could feel the former healer's wounds.

If I hurt myself right now, he wondered, *will she feel it? I haven't felt any of her pain, but I've been trying very hard not to feel anything at all.*

He stared at her face, as entranced by her now as he had been when he first met her in the demolished inn in Talperin. He hadn't known what she was then, only knew he enjoyed her company, this strange girl who fell into his life. Looking at her now, the face familiar but subtly different, her eyes wearier, her smile more worried, he wondered if he was willing to take the risk and feel what she felt. One of their issues had always been communication—her reluctant silence when she should have talked to him; his arrogant refusal to accept her as she was, though he told himself he did. *So many lies,* he thought. *So much pain. And yet ... I still want her. With the bond, I might be able to have her in my life again. Am I willing to risk it, to accept everything that comes with her?*

She saw him sitting in the chair, and for a second, her face lit up, eyes glowing in happiness, lips forming a smile. She pulled back a moment later, face blanking as she remembered everything between them, but the small light in her eyes didn't fade.

Yes, he decided. *Yes, I am.* He reached out then, finally allowing them to connect, embracing the part of himself that he had avoided since he left that tent outside Salva. There was a snap, an echo of magic in his fingertips, then *nothing*.

"Did you? Can you call me to you?" Hannah asked, looking around as she stepped off the balcony and into the room. "Where am I?"

"Firene," he told her, waiting for more from the bond, but feeling the same as he ever did, frustrated and confused. "Where are you?" he asked.

"On a ship," she said, eyes taking in the finery of the room, the plush carpet, the tapestries on the walls. She refused to look at him. Her eyes roamed around the space, pausing when she saw something behind him. She bit her lip, as if keeping herself from saying something, then forced her eyes to look at him. Rory realized he was slowly seeing more into her movements, filling in deeper meanings that would've been simple gestures before. "I think I'm asleep."

Rory suddenly knew what she had seen behind him—Annilyn in his bed. He felt a moment of guilt but swallowed it quickly. Hannah may still be his wife, but they weren't together. She had betrayed him.

He had a moment to wonder why the Valrina would still be there even in his dream, but he let it go. Dreamwalking was an odd thing. Sometimes the real world bled through. He thought of the necklace he now wore,

Klauden's ring, the artifact somehow on the floor of his room a few weeks ago. He knew what it meant—that Klauden could see him now—but he wore it anyway. He couldn't seem to stop himself, to sever the connection with Hannah.

Rory heard Lira's voice in his mind, the elf reminding him that Hannah was bound by magic he didn't understand, but he ignored it.

He may love Hannah, but he was still so angry with her.

"Rory," she murmured, and part of him sang to hear his name in her voice, "why am I here?" She was being so careful, he understood, so afraid of what he would say to her.

"Were you thinking of me?" he asked.

Something flashed across her face, and Rory suddenly knew what it was, could feel it as clearly as he could feel his own guilt and rage. She was thinking of him. She had been thinking of Klauden, the vampire very close to her, maybe even in the bed where she slept, but then something happened to remind her of Rory, and she had gone to sleep thinking of her husband instead.

Hannah nodded, and Rory realized just how little she had shown to him of her inner self, how much she guarded her emotions. He could feel them all now, a swirling wave of guilt and love and anger all connected to him. He hadn't been willing to acknowledge the fledgling bond before. Even for the few precious days back in Severin after she had gotten her body back and they had been alone in the house, he had resisted the idea of the bond, not wanting her to know what had happened while he had been taken, not wanting to know how she had managed to rescue him.

Not wanting to admit he had become a fledgling.

"Why were you thinking of me?" he prompted, soaking in the sensations now, reveling in finally seeing this side of his wife.

Hannah looked behind him again, to Annilyn, then she trained her eyes on him instead, forcing herself not to look at the elf. Rory sensed anger and jealousy, but something else too, something like relief. "I think we're near Kalford," she said. "I heard the sailors talking. We're not supposed to know that's where we are, though." She paused, sighing. "I really wish I could go out and look."

"Why can't you?" Rory asked, suddenly worried about what she was doing on a ship in the first place. "Are you trapped?"

Hannah smirked, shaking her head and rolling her eyes. "It's my fault," she said quickly. "I'm not allowed on deck right now. Not until the captain forgives me."

"Forgives you for what?" he asked. *Gods, Hannah, what have you gotten yourself into?*

She shrugged, biting her lip. "I sort of fell off."

"Fell off ... the ship?"

She nodded awkwardly. "It's a long story." She bit her lip, looking up at the ceiling and shuffling one of her feet on the thick carpet. "I'm bound to all those fledglings, remember?" When Rory nodded, eyes wide open in shock, she continued, "I guess one of them slipped and died."

Rory stared at her, blood suddenly rushing in his ears. Hannah had fallen off a ship, had nearly died, and he hadn't known. He hadn't known anything. He hadn't felt anything. Standing before her now, he could feel her embarrassment, but he could also sense the rest of her emotions, her needs, her desires, in a way he never could before. He assumed it was because she was close to him. When they were apart, he could cut the tie between them, or ignore it well enough to not notice. Still, he hadn't realized she could nearly die and he wouldn't even notice.

But didn't you? A small voice spoke in his mind. *You knew something was wrong, that you were losing her—and you did nothing.*

No, the voice went on, *you did more than nothing. You buried yourself in the Valrina and did your best to forget.*

"And he brought you back again, didn't he?" Rory guessed, for once without the bitterness in his voice.

Hannah shrugged. Rory sensed something else, more behind the movement, but he decided he didn't want to know what it was. Not yet.

"What does it feel like?" he asked instead, curious despite himself.

"It feels like dying," she replied simply. Rory had an idea of what she meant, having come close to death several times in his long life. Now he wondered if he would feel that way again, or if his fledgling body could withstand any damage he would encounter. The idea was exhilarating and terrifying.

He looked at Hannah, the body who had done this to him, the woman who had entranced him before he knew anything about her true nature.

"Hannah," he breathed, staring at her now, his insanely frustrating and completely impossible wife, "what am I going to do with you?"

She gave him a sad smile, exposing only a fraction of her welling grief. "You don't have to do anything with me now," she told him. "It looks like you've already let me go." She paused as ache, guilt, and sadness ran through her. "I need to do the same."

"Is that what you want?" he asked, unsure why he'd even asked. He could feel her answer. "Tell me what you want."

"I want to be free," she said, and Rory felt the truth in her words.

"You are free of me," he told her. "You can be with him." The words stung as he spoke, but he might mean them. *Maybe.*

"Not free of *you*," she snapped. "Free of everything else." She sighed, and for a moment, Rory felt her frustration—her anger at kevna, her uncertainty about Klauden, her fear about Solyn and the baby, her guilt and sorrow about him.

For a moment, he could see Klauden through her eyes, and the image filled him, her need for the vampire crippling, her desire tingling in his skin like the need for blood. He wondered if he had ever felt such a need for anything in his life—and on the heels of that, he wondered if Hannah had felt even a fraction of that for him. He let the thoughts go, though, focusing on her instead of himself. A desire to touch Klauden washed over him, and he closed his eyes, trying to compose himself in the maelstrom of magic. He felt something else, too, something underneath everything, an even deeper desire to be free of kevna, of Klauden and Solyn. To just be herself and make her own choices. The weight of kevna was smothering her, crushing him to even be so close to it.

He pulled away, back into himself, and opened his eyes, continuing to stare at her. Her face revealed none of her inner turmoil, none of the burdens she bore. She just looked sad and wistful as she stared back at him.

"I'm sorry I invaded your dream," she said finally. "It looks like you were having a nice time." She deliberately dragged her eyes away from the bed behind him to turn and face the other direction, staring out onto the balcony.

"Don't," he said quickly, standing up and walking up to stand behind her, wanting to touch her, to grab her and hold her close to him one more time. "You don't have to go."

"But I do," she said, unable to look at him. "I shouldn't be here. I've been awful to you."

He nodded, giving her a low, unexpected chuckle. "And I to you." He shrugged, reaching out to touch her arm and turn her to face him. "We've both done things we regret."

"Yes," she said. "And no." She looked behind him again, then back to his face. He felt her decision to say what was on her mind. "Do you regret it?"

"Regret what?" he asked, not following the wash of emotions fast enough. "Us?"

Her face fell, grief welling in her at the sense of unexpected loss. Rory realized she thought he was telling her goodbye, that things were finally over between them. Part of him wanted to reassure her, to tell her she was wrong, but he remained silent. He didn't know if she was wrong or not. He wanted her, but was that enough?

"Do you regret us?" he asked instead.

She shook her head. "No. Never." And he felt it then, her love for him, still wild and raging and fierce, but she didn't say anything else, didn't move to touch him, didn't ask anything of him.

"And him?" Rory asked, unable to stop himself. "Do you regret him?"

There was another emotion in her, but it felt different. Love, but something more than that—and that same sense of drowning filled her. "I can't regret him," she said quietly. "I'm sorry, but I can't. I won't." She looked away, then back at Rory. "I do love him," she admitted. "It's not the same thing, but it's there, and I don't think it will ever go away."

He felt her resignation, her acceptance, but there was still a small part of her that wanted to fight, to rebel against kevna and fight her destiny.

"And me?" he asked, wanting to hear her say the words. He knew she didn't know he could feel her. Kevna was too strong for her to feel anything else, but he could sense her.

"I love you, Rory," she said simply. "I know I lost you. I know it's over. But I still love you, and I think part of me always will."

"Yet you would choose him?" His voice was quiet, calm, a tone he didn't know he could use when speaking of the vampire.

Hannah shook her head, anger flooding her. "It's not about choice!" she snapped. "I can't not be with him," she struggled to explain, words failing, but Rory suddenly understood. He could feel her, the unending pool of her desire for Klauden, her paralyzing need to be close to him. Rory clenched his fists, restraining his own urge to run to the vampire, just to be near him. Rory marveled at how none of her struggle showed on Hannah's face, no sign of the internal weight she bore.

"But if you could choose?" he asked.

Hannah sighed, looking away from him again, this time turning to the open sea beyond the balcony. "I would choose myself," she whispered. "I would choose to be free." She paused, then looked back at him. "And I would ask if you wanted to come with me—and I would only let you come if you did it for yourself, not for any sense of obligation or duty."

Rory nodded, enjoying this sudden frankness between them. They had been close, but had they ever spoken so freely before? He could understand not wanting obligations and duty—hadn't he fled his duties in Firene a century ago? Granted, he admitted, he had been exiled, stripped of his duties, but nothing felt better than that first night away from the city, free from any orders. He had owed nothing to no one, and it had been glorious. He knew the feeling Hannah sought. After everything was over this time in Firene, he had hoped to find it again.

"Will you fight for your freedom, Hannah?" he asked.

She sighed. "I don't know if I can," she said honestly. "I don't know how."

"What if I fight for you?" he suggested, his anger overshadowed by his newfound need to free her from everything, to let her feel what he had felt that morning so long ago.

"Why would you do that?"

Rory reached around behind her, hands sliding quickly under her jacket at the small of her back. He had retrieved one of her daggers before she could move, the flash of his fingers leaving a tingle on her lower back, through her shirt, to her very skin, echoing what he felt against his back.

He held the blade out in front of her, flipping it easily from handle to tip and back again.

"Because you are worth fighting for, Hannah."

XIX

Hannah stood in the hold of the *Volant*, listening to the sound of the water hitting the hull, eyes adjusted to the dim light streaming down from the stairwell above. She hadn't ventured out on deck again, not wanting to risk either falling off the ship again or upsetting Captain Red with her presence, but the cabin was just too small, the walls closing in around her. Klauden had been sitting on Solyn's bed beside the fledgling, both of them deep in conversation, and Hannah wanted to give them as much privacy as she could, but she didn't want to retreat into the cabin again. She and Klauden were sated, their blood-sharing on the cliff enough to satisfy their hunger, but Solyn still needed Klauden's blood to ease her needs. Hannah didn't want to admit it, but she couldn't ignore the stab of jealousy threading through her at the sight of them together, knowing what came next.

This is ridiculous, Hannah told herself. *I am ridiculous.*

The captain had said they were free to explore the hold and the cargo, so long as they disturbed nothing and didn't set the ship on fire. Hannah hadn't bothered with the lantern hung on the wall near the bottom of the stairwell, preferring to be alone in the dim light. She had already walked around the entire space, winding a slow maze between the barrels and boxes. Some of it she could identify by smell—spices, liquors—and some by label—fabrics, seeds—but there were a few odd unlabeled and magically sealed packages here and there. Hannah assumed the captain smuggled at least a little bit, and the small boxes confirmed her suspicions, but her natural curiosity was not roused. She had enough mysteries in her life without looking for more. She found a corner with three boxes stacked side by side and sprawled across them, stretching out flat on the hard surface, staring up at the wooden beams of the ceiling above.

She thought about Rory and her dream the night before, how he had told her things were over between them. Maybe it had just been a dream, her mind fulfilling her deepest fears.

And it hardly mattered anyway. She would never be free of Klauden, never be able to give Rory what he deserved. Her loss of a husband didn't change her plans. They would still go to Firene and somehow deal with the fledgling army, and Hannah would try to ignore the stabbing pain in her heart every time she looked at him.

She felt Klauden approach before she heard him, the vampire making his way to her side, jumping up easily to first sit, then lay down. She tilted her head automatically to kiss him, her roiling calming in his presence. What did her elf matter now that she was with her mate? The feel of his lips on hers was good, always so good, but Hannah pulled back before his hands could continue wandering, a heavy sigh escaping her as she pressed flat again, the side of her body still touching his where he rested beside her.

"What is it, chaivin?" Klauden asked quietly. She could still feel his passion, the slow-burning desire for her in his soul.

"It's what it isn't," she said after a long pause. She shook her head, trying to understand her reluctance. It was more than her grief for Rory. There was something odd about the way she felt when they were together.

The boat hit a large wave and rocked hard to the right, and Klauden pressed against her. She leaned into him, searching her feelings. Sex with Klauden was good, and after her dream with Rory—where he'd spoken of them in the past tense—she wanted very much to disappear into that pleasure. She'd woken up missing a dagger, though. *What did he mean, he would fight for me?* She tried to forget it, his words disappearing into the image of the naked elf in the bed behind him.

He's moved on. You need to move on. You've made your choice.

Not much of a choice, she grumbled, but she couldn't deny how Klauden made her body sing in ways she hadn't known it could, how she wanted to disappear into the feeling again.

But something held her back. Klauden wrapped his arms around her and pulled her back to him. She leaned into him reflexively, wanting to lose herself again. It would be so much easier.

"Tell me." Klauden's voice was so soft, Hannah thought it might only be in her head, but she could feel the warmth of his breath against her ear. She wanted him to kiss her, then she felt his lips pressing against her skin, one hand wrapping around her hip to press her thigh, the other slipping beneath her side and splaying flat on her stomach.

"This," she managed to say, twisting her neck so he wasn't kissing her anymore. "It's too much."

<What is too much?> This time the voice was in her head, and Klauden's hand was moving down her waist the way he knew she liked, the way she wanted him to, and she grabbed it, freezing him in place. She twisted around to face him, one hand still holding his against her side, the other reaching up to his face. She knew he wanted her to kiss him, and she did, letting the moment linger, understanding dawning as they drew closer.

< This is too much. > She moved her face away from his. *< You want me to kiss you. You want me to touch you here, >* she moved a hand to his back, *<and you want me to grab you here,>* she wrapped her other hand around his neck and tugged him over to her with his hair.

<Yes.>

<And you want me to do this,> she continued, moving her mouth to his neck, *<and take you here. >* She opened her mouth against his skin, feeling her fangs huge in her mouth, the moment almost carrying her away under the intensity of his desire.

But she stopped, pulling away and watching his face as it reddened, his eyes hugely dilated when he opened them to see her.

"Why?" he asked, cocking his head to one side, clearly confused that she had stopped.

"That feeling," she told him, "the one you have right now. That's the difference."

He raised an eyebrow. "I don't understand, chaivin," he admitted. He adjusted himself, pressing against her in a more comfortable way. "This is not a pleasant feeling."

She smirked at him, then leaned back, grabbing his hair at the nape of the neck the way she now knew he liked, jerked him over to her, and sank her teeth into his neck.

<YES.>

She drew back quickly, not wanting to lose herself just when she had figured something out, but there was a moment where she wanted him to pull her close and take her right there, then Klauden was shoving her skirt up and rolling atop her, his mouth covering hers exactly the way she wanted, and Hannah thought of Rory's kiss, sometimes perfect and sometimes awkward, but always passionate, then she remembered her husband in bed with the blonde elf, and she didn't want to think anymore. Her hands were under Klauden's robe, eager, demanding, and he met her every demand without her having to ask.

XX

Later, they sat atop the boxes, Hannah tucked in his arms, her back to his chest as he placed delicate kisses along her neck, soothing the place he had bitten her.

"I think I finally understand," she said quietly, picking up their earlier conversation.

"What is it?" Klauden's voice was soft, but she could feel the sudden tension in him, knowing she was about to say something hurtful.

She took a deep breath, turning to look at him. "I don't mean to hurt you," she insisted. That seemed to be her mantra lately.

He nodded. "I know." He looked away from her face, down to their linked hands. "But still, you do." He shook his head, then let her hands go, lifting her easily aside and moving to face her, kneeling as they had sat when they were young. He nodded, a clear gesture for her to go ahead.

"It's about desire," Hannah said.

Klauden raised an eyebrow, clearly surprised by what she'd said. "What about desire?" he asked, obviously intrigued.

"This isn't desire," she told him.

"Then, what is it?"

"This is satisfaction."

"Isn't desire merely a precursor to satisfaction?" he asked.

Hannah shrugged. "Sometimes. But not always. And that's why this is different. And too much." She reached out to touch her old friend's face, his lips still red from kissing her. "You don't understand because you have nothing to compare it to."

Klauden frowned, and Hannah could feel just how much it hurt him to think of her with Rory. She forged ahead anyway, unable to stop herself. "Desire is about wanting," she tried to explain, "and waiting, and sometimes not getting what you want right away, or even at all. It's about the moments between." Hannah thought of a moment with Rory, when her human body had been new, when she had been frustrated, not knowing what she wanted, and Klauden immediately closed his eyes and looked away.

"I do not wish to see such things," he muttered.

"But you need to in order to understand," she insisted. But Klauden wouldn't look at her, wouldn't let down the wall he had built between them. "Fine," she said, deciding to use words instead, "it's about the time between wanting something and getting it. It's the waiting that makes this matter."

"Why wait at all?" Klauden asked despite his reluctance to talk about this with her.

"Think about before, when I stopped. How did you feel?"

Klauden frowned. "Unpleasant. Frustrated. Hurt."

"And then when I bit you, how did it feel?"

He closed his eyes, the memory swimming over them both, and Hannah almost lost herself in it, reaching for him again. Their fingers tangled together, but she kept herself away from him. "Glorious," he breathed.

Hannah nodded. "Even better because I made you wait for it. I made you want it more and think you weren't going to have it, so when you did have it, it was even sweeter."

Klauden considered. "I am familiar with the idea, chaivin," he admitted. "There are many adages to this effect. But I don't see how it applies here."

"Normal sex doesn't have this connection," she said bluntly, gesturing between their bodies. "Normal sex is about wanting and waiting."

Klauden's face hardened at her words. "I don't want to hear about *normal sex,*" he snarled, grabbing her suddenly and tugging her close to him. "I don't want to hear about how your elf made love to you." He kissed her then, savagely, biting her tongue in the process. "Did your elf know what you wanted?" His hand snaked up under her skirt again, stroking the sensitive skin of her thigh. "Did he know how to satisfy you with his *normal* sex?" He moved so she was lying beneath him, his knees pressed between her thighs. He wiped a finger along the edge of her mouth, then brought the blood to his lips. "Did he know what you really wanted to do with him?" he breathed, then moved so his neck was before her mouth, his blood calling to hers. Hannah pressed her mouth closed, trying to resist, but there was still blood on his skin from when she had bitten him earlier, and she licked it slowly, hating herself as she gave in. She felt him chuckle then as he whispered, "*This* is normal sex for us, chaivin, and you know it."

She rolled him then, her anger giving her strength. She easily pressed him to the boxes as she pinned him down, straddling his waist as she knelt on top of him. "This is about magic and blood," she told him, running a finger along his lips and bringing it to her mouth. "This has very little to do with anything normal."

Klauden moved quickly, sitting up and wrapping his arms around her waist. "We are vampires, Hannah. We are not like their normal."

XXI

They arrived at the docks in Firene in the afternoon, the ship a hub of activity as the crew set to work unloading boxes and barrels. Captain Red seemed too busy to deal with them, so Klauden settled up with Lady Black instead, giving her a little more gold than they had originally agreed on. She handed the extra coins back after weighing the payment in her hand, shaking her head at him.

"Too much," she told him. "We don't overcharge our passengers on the *Volant*." Hannah appreciated the note of pride in her voice. They had chosen a good ship.

"It's not overcharging," Klauden said, handing back the coins. "We caused you trouble, and this is to compensate for the delay."

Lady Black contemplated him for a moment, shrewd eyes debating the money. Finally, she nodded, accepting the coins and gesturing for them to leave by walking down the gangplank. As Hannah passed her, the first mate reached out to touch her shoulder. She leaned down, and Hannah saw she wore a necklace with a small female figurine, the metal seeming to shift as Hannah looked at it. She blinked, trying to clear her eyes. "Be careful on the sea, little one," Lady Black warned. "Not every ship would stop."

Hannah nodded, curious to inspect the necklace closer. "Thank you for not being like every other ship," she said. "I will remember what you've done for me."

Lady Black leaned back and squinted at her, the necklace disappearing beneath her shirt again. "Are you leaving Firene again soon? By ship?"

Hannah shook her head. "No, ma'am," she promised. "I will keep my feet on solid ground from here."

The first mate smiled at her, a real smile this time. "Good choice. You aren't made for the water."

"I know," Hannah agreed.

Lady Black paused, seeming to consider her words, hesitating long enough that Klauden and Solyn were already descending the plank toward the dock below. She leaned close to Hannah and said, "You will find your way, little one."

Hannah raised an eyebrow, wondering who this woman was to call her "little one." Lady Black appeared mortal, maybe in her late 20s, but Hannah wondered how much was going on below the surface. She could sense the woman's heartbeat, but her blood didn't call to Hannah.

Weird, Hannah thought, thinking of the last few weeks aboard the *Volant*. Certainly, the crewmembers had tempted her, and the captain, but now that she specifically remembered, the first mate had never crossed her mind. She wondered if Klauden or Solyn had been tempted by her.

"Thanks?" she replied.

Lady Black nodded a final time, then she was gone, joining the organized crew chaos in port.

Hannah moved swiftly down the gangplank, joining Klauden and Solyn on the dock as they headed into the city. The wooden structure was large and floating, swaying gently up and down as they moved down it to the end where it met a permanent pier hewn from white stone. The buildings were a mix of wooden shacks and ramshackle stone, clearly built from scraps and leftovers from other parts of the city.

There was a variety of smells in the air, fish being unloaded from smaller vessels, foreign spices from the market just beyond the port, a low hum of noise from all of the people. They passed a mix of all races as the streets shifted from mud and wood to sculpted stone blocks. Hannah could sense Klauden's restraint holding Solyn in check, but she knew they didn't have long before the fledgling attacked someone.

They made their way into the middle of the crowd, and both Hannah and Klauden began scanning the people. Nearby, a narrow alley would provide decent cover; they just needed to lure the right victims.

<*Can you restrain yourself?*> Hannah sent the thought out, knowing Klauden would hear it but focusing on Solyn instead.

The fledgling was very hungry, her heart pounding in her ears, the sense of so much blood overwhelming, but she steadied herself enough to reply in kind. <*I can restrain myself.*> Her eyes slid over the crowd, settling on a young man in simple clothing. He had been watching her as they approached, so it was easy for Solyn to lure him closer with a few head nods and smiles. She disappeared down the alley with him right behind, and Hannah and Klauden stood just outside the opening, watching to make sure no one disturbed them. When she finished, the man stumbled out, dazed but not bitten, and Hannah could heal his wound easily.

Klauden and Hannah fed next, careful to heal their victims and send them on their way with a pleasant memory. Both were frustrated, longing for the freedom to bite without consequence. But neither said anything beyond the flashes of intimate memories that continued to leak from one into the other as they fed. Sated enough for now, the trio made their way through the city to the castle at the northern edge.

"So what's your plan, chaivin?" Klauden asked as they drew closer.

"My plan?" Hannah stepped around a small street urchin whose quick hand tried to snatch one of her daggers from her belt. She smacked his hand away with a disapproving frown, but didn't stop to berate him. Instead, she kept pace with Klauden and Solyn as the palace proper appeared, a large building of white spires and balconies that consumed the entire northeastern sector of the city.

"Yes, your plan to get into the palace." Klauden looked up, counting floors and wondering how easy it would be to get lost in such a place.

Hannah shrugged. "I guess we just ask to see Rory when we get there?"

"Of course that's your plan." Klauden shook his head. "I suppose that might work, depending."

"Depending on what?"

"On how much your elf has told them about us."

"Us?" Hannah stared at him, not following. Rory knew all three of them.

"The Houses, chaivin," Klauden sighed, rolling his eyes at her. "Our people." He sighed, eyes widening as he spoke, voice low so no one could hear him. "We've been living in secret there. The elves don't know." He stopped, turning to face her as he continued the conversation in her mind. <*What do you think will happen if these elves find out there's a demon society living not a hundred leagues away in the mountains?*>

Hannah stared at him, the bigger picture sliding into view. She normally didn't think about such things. And she'd been so focused on reaching Firene, she hadn't considered the rest.

<But the Sarkoza?>

Klauden frowned. *<He seeks an alliance, so he'd present us in the best possible light. But Rory...>* He raised an eyebrow. *<He has reason to say otherwise. We are every fairy tale, every bogeyman, every phantom, every curse and disease to them,>* Klauden told her. *<Every child who has disappeared will be blood on our hands.>* He frowned, looking up to where they could see the white stone of the palace ahead. "We have an obligation to our people, Hannah," he said aloud. "*You* have an obligation." He sighed, the motion lifting his shoulders. "I know you like to forget, but you're still First Daughter."

"So what should we do?"

"I'm not sure," he replied honestly. "But we should be cautious."

The buildings around them had grown nicer, the streets more kept, the people more elaborately dressed—and more distinctly Elven—as they drew near the imposing stone structure. Hannah was used to castles, having grown up in one, but the Elven palace of Firene was impressive. Hannah counted at least seven levels of windows, and the building covered all of the land to the edge of the sea. She couldn't hear the waves crashing over the noise of the people, but she thought if she were there at night, she probably could. She remembered Rory's room in the dream, the balcony looking out at the beach and the ocean, hearing the waves from there.

She looked up at the building. He was in there somewhere.

Klauden gave her one last look. "Are you sure about this, chaivin?"

She nodded, and he sighed, then led them to a small line of people in front of an iron gate. Two guards stood on either side of the open gate, both questioning each person. Hannah scrambled for a new plan, realizing her original plan was only to reach Firene and find Rory. Now that she was here, she didn't even know how to find him.

The guards finished with the man before them, then both looked at Hannah. They skimmed her face, focusing on her clothing and shoes. Solyn received the same appraisal, but when they saw Klauden's robes, they gave each other a knowing look.

"State your name and business, please," the guard on the right said, addressing Hannah since she stood before the others.

Hannah decided to go for it. "I am Hannah Tallerin," she told them. "I am here to see the Tallerin."

The guard peered at her, unsure of what she'd said. "Tallerin?" he repeated, eyes scanning her clothing again. Hannah nodded.

The other guard stepped forward, giving his companion a pointed stare. "They look like the Sarkoza," he commented, taking in Klauden's robes. "You're part of his party, then?"

Klauden nodded vigorously. "Of course."

The first guard looked to Hannah. "Visitors for the Tallerin and the Sarkoza. Today is a busy day for imperial visits." He looked from Hannah to Klauden and back again. "So, where shall we bring you? The Tallerin or the Sarkoza?"

"The Tallerin," Hannah said at the same moment that Klauden said, "The Sarkoza."

The guards looked at one another, then back at them. Hannah grimaced. "Fine," she conceded. "The Sarkoza."

Facing Rory right away wasn't high on her list today anyway. She could wait.

XXII

They were escorted through the gate into the palace proper. Hannah noted that the outside walls were thick stone; the elves didn't skimp on security, though they were exceedingly polite to guests. Hannah knew the elves had very specific customs regarding guests and visitors, so she wasn't surprised to be escorted inside based on her words alone. It wasn't obvious, but this part of the palace was well-defended with carefully placed sentries and seeming servants who moved like warriors. The elves were gracious, but they weren't foolish.

The palace itself was bright and airy for a solid stone structure, nothing like the dark stone walls she had been surrounded by in Castle van Kreeosk. Vampires had no qualms with the sunlight, but the architect of her father's castle certainly had preferred dark enclosed rooms. Hannah assumed it was because the castle had been built when the Houses were still being established, the Vanguard Code an idea in Warren van Harner's mind, and an attack from a rival House was a constant threat. The elves may have enemies and had built a stronghold here in Firene, but they hadn't sacrificed beauty in the process. Hannah wondered why she found the palace here beautiful and not her own childhood home. What had changed her perception?

The late afternoon sunlight was golden through the thin slits of narrow windows as they walked down an imposing hallway, making their way to the right and toward the sea. Hannah could hear the distant crash of waves along the beach, the beach she knew Rory could see from his balcony. She wondered how far above her his rooms were. *Does he already know I am here? Does he care?*

Another set of guards took them down a different hallway, the two Elven women still clearly fighters but dressed more casually in black and silver uniforms, a step down from the armor-wearing guards at the gate and the ones who had escorted them so far. Hannah wondered if all guests were taken quite so far inside the palace when they arrived. They had passed several large rooms with elegant furnishings, obviously meeting rooms and parlors, but their escort was taking them somewhere specific. They reached the end of the grand hallway, walked down a short staircase, and turned left down another smaller hall. Hannah could hear the waves more clearly now, this hallway parallel to the beach running alongside the eastern side of the palace. She had been taking in the tapestries lining the halls, committing the images to memory as she built a working map of the building in her mind. She had always been good with directions, keeping her bearings despite new locations. She wondered if this long walk was designed to confuse them, limit them to a certain part of the building. Castle van Kreeosk wasn't particularly designed for visitors, but it was prepared for attack, so the hallways all looked the same, many down to the furnishings and tapestries, a last-ditch attempt to confuse the enemy during an invasion.

The guards paused outside a smaller set of open double doors on the left-hand side of the corridor, opposite the beach, gesturing for them to enter. Hannah felt Klauden's reaction as he walked through the doorway, and she understood a moment later. Every wall in the room was lined with books.

Hannah shared a look with Solyn as they entered, both of them knowing they would lose Klauden to this room as they allowed their newest escort to lead them to a small area with plush chairs and small tables. "Ladies," the Elven guard said, both women bowing to them before taking their leave. They gave Klauden a nod. "Sir."

They were joined immediately by two elves in fancy dress, both servants by the demeanor but clearly dressed to impress any visitors. Hannah was reminded of Lira, the elf she had met on the road when she'd first met Rory, and her perfect pants despite the days spent out in the open. The material was fine, the design elegant without being ostentatious. These servants had the same look. "What can we get you, Madam Tallerin?" the first asked, addressing Hannah. They were quick, Hannah thought. She had only given her name to the guards at the gate—three sets of attendants before these.

"I'm fine," she told them. "Nothing, thank you."

The man nodded at Solyn while still looking at Hannah. "And your lady?"

Hannah smirked at him. "She's not my lady," she told him, wondering what about Solyn made him think she was a servant.

"Oh!" he seemed genuinely shocked, instantly afraid he had caused some offense. "My apologies!"

"It's fine," Hannah reassured him. "Solyn, you want anything?"

"Nothing, thank you," Solyn told them, echoing Hannah's words and tone. She seemed as fascinated as Klauden by the books, though Hannah knew she could barely read. Klauden had been teaching her, but she wasn't ready for the books in this room yet. Hannah reached out, realizing that Solyn was swept up in Klauden's awe, the bond overwhelming her as he forgot to shield himself.

She looked at him, watching as the other servant approached with deference, no doubt to ask the same question, but Klauden ignored him. Standing in the library, his robes clean, his hair long, his face glowing, Klauden was lovely to behold. Hannah stared at him, seeing him beyond the magic for a moment, her old friend, her companion, the boy who had always loved books more than anything else in the world. Except, maybe, her.

She caught a wave of him then, the idea of so much knowledge available, and she sat down in the chair, echoes of memories running through her. He was calculating the number of books in the room and the amount of time it would likely take the army to arrive, deciding how much of this information he could get through to find a way to break Hannah's connection to the fledglings—if the books they'd gotten from the library didn't end up holding the answers he needed.

Here we go again, she thought. *Now he will spend every day in this room, and I will learn exactly how many ceiling tiles there are or how many different patterns make up the carpet.* She looked up. The ceiling was far above them, the rows of bookshelves reaching up and up, connected by a series of small ladders and walkways. It was truly a beautiful room, a perfect place to put guests at ease while they waited to meet with those in charge.

Hannah examined the setup with her father's eyes. The books were a show of wealth and power, the furniture a sign of comfort, but also a reminder that the guests were there by the mercy of those managing the palace. The servants were a sign of courtesy, but also spies guaranteed to keep the visitors honest until they could be assessed. Solyn sank into another chair, leaning back and closing her eyes, a hand over her belly. Hannah could feel her exhaustion, her hope that tonight would find her sleeping in a comfortable bed again.

Klauden had wandered off to examine the shelves, his fingers sliding along the titles there, brain already recording which titles he would ask to read. Hannah had just about resigned herself to the next few days spent in this room when she realized that this was not her father's castle, that she was not bound to stand by Klauden for every moment.

She was in Firene. Rory was in Firene. She could see him. Even if it meant seeing his Elven lady, she could still see him. And no doubt the castle was filled with things to divert her attention. She could train with the elves here. She could explore the grounds as much as they would let a visiting dignitary.

Her thoughts ran cold at the thought—was she a visiting dignitary, then? A part of the Sarkoza's retinue? She wasn't the vain girl she had once been, but part of her longed to be something else. To be the Tallerin's wife as expected, whatever that meant among these people. Rory had been exiled, but then welcomed back when he brought a warning of the army and Herrick—would they treat her as the companion of an exile or as a proper Consort?

Hannah scanned the room again, taking in the two servants who hadn't left their door posts. She reached out with her senses, trying to get a feel for others nearby. She could sense movement in the hallway outside, but they scurried along quickly, more like servants than anyone coming to see them. Another group moved by in a more orderly fashion, likely a guard patrol, and Hannah turned away from the obvious lure of the doorway. This room seemed to take up the entire side of the castle, ending with thin narrow windows overlooking a lush garden. There was a stone fireplace in the far corner, but no fire burned in it. Hannah wondered if it normally had flames or if they had left it cold today because they weren't expecting visitors.

They had been in the room a few minutes when a group of people entered. Hannah was slightly surprised—she hadn't sensed their approach at all. Looking them over, she understood why immediately. Four vampires stood before them. She recognized Milo van Reegan even though it had been years since she had seen him. He may be a plain-faced man who could easily fade into a crowd, but the Sarkoza was famous. The woman standing beside him was unfamiliar, but the lines of her face mirrored Milo, and Hannah recognized her as his twin sister, Millani, a member of the Kargin as a second child. The other two men were clearly members of the same family, but much older. One looked about the same age as Klauden's parents, his hair thick and dark, framing a face that distantly echoed Klauden's eyes and cheekbones. The other looked like he was in his 900s at least, his hair steel grey but still full, his eyes bright blue and the expression on his face one Hannah recognized from Klauden. Something about him was vaguely familiar, but Hannah couldn't place it.

Milo might be her distant cousin on her father's side, but he was descended from the van Tarkinets, just like Klauden. Twins were common in their family, something Hannah hadn't thought about but did now, glancing quickly at Solyn's belly. The fledgling hadn't moved from where she sat in the plush chair, clearly waiting on her master's reaction before making herself known.

Klauden reacted first, a hand to his shoulder, then to his chin, the greeting for equals. The Sarkoza nodded. "Master van Sherinak," he said, his voice low. "I've been expecting you."

The older man gave Milo a glance, quickly hidden, then turned back to observe the trio. Klauden nodded, then gestured to Hannah. "May I present Lady van Kreeosk?" Hannah gave him the same greeting, adding a small dip of the head as was customary, trying not to frown when he used her old name. <*Hannah Tallerin,*> she thought to Klauden, letting him feel her annoyance.

<*Not right now,*> Klauden responded in kind, then turned to where Solyn sat on the chair. She rose gracefully as Klauden spoke, her hand touching her chin, then her forehead before executing a deep curtsy, the appropriate greeting for a superior. "And my fledgling, Solyn." Though the fledgling's face revealed nothing in that moment, Hannah felt how much Solyn wanted him to claim her with a last name. But it wouldn't happen.

Solyn had status as Klauden's fledgling but was a pale comparison to the Kargin in this company.

Fledglings were always respected but never honored among the pure-blood families.

<*Except I'm not even pureblooded,*> Hannah thought, unable to stop herself.

<*Not now,*> Klauden reminded her.

<*Of course not now,*> she snapped back at him. <*You think me a fool?*>

The Sarkoza nodded, then gestured to his sister. "And I present Millani, Secondborn of House van Reegan."

Klauden nodded cordially as Millani touched her chin and her forehead, but she didn't curtsy as Solyn had done before a superior. Hannah didn't miss this flaunting of custom, nor did she dismiss the oddity of introducing a Kargin before the other men at his back. The Sarkoza was adhering to some traditions while flouting others. <*Interesting.*>

"And my uncle, Eriken, Secondborn of House van Tarkinet," he said, nodding to the older of the other men. Hannah understood. Milo's mother had been a twin as well; this was her brother, no doubt protective of his nephew especially after the death of his sister. Secondborn was not a title used in Castle van Kreeosk; Hannah wondered what it meant in the context of Castle van Lartner. Eriken nodded, touching shoulder and chin in an echo of the Sarkoza, but adding a dip of the head in their direction—another break with the rules.

"And Nicolo," Milo gestured, "Thirdborn of House van Kistling." The old man simply nodded at them, cordial enough, but definitely not following custom. Hannah racked her brain, trying to identify the old man, to fill in that tickle in her memory, but Klauden's knowledge filled her. His elder sister Dara had married Hannah's grandfather, while his middle sister Elana had married into the van Tarkinets as Lana, Milo, and Millani's grandmother. The Houses of the Vanya often intermarried, mingling bloodlines. She and Klauden's ancestors were connected through marriage, not blood, and Nicolo was the generation where the families had joined.

She had expected the Sarkoza and perhaps some Kargin soldiers, not that he needed them; the elves probably didn't guess his ability. She hadn't expected this odd assortment of relatives, all looking at her trio with expectation.

"Well met," she said. She was still the highest-ranking person in the room, so it fell to her to begin, though given the lax adherence to custom so far, Hannah hoped they could dispense with the rest. She was uncomfortable being Lady van Kreeosk. She may be back in her body again, but she wasn't that woman anymore.

She looked at Klauden. *<So,>* she prompted, *<how do we do this?>*

Klauden shrugged. *<You wanted to come to Firene.>*

<To see Rory,> she reminded him, though she felt how the name hurt him. *<The Sarkoza was your plan.>*

Everyone continued to stare at her, and she looked at Klauden, trying to divert the attention. "So what brings you all to Firene?" she asked to fill the pause.

Milo and his sister exchanged a look, clearly holding an entire conversation in a glance. Hannah knew that kind of connection—she had it with Klauden, and to some extent with Solyn. "We are hoping for an alliance with the elves," he said neutrally, glancing at Klauden. Hannah assumed Milo was thinking of their dream. He wouldn't know that Hannah had seen it too.

Klauden looked at the four of them. "You wish to start a new House," he said quietly, "allied with the elves." When Milo nodded, Klauden asked, "Why?"

"It's time," Milo replied, and Hannah thought he would leave it there, but he continued, "for something different."

"Different?" Hannah echoed.

"You haven't been home in quite some time, Lady," Milo observed. "Perhaps you've found the customs of others more palatable to your preferences."

Hannah smirked. "Please call me Hannah," she told him, "since we're dispensing with pleasantries here." She looked at all of them, Kargin, Second and Thirdborns. "What customs might you want to avoid?"

"Customs that would have you bound to Castle van Kreeosk rather than standing in this room," he replied quickly, and Hannah smiled again.

"But why the elves?" she asked. "Why not just start a House farther north?"

Milo looked around, pointing out the finery of the room. "This is a wealthy city. Well-appointed. Well-stocked. Well-guarded."

"Trade." Klauden nodded. "And allies."

"Among other things," Milo said.

"And Gerter van Lartner will just let you go?" Hannah asked, thinking of her father, who would never have let her go if he had a choice. The Sarkoza was far more valuable.

Milo frowned. "Having allies can be crucial, but these ties need to grow from strength."

"So you help them with the army, and they agree to let you set up nearby," Hannah guessed, assuming Milo had assured the elves of his ability to render aid.

"We may be few, but we are strong," Milo offered.

"Do they know how strong?" Hannah asked bluntly.

Klauden shot her a look and Milo frowned, glancing at the door. "They know we are willing and able to help at a time when they need it."

Hannah nodded, letting it go for the moment. "So what's the plan, then? Start a new House without Kargin?" Solyn looked up, her attention hooked despite her desire to keep herself quiet and unnoticed. In the presence of so many purebloods, especially so many men, she was having a hard time keeping herself calm. Hannah knew what had happened to her back in the castle, knew that being around so many others like them would be challenging. *<But you're strong now, Solyn. You're no longer mortal.>*

<No, but I'm not as strong as you,> Solyn thought. *<I was when I was new, but not anymore. They could do whatever they wanted to me, and I couldn't stop them.>*

Hannah frowned at the idea, unable to conceal the expression. She didn't understand. She had been hurt as a human, but she was still alive. She tried to put herself in Solyn's place, a fledgling among powerful vampires, and failed.

I wouldn't be afraid, she told herself. *Would you, though? You don't know.* For all that Hannah had shared Solyn's body both as a mortal and as a fledgling, there were still things about Solyn she didn't understand, would never understand, even having seen the former slave's memories.

Hannah could understand the appeal of a new House. She had been wondering where they would live when this was over.

"Start a new House," the Sarkoza echoed, "and decide what we want it to be."

"And by we, you mean...?" Hannah looked at Millani, Eriken, and Nicolo, all of whom had remained silent, letting Milo do the talking.

"You wish us to join your House," Klauden said from behind her. "You need us so van Lartner will release you without a fight." He took a few steps to stand at Hannah's side, Solyn partially hidden behind them. No doubt he could feel his fledgling's fear and excitement. "And with the elves as allies, no one else in the Vanya would dare challenge you."

Milo nodded, looking at both of them in turn. "And what will you require to join us?" The question was simple, but everyone else in the room was waiting for their response.

<*This is what you meant,*> Hannah thought to Klauden, <*when you imagined us in a House. This alliance is part of your plan. What will you negotiate for it?*>

"We require certain magic," Klauden offered. "A spell to break bonds."

"No spell created can sever kevna," Milo said.

Klauden shook his head. "Not kevna. The fledgling bond between Hannah and Herrick's followers."

Milo frowned. "I don't know of such a thing, nor is it in my possession." He looked at his sister, who quickly shook her head. His uncle made the same quick gesture, but a look at Nicolo gained a different response.

"A magical bond," the old vampire repeated. "Between a physical body and many fledglings," he mused. Hannah tried to recall what she knew of Nicolo. He was a magic user like she and Klauden, and his eyes had also been scanning the books in the library as they spoke, so he probably had the same thirst for knowledge. Klauden had heard whispers of a van Kistling Kargin from many years ago being a seer, but he didn't know if they referred to Nicolo. They could both feel the low burn of his magic, a power like their own, and yet slightly different. The old vampire was silent for a moment while they all waited for him. "I think I may have a solution."

"What is it?" Klauden demanded, more heat in his voice than he intended. He had been studying the books from the castle every spare moment, but he couldn't put the pieces together. He was missing something. And now, since they were in Firene, time was running short.

"What do you know of the Book of Samander?" Nicolo asked, and information flooded Klauden's brain, possibilities considered and rejected. He knew the Book was supposed to contain whatever magic the user required, an ancient artifact of dangerous power. "I know only that I've never seen it, nor read anyone who has," Klauden said neutrally. "No one that survived, anyway."

"What if I could let you see it? Would that be enticement enough to join our House?" The old vampire's face was crafty, eyes darting from Klauden to Hannah and back again.

"That depends," Klauden replied, his voice masking the eager excitement building in his chest. He would have to spend some time thinking about Nicolo after this meeting, recalling everything he knew about the van Kistling family. He frowned, wondering if this too-good-to-be-true offer was a delaying tactic. They had perhaps two weeks before the army arrived, and Hannah's tie to the fledglings would prove her end. He wouldn't let that happen, not when he finally had her. Hannah stared at him, warmth filling her at the determination in her mate. "Time is of the essence," he said. "I would need it soon."

The vampire nodded. "Allow me to consult an old friend," he suggested.

Klauden agreed. "Very well." He looked at Hannah, who sent him a silent agreement, though part of her felt like they had just willingly stepped into a subtle trap. "If you can locate the Book for us, we will join your House."

"It must be House van Sherinak," Millani said, looking at Hannah and Solyn in turn before back at her brother. Hannah understood. They were trying to break free from their own House but couldn't under their family name. The van Reegans were still Second Family despite Milo's ability. "You must be First Family."

Klauden nodded, not thrilled with the idea, but understanding enough of custom to expect it. "Both of you," Millani insisted quietly. "Lady van Kreeosk and Master van Sherinak."

Hannah nodded, wondering why she was repeating herself. "Yes, we already said we'll live in your castle."

Millani smiled, showing her fangs, giving her brother a pointed look. The Sarkoza turned to them again, not smiling. "You will be married as soon as this army business is taken care of."

Hannah stared at Klauden, the vampire staring right back at her. They had discussed a lot of things in the last weeks, but getting married was not one of them, though Hannah now realized how foolish she had been in ignoring the question. She looked back at Millani, blurting out the first thing coming to mind. "This is probably a bad time to tell you that I'm already married to the Tallerin, then," Hannah said.

"Married to the Tallerin?" a voice echoed. "Damn it, Rory, you couldn't even invite your brothers to your wedding?"

The vampires all turned to see the trio of elves who had arrived on silent feet. Hannah's gaze slid past the other two elves to settle on Rory, her heart pounding as she stared at her husband in the flesh. He looked well, skin flushed with vitality, his hair a bit longer and tied into a braid that reached his collar. He was wearing familiar clothes, a plain, black shirt and dark pants, but the material was finer, the cut more flattering. His long ears each had a silver hoop at the top, something Hannah had only seen in dreams.

Staring at him, she sensed a hint of his emotions—excitement, anger, lust—when he looked at her, but the feeling quickly disappeared as Klauden stepped to her side and took her hand. She looked at him, surprised at the gesture, especially given that she had just said she was married to Rory, but her words were lost as she looked at him, familiar desire creeping through her at the touch of his hand to hers, the confident expression on his face, the politician at work already.

He bent his head in a cordial greeting, and Hannah finally saw the other two elves. They both resembled Rory, clearly brothers, though one wore what Hannah recognized immediately as a royal insignia on a chain around his neck, the gold medallion a clear indicator of his position. *That must be Jasper,* she thought, taking in the dark hair also tied back in a braid, though his reached partway down his back. He was thinner and slightly taller than Rory, the middle brother, his face handsome and cunning.

The other elf was shorter than both of his brothers, his wavy dark hair hanging free around his face, bright eyes taking in the scene as he smiled. *Linus,* Hannah thought, *his youngest brother.* Linus had been the one to speak when they entered, and now, all of the vampires turned to face Rory, clearly wondering what his response would be, no one missing the way Klauden held Hannah's hand.

"We never had an official wedding," Rory said, face impassive. Hannah felt like he had stabbed her, but then he added, "But I did promise her my name."

"He did," Klauden agreed, lifting Hannah's hand and releasing it, pointing her in the elf's direction, effectively handing her off to him, waiting to see if he would take her hand. Hannah stood in the middle of the room, unsure of what to do.

"I really need to learn more of your customs," Linus commented, staring at both Klauden and Rory before turning his charm to Millani. "Perhaps the lady would care to explain the ways of the Vanya at another time." He winked, easily refocusing the tension in the room.

"I would gladly shed light on our customs for you," Milo gritted, and Linus laughed.

"Clearly, brothers are the same everywhere." He turned to his own brother. "Now that everyone is finally here, how would you like to begin?"

Jasper scanned the faces around him, no doubt noting that Rory hadn't moved toward where Hannah still stood amid both groups and was not claiming his supposed wife. "This is not the ideal place for such things," he announced, glancing at the scattered groups of chairs, none of them large enough for everyone to sit at once. "Come with me." He didn't wait, expecting to be obeyed as he turned and left the room.

Linus gestured for the Sarkoza's group to follow, then stepped into Millani's other side. "I think I missed something important," he said to her, "about how your Houses work. I thought bloodlines were critical." Hannah missed what Millani said, watching Rory instead. Klauden took Solyn's arm in his and led her after the group, leaving Hannah alone with her husband.

Hannah wanted to say something, anything, but words failed her, so she stood there instead, biting her lip and waiting for him. He only paused for a moment, then gestured to the door and raised his eyebrows. She nodded, stepping quickly after the others, trying to ignore his presence at her side. He didn't touch her or say anything, his gaze fixed on the backs of the vampires before them. Hannah did the same, trying to ignore the frisson of jealousy that ran through her at seeing Klauden touching Solyn but willing to face that instead of the huge hole inside of her where Rory was supposed to be. The vampires did look great together, his hair slightly darker than Solyn's, their bodies pressed close as they walked down the hall, his grip gentle as they went up a flight of stairs.

150

She suddenly wanted to be on his arm, to feel him touching her, to be all that he wanted from her, to accept her life as Lady van Sherinak, but the desire fled as quickly as it had arrived, a small voice inside reminding her that she had decided long ago to abandon that life. She gave Rory a quick look where he walked beside her, but he wasn't looking at her. His face was focused on Klauden's back with an oddly confused expression, and slow red crept up from his chest to the bottom of his neck, where it stood out in bright contrast to the white scars on his skin. *It's true, then*, Hannah thought, releasing the tiniest bit of hope she had held onto that everything she had seen, everything Klauden had said, was in her mind. Rory was her fledgling, and that meant everything else was true. He was with someone else now.

She had seen that red work its way up his chest before, either in anger or in excitement. She wondered which it was now. She focused on him, testing the bond, and for a second, she caught a wave of something that shocked her—lust. He was staring at Klauden's hand where it rested on Solyn's arm, and memories of the night in Severin when Klauden had changed her into his fledgling flooded her, when she had first felt that rush of desire for Klauden, only to be replaced at the last moment with Rory.

Her husband faltered on the step, breathing ragged, then Hannah was outside of him again, the quiet need for Klauden pounding in her fingertips, kevna ever present and demanding. She gave Rory a questioning look, but he refused to look at her, blinking several times and clenching his hands. He bit his lip, and Hannah saw his fangs. A different series of emotions filled her at the sight—desire, pride, love—but she looked away. Rory was clearly having a moment, and he needed some privacy to contain himself.

Did I do that to him? Can he feel what I feel for Klauden? The idea was entertaining. Rory was definitely open to certain things in the bedroom, but she didn't think he'd ever truly desired another man. The feeling must be confusing for him. She kept following the others up the stairs, letting Rory fall a few steps behind. He knew where they were going.

She continued to watch Klauden's hold on Solyn's arm, another thought surfacing: *If Rory can feel my desire for Klauden through our bond, can Solyn feel Klauden's need for me through their bond?* She looked at Solyn's back, the fledgling's body a lovely set of curves in her pants and shirt. Her body had bloomed in pregnancy, her breasts full and her skin glowing. Hannah could appreciate her beauty, could admire her body, but she didn't feel anything more than that.

Can the magic make me desire Solyn if Klauden does? She looked back at the fledgling. She hadn't felt anything for her, but she doubted that Klauden never wanted her. Even back in the castle before all of this, he had found Solyn attractive. But Hannah felt nothing beyond loyalty when she looked at her, a feeling she was surprised to find, but joined by guilt, which she expected, and a slowly fading pity. There was pride too—Solyn grew stronger every day, becoming more herself than she ever had before. But there was no desire to touch her.

So the magic does have limits! Hannah tried to calm the growing excitement inside, the hope that began to glow fiercely inside at the idea that magic with limits might also have flaws, cracks that could be exploited with the right pressure.

Maybe I could be free.

Klauden turned to look at her over his shoulder at the thought, face creased in curious thought. No doubt he had heard her revelation. He looked beyond her to where Rory followed a few steps below and smirked, clearly enjoying the effect kevna was having on the elf.

<*Maybe it's possible, chaivin, if it's what you want. But for now, I need your help. I need to be part of the new House, whatever it takes.*>

Hannah nodded. <*Of course. I wouldn't take that from you.*>

<*Even if it means marrying me?*>

Hannah swallowed hard, trying not to look back at Rory, the elf composed again and following as they turned down another hallway.

<*I'm already married.*>

<*Are you? I'm starting to think there are a lot of Elven customs your elf never told you.*>

XXIII

They settled around a round wooden table in the War Room, Jasper surrounded by both of his brothers, Milo with Millani on one side and the men on the other, and Klauden seated between Hannah and Solyn. There were two more elves already at the table when they arrived. The first was male with tattoos covering his exposed skin in swirling arcs of power, and though Hannah had heard a lot about Caganasti, this was her first time seeing him in the flesh. The female sitting beside him was a stranger, though her official dress and bearing marked her as a member of the royal household and a soldier with years of training. She looked mildly annoyed as they entered, as if they were all late for a planned meeting.

"My Royal Advisor, Caganasti." Jasper introduced the elf to Klauden's party, but Klauden only nodded, face blank of the surprise that meeting Caganasti for the first time usually elicits.

"We've met," Klauden told the ruler, nodding to the old mage.

"And Saria Kelharin," he gestured to the female elf, "our Warmaster." Hannah nodded at the elf who had taken over Rory's position. The woman nodded politely back, clearly no stranger to politics, keen eyes assessing each of the people in the room.

"So," Jasper began, looking at the faces around the table, "we find ourselves in a situation." He paused, gathering his thoughts. He looked at Milo first. "You come seeking an alliance just as we find ourselves in need." He looked at Rory. "An army approaches the city. The goblins are not a huge threat, though they too must be dealt with, but these other creatures you speak of seem troublesome. You say they are stronger and much harder to kill, the equivalent of thirty seasoned soldiers for each one, and led by Herculindarus, himself now one of them." He looked at Klauden and Hannah in turn. "And you bring us a connection to Herrick that can help us defeat him." He sighed, then looked around the room, scanning the tapestries with their depictions of Elven victories over the years.

"Let us begin with the army."

Saria nodded, taking the lead. "Scouts tell us goblins have been sighted near Lake Versin. That's about ten days from here. Depending on how they cross the Marin, they could be at our borders in a fortnight."

"And the creatures?" Jasper asked.

"We have no real reports of the creatures. Only distant sightings of male humans among the goblins."

"And Herrick?" Hannah asked. "Has he been seen?"

Saria looked at Caganasti. "Only through magic."

The old elf smiled. "Herrick is strong with his new abilities, but he has lost his connection to his god. He has no protection from scrying now."

"What does he want?" Hannah asked, searching the Elven faces at the table.

"Revenge," Linus said quietly. "He feels ... slighted."

Hannah raised an eyebrow, waiting for the rest of the story.

"He thought he should have been head of the temple here," Rory answered. "Our father disagreed." He shrugged. "Herrick left a long time ago."

"So ... he wants to destroy the temple, then?" Klauden prompted. Rory stared at the vampire's face for a moment too long, as if unable to stop looking at Klauden's mouth. Hannah bit her lip, hiding a grin, delighted that kevna was bleeding into her bond with Rory. *Let him understand what I deal with every day now.*

Caganasti nodded. "It would appear so. He seems to think that Valerius can smite him now, and he wants to destroy the temple so there won't be any more acolytes."

Hannah snorted. "That's dumb. Wouldn't you just rebuild the temple? And not having a temple wouldn't remove the god or his followers."

"I never said Herrick was the brightest," Caganasti said. "Only the angriest right now." He sighed. "And he also wields an army of very strong creatures." He turned to Saria. "What do we know of these fighters?"

The Warmaster frowned. "Not enough for my liking. They are incredibly strong and fast, moving like nothing we've seen before, even with magic-enhanced fighters. They are magical, but it is a type of power the mages cannot identify." She paused, shaking her head. "Some reports suggest they drink blood."

Linus raised his eyebrows. "What manner of blood?"

"Apparently, they prefer Elven blood if they can get it, human if they cannot. No one reports seeing them drink animal blood."

"Vampires?" Jasper asked, turning to Milo and Klauden in turn, face concerned but not outraged. "Are the stories true, then?"

Klauden nodded to Milo, letting the Sarkoza explain. "Stories often have a grain of truth," the vampire said.

"What grain might that be?" Linus prodded. "The blood-drinking part or the demon part?"

Milo paused, considering his words. "The blood-drinking part is true," he said finally, "a dietary quirk of our makeup. The demon part is myth."

Jasper scanned the table of faces, sliding over Milo and Millani's bright eyes, Eriken and Nicolo's neutral expression, eyes skipping to Rory's scarred neck, to Klauden and Hannah's pale skin. "And your purpose in coming here is to secure an alliance with our people?" Jasper asked. "What connection do you have to this army?"

"None," Milo answered quickly. "The army is merely a coincidence of timing."

<*Not likely,*> Klauden thought, giving Nicolo a curious look.

<*Why do you say that?*>

<*He's a seer,*> Klauden reminded Hannah. <*He knows when some things will happen. He knew when to come here.*>

"A very convenient coincidence," Saria observed. "What do you offer in your alliance?"

"Our strength," Milo offered.

"You are but four," Saria said, then glanced across the table at Klauden, "perhaps seven. What can you do against so many?"

"We are stronger than the creatures you saw," Milo told her.

"Are they not vampires, then?" The Warmaster's eyes narrowed.

"We call them fledglings, and they are fierce, but nothing compared to their Makers."

"Are you their Makers?" Jasper asked, the question filled with intent.

Milo sighed. "Not of this group of fledglings," he told them, glancing at Hannah, "but in general, yes, our people can create creatures such as those."

"As you have explained," Jasper said speculatively, and Hannah wondered how many conversations they had already had about her people. How much did the elves know? The prince looked up at Milo again. "Do you plan to single handedly kill them all, then, plus the goblins?"

"Not exactly. Not yet," Milo said carefully. "There are ... complications," he added, looking at Hannah again. She took a deep breath and frowned at him.

"So if you aren't here to destroy the army, what else can you offer?" Saria asked, face skeptical.

"Trade with the north, treaties with the wolves, a cease-fire with the creatures who hunt your mountains. Is that enough to satisfy?" Milo's tone suggested he found this more than reasonable motivation.

Saria looked at Jasper, letting the prince decide. Jasper frowned. "I need to know more. I'm told you're Herrick's Maker," he said, addressing Hannah.

"Unfortunately," she admitted, "I had a part in his creation."

Jasper looked at the Sarkoza and back to Hannah. "Though I don't pretend to know what all that entails, I do understand this means you share a connection with him, that you are magically bound in some way." Hannah wanted to laugh, thinking for a moment if only her biggest problem was being bound to Herrick. Who wasn't she bound to? She nodded at Jasper. "Can you control him?" he asked.

She shook her head. "No. Some fledglings can be controlled, but Herrick is a special case." She sighed, embarrassed to admit her failure in front of her cousin and his family. She knew what her father would say at her sloppiness. "I thought he wouldn't survive," she said, hoping none of the elves would get angry at the fact that she was talking about killing another elf. Herrick didn't seem very popular among the elves present, though, so she added, "And he wouldn't have if another hadn't found him to complete the transition."

Jasper frowned. "So can we simply kill him?"

Hannah lifted her hands, shrugging, unsure of how much to admit. "He can die."

"And what happens to you if he dies?" Linus asked, picking up on the subtext.

"I really don't know. I might die with him."

"That is problematic," Jasper told her. "I would rather not begin my alliance with House van Sherinak by inadvertently slaying the Lady of the House."

"Wait," Linus said. "I thought you said you were married to my brother. How are you also Lady van Sherinak?"

Hannah wanted to crawl under the table. "It's ... complicated," she managed, looking at Klauden, then at Rory.

"Clearly," Linus said. "Can someone please clarify for me? I'd like to know with whom we are making an alliance." He looked at the Sarkoza. "You came here with the request, but you say your House wouldn't be in your name. You would be Second Family." He said the title like he didn't quite know what it meant. "So presumably, we would be dealing with Klauden instead?" He frowned. "And his lady?" He shook his head. "I feel like I'm missing something pretty significant here."

"Hannah has been betrothed to Klauden van Sherinak since childhood," Rory said quietly. "But she lived with me for a year." He added, "As my wife."

"In Solyn's body," Klauden added quickly, looking at Milo and Millani, and Hannah wanted to kick him under the table. She could sense where this was going. She had told Klauden that she wouldn't stand in his way, wouldn't prevent him from getting his House, and she had meant it. She just didn't realize what it might mean for her.

"But now she's back in her body," Milo observed. "And you are here," he addressed Rory, "with the Valrina."

Rory flushed, looking away from Hannah, but then unable to drag his gaze from Klauden. Milo raised an eyebrow, clearly wondering why Rory kept giving Klauden those looks, not the expression he would've expected the elf to give his wife's new lover, but he continued, "So Lady van Kreeosk is free to uphold her betrothal to Master van Sherinak. The bloodlines remain pure."

Hannah stared at him, too shocked at this frank discussion of her purity in front of everyone in the room to contradict the words. She waited for Rory to correct him, to explain that though she had been in another body for most of their time together, they had spent that first night together in her body. She remembered the night in Kalford. She remembered Rory's confusion when she told him what staying with him meant for her, for her people, their beliefs about purity and bloodlines. He wouldn't have forgotten.

But he didn't speak, staring at Klauden instead. She opened her mouth to object, but then Klauden's will clamped down and the words died in her throat.

<NO. You will not tell them. You will not ruin this for us.>

<But—>

<NO.> He drowned her in his feelings, his absolute need for this alliance to keep her and Solyn and his child safe, and her ability to contradict him fled. She stared at his face, familiar and beloved, but in the moment, he reminded her of her father, and she remembered telling him a long time ago that, one day, he would look at her that way, tyrannical and merciless.

<I'm married to Rory,> she told him in a very small voice. *<He will say something.>*

<He will not.> Klauden shoved memories into Hannah, his body moving with hers, his lips against her neck, his hands on her skin. Her body reacted immediately, hands aching to touch him, needing to be closer to him, and her mind immediately caved to his wishes. She wanted him to be happy, wanted to please him, would do anything he wanted.

<Say nothing.> This time Klauden's command was gentle, though still an order. She dipped her chin in a brief acknowledgement, then looked across the table at Rory. The elf was turning red again, hands splayed across the table.

"Of course," Klauden replied. Though it seemed like a lot of time had passed, her exchange with Klauden had been no more than a few seconds. She could feel kevna slowly receding again, her need to please Klauden fading to the background.

"Very well," Milo said. He addressed Linus and Jasper, "Your alliance is with House van Sherinak."

"But..." Linus began, looking at Solyn now, drawing everyone's gaze to the fledgling, "that one is with child." He looked at Rory, then at Klauden. "She lived with you in that body before she became one of these fledglings, and now she's clearly with you. Whose child does she carry?"

Hannah was glad that the focus wasn't on her, but she felt awful for Solyn, the former slave wilting under the scrutiny of so many male gazes. The elves seemed curious, sympathetic even. The vampires didn't seem to think the question mattered at all. It wouldn't to them. Solyn was a fledgling, beneath notice beyond her protected status. Her child wouldn't have a rank. Solyn seemed to pick up on Hannah's thought, and suddenly, she straightened, raising her chin and tossing back her glorious hair, flaunting her healthy glow, her obvious beauty. She took Klauden's hand and let them both rest on the table's surface, the gesture clear in its meaning.

Linus looked at Rory.

"I ... left many months ago," he said.

Linus frowned, nodding. "I see." He looked at Klauden where he sat between Hannah and Solyn, something like admiration in his expression. "Very interesting!" He looked at Milo. "Do your people customarily have harems, then?"

Hannah choked, unable to stop herself. "Can we not talk about this?" Milo's normally pleasant expression had started to darken as his head tilted to the side, gaze fixed on Hannah.

Linus raised an eyebrow, confused by her embarrassment, but nodded agreeably, holding his hands up in a peaceful gesture. "I meant no offense, my lady. I'm still learning your ways."

"These aren't our ways," Hannah grated. "These are exceptional circumstances."

"Glad we got that cleared up, then," Linus said sarcastically, rolling his eyes in Rory's direction, but clearly willing to let the topic go for the moment. "It doesn't solve our problem. I'd rather not be responsible for the death of a brand-new ally."

"We're working on a solution," Klauden told them. "We will break the bond. Then you may kill them all."

"Break the bond?" Rory asked. "I didn't think that was possible."

"Not all bonds," Klauden said. "Just the one with the army." Rory hadn't misunderstood the meaning, eyes darkening as he looked at them both. Klauden looked at Jasper. "I would request access to your library."

Jasper nodded. "Of course. I'm sure Rory can help you with whatever you need."

Rory was staring at Hannah now, face hardening in anger. He nodded at his brother's words, though, a sharp gesture.

He's coming out of Klauden's influence, Hannah thought. *And he remembers what I just felt.* The sensations echoed through her again, distant but still powerful, Klauden's body against hers. *He knows I've been with Klauden now. He knew it before, in Solyn's body obviously, and he must've assumed, but now it's confirmed.*

He doesn't just know it, she thought. *He felt it.*

She felt her own face growing hot with even more embarrassment and the slow build of anger. Not only had Rory refused to acknowledge his marriage to her, he had lied about their time together, basically relegating her to the status of another fling in a different body, then dismissing her when that body got pregnant. *So much for him fighting for me.*

"Very well," Jasper said. "This has been most enlightening." He looked at Milo. "We accept your alliance under the condition of aid destroying this army." He looked at Klauden. "You have six days to sever your bonds. We need four days to get our defenses in place. After that, the city comes before everything else." He gave Hannah a sympathetic look. "I do hope we can find a solution," he told her. "I don't want to be responsible for the death of my one-time sister either."

Hannah remained seated as the others began to rise, Jasper leaving immediately, followed by Saria. The Sarkoza stood next with his family, though Millani seemed to linger long enough to be the last to leave. Linus was quick to stand near her, the charismatic elf making small talk as they exited the room. Caganasti stood slowly, giving the four of them long looks in turn. Finally, the old elf sighed, rolling his eyes.

"You all are the most tangled mess I've ever seen," the elf declared, "and I've been alive for five centuries." He chuckled. "This is fascinating!" Klauden's face darkened, nearly matching Rory's, and the elf raised his hands. "But you definitely need to work out a way around this," he added. "What's your plan?"

"Do you know of the Book of Samander?" Klauden asked bluntly, and Caganasti's face paled beneath his tattoos.

He shook his head. "No. Bad plan." He glanced at all of them. "Tied together you may be, but you're all alive. Enjoy living."

"I plan to," Klauden said, "with Hannah."

"What's the Book of Samander?" Rory asked, ignoring the jab as he stepped around the edge of the table to stand closer to them. His hand reached out, seeming of its own accord, to touch Klauden's arm, but he yanked it back.

"Awful business," Caganasti replied. "You know I love dangerous toys, but that book is blasphemy."

"Why?" Hannah asked, skin prickling at the warning.

"It gives you whatever spell you need," Caganasti told them. "No matter the cost." He shook his head. "No one ever truly benefits from that thing."

"What else would you suggest, then?" Klauden prompted. "How else can we break the bond?"

"It's magical, right? You need something that stops magic," Caganasti said simply.

Hannah stared at him. The answer was so simple. If she could stop magic, she wouldn't be tied by kevna. She wouldn't be connected to the fledglings. She would be free.

"Stops magic?" Klauden echoed.

"But Hannah is magical," Rory said, surprising all of them. "Without magic, what happens to her?"

"She won't disappear if that's what you mean," Caganasti said. "She's flesh and blood and bone."

"No, I mean she's a vampire. There's magic in her body. She's a spell-caster. Even without the bonds, Hannah herself is a magical being. What would she be without magic?" Rory paused, the words flowing out of him. "*Can* she be without magic?"

Caganasti shrugged. "I assume so." He looked her over. "There are vampires without magical ability, yes?"

Hannah and Klauden nodded. "So you would likely remain what you are."

"Likely," she echoed, disliking this idea. "Can't something in my life be certain?"

"You will certainly die if we cannot break your bond to the fledglings," Klauden said quietly. "I cannot save you from that."

"Why not?" Rory asked, hand reaching out to touch Klauden's sleeve, fingers sliding down his arm to touch the back of his hand. "You've done it before. Why can't you save her now?"

Klauden looked down at the hand touching his, glanced at Hannah, and smirked, turning to face the elf. "Because I can only pull her back from the abyss so many times before I, too, am lost," he said, gently lifting Rory's hand from his. "Because my power has limits." He turned Rory's hand, taking it and pressing it flat against his own chest while sending Hannah a memory of her touching that chest when they stood on the cliff in the Vanya. Hannah gasped, pleasure building as she recalled what happened next. Rory's face reddened as he bit his lower lip, unable to look away from where his hand rested on Klauden's robes.

Klauden slowly shifted the image in Hannah's mind: instead of her hand on his chest, it was her foot, then he was yanking her to him, throwing her leg over his shoulder. Rory choked as the pleasure hit him, and he jerked back, hitting the edge of the table between two chairs, breathing hard with his eyes jerking back and forth between Hannah and Klauden.

He looked at Solyn then, the fledgling still sitting in her chair, though she had turned it to face the discussion. A different memory filled Hannah then, floating in the water in Solyn's body, her legs wrapped around Rory as they swam in the pond behind the house in Severin, her lips tasting of berries as they kissed. It was gone quickly, buried by kevna, but Klauden had felt it too. He frowned, clearly not enjoying the image of Hannah or Solyn with Rory. He glanced at his fledgling, and Solyn smiled sweetly at him but said nothing, clearly not getting in the middle of this memory contest.

"How..." Rory breathed after a moment, "can we break this bond?"

"Between us?" Klauden asked. "I don't think we can. I did tell you that the fledgling bond was forever. You didn't seem to care back then." He glared at the elf. "I warned you. I warned all of you."

"You did," Hannah said in a small voice, emotionally exhausted from the barrage of memories, "but it doesn't matter now." She looked at both men. "We're here now. I don't want to die," she said simply. "Let's break the bonds so that doesn't happen."

"A wise woman," Caganasti said, giving Rory a pointed look, then Klauden. "Let me know how I can help."

"Show me the books in the library about spell-breaking. I'll start there," Klauden said, and Caganasti waved for him to follow.

Klauden looked at Solyn. "Will you come?" The fledgling looked at Rory and Hannah, both still standing beside the table, and stood quickly, hand going to her belly.

"Gladly," she said, stepping to Klauden's side. "The tension in this room is exhausting."

The three of them left, leaving Rory still leaning against the edge of the table. His eyes were haunted, dark with wanting and anger and something that Hannah wanted to think was love. They stood there for a long moment, staring at one another, unwilling to break the silence. Finally, Hannah couldn't stand it.

She may be with Klauden, bound by destiny and ancient magic, but she still wanted Rory, wanted him the way she had since that night in the cave during the storm when they had first met on the road from Talperin. She remembered how he had looked at her then, interested in her stories, laughing at her silly jokes, gazing into her eyes. *How did we end up here?*

"Rory," she breathed, an ache spreading through her. For a moment, she thought he would move to her, gather her in his arms, and kiss her senseless, but then another person entered the room, a familiar blonde elf, and Rory's gaze slid off Hannah to the newcomer. The woman walked up to Rory, tucking her arm into his with familiarity, and stared blandly at where Hannah stood alone. Any remaining hope fled Hannah's heart, and she stared at where the elf held onto Rory, that grip so comfortable.

She recalled Klauden's words: *I can show you how he touches her, how he moves in her, what he says to her as they lay naked together.*

"Here you are!" the elf exclaimed, leaning into Rory's side. "And with a guest!" She looked at Hannah, then to Rory expectantly.

Rory looked from the woman to Hannah and back again, his eyes growing bigger. "This is Annilyn," he introduced awkwardly, his ingrained manners catching up, "the Valrina."

"And who is this, my Tallerin?" the Valrina asked in a syrupy voice that Hannah hated immediately. "I don't believe we've met."

Hannah looked at them together, knowing she was a complete hypocrite, knowing that she had given this up when she gave in to the magic, but still hating Rory a little for his choices, and hating herself even more for hers.

"Apparently, I'm Lady van Kreeosk," she said, shaking her head as she left the room, trying not to cry.

XXIV

The suite Hannah had been given was on the top floor of the palace, two rooms and a balcony overlooking the beach with its black sand. She kept several windows open, enjoying the breeze despite the coolness of the autumn air. The nights were growing longer this far north, the leaves on the trees turning gold as the season changed. Hannah felt like she had skipped a summer, having travelled from the end of winter in southern Severin to the far northern Firene where it was already turning cold again. Hannah didn't mind the cold; she hadn't enjoyed the summer in Severin. The heat on her skin made her sticky with sweat, a feeling she never enjoyed, though she was familiar with the sensation from her time over the forge.

Sitting in the silver bathtub with the water still slightly steaming, Hannah flexed her fingers, suddenly missing the feeling of her hammer, the satisfaction of working with metal. It had been so long since she'd had any kind of routine beyond traveling. She knew she would probably miss the chaos of this time one day in the future when she was settled somewhere, but for now, it was nice to pause for a moment.

Six days, she thought. *I have six days to figure this out.*

She let herself sink down under the water, enjoying the feel of her hair sliding around her face and shoulders. She hadn't expected to have a bath when the servants led her to her rooms, but when they showed up with a long parade of pitchers and filled the tub, she didn't object. It had been so very long since she had a proper bath. The warmth of the water sank into her bones, settling her nerves as she let herself relax. It was easier under the water, all outside sounds muffled, and even her connection to Klauden seemed farther away. She knew where he was, settling into the library and new books, while Solyn rested in their rooms on the floor below hers.

Now that they were officially betrothed again, she and Klauden weren't allowed to share quarters. He could do what he wanted with Solyn, his right to do as he wished with his fledgling, but Hannah was bound to him alone now, at least until she had a child. His child. Hannah scowled. For someone determined to start a new House with new rules, Milo van Reegan was certainly sticking to tradition when it came to marriage. Hannah assumed the way Linus kept looking at Millani had something to do with the Sarkoza's insistence on protocol.

She sat up, water streaming down her face, an ache building in her chest as she remembered once more how Rory hadn't spoken up for her when it mattered. He had let her go. Hannah knew it was because of Klauden's influence, because kevna made her want to please the vampire, and Rory had been affected by the magic, but it still hurt. She tried to think of him now but could only imagine him in his rooms with that woman. She immediately tried to think of something else, anything else, and caught sight of her reflection in the full-length mirror across the room from the tub.

Glancing around to be sure she was still alone, she sat up straighter, leaning on the edge of the tub to look at herself. It had been a very long time she had seen her reflection. She still had the small mirror from her mother, the relic tucked at the bottom of her bag, but she hadn't seen her entire body in a mirror since her rooms in her father's castle. She looked at her face, familiar and yet also strange now, her green eyes, her red hair falling past her shoulders now that it was wet. Standing up and stepping over to the mirror, Hannah let the water drip onto the floor, not caring about the mess, knowing that there were servants here who would clean up after her, reveling in old habits.

She stared at her body, so familiar and yet slightly different. She didn't know if the change was because she spent a year out of it or if it was because she hadn't really seen herself in a mirror like this since leaving home two years ago.

I'm older now, she thought, *but that's not it.* She studied her face, her skin still smooth, but there was something else in her eyes now. She hoped it was wisdom, but more likely just experience. Her hair was the same, even now pulling back up into curls that brushed her shoulders. She let her eyes move down her body, a hand reaching up to touch the scar on her shoulder from the goblin attack so long ago, the burn mark from Gorn's blade a permanent reminder of how her friends tried to save her from bleeding out and only succeeded in nearly killing her. Her breasts were slightly different, but she couldn't explain how or why. She wondered if it was because she had spent a year inside Solyn's body, the fledgling endowed with a much larger bust. She ran a finger over the scar on her chest, admitting that perhaps the healed wound might have shifted the way they rested on her chest. Her lower stomach seemed different too, slightly stretched, and she let herself wonder what Anna had done to her body during that year. Hannah had always been fairly active, her body trim and muscled, and she certainly still was, but it seemed like at some point, this body had gained weight, then lost it again.

Her thighs were still toned and unblemished, her feet familiar. She held up her hands, staring at the reverse image of the divine sigil burned into her palm. The back of her hand was smooth, the wound from Malbrek's rapier healed completely, but the sigil would always remain. She reminded herself to keep that hand fisted at all times while in the palace. Those with divine power who followed Valerius would recognize the mark and what it meant. Jasper may be fine with allying with a new House of the Vanya, but Hannah didn't know how much the average elf knew about her people.

She knew she could ask Rory, but she didn't want to think about him, never mind be in the same room with him. *It can wait*, she decided, *at least until tomorrow.*

She stood there for a long moment, letting the night breeze dry her body, trying to focus her mind on something other than the magic drowning her. Pressing her hands to the cool surface of the mirror, she only allowed the sensation of cold against her palms to fill her mind. She pictured a glass floor beneath her feet and tried to push everything not directly related to her body underneath it, hoping she could trap the magic somehow.

Hannah didn't hear him come in, but suddenly Klauden was standing directly behind her, body pressed against hers, head above her shoulder, and eyes drinking in her reflection in the mirror.

"Klauden!" she shouted in surprise, immediately pulling her hands over her breasts to cover herself as she spun away from the mirror. He trapped her against it, the cool surface against her naked skin of her back, and ran his hands down from her shoulders to her waist, pulling her in for a kiss. She pushed him away, too shocked by his presumption and force-fulness to let herself be kissed. "Stop!"

Klauden jerked his head back, looking down at her in confusion. His hands didn't release her.

<What?>

"Words," Hannah demanded, glaring at him. "Words work."

<We have no need of words,> he repeated in her mind, leaning down again. Hannah felt his desire as it flooded through her, realizing with a start that she hadn't felt it before then. She hadn't felt him approach, hadn't heard him come into her rooms, hadn't been affected by his need. She thought of the glass floor beneath her feet again but dismissed it quickly, filing it away to try again later.

For a moment there, I couldn't feel him.

And I didn't want him.

Staring up at him now, she wanted him to kiss her, wanted to tug her arms free and show her naked body, but she held herself in place, watching his face, hearing his thoughts.

"You..." he said slowly, as if just realizing it, "aren't thinking of me."

Hannah bit her lip and looked away. "Not really," she said honestly. "I wasn't thinking about you at all."

Klauden looked at the mirror behind her, then down at her naked body, an eyebrow raised. "Then, what are you doing?"

Hannah shrugged, slipping out from under his arms. She moved to the bed where a silky robe had been laid out for her use and slipped it on, quickly covering herself.

"Chaivin," Klauden said, following her to the bed but still giving her space, using words because she had asked him to, "what is going on?"

"What do you mean?" Hannah deflected, shaking her head at him. "What are you even doing here? I thought you were down in the library studying."

Klauden nodded. "I was."

"So did you find something?"

Klauden shook his head, looking at her curiously. "No, I abandoned my book."

It was Hannah's turn to give him that look. "Why would you do that?" Klauden rarely let himself be interrupted for anything; he certainly wouldn't leave now that they had so few days left to find a solution.

He glanced at the tub, then at the mirror, then let his gaze drift back over to where she sat on the bed. "You took a really long bath, chaivin," he said finally, "then stared at yourself naked in the mirror." He paused, then added, "What did you think I would do?"

Hannah laughed, the sound escaping before she could help it at the thought of Klauden sitting in the library, struggling with his desire until he abandoned his book and came to find her. "Oh, Klauden!" She giggled as she hadn't in many months. "That is so far off from where I was." She cocked her head at him, studying the lines of his body. "You thought I was... what? Teasing you from up here?"

His eyes darkened, a wash of desire spilling into her at the idea. Just as suddenly, the feeling faded, replaced by hurt and embarrassment. "So ... what were you doing?" he repeated.

Hannah pursed her lips. "Actually, I was trying to block the bond, to focus on myself for once."

"I see," Klauden nodded, embarrassment morphing into slow resentment.

"What?" she asked. "You know I don't enjoy this."

He filled her with a memory of her face seeming to enjoy him very much, and she frowned at him despite the echo of pleasure in her skin. "You know what I mean," she told him coldly. Staring at him, she had another thought. "You know what I mean," she repeated. "You always know what I mean, what I want, what I need." She frowned. "How were you just so completely wrong?"

Klauden stared at her, and a sudden frisson of fear slid up her back, Klauden frantic at the thought of losing her. He pulled it back immediately, but she didn't imagine it. She wondered if she felt the same for him. She loved him, desired him, often enjoyed his company, but she could live without him. He heard her thoughts, and his face hardened, resentment morphing into anger as he glared at her.

"Glad to see I'm *so* disposable," he snapped.

"That's not what I meant," Hannah tried to say, but he was already walking away. "Klauden!" she shouted, and he stopped, his back to her, breathing heavily as he waited for her to speak. She stared at him, eyes narrowing. "We're fighting," she said quietly. "This is a fight."

Klauden turned back to face her. "This isn't a fight," he said quickly. "This is..."

Hannah raised an eyebrow and grinned. "This is...?" she prompted.

"Something else," he finished lamely. "This shouldn't have happened."

"You don't know that," Hannah said. "It just hasn't happened before now." She paused, remembering their childhood. "Well, not since this really kicked in," she amended. They had fought before, years ago, often because she pushed him too far, but he always forgave her soon enough. And they had bickered since he had found her in Severin, but they had never truly argued.

She sighed, frowning. "Come here, Klauden," she said, patting the bed beside her. "You didn't really think that kevna meant we would never fight, did you?"

He sat reluctantly, sinking into the soft mattress but leaving space between them. "I guess not," he admitted sheepishly. "I just assumed it meant we would always be in tune, though, connected." He bit his lip, looking at her with regret. "I didn't mean to force myself on you," he said in a low voice, red creeping up from the neck of his robe. "I would never."

"I know that," she said, quickly reassuring him. "Of course I know that!" She looked away. "I didn't expect you. That's all. I was surprised."

"And I was oblivious," he observed. "I'm a fool, throwing myself on you, assuming you'd want me."

She grabbed his hand, not wanting him to feel this way. "You're not a fool," she said firmly. "You are Klauden van Sherinak. The last thing you could ever be is a fool." He smiled at her; a small movement of his lips that showed he believed her. "Now," she added, sitting back, "you can be foolish sometimes..."

"I can accept that," he said, his voice low, filling with heat as he looked at her in the silky robe. "Can you?"

Hannah sighed, thinking about the vampire and her promise to marry him. *Is this what my life will be?* Klauden caught the thought, scooting closer to look at her, a hand catching her chin when she would look away. "Can you?" he repeated.

"Can I what?"

"Accept me," he said, steeling his shoulders as he faced her. "Do you want to be with me?"

"I..." The words trailed off. Hannah wanted to reassure him, to say *yes*. The magic filled her, pushing her to agree, but she couldn't say it. "I want you," she said instead, watching his mouth, seeing how his fangs were huge in his mouth.

"I know," he said. "Now. But that's not what I mean, and you know it." He gave her a serious look. Hannah considered it, biting her lip as she tried to separate her desire from the magic.

"I don't know," she said finally. "I mean, this part is definitely real."

"What part?"

"The misunderstanding part," she scoffed. "That I can trust. But the rest is still just kevna."

"You really think everything you feel for me is from the magic?" His voice was cold as he slid away from her, standing up.

"Isn't it?"

"Not for me," he said.

"You don't know that, Klauden. You don't know anything but this." She rolled her eyes. "I've told you that normal—"

"Do not tell me about normal sex, Hannah." He was angry now.

"But—"

He shook his head. "No. I'm done talking about this." He looked around her room, clearly wishing the evening had gone differently. "Good night," he said formally and left. Hannah heard the door close behind him, and she felt his angry resentment all the way down the stairs and into his rooms below.

XXV

Hannah lasted most of the morning in her rooms, using every last bit of her patience in forcing herself to stay put. The servants had brought her hot tea at breakfast, and she had savored each sip sitting on the balcony, letting the sound of the waves soak into her. But eventually, she had finished the tea and grown tired of sitting still. She went back into her rooms to do something, anything.

She studied the lines of the designs on each wall, the delicate twists of embroidery on every single pillow, the titles of every book on the shelf against the wall, and the dozen or so possible escape routes if things got tricky and she had to leave in a hurry. She was on the fourth floor of the palace, and the balcony overlooked the sea, but she could climb down easily enough, or jump if she had to. She stood outside again, glancing directly at the sun overhead. *Yes*, she decided. *This is a good time to try out my magic.*

She had seen Klauden fly any number of times, but the spell had always eluded her, the words she needed just out of reach. But now she no longer needed words, the magic simply forming to her desires, and she imagined herself lifting off the balcony just a few inches. She could feel the familiar thrill of the power against her skin, and a smile crossed her face, the first genuine smile in days. She felt weightless and, looking down, saw that her boots were no longer resting on the stone floor of the balcony. She concentrated, and she slowly rose a few more feet in the air. The wind gusted then, and she blew backward, body hitting the wall of the palace a few feet above the doorway, and Hannah grunted. Focusing, she used the magic to bring her back down, her landing a bit rough but still successful.

I did it! The surge of confidence and pride filled her, and she wanted to tell someone, anyone. She thought of Rory but couldn't face him, not now, not with this, and reached out for Klauden instead.

He was distant, but always present, and she got a sense of satisfaction from him, a quiet comfortable feeling that she soaked in for a moment. He didn't seem annoyed with her, so he must've gotten over their argument from the night before. In fact, he seemed very relaxed and content. She thought to find him in the library, but he was in his rooms with Solyn instead.

Deciding that she could at least share this victory with him, Hannah abandoned her rooms and walked down the stairway to the suite he shared with Solyn, feet silent on the padded carpet. Her quiet knock went unanswered, but she got a sense of welcome from Klauden, so she opened the door and walked inside. His rooms were nicely appointed like hers, fancy furniture showcasing Elven finery and delicate tapestries on the walls.

She had taken two steps inside, mouth open to call a greeting, when she heard a sound that stopped her. Someone was moaning softly, and Hannah heard the unmistakable sounds of bodies moving together. Unable to stop herself, she took a few more steps into the entry room and peeked through the open doorway into the dining area. Klauden was facing her, sitting in a high-backed chair, a naked Solyn wrapped about his hips, the fledgling clearly riding him, her face buried in his neck. Klauden looked up slowly as Hannah came into view, his hands on the curve of Solyn's ass, and as she stood there, frozen, he smiled at her and bit Solyn.

The wave of pleasure hit Hannah from across the room, and she backpedaled wildly, her warrior training allowing her not to crash into anything. Freed from her paralysis, she turned and ran from the room, shutting the door quietly, then sprinting down the hallway and as far away from them as she could. Even as she put physical distance between them, she could still feel Klauden in her mind, his satisfaction as Solyn moved, the taste of her in his mouth, and she ran even faster.

By the time she reached the kitchens and the doorway onto the beach far below, she had managed to build a brick wall between them, but even that was not enough to block Klauden's thought.

< *This feels quite* normal *to me, chaivin.* >

XXVI

That evening found Hannah still down on the beach, boots abandoned by the rocks, bare feet enjoying the waves that crashed on the shore, the cool water a diversion from her angry thoughts. She was still furious.

She knew why he'd done it, to get back at her, to show her that he understood what she had been trying to tell him, and that he thought she was wrong. Klauden didn't understand why she kept trying to separate her feelings into physical desire and magical devotion. He couldn't see the difference between sex and love and wanting. He would never truly understand what she was trying to tell him.

He couldn't.

Standing on the shore, watching the sun set, Hannah wasn't sure she understood it either. But she knew that the distinction was important to her, that even though she may desire Klauden, even though kevna may bind them together, even forever, she was sure that the magic was a physical thing, powerful yes, but not something she had chosen. She could choose to have sex with Klauden, choose to satisfy the magic, but she was still in control of her desires, could still choose what she wanted, free of the magic. And as ridiculous as it was, as doomed as it was, as much as the memory of Annilyn's clothes strewn about Rory's rooms hurt, she still wanted the elf. She chose the elf. She clung to the idea like a drowning sailor, sure that if she let him go, she would lose herself completely to kevna, to Klauden, to everything destiny had planned for her.

"No," she said quietly, kicking the sand and watching the water spray, a kaleidoscope of color and light in the setting sun. "I will not." She looked up at the palace, trying to avoid seeing the balcony that was probably Klauden's, unable to stop wondering if he and Solyn had finished, both satisfied and dressed again and talking about whatever it was they discussed when they were alone.

Fine, she finally admitted to herself. *Fine*. She pictured Klauden's hands on Solyn's skin, of his face as he bit his fledgling, of the feelings she couldn't escape. *I'm jealous. I don't want to think about him with her.*

I'm an idiot, she told herself sternly, retreating from the shoreline and sitting down in the black volcanic sand a few feet above the waves. *I'm ridiculous and spoiled and unreasonable and everything else.*

She buried her face in her hands and let the tears come. It had been a long time since she cried. The night that Rory left, she had cried alone in their bed, knowing that it was her fault he was gone. But then time had softened the blow, and now, she knew it wasn't entirely her fault. That mystical ancient magic and forces of destiny were also to blame. She thought of the way Annilyn had casually put her hand on Rory's shoulder, a claiming gesture, a marking.

Hannah still had her face buried in her hands when she felt the slightest brush of something against her bare foot. She thought it was the water for a second, surprised to find that the waves had crept up so far onto the beach, but then her foot went numb, and she jerked her eyes open.

A long snakelike creature was near her feet, body still partially in the water. Wispy tendrils stuck out from both sides of the translucent body just under its mouth, and it was one of these strings that had brushed her foot. As she sat there looking at it, the creature twitched, and another tendril brushed her other foot. The wave of numbness washed up her foot to match the other, then she was shoving herself backward and away from the creature, hands sinking in the soft sand as she shuffled away, aware that her leg below the knee was paralyzed. Her other leg quickly joined, and she scooted back farther. The creature followed slowly, a lazily graceful arc to its body as it slithered with her up the beach.

Hannah plucked a dagger from the small of her back, and threw it, but the blade sank into the nest of tendrils and not the main body, and the creature simply swirled around it, head moving toward her, jaws widening to reveal a line of intimidating teeth. She scooted back again, noting that her thighs were starting to numb, but not as quickly, and the creature continued to slide toward her, its body straightening out as it came, instead of the curving approach it had used before. Hannah noticed that its tail was still in the water, but barely. It seemed reluctant to leave the ocean, stretching out its body to reach her instead. Her legs were mostly numb now, deadweight attached to her, and she could feel her lower body growing heavier.

Fire! She thought desperately, feeling the magic coil up in her slowly, as if stunted by whatever the creature's poison had done to her. A small spark left her hands and struck the creature, and it recoiled but didn't leave. It stayed out of reach of her hands, waiting for the poison to do its job. Hannah's fingertips went numb next, and she grabbed another dagger, this time taking a moment to aim carefully, knowing she might not get another chance, then she flicked the dagger at it, seeing the blade bury itself in the creature's head, stabbing deep into the sand beneath. The body stopped moving, and Hannah took a deep breath.

She could still breathe, though she knew it didn't matter. She considered her legs, touching them with hands that were quickly losing sensation.

Well this is new, she thought dreamily and instinctively reached for Klauden. In the place where he normally lived, though, there was emptiness. Sheer panic filled her, and for a second, she could feel every part of her body again, but then the paralytic numbness returned, and she fell back, curious at how the sand seemed to stop at her lower back, her body disappearing into nothingness. She reached for her magic then, assuming that she could probably cast something to counter the poison, but found the same emptiness.

It's gone, she thought slowly. *My magic is gone. Klauden is gone.*

The hollowness inside her spread, sinking into everything, then she jerked upright, suddenly afraid that she would die right there on the beach. *I can't keep doing this,* she thought, and anger rushed through her, again burning through the paralysis. Her feet were there for a moment, then nothingness again. Hannah used her arms to prop herself up, her hands feeling like a stranger's attached to her body and focused on the anger again.

It was different than calling her magic, but the mechanism was the same. Her fury at her helplessness rushed through her, bringing sensation back to her body in small waves. Her hand collapsed, she fell back again, and she stared up at the now dark sky, the first stars peeking through.

Klau—she began, but then stopped. She had to stop calling him every time she was in trouble. She had to stop assuming he would be there to save her.

She paused, listening as waves crashed on the shoreline below, the soft wind caressing the sand.

He wasn't there now. He wasn't anywhere. She sobbed with the relief, the sound escaping her in a harsh cough, then she could sit up again, joy filling her as feeling streamed back into her body. She could feel her hands again, and she leaned down to examine her feet. Both tops were burning.

There was an angry red mark on her skin, but at least she could feel again. She wanted to get a better look in the dim light, instinctively calling her magic for a small flame, but nothing happened. She stopped, focusing, and found that her magic was gone. She stared at the sea creature, its head still pinned to the sand with her dagger and considered.

It had paralyzed her and stolen her magic.

Dawning realization made her giggle.

Without her magic, she was no longer bound by kevna. She was free from Klauden.

She scooted forward slowly, careful to avoid touching any of the creature's tendrils as she moved to retrieve her knife, then she carefully cut one of the tendrils free. Using the blade to ball it up, she flicked it onto a small swatch of fabric from her belt pouch, and wrapped it up, tucking it inside a small pocket. She was still studying the creature when a voice caught on the wind.

"Hannah!"

She looked up, instinctively pulling for her nightvision and relieved to find it still there. The beach disappeared into a wash of grays and blacks, and she could see a figure running toward her on the sand. The figure jerked for a second, as if stepping on something sharp, and Hannah felt it, an echo in her own foot. There was a pull to him, something physical that almost hurt, then she was examining the bottom of her foot, wondering why it felt like when the fledgling had been hurt. She glanced up, and for a split second, she was sure it was Rory running to her, connected to her, but then she remembered Annilyn and his room and everything between them, and she closed her eyes, knowing it for the trick it was.

"I'm here," she said, and when she looked up again, she could see Klauden coming toward her, farther away than she had thought him but still her old companion. She would recognize him anywhere.

But, she realized, she could no longer feel him everywhere. She looked back at the creature dead on the sand.

"What happened?" Klauden asked, spraying an arc of sand as he slid to his knees beside her. Hannah brought up her hands to block the spray.

"I'm fine," she reassured him. "It's dead."

Klauden looked at the creature and back at Hannah, taking in her bare feet. "What is it?"

"I'm not sure," she said, gathering her legs beneath her and standing up, feet a little sore but nothing serious. "It paralyzes and takes away magic, though." Klauden seemed ready to examine it further. "I would be careful touching it."

"Takes away magic?" Klauden repeated, looking from it to her and back again. "It touched you?"

Hannah nodded. "I tried to use my magic, but it barely worked, and now it's gone." She paused, then added, "All of my magic is gone."

"How... how do you feel?" Klauden got to his feet, a hand reaching out to touch her face, as if to reassure himself that she was not hurt. Hannah remembered where his hands had been earlier that day and jerked away from him. The thought of him with Solyn still stung, but it was not the same kind of pain she expected. It was smaller, petty even.

"I feel empty," she told him truthfully. "Hollow." She looked out to the sea, where the low rising moon had begun to show over the horizon. "Alone."

Klauden jerked as if she had struck him. "I see." He took a step away from her.

"Do you still feel it?" she whispered. "Kevna?"

He turned to face her, anguish in his eyes, and Hannah knew he did. "I will always feel it," he grated, "because it is what I feel."

"But it's not real!" she shouted at him. "This thing between us isn't real!" She gestured between them.

"It is the only real thing I know," he snapped, stepping back toward her and grabbing her hand. He pressed it to his chest. "You feel this?"

Hannah left her hand there, thrilled to feel nothing beyond his heartbeat. Klauden was her oldest companion, her childhood love, her friend, but nothing more. Her heart burned for another. "I feel you," she said after a moment. "Just you."

"Just me," he snarled, then he jerked her to him, pressing his lips to hers savagely. Hannah let herself be kissed, reveling in the feel of warm lips, lovely lips, but still just lips against hers. There was no overwhelming need to be with him, to devour him. She was aware of the blood in him, could feel its pull as she always did when around another creature, but it was a pull she could resist. She didn't want him without the magic.

He broke the kiss, stepping away from her. "You." The word was quiet, nearly lost to the wind. "You don't want me."

"I will always love you, Klauden," she said, knowing his heart broke even though she couldn't feel it. Again. "But it's not more than that. It's not what you feel." She sighed, tucking her hair behind an ear. "I don't feel what you feel without the magic." She reached for his arm. "You probably don't feel this way either. It's all kevna messing with us!"

He sighed, the sound broken. "<Were I drained of every ounce of magic, chaivin, I would love you still. Were I no longer myself, stripped of all that I am or ever have been, my love for you would remain.>" He had reverted to their native tongue in his despair, and Hannah replied in the same tongue.

"<You could be free of this,>" she said softly. "<You could be only yourself.>"

"<I have always been myself,>" he told her, "<kevna or no, magic or no.>" He looked away, unable to face her. "<But it has never been enough for you.>"

"It's not about being enough!" she yelled in the common tongue, not wanting to share anything else with him. "It's about what I want!"

He gave her a cold glare. "Oh, I know all about what you want," he snarled, the language clipped syllables in his accent. "My entire life has been about what you want."

"It has not," she insisted. "You've done plenty that you wanted."

"Have I."

Hannah tried to shove the image of Solyn wrapped around him into his head, but found that she couldn't, their connection broken. "You seemed to be having a fine time getting what you wanted earlier."

"But that, too, was about you," he admitted. "You must know that." He moved as if to reach for her, then turned away, shoulders slumping. "Everything I do is about you."

Hannah sneered. It was easier to be angry at him than show him pity. "And how would shoving Solyn in my face be about me?"

"You said it was about desire," he said, the words so quiet she barely heard him. "About wanting and not having satisfaction." He sniffed, then shook his head. "But it doesn't work like that. It never does." He paused, then continued, "Solyn does everything I want her to do because she knows what I want her to do. She's my fledgling. We are bound."

"You are bound to everyone and everything, Klauden. When are you bound to yourself?" The question came out unexpectedly, and he turned back to her. "Do you not wish to be free of it? Do you not wish to be yourself, alone and free?"

He tilted his head, and Hannah had a flash of what he wanted, his desire to fall into her and lose himself completely over and over again, and she closed her eyes, knowing that kevna was returning, as she knew it would, and feeling her heart sink in her chest.

Klauden shook his head. "No." He leaned his head back, and Hannah saw that he was crying, wetness streaking his face in the moonlight. She had never seen him cry. She had heard him sobbing, screaming for her in desperation, but she had never seen him like this, broken.

And she had done this to him. Again.

"Do you not wish to be free of me?" she whispered. "All I do is hurt you."

"You are part of me," he replied. "I will never be free of you." He looked back at the palace. "Even if you get what you want, if your elf takes you back and you leave with him, abandoning me with Solyn to make our own way in the world, I will never be free of you." His voice grew strong. "And I don't want to be. Ever." He gave her a look that burned her heart. "I will hold onto you with everything in me, Hannah van Sherinak," he said, using her name as if they'd been wed as promised. "I will never let you go."

"You're afraid," Hannah spat suddenly. "You don't know who you are without me." She glanced at the dead creature on the sand, the end of its body drifting in the incoming tide. "Why don't you touch it and find out, Klauden?" she taunted. "See if I'm truly the everything you think I am."

He stared at her, and for a moment, she thought he might actually do it, but then he shook his head. "No."

"Why not?" she yelled. "Don't you want to be certain?"

"I already know," he said simply.

"But what if it's all kevna?" she asked. "What if it's all a lie?"

He shrugged. "Then it's kevna," he said. "It doesn't matter."

"Of course it matters!" she screamed. "It's the only thing that does matter!"

"Not to me," he told her. "I love you, whether you will or no, whether you care or no, whether you're here or no. I. Love. You. And that will never change."

As he spoke, she could feel him again, slowly creeping back inside of her, the magic returning as the poison faded. She knew he spoke the truth. He would never stop loving her. He couldn't understand her determination to run away from the magic.

"Oh, I understand you just fine," he said, their connection back. "I just don't agree with you."

"I'm going to keep trying," she said. "I'm never going to stop trying to control the magic somehow, to be free."

He nodded. "I know."

"How can you love me knowing I'm trying to break free of you?"

"Love isn't a choice, chaivin. It never was about choice for me."

XXVII

"So I hear you encountered the famous Manawyrm," Jasper said to Hannah, tilting his glass in her direction. The wine moved smoothly, the gesture practiced, and Hannah nodded in return.

"Is that what it's called?" she asked. They sat at the head table in Firene's dining hall, Hannah doing her best to eat only the liquid from the soup in front of her, hoping the ruler wouldn't take offense at her odd dietary habits.

Down the table, Rory and Solyn were eating easily, their fledgling bodies able to ingest both normal food and blood, but Hannah, Klauden, and the Sarkoza's party were all politely spooning liquid from the soup. Klauden was far away from Hannah, sitting with Solyn across from Milo, Eriken, and Millani. Rory was at the other end of the table as well, keeping up a polite stream of conversation with the other vampires. Hannah wondered where the Valrina was tonight but tried not to think about it.

Jasper sat at the head of the table at her end, with Linus across from her and Nicolo to her right. The old vampire had been cordial, making small talk as the meal progressed. "I've never seen a creature like that before," she added.

Jasper nodded. "It's been a long time since we've had one on our shores," he told her. "They normally stay far to the north where the volcanic waters are warmer, but they occasionally venture this way."

"Interesting," Hannah said, not really paying attention, failing to ignore Rory's face as he laughed at something Millani said. "I wonder what brought it out now."

"Normally, they are attracted to great fonts of magic," Jasper offered casually, and Hannah focused on him. She shrugged, trying to put him off.

"I'm no great font of magic," she insisted. "I'm a caster. Nothing more."

"Destiny surrounds you, child, which is a power unto itself," Nicolo said quietly. "You must know that."

"But destiny isn't magic," Hannah argued.

"Isn't it?" Linus smirked. "What else would it be?"

Hannah frowned. "I don't know. Some powerful force that insists on bullying people into doing things they don't want to do?"

"Tell us how you really feel," Linus quipped, then held his hands up apologetically. "I didn't mean to strike a nerve."

"I'm so tired of hearing about destiny," she admitted. She looked down the table at Rory, then back at Jasper, deciding to flip the conversation. "I mean, would you say it was your destiny to rule Firene?" she asked. She felt Nicolo stiffen beside her, but she decided to keep going. If they were going to discuss her personal life at the dinner table, she could bring out their personal experiences too.

Jasper frowned, considering. "I don't think of it in terms of destiny," he said finally. "Not all elves live by prophecies."

"But some prophecies are too great to ignore," Nicolo countered.

"Really?" Hannah prompted. "And was there a prophecy about Rory? Was he meant to leave this city?"

Linus gave her a sly look, understanding what she was doing. Jasper shook his head. "Not that I was ever aware of." He looked at Linus. "How about you, brother? Had you heard such things?"

"I think we should ask Caganasti," Linus suggested. "He would know all about prophecies." The elf wasn't at dinner, though, returning to his shop and his life as often as possible.

"Are your people usually believers in such things?" Hannah asked, moving the conversation to more general topics.

Jasper shrugged. "Some of them. Are yours?"

Hannah laughed. "I don't think so. Not at my father's castle anyway. He wouldn't enjoy the idea that his fate wasn't his own." She looked at Nicolo. "What does Gerter van Lartner think? Does he think everything is predetermined?"

Nicolo chuckled. "Not everything, no. But some things are fated, and all the squirming in the world will not change the outcome."

"Well that's cheerful," Linus said with a laugh. "Are all of your people so depressing?"

Hannah laughed with him. "Not like that," she said.

"You can laugh all you like," Jasper said seriously, "but the Manawyrm has not been seen in almost a hundred years, and it found you on the beach tonight." He looked her over. "And yet here you are, no worse for the experience."

Hannah shrugged. "I killed it. No big deal."

Linus snorted into his food. "No big deal, she says," he repeated, "like slaying a Manawyrm isn't something from the great tales."

Heat rose in Hannah's face. "It's not like I slayed the dragon or anything," she said. "I got lucky and killed it." She paused, then asked, "Do people not normally survive?"

Jasper laughed. "No, lady, they don't. The Manawyrm paralyzes with its touch and absorbs magic. Both fighters and spellcasters are defenseless as it drags them into the water and drowns them."

"I just used my dagger," she said.

"You must be a fearsome fighter," Linus told her, then looked down the table to where Rory sat. "No wonder my brother likes you."

Hannah noticed his use of the present tense, and her heart ached a little more. "Well," she said, "he's a great fighter himself."

"Not all fights are with creatures," Nicolo said. "Sometimes the hardest fights are fought in the mind." Hannah squinted at the old vampire, wondering what he knew. They were supposed to meet with him in the morning about the Book of Samander.

"True," Linus agreed. "Are all of your kind such fighters?"

Hannah wondered again how much he knew about her people. She said only, "Some of us fight, some cast spells, some do other things. We are all different, just like your people." She really needed to talk to Milo and learn what he had shared with the elves.

"I do hope our people can thrive together," Jasper said. "That our alliance continues for many generations."

"As do I," Hannah replied, still enough her father's daughter to play politics. She glanced down the table to where Klauden sat.

Am I still enough of my father's daughter to marry Klauden despite knowing it's kevna making me feel this way?

XXVIII

T he next morning, Hannah walked down the long hallway of the ground floor of the palace. It was too early to go to the library for her meeting with the other vampires. A quick glance into the room showed it was empty. Hannah had already been awake for hours, using her night-vision to stare at the intricate designs on the ceiling above her bed, filled with nervous energy. She spent some time mentally preparing the questions she had for Milo and Nicolo, but after that, the empty room had her pacing angrily around the perimeter of the space. She had to get outside, she decided. Practicing would help calm her nerves.

She had maintained her training routine even on the road, though the lack of open space on the *Volant* had made it difficult. Since arriving in Firene two days ago, she hadn't practiced at all. After considering the available options, Hannah decided to head for the beach. The sand would make her workout difficult, dragging her feet down and making it harder to move. She relished the challenge. Focusing on her body's movement seemed like the perfect way to forget everything else.

She stepped outside into the predawn light of the thin autumn sunrise, the air cool on her face, feeling the tension in her body drain away. She moved away from the palace, walking up the shore as she followed around a low rock wall at the top of the beach until she could see the sunrise over the Vanya mountains on her left. Homesickness filled her for a moment at the sight of the mountains, a sight she never thought she would miss, but she stood there until the soft light touched her face.

Nodding, she considered the area of the beach she was in. The waves were far away at her back, the tide low. Nothing stood on the beach to the north, only glittering dark sand up the coastline to the distant northern mountains. The low wall dipped eastward, creating a sizable alcove large enough for her to run through a few of her morning exercises. She stepped back to the opening, peering back down the beach to see the palace coming to life with the sun, smoke puffing from the lower windows as the kitchens started breakfast. She was far enough away that she didn't think anyone would spot her from the balconies facing this way. Klauden's eyes definitely weren't up to the task. She should be undisturbed here.

Hannah returned to the space, removing her jacket and laying it on the ground beside the wall. A mark on the stone caught her eye as she rose, stretching in her white shirt. She leaned forward to examine it: a small symbol carved into the wall. It looked like letters, but Hannah didn't recognize the significance. Apparently, she wasn't the only person to use this place.

Hannah moved to the center of the space, hiking up her skirt and tucking the length into her belt to free her legs. She drew a dagger from the small of her back, flipping it freely in her hands, enjoying the feel of weapons again. Her body began to move, automatically falling into the rhythm of the practice, tension draining from her as each step grew more surefooted. She closed her eyes, focusing on how she held her arms, the angle of her back, the placement of each foot as she moved. Time stopped, and she relished the movement, allowing herself to just be for the moment.

A sharp intake of breath made her open her eyes, and she immediately turned to face the source of the noise, the dagger in her hand flinging at the target without thought. She watched, mouth open in surprise, as Rory caught the dagger, spun around, and flung it right back at her. Hannah caught it by the tip easily, allowing the motion to swing her arm behind her body and sheathing the dagger in a practiced swipe.

She couldn't help the smile on her lips at the sight of him. She was angry and disappointed and hurt, but she loved the warrior in him, loved that his confidence in her allowed him to return the weapon without worry that she would hurt herself. It was a relief, this shift in his attitude from the careful way he treated her in those first few months in Solyn's mortal body. Seeing her as herself once more had reminded him of her strength, her abilities, enough to rely on her again.

"Rory," she breathed, the word filled with longing. He was wearing a simple white shirt and black pants, his hair loose and long around his face, so different from the formal presentation she had seen in front of his brothers. Both of his blades hung along his hips, toned thighs hugged by pants that disappeared into familiar boots. The sun was shining on him, glinting off the silver hoops in his ears, the lines of his chest and arm easily visible through the thin shirt.

Hannah thought about her own shirt, the material fine but too transparent to wear without the jacket and wondered just how much of an eyeful the elf was getting as she stood there backlit by the sun.

"Hannah," he replied and she was so glad to hear him say her name, not chaivin as Klauden called her. Rory stared at her for another long beat, then shook his head, looking around in the alcove as if making sure she was alone. "What are you doing here?"

"Practicing," she said, wanting to ask him the same question. "I had to get out of there and move. Just for a little bit."

"I see that," he replied, head cocked to one side as he considered her, "but why are you *here*?"

"Here like Firene, or here in this little spot?" she asked, walking to the wall to reclaim her jacket.

"In this spot," he clarified. "What made you come here?"

Hannah picked up her jacket, sliding into it swiftly and lifting her hair out of the collar. "It seemed like a good place to practice," she shrugged. "Why? Am I not supposed to be here?" She wondered if she had stumbled into some kind of Elven sacred space and had desecrated it with her exercises. She didn't think Rory would be offended—he wasn't one for divine worship. She glanced at the carving in the wall. "What does this mean?"

Rory's face reddened as she pointed out the mark. "It's nothing. Foolishness."

"I didn't mean to upset anyone," Hannah said, trying to understand what he meant. "I will go." She couldn't stand being next to him. It was too hard not to say what was on her mind, too hard to keep this odd civility between them.

"You're not upsetting anyone," he reassured her, voice way too calm for Hannah's returning nerves. "It's just..." He paused, then shook his head at her with a small grin. "This is where I always came to practice."

Hannah glanced around at the space. "You mean ... when you lived here?" She tried to picture a younger Rory running through his morning exercises in this space, face rounder, ears shorter, eyes squinting in determination to get it right.

Rory walked to where she stood by the wall. He dragged his fingers over the mark on the wall. "This was where I came to escape," he admitted.

Hannah agreed. "I can see that. It's a good place. Hidden from view." She looked at her once husband, not wanting to trust this new easiness between them but unable to stop herself from hoping again. "Did you often want to hide when you were younger?"

"I don't know anyone who didn't," Rory commented with a shrug. "Sometimes the weight of the future is too much."

"Tell me about it," Hannah said. She looked up at him, fisting her hands so they didn't do anything stupid like reach out to him. "Look, I can go. I didn't mean to invade your space."

"I don't mind," he said quickly, body blocking her way just enough so she didn't walk away. Hannah looked at him, and longing filled her, but it was quickly buried by a wave of kevna, a need to return to the palace. Klauden was looking for her. She looked down at the sand, realizing her skirt was still tucked up into her belt, her thighs exposed. Her hands worked quickly to pull her skirt back down.

"I should go," she said quietly. "We have a meeting with Nicolo."

Rory nodded, but he didn't move, still standing so close to her.

"Rory," she whispered, "I..."

"I know," he said simply, then he was tugging her into his arms, the smell of him overwhelming her senses. She sank into his embrace, the familiarity of him enough to make her want to sob in relief. She wrapped her arms around his back, gripping him with more strength than she would have before, careful of his mortal body. But he was a fledgling now, strong enough to hold her just as tightly, and they stood that way for a long moment, the waves crashing in the distance, the cool morning breeze twisting their hair together.

Yes, Hannah thought. *This.*

<*Chaivin?*> Klauden's voice was distant.

<*I'm coming,*> Hannah thought quickly. <*I was on the beach.*> She pushed out of Rory's embrace, looking up into her fledgling's face. "I have to—"

He cut her off with a kiss, gently touching his lips to hers, pressing himself to her the careful way he had that first night in Kalford. It was a sweet kiss and over too soon as he leaned away from her.

"I..." Hannah stared at him, words failing her as she struggled to understand what this meant.

"I know," he repeated with a nod, face revealing nothing. "Go."

"But—" she tried again, eyes wide as she looked from his mouth to his eyes and back again.

He smirked at her, shaking his head and rolling his eyes. He slid aside, taking her shoulders and pointing her back toward the palace. "You need to go."

She looked back at him, a fragile smile on her lips, her mouth still tingling from where he'd kissed her. "What—"

"Just go," he repeated gently, still smiling. "He's waiting for you." He bit his lip, then added, "We can talk after your meeting. I'll come find you."

Hannah nodded slowly and let him push her a few more feet, then let her feet carry her down the beach and away from him. She put a hand to her mouth, emotions roiling through her.

What in the nine hells was that?

XXIX

When Hannah arrived in the library, she found Klauden already waiting for her. She looked around the room. "Solyn?" she asked. He shook his head. "She's sleeping."

"This is my surprised face," Hannah retorted, nodding at the books he had piled on the table in front of him, one already propped open with a long brass rod across the page to the left of where he sat. "What's this?" Directly in front of him was another book, his right hand already writing in the middle of a page. Hannah recognized his journal from the secret stash in the castle library. "Looks like you've been here a while. Find anything useful?"

He frowned, laying the small magical rod he used to write between the pages and closing the cover over his words. "Not particularly." He took in her windswept hair. "Find anything useful on the beach?"

Hannah bit her lip, wondering how much he had seen, then sighed. Of course he had seen everything. Between his connection to her and the ring Rory still wore, Klauden probably saw it from every angle. "I don't know," she answered truthfully, remembering the feel of Rory's lips on hers, fleeting but real.

Klauden sighed, then shook his head. "We can talk about it later," he said. "For now, let's get the book and break your bond to those fledglings."

Hannah nodded, releasing a relieved breath. "And we need to know how much Milo has told the elves about our people. I don't want to share the wrong thing," she said in a low voice, very aware that the palace had many wandering ears. "Do you really think Nicolo can get the Book of Samander?"

Klauden looked at the books piled on the table, then toward the ceiling. "I don't know, chaivin." He leaned closer. "I do know that he was renowned for his prophecies, his visions of the future." He scoffed, "Though the gift didn't prevent his own fate."

"What fate is that?"

"He's Kargin, chaivin, thirdborn in a House that can claim the Sarkoza." Klauden leaned back again. "I wonder what it would be like to see one's future and be unable to prevent it," he mused. Hannah gave him a look, unable to miss the irony. Klauden didn't miss her thought. "You think it's inevitable, then?" he asked. "That I will lose you to your elf?"

Hannah remembered Rory on the beach, tried to decipher his motives, and failed utterly. She didn't understand him at all. He had essentially set her free to marry Klauden for a political alliance, releasing any claim he had on her. Why show up this morning and kiss her? She shook her head.

"I don't know anything anymore," she admitted. "I don't know what's inevitable." She scoffed. "Unlike some, I cannot see the future. I can't even predict what I think might happen this afternoon." She thought of the fledglings, remembered that feeling as the fledgling fell into nothingness, and she shivered. Would her death be like that? Or would she be more aware? She had vague memories of what happened in the tent outside Salva: Klauden's voice, pain in her chest, movement and echoes, but nothing of the worlds beyond this one if they existed.

Hannah had never given much thought to the afterlife. Given she had only five days remaining to sever the bond, she wondered if she should start. Then she quickly dismissed it. She had never been keen on worshipping Cairn, the bloodthirsty god her father appeased with his tournaments. She doubted any of the other gods would grant her an afterlife, given what she was.

No, she decided. *There's only the here and now.* If she couldn't figure out a way to break free, she would cease to be in a few short days. Thinking of it that way, she was glad Rory had kissed her. At least she wouldn't die feeling so disconnected from him.

<I never thought I'd hear you complain about not being connected to something, chaivin.> Hannah looked up at Klauden, coming back to herself and the room. *<And you will not cease to be. I won't let you.>*

She felt the strength in his words, the determination, and hope blazed again. She shouldn't give up yet. There was still time.

<*I know.*>

Noise from the hallway caught their attention, and they both turned to face the doorway, Klauden picking up his journal and tucking it inside his sleeve in a swift motion. Nicolo and Milo entered the library. Hannah looked behind them for Eriken and Millani, but it seemed the vampires were alone. They exchanged greetings, modified nods and gestures, but it was half-hearted at best, all of them clearly uninterested in protocol.

"So," Klauden began abruptly, "the book."

"The book," Milo agreed, looking at Nicolo, "of course." He pulled up a chair to the table where Klauden had been sitting, gesturing that Hannah do the same. Nicolo slid a plush armchair across the carpet and settled in gracefully. "But first," Milo said when they were all seated, "I need to clarify something."

Hannah raised her eyebrows, nodding for him to continue, wondering what this new angle would be. Klauden gestured for him to go on, impatiently waving his hand.

"It is a matter of some delicacy," Milo began.

"Seriously?" Hannah asked with a sigh, glancing around at the three men. "You guys were discussing my purity at a War Council. I think we're beyond delicate at this point."

Milo dipped his chin in acknowledgment, "Very well." He looked at Hannah directly. "This time last year, where was your body ... when you weren't in it?"

Hannah frowned, not expecting the question or understanding why he would ask it. "What?"

"Your body," he repeated. "This body," he pointed at her.

"What do you mean?" she asked, narrowing her eyes. "Another was in it if that's what you're asking. I don't know what she did with it while I was gone."

Milo frowned, clearly disliking that answer. He shook his head though, closing his eyes for a moment. "*Where* was it?" he repeated.

"We think it was with Kelvin Malbrek for a time," Klauden offered, "but at some point, she came south to Salva, gathering an army along the way."

"And how long did she stay with Malbrek? Was she at Castle van Kreeosk?" Milo pressed, looking at Nicolo and back at Hannah.

Hannah shrugged. "I have no idea." She frowned, calculating the timing. "She was in Salva for about a month before attacking Severin." She glanced at Klauden. "She would've walked or ridden there, so probably two or three months to travel? When did you leave the castle?"

Klauden pursed his lips, head tilting as he recalled. "Mid-Nightal," he said, naming their winter months, "almost a year ago now. I got to Severin three months later to what should have been spring in Ches." He shrugged. "Except the seasons are different so far south, so it was cool instead." He contemplated. "She probably arrived just before I did." Hannah noticed that neither of them had used Anna's name, as if saying it would conjure her dead half-sister. "She certainly wasn't at the castle while I was there," he added quickly. "I don't think Malbrek could have hidden her from me."

"And when did you lose that body?" Milo asked, keenly searching her face.

"Why?" Hannah sputtered. "Why does any of this even matter?"

"Merely trying to understand a riddle," Milo told her. "When did you enter Solyn's body?"

"The Nightal before that!" she said heatedly, thinking of that year spent with Rory, first traveling south, then settling in the small house in Severin. She glared at them, suddenly missing those days. "And I left the Castle the Ches before that since apparently you're keeping track of my life now!"

Milo and Nicolo were having a silent conversation, one that Klauden suddenly seemed to follow. His face paled, and he looked at Hannah, eyes sliding down from her face to her body.

"It is what was foreseen," Nicolo said finally. "The timing is right."

"Will someone please tell me what this is all about?" Hannah demanded.

"In Ches," Milo said quietly, referring to the spring, "Magnus van Kreeosk announced an heir to House van Kreeosk."

Hannah felt the blood drain out of her face. "An heir?" she whispered. She looked at Klauden, remembering the conversation they had overheard in the tunnels beneath the castle.

The baby! But who?

Klauden was silent, staring at Milo and Nicolo. He calculated the timing, adding it to what he knew of babies and children. All three vampires were staring at her now.

"Who?" she said out loud. "Livenna is Kargin..." Her voice trailed off, trying to imagine that her father's other daughter would have a child acknowledged by Magnus van Kreeosk. Had the world shifted that much? "Who?" she repeated.

<*You*,> Klauden replied inside her head.

<*Me? But how...*> The thought disappeared as she put it together. The night in Kalford, the difference in her body, the time between. <*So ... I have a baby nearly a year old?*> The rest of the blood left her head, and she sank forward, falling out of the chair.

Three vampires reached out to catch her easily, lifting her up and placing her on Klauden's lap, the vampire's strong grip around her shoulders keeping her upright as her head lolled on his shoulder.

"I didn't think she knew," Milo said quietly, confirming something clearly long suspected. "Did you?" This last was directed at Klauden. She felt him shake his head, and she knew he was telling the truth. This was not something he would've kept from her. "And yet you tried to reassure me of the bloodlines with talk of Solyn's body," he mused. "We cannot begin an alliance this way, Klauden. You must trust me."

Klauden sat up straighter, adjusting Hannah in his lap. "Would you have contradicted what was said if it had been your sister's honor in question?"

Milo blanched and Nicolo let out a low chuckle. Milo glared at him, but Nicolo was smiling. "Master van Sherinak makes a valid point," the old vampire said. "You would say anything to protect your sister. Why wouldn't he say anything to protect his kevnisha?"

"I'm not his kevnisha," Hannah managed, forcing herself to sit up despite the pounding of her heart in her chest.

"Yes, you are," both vampires said in unison.

"I have a baby in my father's castle," she said, marveling to hear the words spoken aloud. "I am nothing right now except a mother." She turned to look at Klauden, though he already knew what she would say. "I have to go."

She heard him entertain and discard arguments, shuffling through the reasons she couldn't go. It was too dangerous. Malbrek would kill her. The fledgling army was too close. She was tied to Klauden and Solyn—what would happen to them if she died? She had obligations here. She nodded, knowing that everything he said was true, but that she was going anyway.

"Wait," Klauden said out loud, his voice jarring her out of the frantic plans she was making. "Listen."

"Listen to what?" she yelped. "I have to get her!" She looked at Milo. "Him?" She put her face in her hands. "I don't even know if I have a daughter or a son!"

"It's a daughter," Nicolo supplied helpfully, "as foretold in the prophecy."

Hannah stood up. "No." She stepped away from all three vampires. "Hell no." She took a deep breath to calm her racing heart, then turned back to face them. "You're not involving my daughter in any krangesh prophecy," she told them. "I'm going to get her, and she will live her life the way she chooses to, not according to anyone else's damned destiny."

"But the book?" Klauden tried to sway her.

"You get the book. Tell me what you find." She didn't let them say anything else to keep her in the room, running out of the door and down the hallway. Her thoughts raced, a plan forming, a litany repeating in her mind.

I have a daughter.

We have a daughter.

She skidded to a halt halfway up the second flight of stairs, her chest tightening in panic. *Our daughter. My and Rory's daughter. I have to tell him.*

She closed her eyes, fear and excitement flooding her, then she was sprinting again. Her room had been cleaned, the bed made and pillows perfectly fluffed, and it didn't take long to jam all of her belongings into her travel bag again. She turned to leave and nearly smashed into Rory as he ran through the doorway.

"What is it?!" he asked, frantically looking at her. He must've felt her reaction through the bond and ran here. "What happened?"

"Uhh..." Hannah said, waiting for her mouth to find the words.

"You're freaking out," he observed, pulling her into him for a hug to calm her down. "Is it Klauden?" he whispered into her hair. "Solyn? The baby?"

Hannah choked at the last question, then leaned back far enough to see his face. "It's about a baby."

Rory raised an eyebrow, waiting for her to continue.

"Um... Apparently, we have a baby." Rory's arms stiffened around her body as the color dropped out of his face.

"What?" he breathed.

"Yeah," Hannah said, grinning in nervous excitement. "Apparently, my body had a baby about ten months ago."

He looked around, as if expecting the baby to magically appear. "But... Where..."

"Oh, my father's castle," she said brightly. "He's announced her as his heir."

She felt Rory's grip let go, and suddenly he was sliding to the floor, face white and eyes wide. She followed him there, panting as her heart did strange cartwheels in her chest. "Yeah," she commented, nodding at him, "I know."

XXX

"Anything specific I should do?" Rory asked, checking his weapons one more time, hands patting his belt. He tucked his winter cloak slightly under the straps of his pack before turning back to Hannah, clearly ready to go. Hannah was going through her own checklist, making sure her daggers were easily accessible in her belt, adjusting her new winter cloak over one shoulder as she tightened her pack. She didn't need the warmth, would be fine in her plain jacket even in the cold mountains, but the elves had insisted she take the warm gear, and Hannah had been too distracted to say no.

She ran through the spell in her mind again, slightly nervous about performing it without Klauden but knowing it was the fastest way to get to the castle. Traveling on foot would take at least two weeks this time of year, and she only had five days until the elves started slaughtering the fledglings. She had to be back before then so they could break the bond.

Back with my daughter. The thought was still shocking. *I have a daughter,* she told herself. Before she could start wondering what she looked like and what her life had been like for the last few months, Hannah forced her attention back to the room.

"Do?" she repeated, looking at Rory. "Don't do anything. Just hold on."

"And if I let go?" he asked.

Hannah bit her lip. "I'm not sure, but that would probably be bad." She frowned. "I've never done this spell before. I've only been part of it with—" She stopped talking, not knowing how Rory would react to her mention of Klauden. It had been after that first teleportation trip that she and Klauden had first been together.

"With Klauden," Rory finished for her, and he didn't spit the name as he sometimes did. Something had shifted in his appraisal of the vampire since he could feel what Hannah felt. There was a grudging respect there now, a reluctant acceptance bordering on admiration.

"I'm aiming for the lower tunnels," she told him. "We can find her from there."

He nodded, ready to go, and Hannah's heart swelled with love for him. Here he was, willing to return to her father's castle to rescue their daughter. He hadn't pestered her with questions about the how as Klauden would've done. Hannah didn't have a clear exit strategy worked out yet. Beyond getting her hands on her daughter and getting away from the castle, she didn't have any plans. They could teleport into the castle, but the spell only took one person, so Rory would be left behind when they got the baby.

While they were gone, Klauden should be able to update her on his search for a spell.

Five days, she told herself. *It's enough time. It will have to be enough time.*

Hannah stepped forward, taking Rory's hands. She was about to begin when the door to her rooms flew open. Klauden and Nicolo came inside, clearly hurrying to catch them. Hannah sighed, waiting for Klauden to tell her all of the reasons why this was a foolish plan.

"Let's hear it, then," she said, dropping Rory's hands and turning to face Klauden.

"She's been there for months," Klauden tried. "A few more days will not make a difference. And the fledglings are far more pressing."

She knew he was right, but now that she knew her daughter was out there, any amount of time waiting was too much. "Too long," she said. She paused, then looked at Klauden. "If it were Solyn in the castle with your child, would you wait a few more days?"

Klauden frowned. "That is entirely different! Solyn would be in danger. Your child has been named heir apparent."

"Exactly," Hannah agreed. "And how many heirs apparent have had mysterious accidents in our families, Klauden?"

He sighed, looking away, but she knew he would let her go. He grabbed her hands, pressing one to his chest. Hannah heard Rory's sharp intake of breath, but she didn't look at him, staring at Klauden instead, a well of love and longing rushing through her.

"Come back to me," he said.

"I will," she promised.

Klauden looked away from her to where Rory stood, the elf's face unreadable. "Bring her back to me," he ordered.

Rory nodded. "I will."

Satisfied, Klauden leaned down and kissed her, the gesture surprising but not unwelcome. He released her quickly, pushing her gently back to Rory. "I will find the spell to break the bond, chaivin. But you need to be here for me to cast it."

Hannah nodded, taking Rory's hands again.

"Wait!" Nicolo had stood near the door, hanging back and letting them talk, but now he stepped forward. "The necklace."

Hannah thought he referred to Klauden's ring, the artifact still on a necklace around Rory's neck, but Klauden was reaching inside his robe, tugging something out from an inner pocket. He held out a small silver chain to her, a small pendant in the shape of the moon dangling from the end. Hannah recognized it from years ago—the pendant they had recovered from the hidden cubby that held her grandmother's journal.

"Take this," Klauden urged her. "Put it on."

"Have you really been carrying this the entire time?" Hannah accepted the necklace, then put it over her head, lifting her hair so it rested against her skin. "Why?"

Klauden looked at Nicolo, who shrugged. "It's old magic, and it belonged to your family."

Part of my family, she thought, but didn't say the words out loud, not wanting Nicolo to know about her heritage if he didn't know already. She hadn't worried too much about the other vampires being able to read her surface thoughts; kevna tended to drown everything else out. She doubted anyone could read her mind now. Except Klauden. But that wasn't reading her mind. He was inside her mind.

She shook her head at the old vampire. "Let me guess," Hannah said, "you saw it in a vision."

Nicolo nodded graciously. "Some things are foretold in the stars," he told her. "You will find need of it."

Hannah lifted the moon up to look at it, the thrum of old magic echoing in her fingers. She shook her head, not wanting to explore the mystery at the moment. "Whatever," she said finally, letting it fall. "Thanks, I guess?" She looked at the vampires. "Anything else?"

"Be well, chaivin," Klauden told her.

"I will." She took Rory's hands, taking a deep breath to prepare herself. "We will."

The magic came more easily than she expected, a swell of power filling her as she thought of the tunnels beneath the castle, focusing on bringing them both there. She knew it was working, her body enveloped by the magic, her hands tightly gripping Rory's, but then something snapped, and she was being tossed sideways in the void.

Wards, she thought as the world spun around her. *I'm not strong enough to get through them.*

She still held one of Rory's hands, and she searched frantically for the other one. *Rory! Hold—*

But then her body hit something hard, and he jerked out of her grip. Cold earth touched her face, and she managed to roll over, body rigid with redirected magic. The last thing she saw was a face leaning down to look at her before everything disappeared.

XXXI

"<I don't like it,>" a voice said in her native tongue. Hannah heard it, but she didn't open her eyes. She took quick stock of her situation first. She remembered the spell going awry and falling and landing hard on something. She even remembered a face peering down at her curiously. "<It smells like a trap,>" the voice continued.

Hannah was laying on her back, but her hands were bound in front of her, resting comfortably on her stomach. There was something soft bundled under her head and neck, but the rest of her body was on the ground. She could feel the heat from a fire nearby. She tried to reach out to Rory but found Klauden instead.

<What happened?>

<I think I hit Malbrek's wards,> she told him, relieved that kevna was still working despite herself. <We bounced out.>

<Are you alright?> She appreciated that Klauden didn't berate her for not being able to get around simple ward magic. Klauden clearly could do it with ease. She really should have paid more attention during her classes.

<I think so?> Steeling herself, Hannah opened her eyes. She was in a rough camp, her body resting on a thin woven blanket. A quick glance to her right showed Rory laying in a similar position to her own, his hands bound. She saw that he still wore his weapons belt, but both blades had been removed from it. She could still feel her own dagger sheaths around her back, but she couldn't feel the handles; her blades had also been taken. They were both restrained but didn't seem to be injured.

Hannah reached for her magic, relieved to find that it was still there, though notably weaker. She had known that the teleportation spell would use most of her power. Klauden couldn't cast anything for the next day after teleporting, and he was stronger than she was. But Hannah had never actually run out of magic; she just couldn't access it without reciting words like the humans. Since kevna had exploded between them, Hannah could now cast like a normal vampire, simply pushing the power in the direction she needed. She may not have her daggers, but she was most definitely still armed. Her magic may be weaker after the teleportation spell, but she could still feel it inside, a low well of power waiting for her command.

Two men dressed in simple clothing sat nearby, likely the source of the voice she had heard. They both stared at her as she took in the scene, faces suspicious and bordering on hostile. Two more men were on the other side of the fire, one kneeling on a blanket and the other squatting with a plate of food on his knees. Their clothes were plain, browns and blacks, but their boots were fine, clearly made by a master. Hannah wondered where these people came from. They were hardened travelers, clearly not new to the wilderness, but they must have some connections to a town or city. A woman knelt near the fire, poking at the flames and stirring something in a metal pot. Hannah caught a whiff of rabbit, thick and rich. The smell wasn't appetizing to her vampire senses, but it wasn't unpleasant. They had hunted that day, and the camp was clearly temporary. Who were these people? They didn't seem like the villagers Hannah had known from Valrane.

She looked up, trying to see the lines of the mountains beyond the trees overhead, but she didn't recognize any landmarks. They were definitely in the mountains surrounding the castle, but not close. She assumed Malbrek's wards had tossed them out beyond the edge of the property surrounding the castle grounds. She wondered if Malbrek knew she had tried and failed to get inside the castle, if even now he had sent out guards to find them.

The two men were staring hard at her, clearly waiting for her to speak. Hannah returned their gaze without speaking, knowing that the language she chose to reply in would be a clue to her identity, not to mention the accent she never really lost. Men who traveled these roads would be familiar with the castle and her father, and from the sound of the conversation, they already suspected her. They had bound her hands, so likely had already seen the divine symbol burned into her palm. She wasn't sure they would know what it meant. The fact that she and Rory were still alive was a good sign.

She glanced over at him again, seeing that his eyes were now open, taking in the situation as she had, and he nodded in her direction.

The man who had been eating by the fire finished his last bite, tossed his plate down, and stood up, easily topping six feet with a broad frame. His face was pleasant, his hair wild, his cheeks scruffy with a few days of beard, and Hannah felt a rush of hunger for him, the strength of his blood. She swallowed hard, pushing the feeling down, reminding herself to feed as soon as she could. The woman who had been kneeling at the fire shuffled over and quickly picked up the plate, adding it to a small pile off to the side.

Hannah didn't want to kill these people, but she assumed that five humans against a vampire and fledgling were very good odds in their favor. If this went poorly, she and Rory would survive. She reached out with her senses, trying to get a feel of their intentions, but she was stopped by a sense of emptiness. According to her innate magical ability to sense people, these five didn't exist at all. She looked at them again. They weren't vampires—she could sense her people as well as mortals when she focused—nor were they regular humans. Hannah had never met anyone who didn't register with her magic. Perhaps it was some kind of cloaking spell. She rapidly re-evaluated her assessment that she and Rory could easily escape if they wanted to.

"So," the big man said in a pleasant voice, speaking in the common tongue as he stepped over to stand between Hannah and Rory, looking down at both of them in turn, "you want to tell me what you're doing here?"

"That depends," Rory replied, looking at Hannah. "Where is here?"

The man nodded, one eye narrowing. "Don't even know where you are," he mused. "You should probably rethink using magic like that if you don't know what you're doing."

"I know what I'm doing," Hannah snapped in annoyance. "I didn't know there would be wards."

The man smirked. "Heading to the castle, then, I see." He chuckled. "You honestly thought van Kreeosk wouldn't have some kind of defenses?"

Hannah opened her mouth to reply, then closed it. Klauden hadn't seemed to have any issues getting into the castle. Perhaps there had always been wards, but Klauden knew how to avoid triggering them. It made sense. Hannah should have realized it before, but she'd been in such a hurry to get there, she hadn't thought of much else.

"And where would you stand on the topic of van Kreeosk's defenses?" Rory asked quietly.

The big man smiled, showing large white teeth. "I think such creatures can do what they like in their own castles." His face darkened. "But when they come around bothering what's not their business, it can become ... problematic." He looked at both of them in turn, taking in the scars on Rory's neck, no doubt recalling the mark on Hannah's hand. "So what I want to know is what a vampire and fledgling are doing trying to sneak into Castle van Kreeosk," he continued conversationally.

Since he already knew what they were, Hannah decided to just be honest. "They have something of mine," she told him. "I need to get it back."

The big man nodded. "Must be something worth a great deal to you to trifle with the likes of van Kreeosk." He looked around at the other two men, who sat still, watching their leader speak. "What is it?"

"Something of great value to us," Rory answered. "Not to anyone else."

"Clearly valuable to old Magnus," the man observed, "if he's got it." He narrowed his eyes. "So you mean to steal it, then?"

"It's not stealing," Hannah replied. "It's..." She looked at Rory, uncomfortable discussing their child in such a way. "Ours."

"So why not enter through the main doors, then, if it's rightfully yours?" he prompted.

"Because we are not fools," Hannah said, sitting up. The two men stiffened but didn't move, clearly trusting their leader. "Magnus van Kreeosk is not known for his hospitality."

"You know him well, then?" he asked, kneeling down to look at her more closely.

"Well enough to know not to knock on his door," she snapped. She rolled her eyes, thinking of Rory's last visit to the castle when he had done just that. The Vanguard Code wouldn't save them now. She lifted her bound hands in his direction. "Is this necessary?"

The big man shrugged. "Is it?"

"We mean you no harm."

"Clearly," he said. "That's why you appeared out of nowhere and crashed into my campsite."

Hannah frowned. "Magic can be … unpredictable. It was an accident." She looked around. "It doesn't look like we broke anything, and if we did, I can pay to replace it."

"Pretty dangerous to tell me you have money to pay," he commented, "given that your hands are bound."

Hannah scoffed, flexed her muscles, and snapped the rope that bound her wrists together, offering the man a fanged smile in the process. Grinning, she tugged the last of the ropes free, letting them fall to the blanket. After a moment of struggle, Rory managed to break his ropes as well. "Speak plainly," Hannah sat, folding her legs and sitting up to address the leader. "You can't hold us here. Even though you took our weapons, you must know it doesn't matter."

"You think us weak, then, vampire?"

"What do you want from us?" she retorted, not willing to get into a contest of strength when her daughter waited inside the castle nearby.

"I think you will find it is the other way round, vampire," the big man said, then reached out with startling speed for Hannah's neck. She could have stopped him at the last moment, but she didn't move when he only lifted her necklace out so it rested over her shirt. "But first, you must tell me about this."

Hannah frowned, looking down at the pendant she had retrieved from so long ago. "It's a necklace?" she tried.

He rolled his eyes, lifting it higher so the silver moon glittered in the reflected firelight. Everyone in camp stared at it, transfixed. "Where did you get it?"

"What does it matter?" Hannah asked, snatching it out of his hand and scooting over to sit near Rory, preferring to be near him rather than have the big man in between them like this. The elf put a hand on her shoulder, and Hannah could feel how ready he was to leap into action at any moment. Love rushed over her, gratefulness and appreciation for the elf who had her back, who understood her without needing ancient magic to do it. Then again, he was her fledgling, so maybe it was the bond telling him how to behave. She ignored the thought, unwilling to face what it would mean, focusing on the current situation. They could work out their issues later.

Something shifted in the big man's eyes, a darkening, and Hannah felt the swirling magic rise, a power different from hers, but familiar somehow. "It matters a great deal, vampire."

"I found it," she admitted, not wanting to test her skills against whatever that was in her weakened condition. "I think it belonged to my grandmother."

"Lies!" one of the men sitting shouted.

"Blasphemy!" shouted the other. Both were silenced by a glare from the leader. The man sitting across the fire said nothing, only watched with astonishment. The woman had stopped moving as well, mouth open in a small circle as she stared at Hannah.

"Who is your grandmother?" the big man asked, studying her face.

Hannah sighed, tensing for the attack that might be coming. "Isla van Gerter."

The leader nodded while the other two men hissed their disapproval. Hannah relaxed. "I see." He gestured to the necklace again. "And you don't know what that means," the big man said quietly, shaking his head. "She didn't tell you."

Hannah shook her head. She hadn't seen her grandmother more than a handful of times her entire life, the last being when she was still a toddler.

The leader stood, pacing a little. Hannah could see the indecision on his face, an internal debate quickly settled with a resigned sigh. "So I must tell you."

"No," the first man insisted. "She lies!"

"And where is your proof of that?" the big man asked. "Look at her face. Do you not see it?" The other man cringed, hunkering back down.

"I'm not lying," Hannah said, thinking of her grandmother's journal and the secret within. "I found it hidden in a secret place. What does it mean?"

"It belonged to your grandfather, Kerrin."

Hannah's mouth fell open. She had thought it might have something to do with her grandfather when she and Klauden found it so long ago, especially given that it was in the secret hole with her grandmother's journal, but she didn't expect these people to recognize it. "How do you know that?" she breathed. Rory's hand tightened on her shoulder, offering support from behind her.

The man reached into his shirt, pulling out a similar necklace, the moon pendant a full circle instead of the half-moon Hannah's had. He gestured to the other men, who reluctantly pulled out similar pendants, all in various shapes of the moon. The man across the fire held a nearly full moon; the woman barely a crescent.

"What does it mean?" Hannah asked, staring at the faces around her. A theory was whispering in her mind, something ridiculous, too silly to even contemplate, but the word broke free despite her protestations: *wolves. Shapechangers. Werewolves.* Saying the word in different languages didn't help.

My grandfather wasn't just a human, she thought dully. *He was a freaking werewolf. I'm related to animals.* A shiver ran down her spine as she fought to keep her face impassive.

She lost the battle, a soft gasp escaping when the others in the campsite knelt, the two men angrily falling to their knees, the man across the fire respectfully nodding in her direction, and the woman hunkering down and folding forward at the waist, putting her face to the ground. The big man nodded at her in respect, but he didn't kneel. "It means you belong to the pack," he told her. "And we belong to you."

At Hannah's astonished expression, he added, "We will help you." He reached out a hand to shake hers. "I am Colby, leader of the Grilamon." He turned to acknowledge the man across the fire. "Bastan," he introduced. "My second." He waited, clearly expecting Hannah and Rory to go next.

"Hannah," she said, then looked at Rory. *What should I say now? Tallerin? Van Kreeosk? Van Sherinak?* She thought of the mountains and her father's castle and decided to own what remained of her heritage. "Hannah van Kreeosk," she repeated. Bastan nodded, as if expecting the name. The other two wolves sputtered, clearly shocked at the revelation.

Hannah gestured to Rory. "Rory," he said simply, deciding not to identify himself further. These wolves may be loyal to Hannah for her grandfather's sake, but he had no such guarantees.

Colby dipped his chin at her, expression warm. "Lady." He gave Rory a shorter nod, polite, but definitely different.

He turned around and gestured to the other two men. "Luc and Han," he grumbled. "Please ignore them. They talk more than they think." His gaze finally landed on the woman who was still laying with her face on the ground. Hannah was glad to see his expression held kindness as he looked at her, not derision. "And this is Bess," he said gently, stepping over to lift her from the ground. She wouldn't meet his eyes until he put a hand under her chin and lifted it. She gave him a watery smile, then looked at Hannah and Rory, dipping into a gentle curtsy. Colby let her go, and she quickly went back to her cooking, gathering dishes and busying herself with tidying the camp.

"Pleased to meet you," Hannah said politely, wondering when she could ask Klauden to tell her everything he knew about wolves and their culture.

"Likewise," Colby said. "So," he continued, rubbing his hands together, "how can we help our new sister?"

"We need to get into the castle," Hannah told him, deciding not to question her good luck. "Now."

"What does Magnus have of yours?"

Hannah looked at Rory, who dipped his chin in agreement. "Our daughter."

Colby took a deep breath, then nodded. "Kerrin's great-grand-daughter." He scanned the campsite, taking in each face. "She is also pack." Han and Luc frowned, but nodded.

"We can't get in using magic," Hannah said.

"And we can't use the front door," Rory added.

They looked at the wolves.

"No matter," Colby said, glancing over at Bastan. "We can get you in the lower levels."

"How?" Hannah asked, thinking of the wards.

"Through a door, vampire sister." Colby laughed. "How else?"

XXXII

"So," Rory said, squatting beside where Hannah sat under a large tree, "shapeshifters, huh?" He used the Elven word for werewolves, and Hannah let out a long breath.

"I thought him being human was bad," she said, "but this?" She gestured in the direction of the campsite, the wolves clustered around their fire hidden by the trees. She rubbed her face. "I don't know what to think anymore."

Rory cocked his head, face speculative, then shrugged dismissively. "So your grandfather was a werewolf," he said quietly. "So what?"

Hannah's eyes grew wide. "How can you be so calm about this?" She tugged the necklace up to stare at it in the fading afternoon light. "I'm practically an animal."

Rory frowned, gesturing at the pack. "They don't seem like animals. They seem like good people." He grinned. "Magical people. They can really turn completely into wolves?"

Hannah shrugged. "According to the legends," she said. "I've never seen it."

Rory narrowed his eyes at her. "Can you turn into a wolf?"

Hannah choked. "No."

"Are you sure? Have you tried?"

Hannah shook her head. "No," she admitted. "But I think if I could, I would have figured it out by now."

"Would you, though?" he asked, and she glared at him, loving his honesty but hating it at the moment. Rory knew just how to cut through everything to the point.

She sighed. "Maybe not. I can't even begin to think about this now." She looked up and to her right, the direction where she now knew the castle lay. The wolves had said they would leave at sunset.

"Okay," Rory said, "then let's talk about tonight."

Hannah nodded, focusing her attention. "They mentioned going through a door. I know there are a few doors leading into the mountains, but I only know them from inside the castle. I don't know where they are from here." She frowned, frustrated at the limits of her knowledge. Eighty years spent exploring the castle but neglecting the surrounding countryside on the ground—she had been so foolish. "I don't know what we would do if we hadn't found them," she admitted. "We're so lucky."

Rory snorted. "I wouldn't call anything luck anymore." He looked at Hannah. "Nicolo gave you the pendant as we left. Clearly he knew what would happen."

Hannah scoffed. "I don't care what he sees. My fate is my own."

"Do you really believe that?" he asked, hand reaching to his belt to retrieve a small dagger, hands idly flipping it end to end as he spoke. Hannah recognized it as one of hers, the one he had taken from her in a dream.

"Can't I believe that?" she asked, watching the blade and its hypnotic motion. "Can't I believe that something in my life isn't foretold somehow?"

"I don't know about foretold," he commented, flipping the dagger a few times and managing to catch it at the last second. "But you seem fairly bound by destiny, Hannah."

"I didn't know that," she said, wanting desperately for him to believe her. "When we met, I didn't know any of this."

"I know." He nodded, chuckling. He looked up, face speculative. "I wonder how much he saw of me."

"You?" she asked.

He nodded. "Yeah, me. I'm as bound to you and your destiny as you are."

"But..." She let the words trail off, not knowing what to say. *But you left me. But you're with someone else. But you don't want to be with me.*

But I'm with Klauden. It was her last thought, but it was still there. Guilt surged through her.

"What am I doing?" she whispered fiercely, ducking her face into her hands. Grief and fear filled her. What was she doing here? Rescuing her daughter, but then what? Klauden was right—she never thought about the future.

Rory's hand touched her, fingers pressing hard against the back of her hands, tugging them away from her face. He had dropped the dagger to stick in the dirt at their feet. "You're doing what needs to be done, Hannah."

"But—" The swirl of emotions filled her chest with an ache that continued to grow.

"Stop," he said gently, face cradling her cheek. "Just stop."

"Stop what?" she burst in a loud whisper, turning her face away from the direction of the camp. The wolves were out of sight, but she didn't want them to see her like this. "Stop being the ridiculous person I've always been?" She stared at Rory, and the first tears fell. "I never stop. I just do whatever seems good at the time without thinking. I'm so stupid."

"Hey," he said, tugging her up and over into his arms. He pulled her onto her knees, wrapping both arms around her back and squeezing her tight, then leaned back so he could look at her face. He smiled, eyes filled with strong emotion, then pressed his forehead to hers, one hand sliding from her back to press against her chest between them, feeling the pounding of her heart. "It's okay, Hannah," he told her. "Just let it go."

Hannah sagged against him, letting the emotions wash her away with them. She could feel Klauden for a brief moment, his concern, then a wall rose between them as he realized that she was not in danger. "I don't know what I'm doing," she whispered. "I don't know what to do."

"Well that's totally not true," Rory replied, and Hannah could see the small edge of a grin teasing his lips through her tears. "We're allied with a wolf tribe to get inside the castle and rescue our daughter," he said. "You know exactly what you're doing."

"But what are we going to do once we get inside?" she whispered, the fear spilling out of her. "I don't even know…"

"We'll figure it out when we get inside," Rory assured her. "Our plan is simple. Get in. Get our daughter. Get out. Done." He paused. "See? Simple." He laughed a little. "We really need to talk about a name, though. I hate referring to her as a thing."

Hannah sniffed, taking a deep breath, letting the idea distract her. "What kind of names were you thinking?"

Rory considered, lips pursing. "Do you think your people have a name for her already? Will it be weird if we change that? She has to be ... what, eleven months old by now? Will she be walking? Elven babes don't walk until they're a few years old, but human children start very young."

Hannah shook her head. "I don't know," she said honestly. "I don't think so, though. We grow very slowly. My first memories are from when I was five or six, walking and learning to talk." She remembered her mother's voice, softly singing as she brushed Hannah's curls and braided her hair. "They probably haven't named her yet, not until she reaches a year."

"So what would they call her?" he asked.

Hannah thought of the baby endearments she had read in books over the years. "Dearest," she offered. "Sweetling, Hobskin, Apple..."

Rory laughed, the sound lightening the ache in her chest. "Hobskin?" he repeated. "What is a hob, then? Do babies often wear their skin?"

It was her turn to laugh. "Hob's Kin," she said, enunciating the words more clearly. "Hob is a minor god of clever children."

Rory nodded. "And Apple? There are no apple trees this far north."

Hannah sniffed, emotions settling. "My mother called me Apple." She lifted a hand to tug on her curls. "Because of my red hair."

"And chaivin?" he asked, voice carefully neutral.

Hannah leaned back, her forehead leaving his, looking at him with guilt and longing and love. "Chaivin means fire-spirit or fiery temperament," she said quietly. "Sometimes, it means red."

"Did no one in your life use your name, Hannah?" Rory asked gently.

Hannah laughed darkly. "Actually, no. My father always calls me Daughter or Girl. The Kargin called me lady. The others..." she paused, then finished, "called me nothing at all." She looked at him. "What about you? Were you always the Tallerin?"

Rory grinned, leaning back on his haunches a little, giving her space. "I was *a* Tallerin, not *the* Tallerin. And in title, yes, I was. In behavior ... not so much." He shrugged. "I was never suited to be the ruler. I was glad that Marten was in charge." He looked up. "Soldiering came naturally to me. I can solve problems like armies; I cannot negotiate treaties." He looked up, then plucked his knife from the dirt and held it loosely in one hand. "I am a Tallerin in name only now."

"What will you do when all this is over?" Hannah asked quietly. "Will you stay in Firene?"

Rory frowned, shaking his head. "I don't know." He cocked his head at her. "Where will you go?" He flipped the dagger again, the motion a nervous habit now.

Hannah shrugged. "I don't know." She sighed, watching the blade. "We have a daughter, Rory. Where will she sleep at night?"

"I imagine she will go wherever you go," he said quietly.

"My life is dangerous," she whispered. "I'm bound to fledglings in an army. I might be dead in a few days. What will happen to her then?"

"You aren't going to die," he said fiercely. "We've been through worse before. We will figure it out."

"Will we?" she whispered. She looked skyward. "Perhaps she's better off with my father. She will be safe there."

Rory was quiet for a moment, then he asked, "Do you truly believe that?"

Hannah thought about it seriously. Her father's castle was a stronghold, and if he named her his heir, she would live a protected life, the kind Hannah had enjoyed before leaving home. There would be trials—she hadn't lied when she mentioned fatal accidents to Klauden—but there were still some in the castle who would defend her child. Klauden's mother Keller would help her. Her own father would try his best to keep her safe, needing the security of her lineage. It wouldn't be a bad life.

But her daughter was only half vampire, she reminded herself. Half of her was Elven, pure Elven since she had been conceived long before Rory became a fledgling. What if, as she grew, her lack of abilities or breeding grew too obvious, too embarrassing? Would she meet a similar fate to Anna?

"No," she admitted. "I don't believe that." She looked up at Rory again. "But we're a mess. How can we be parents?"

He snorted. "I can remind you how if you want, Hannah," he joked, smirking at her. Hannah laughed in response, soul lighting up at the connection that still burned between them.

"I remember," she said, face reddening slightly, thoughts receding to that room in Kalford, his gentle touch, his soft kisses.

"You're right, though." He nodded, face growing serious. "We are messy." Tilting his head to one side, he stared at her. "Hannah, do you want to be with me?"

It was the same question he had asked her back in their house in Severin, after the awful time in the tent.

Hannah stared at him, wanting to answer right away, jumping in with both feet like she always did, but this time, she paused, forcing herself to think it through.

She was bound to Klauden. Part of her loved him, would always love him.

She and Rory had a child together. He was her fledgling. They were bound in so many ways.

Klauden needed her for his alliance with the elves, needed her to marry him to satisfy Milo's traditional demands. He was waiting for her to come back to him, trusting kevna to keep her at his side, no matter how she truly felt.

There was also Solyn to consider. When the baby came, Klauden would likely spend most of his time with his fledgling and child. He would be occupied, content even.

Stop, Hannah commanded herself. *Stop.*

Answer the question, she told herself. *Stop thinking about everything else and answer the damn question.*

The answer was just as simple. She knew it, had always known it, even when everything else in her life threatened to sweep her up in the turmoil.

"Yes," she said, voice firm as she looked at him. "I want to be with you." She wanted to add the rest, list the complications, the impossibility of it all, but she didn't.

Rory nodded. "Then be with me."

"It's that easy?" she asked, smiling as more tears slid down her cheeks, joyful ones this time.

"Sometimes," he said. "Not often with you, but yes." He took a deep breath, settling himself on one knee and reaching for her hand. She let herself enjoy the feel of his skin against her fingers.

"Hannah van Kreeosk," he said formally, lifting her hand and pressing it to his, palm to palm, "will you tie yourself to me?"

"I..." Hannah stared at him, unsure of what he meant, remembering the words from that night in Kalford. "Are you asking me to marry you?" she whispered.

Rory chuckled. "I get the distinct impression you're thoroughly engaged to another," he said. "I don't know how your people feel about bigamy, but mine are ... particular about who their princes marry."

Hannah had a fleeting thought, wondering when he started caring about such things again, but she let it go. It doesn't matter now. "So what do you mean, then?"

"Be with me," he repeated. "When you can, as long as you can, choose to be with me."

"But the Valrina—"

"Is over," he said quickly.

"Since when?" Hannah asked, frowning.

"Since right after the War Council," he said.

Hannah stared at him. "But you said—"

"I know what I said," he interrupted. "And you must know why I said it, Hannah." He frowned, pressing his hand against hers. She remembered the moment Klauden had forced her to stay silent, the way Rory had looked as he too said nothing. "You need the alliance to work out."

"It was you, wasn't it?" she asked, changing the subject as the pieces fell into place, her voice low as she ran through the last few days. "That night on the beach. I saw someone running." She peered at him. "Klauden showed up, but only after I thought I saw someone else."

Rory nodded. "I felt your pain," he said. "I had to see you."

"So why didn't you come?"

He bit his lip, embarrassed. "I stepped on a rock and stumbled. I wanted to get up and keep coming, but he came running behind me. He seemed upset." He bit his lip. "I thought maybe you needed to see him more. That he was what you wanted." He paused, shaking his head. "But then..."

"Then you heard us talking," Hannah finished. "You heard what I said when I couldn't feel the magic."

Rory smiled softly. "And then I thought maybe ... there was hope." He shook his head. "I was going to break it off with her anyway, but after her behavior with you..." He rolled his eyes. "Annilyn was always petty. I should have known better." He looked at her, face searching, fingers pressing against hers. "She was convenient, Hannah. A warm body and some comfort—nothing more. You must know that."

Hannah sighed, a weight leaving her heart. She hadn't thought he loved the Valrina, but part of her was glad to hear him say it. She wanted to be angry at the idea of him sleeping with someone else, but she thought of the release she had found disappearing into Klauden's arms on occasion and knew she couldn't begrudge him the same relief.

Klauden. Her heart sank.

"But Klauden—"

"I know." He nodded, but there was no anger in his voice. "Believe me, I know."

Hannah cocked her head at him. "What do you know?" she asked.

"Hannah, he's several hundred leagues from here, and even I can't wait to see him again." He chuckled, shaking his head. "I feel the pull of him constantly, his need for you." He smiled. "And I get it. Believe me, I get it." He smiled at her again. "You're worth it."

"So ... you'll what? Share me with him?"

"I will take what I can have of you, Hannah, and damn the rest." He brought the dagger up slowly, watching her face as he first slid his palm away from hers, then drew the blade across his flesh in a swift motion. He held the dagger out to her, putting his hand back up near hers, but not touching, letting her decide. "Will you have me?"

She didn't speak, instead taking the dagger and sliding the blade down her palm. Her skin began to heal almost immediately, faster than Rory's, but not before she pressed her hand against the elf's. "I will have you," she told him. "For as long as we can, for as much as we can, I choose to be with you." Their fingers folded into one another, hands clasped. Hannah smiled at him, tears falling down her cheeks.

Rory leaned down, but instead of kissing her lips, as Hannah expected, he placed a chaste kiss on her forehead. "<My Hannah,>" he whispered in Elven, "<mother of my daughter.>"

"<My Rory,>" she replied in the same tongue, "<father of my daughter.>" She stayed there for a long moment, her hand still holding his, his lips on her forehead, hearts beating together. "You're right," she said after a while, "she really needs a name."

"What are you thinking?" he asked.

Hannah thought, then said, "I always liked the name Kira."

Rory nodded. "That's nice. What else?"

"What do you mean?"

"What's the rest of it?"

"The rest of it?"

He pulled away to look at her, tapping his chest. "Rorinvalranus Tallerin," he said. "Rory for short."

"Oh," Hannah breathed. "You want a hundred-syllable-long Elven name."

"She's half-Elven," he commented.

"Okay," Hannah said, thinking, "well, what does valranus mean?"

"Moonrise," he replied. "I was born at night."

Hannah wondered what time her daughter had been born. "That's nice." She paused, decided it didn't matter, then suggested, "Kiravalranus? Is that too much?"

"That's perfect," he agreed.

"And her last name?" Hannah asked. "She is First Daughter. She should have a family name."

"Right," Rory said. "Well, she isn't staying here, right?"

Hannah shook her head. "No. She's coming with us. Whatever that means, wherever we go, she's coming with us." She looked at him. "And if this goes badly in a few days with the army, she stays with you. Don't let any of the vampires take her from you."

Rory nodded, accepting her decision. "As you will." He paused. "Can she have my name, then?" he asked quietly.

"Kiravalranus Tallerin? But she's not a prince."

"She's my princess," he said firmly. "Always."

Hannah nodded. "Yes." She tried to picture their child, Kira, and failed. Would she have red hair or black hair? Green eyes or brown? Whose nose would she have? "Oh Rory," she whispered, "how am I going to be a mother?"

"You will be a fine mother," he assured her. "We will figure this out."

She looked at him, biting her lip. "We can do this," she repeated. She looked down at their linked hands. "Together."

Rory bit his lip, then slid his fingers slowly from hers, a small smear of their blood on their palms, the cut already healed for both of them. "Hannah, I have to ask you something."

"Something more than this?" she asked, leaning back and raising an eyebrow.

His face was serious. "I spoke to Caga, and he has a possible solution."

Hannah sat up. "Magic to break the bonds? How does it work?"

Rory frowned. "That's just it. It really works." He reached into his belt pouch, fingers searching for something tucked into the small pocket near the top. He withdrew a small metal band.

Hannah frowned at it. "I thought rings were customary *before* agreeing to not-marriage."

"I know. Bad form," he said. "It just happens to be in a ring right now." Hannah reached for it, but he pulled it out of reach. "Listen," he told her, face serious, "this is a last-ditch effort solution. I hope we don't have to use it."

Hannah's fingers folded down and away from the ring, face scrunching up in surprise. She couldn't feel any magic from the ring. It seemed like a perfectly normal ring of metal. "What does it do?"

"It stops magic," he said bluntly. "All magic. Like the Manawyrm but without the paralysis."

Hannah frowned more deeply, staring at the ring, trying to feel any kind of power from it. "Are you sure?" she asked, reaching for it. "It just seems like—" Her voice broke off as her fingers touched the edge where it rested on Rory's palm.

There was a sucking sensation, a draining, and a loud explosion of silence inside her head. She gasped, ears ringing, then took a deep breath before opening her eyes.

Rory sat before her, face handsome as ever, eyes concerned, skin warm where she could feel it against her fingers. She wanted to touch him, to kiss him, to lean into his embrace and never leave.

Wait.

She reached for Klauden. Emptiness. Blessed empty space. Solyn was gone, even the distant echo of her a blank space. Hannah remembered how it had felt on the beach that night with the Manawyrm, recalling this feeling of magical emptiness.

She reached for her magic, the well of power always lurking somewhere inside of her. And found nothing. Not even emptiness, just nothing, as if her magic had never even existed.

She looked at Rory again. "Do you feel that?" she whispered.

He tilted his head, considering. "I feel you," he said. "I feel your emptiness." He paused, taking more time to experience the sensation. "I think my bond to you is still there. I can feel you." He paused again. "I don't feel him anymore." He searched her face. "How are you? Is it awful?"

Hannah frowned. "It's weird," she admitted. "I'm still me, but I'm missing parts."

"And the fledglings?" he prompted.

Hannah concentrated, searching for those strings that bound her to those creatures. "Nothing," she breathed. She focused more, willing herself to find them. A ghostly tendril of a cord brushed against her. "Wait." She followed it, seeing a handful of ghostly fledglings making their way through a forest of ancient trees. "I can see them, sort of, but I cannot feel them." She opened her eyes to stare at Rory. "This might work," she breathed. She considered him. "How does this feel for you?"

Rory shrugged. "I still feel you, but that is all."

"So you'd still be connected to me, but I can't feel you." She frowned. "Or anything." She sniffed, listening to her body. "Can you live like this?"

He smiled. "This is fascinating, Hannah. I will spend years appreciating how all of this feels." He looked at her. "Can *you* live like this?"

Hannah frowned again. "It seems to work."

"But at what cost?" he asked.

Hannah considered. "Could I just wear it until after the army is gone? What happens if I take it off again after?"

"I don't know. Caga isn't sure." Rory paused, frowning. "The only way to be sure it works is to keep it on … forever." He sighed heavily. "I don't want this to be the solution."

"So I would live like this," she said. She flexed the fingers on her other hand, reaching out for the dagger resting on the ground and flipping it easily. With a flick of her wrist, she flung it into the tree behind her, hearing the satisfying *thunk* as it sank into the target. "I'm still me," she declared. "I'm strong and fast and efficient." She breathed, keeping her hand on the ring's surface, not willing to let go yet. "This could be enough."

Rory nodded, but his eyes were sad. "Could it?" he asked. He shook his head. "I'm sorry, Hannah. I'm so damn sorry that you always have terrible choices."

"I'm not sorry," she told him, getting up on her knees so her face was near his. With her finger still touching the ring, she couldn't feel Klauden at all, her love for the vampire an old feeling, part of her history and childhood, but nothing in her present. "This is my choice," she said, then leaned forward to kiss Rory. He let himself be kissed at first, careful not to move, but then he was wrapping his free hand into her hair and holding her close, the hand with the ring folding into hers so they both touched the metal.

His mouth moved against hers, igniting a fire under Hannah's skin. She lost herself in the feeling, reveling in the freedom of kissing him without fear of hurting him. Her free hand wrapped around to grip the back of his head, not worrying about her strength or her fangs. Rory seemed as caught up as she was, strength not matching her own but much more than when he had been only an elf. He moved his mouth against hers, tugging her lower lip into his mouth, then he bit it, a small nip, but enough to draw blood. Hannah shuddered, pleasure shooting through her, then she returned the gesture, nipping his lower lip and tasting his blood for the first time, the sweetness satisfying her senses. She reveled in it, in him, in this new intoxicating freedom to be in control of her own desires. Both of them smiled then, lips still pressed together. Finally, they moved apart.

"Well," Rory breathed, sucking in his lip and swallowing the rest of the blood there, "that answers one question."

"What question is that?" Hannah asked.

He looked down at her, hand releasing her hair and resting on her shoulder. "You definitely want to be with me."

Hannah nodded, then looked down at their linked hands, the ring pressed between them still. "But when I let go…"

He reached out with his other hand to lift her fingers free one by one. "When you let go, everything comes back," he said. "And I'll still be here."

"Will you?" she asked, face a little desperate, remembering how quickly he had abandoned her in Severin, how easily he had dismissed her in the War Room. "Will you be here?"

Rory nodded, lifting the last finger and laying his hand flat, the surface of her palm still barely touching the ring's edge. "I swear it," he promised, his free hand moving to draw two lines across his heart, the ancient gesture for an oath. "No matter what, I will not leave you again, Hannah."

XXXIII

The afternoon light waned, the sun dipping below the mountains to the west. Hannah stood beneath the large oak tree, thinking of Rory's oath and her promises. It was almost time to go, but she had something left to do first.

You know what you have to do, she told herself. *Suck it up.* She closed her eyes, wanting privacy for this conversation.

<Klauden.>

<Hannah.> He used her name, sensing the gravity of the situation.

<I...> She paused, not knowing how to continue. She knew what had to be said, had walked through this discussion so many times in her head, but now that it was here, she couldn't make herself say it. *<Any luck with the spell?>*

She could feel the frustration surge through him, followed by a bone-deep weariness.

<I guess that's a no, then. What about the Book of Samander? Nicolo couldn't get it?>

<Oh, he got it alright.> There was a pause, a steel wall between them as he chose his words as carefully as she did. *<I saw it.>*

Hannah's heart sped up. *<But it's supposed to have what you need!>* Her chest deflated, the impact of his words sinking in. *<So, it's impossible, then. Breaking the bond cannot be done.>*

Klauden was silent, agonized guilt washing over the wall between them. Something dark filled the space between them, a temptation and a promise that Klauden shoved ruthlessly aside. *<I cannot, chaivin,>* he told her, sorrow infusing his words. *<I am sorry.>* A long pause. *<I have failed you.>*

<There is another solution,> she told him.

<Caganasti's ring?>

<It ... works.>

<I know.>

<How do you know?> Hannah thought of the time she had spent touching the ring, time without her connection to Klauden, time spent alone ... kissing Rory. She remembered her hands in his hair, sliding up his neck. His neck, where he still wore the chain—the chain holding Klauden's ring. *Malfek.* So Klauden had seen everything anyway. Guilt and regret filled her. *<I'm so sorry, Klauden. I didn't mean—>* She stopped herself, hating that she was always hurting him. *<I'm sorry,>* she repeated, knowing how little the words mattered.

<I know.>

<I love him,> she told Klauden simply. *<I want him.>* The magic surged, filling her with love for the vampire, their bond wrapping around her. *<And I love you,>* she added.

<Perhaps. But not enough.>

<If things had been different ... if I had stayed in the castle ... it would've been enough.>

<No. I would never have been enough. You might not have known it, but I would.>

<How?>

<Because I love you, chaivin. Without bonds. Without magic. Without any of this. I will always love you.> There was a soft sigh in his voice, a deep sadness. *<And I know you. I've seen you truly happy. And ... it wasn't with me.>*

<I'm so sorry,> she told him again. *<I want to feel the way you do.>*

<No, you don't,> he snapped. *<Don't tell me lies to soothe my ego.>*

<It's not your ego I'm worried about,> she snapped back.

<I will be fine,> he told her, as if she couldn't feel his heart breaking through the bond. *<Now tell me your plan.>*

Hannah bit her lip, knowing he was about to get angry with her. *<Umm ... get in, get Kira, get out again? The wolves are helping us get in,>* she added helpfully.

There was a beat. *<And?>*

<And what?>

<Please do not tell me that is the sum total of your plan, chaivin. Please tell me that your elf is smarter than that.> There was a pause, then the questions rolled in. *<How are you going to take the baby from Magnus? He will try to stop you. And what about Malbrek? Assuming you can defeat them and get to the child, how will you get out again—teleport? How will your elf get out if you leave him there?>*

<We'll figure that out when we get there,> Hannah told him. *<Besides, planning has never worked out for me anyway.>*

<Planning prepares you for most eventualities,> Klauden insisted. *<Your elf knows this.>*

<Yes, and he also knows that too much planning can get in the way of acting. We don't know enough to plan properly, so imagining all these scenarios just makes it all seem impossible.> She paused, then added, *<I'm going to be around my father and Malbrek. There's a good chance they can read my thoughts, Rory's too. I may be protected by kevna, but I don't know that for sure. Any plan I had would only work against me.>*

She could practically feel Klauden rolling his eyes. *<A likely excuse,>* he chided. *<But still a possibility.>* There was another pause, a sense that he was organizing other issues in his mind, making plans for other problems. The wall he had built was starting to grow thinner, and she could see into him again, feel his need for order amid the chaos that she brought into his life. *<Very well.>*

<Very well what?>

<You clearly need my help. And since I'm useless to you here, I'm coming to you there.>

<But Solyn...?>

<I will handle Solyn,> he snapped. Then he eased, softening with her again. *<If you plan to put on that ring in a few days and cut me off forever, I would like to spend the rest of our time with you. Our bond is incredibly useful right now. Let me help you.>*

She nodded, though he couldn't see her, a warm tear running down her cheek, gratefulness welling up.

<I will meet you in the tunnels,> he told her, *<because I like to have a plan.>*

<How will you get in? Malbrek's wards...>

He scoffed. <*Honestly, chaivin, for the amount of power you wield, you are incredibly lazy.*>

<*In a few days, it won't matter anyway,*> she reminded him, trying not to think of her life without magic. It was better than dying.

<*Not yet, though,*> he told her. <*There is still time. Wait for me.*>

XXXIV

Colby and Bastan led Hannah and Rory down a narrow descending mountain path. The men moved efficiently, feet making no sound as they stepped easily around smaller rocks and pebbles on the tiny path. Hannah and Rory followed just as silently, easily keeping up with the pace. The sun had set, but the last of the evening light still allowed her to see enough of her surroundings to move without danger of injury.

Hannah looked up, the side of the mountain on her right rising to where she could see the base of her father's castle. She could probably climb the wall and get up there, but the stone wall was solid—and no doubt warded against anyone who dared touch it. There was no way there. Even down here, Hannah could feel the soft brush of the magic against her senses.

They followed the path down around a slight curve, then both men slowed, stopping to peer around a sharp edge of rock. Colby nodded once, then Bastan gestured for them to continue, but the pace was slower now, both because of the growing darkness as well as their closeness to the castle. Hannah thought she could see a pale shine on Colby's eyes as the big man looked ahead again. Maybe the wolves had a similar ability to her nightvision that allowed them to see. She took a few more steps, but then the last of the light disappeared, and the world turned to darkness. She called on her nightvision, not caring if the wolves could see it, and the world came back into focus in a blend of blacks and grays. She turned to see Rory's eyes glazed a similar color, the elf nodding at her as they continued down the mountain. The path had vanished, and now they followed a cut formed by winter run-off, the ground uneven and cracked.

Colby and Bastan paused again, this time at another edge, peering around quickly before signaling the all clear. They gestured for Hannah and Rory to move past them, and in the darkness, Hannah's eyes made out the small outline of a wooden door in the base of the cliff face in front of them. Colby jerked his head, eyes raised to see if she had any questions. Hannah bowed her head, mouthed "thank you," and stepped around the corner, finding her way to the small opening. Rory followed behind her. They approached the space before the entrance, just enough flat dirt for the swing of the door itself, but Hannah did not try to open it. There was no handle on this side. She reached out with her senses first, seeing if the door had any magic on it. Finding none, she pushed Rory back with a gentle hand, then concentrated.

Open, she commanded, the word infused with power.

To her surprise, the door obeyed at once, opening wide and revealing a long hallway. Hannah smiled, pleased to find her magic so effective, and grabbed Rory's hand before stepping inside. The door fell shut behind them with a small thud, then they were in a long tunnel. Hannah examined the walls, trying to identify where she was. The walls were rough, hewn from the mountain rather than built like the tunnels above. She nodded. She knew the tunnels ran deep on the south side of the castle, so that must be where they were.

She was surprised that she didn't recognize the door, though. Glancing behind her, the reason became clear. To her vision, the tunnel ended in a blank rock wall, whoever had carved the stones clearly giving up at this spot. She gasped, then reached out a hand to touch the stone. It felt real.

"That's good work," she said, her voice loud in the quiet. Rory had turned to see what she was doing, then he did a slow circle, face confused. "It's a spell," she told him, "to hide the door."

"Hide it from whom?" Rory asked.

Hannah shrugged. "I have no idea." She turned, leading him down the tunnel. "The castle is ancient. I explored most of it, but that spell explains why I never found this door."

She led him down the tunnel, eyes scanning the walls for the telltale shift from carved rock to the smoother surface of the tunnels she knew. They reached a T-junction and Hannah studied the walls, eyes scanning the options. Feeling fairly confident, she turned right, her direction sense rewarded a few moments later when they reached the bottom of a winding staircase. She turned to Rory, whispering, "We're going to pass the dungeons this way. Be quiet."

Rory nodded, his footsteps silent on the stone steps behind her as they climbed. She ignored the first two landings, knowing they led to the lower and upper dungeons in the fourth level, listening hard for anyone coming in the other direction. They were lucky and met no one. Hannah took the third landing, setting off to the right automatically, leading them to the spot where Klauden had said he would meet them.

"We should be fine here," she said quietly when they reached another tunnel. "No one comes this way."

Rory nodded, marveling at the tunnel system she had navigated. "We have tunnels under Firene," he commented. "But no one in the army could ever make an accurate map." He looked at Hannah. "If we get back there and you need something to do, Hannah, you'd be a wonderful mapmaker."

Hannah smiled. "I had a lot of free time as a kid," she told him. "These tunnels were my life for years."

"Clearly," he agreed.

Hannah slowed as they turned another corner, slipping down a finished hallway. She could see the dim outline of a person ahead, and she knew it was Klauden, feeling his presence before she could actually see his body. They reached him, all three awkwardly standing in the center of the hallway, magic and desire swirling around them.

"So," Hannah said, then stopped, not wanting to make the awkwardness worse.

"So," Klauden echoed, red gaze moving from Hannah to Rory and back again, thoughts filled with memories of Hannah's mouth, doubled with the image of Rory kissing her.

"Yeah," Rory said, "this is super uncomfortable." He coughed, looking down, clearly trying to tear his gaze away from Klauden's mouth. Looking up again, he shook his head, staring at Klauden. "Get it together, man," he snapped at the vampire. "We're on mission now." He looked at Hannah. "Yes, she's gorgeous. I want to think about nothing but her too." He shook his head. "But this is not the time for that." He poked Klauden in the chest, finger poking a second time seeming without his permission. "Get your head in the moment."

Klauden looked down at where Rory's finger had paused, resting against Klauden's chest. "It seems I'm not the only one having ... difficulties focusing," he commented.

Rory pulled his hand away, reaching down to grip the handle of his blade. "It's you," he snapped. "Stop drowning everyone with your need." He looked at Hannah. "Which way from here?"

Hannah felt Klauden's pull recede the slightest bit, clearing her mind. "I'm not sure," she said, "but I think we should start near the servant's quarters. I don't think he would keep her there, but it's far more convenient if she has mortal nursemaids." She took a few steps down the hallway, leading them in the opposite direction from the library.

"And if she's not there?" Rory asked.

Hannah sighed. "Then she's probably on the first level, near my father's rooms." She glanced at Klauden. "We can use the tunnels to get close, but I never found one into his rooms. I can get into Malbrek's suite but not my father's. It's too well hidden."

"Can we find one of these servants," Rory asked, "and question them? Would many people in the castle know where she is?"

"Probably," Hannah said. "The servants were gossiping about it the last time we were here."

"Wait, what?!" Rory sputtered. "You knew—"

"I didn't know!" Hannah assured him. "We overheard them talking about a child, but I didn't know what they meant. *Who* they meant."

Rory glared at Klauden. "You didn't know," he said. It wasn't a question.

"I didn't know," Klauden insisted. "I should have guessed, but I didn't know."

"Your good friend Nicolo didn't tell you that part?" Rory asked, and Hannah turned to look at him, slowing her pace as they moved through the tunnels.

"What are you talking about?" Hannah asked. "He just met Nicolo a few days ago."

"Okay," Rory said casually. "That explains why they had so much to say to one another down in the library."

Klauden narrowed his eyes, red glare focusing on Rory. "How do you know what we spoke of in the library?"

"Your castle isn't the only one with secret doors," Rory commented. "I wonder how much he left out of his little story."

"What are you talking about?" Hannah demanded.

"There's a whole prophecy," he told her, "about you and the new House of the Vanya. It's very specific."

Hannah turned to Klauden, suspicion burning through her. <*What haven't you told me?*>

"This is not the time, chaivin," Klauden said out loud. "Later, I promise. I will tell you everything."

"So many secrets," she muttered, turning to stalk down the tunnel again. "All this time and still so many damn secrets."

They encountered no one on their way to the kitchens, and Hannah listened for the sound of a baby crying.

A baby crying.

Hannah stopped dead in the center of the hallway, a memory unfolding.

"Ha—" Rory whispered, but she shushed him, closing her eyes to snatch the hint of memory she had stumbled upon. The images flooded her, slow at first, then with rapid accuracy.

She had been standing in the tunnels outside Klauden's rooms, waiting for the servants to finish cleaning up so she could go back inside. Feelings overwhelmed her as she recalled what had just happened in his room, their first time together, and she'd taken a walk to get away from him.

A walk down to the library, then to her old rooms.

Where she had heard a sound like a child crying.

"My rooms," she breathed. She turned to face Klauden, fingers throbbing in sudden excitement. "When we were here that night, I heard a child crying near my rooms." Her face grew hot. "And you were afraid when you found me." She stared at him, not wanting to believe what she suspected. "You thought I would be found..." she trailed off, "or were you afraid of what I might find?" She stalked to Klauden, eyes peering into his. "Did you know that she was here? *Did you?*"

Klauden sighed, face sad. "I know how it looks, chaivin," he said quietly. "I should have known." He paused, and she could feel the truth in his words. "But I did not."

"Okay," Hannah said. "I believe you." She turned to Rory. "I think I know where she is."

XXXV

They stood in the tunnels outside of Hannah's old rooms, all three staring at the small panel of stone that would slip aside to let them inside. They had been listening for a while now, growing increasingly unnerved by the utter silence around them.

"Nothing," Klauden repeated. "Absolutely nothing."

Hannah frowned. "It's a trap, then."

Klauden nodded. "Magic-dampening field, likely." He turned to include Rory. "That's when—"

"No magic inside the field," the elf said quickly. "I get it." He looked at Hannah. "Could she have magic that they are keeping under control?"

Hannah considered. "Maybe? My magic didn't manifest until I was older. It's not like I set the blankets on fire or anything. I had a hard time getting my power to come out at all." She turned to Klauden. "You?"

Klauden shook his head. "It's always a possibility," he admitted. "Not likely, but with you, unlikely seems to happen a great deal."

"Could this just be Livenna protecting her rooms from intruders?" Hannah offered. "If you thought she had my rooms…"

Klauden frowned. "I assumed so, chaivin. I didn't actually know." He paused, frowning. "You'll recall, I was a little preoccupied at the time with walking across the continent and all."

"Good point," she allowed.

"But you heard something when you were here. It's probably where she is," Klauden added. "The magic field is probably a precaution, keeping another from teleporting in here and snatching her for their House."

Hannah nodded, trying to remember that everything wasn't always about her. Her father did have many enemies among the Houses, people who had a vested interest in seeing House van Kreeosk fall.

"So if magic doesn't work inside there," Rory said, looking at Klauden, "what can you do?"

Klauden sniffed, an eye twitching. "I'm sure I will find something useful with which to occupy my time," he snapped. He may have been weakened from teleporting, but his connection with Hannah allowed him to pull from her magic.

Rory frowned. "Stay behind me."

"Listen to him, Klauden," Hannah agreed. "Are we ready, then?"

Rory shrugged. "Let's get our daughter."

Hannah reached for the hidden latch that released the secret door, slipping inside quickly, Rory right behind her. She jerked to a stop immediately, eyes widening at what she found inside.

Her bedroom had been redecorated, her old bed gone, replaced by an elaborate crib against the far wall. The same red tapestries covered the walls, the same soft red rug on the floor, but her dresser had been replaced by a matching bureau next to the ornate crib, and another low table sat next to the crib, an assortment of fabric and bottles on top. Hannah's old rocking chair still remained in one corner, the battered footstool re-covered with new material in bright colors.

Sitting in it was Kelvin Malbrek, the magician relaxing comfortably with his feet up on the stool, a dark-haired baby nestled in one arm.

Klauden stepped into the room last, the door sliding shut behind him with a soft *snick*. He took in the scene immediately, reaching for his magic to assess the situation. His normal magic was out of reach, locked behind a barrier, as he expected, inside the spell laid on the room.

<Hannah?> He sent her the thought.

<I'm here,> she replied silently, feeling the bond still strong around them, kevna unaffected by the spell. *<So, not stronger than that,>* she thought. *<Just a spell.>*

<And I can deal with just a spell,> Klauden told her. *<Keep him talking.>*

Hannah turned to see Rory looking at her. He gave her a slight dip of the chin, a sign that he could still feel her, feel them, and they both turned to face Malbrek together.

"My dear Hannah," Malbrek greeted in a cheerful voice, "how nice of you to finally join us."

"Malbrek," she replied, "how unpleasant to find you here."

The magician kicked back in his chair, one foot rocking the chair slowly. "You are so utterly predictable, my lady." He glanced over her shoulder to where Klauden stood behind them, his mind frantically running through arcane words, clearly working on a counterspell. "And you, Lord van Sherinak, you never learn, do you?" Malbrek glanced at Rory, dismissing the elf as unimportant. "And you, well, I thought you had abandoned her back in Severin." He frowned, then studied Rory's neck. "I see, bound again." He tisked, his gaze returning to Hannah. "You're very greedy, my lady. So many bonds are dangerous. Did no one ever tell you?" He paused. "Wait, I did. Many times. But you never listened to me." He glanced down at the baby he held: a hand poised over her face. "Will you listen now? Will she?"

"What do you want, Malbrek?" Hannah asked, voice louder than she intended. Rory took a small step to his left, away from her. Klauden mirrored his movement, staying hidden behind the elf.

"Keep your voice down," Malbrek chided, eyeing the elf for a second before turning back to Hannah. "You'll wake the baby. And trust me, you don't want that, do you?"

"What do you want, Malbrek?" Hannah repeated, taking a small step to her right, widening the gap between her and Rory, forcing them into separate targets. She had already studied the room, analyzed the angles, the possibilities. She could have reached Malbrek with her magic, but he was too far away for her to jump on him before he could act. She wasn't willing to risk an attack until he moved his hand away from her daughter.

"You, of course," he said with a creepy smile.

Hannah frowned, sliding slightly more to her right. "Me? For what?"

"You know for what," he said, voice low and personal. "Come with me, Hannah. Rule at my side, and we will be unstoppable."

Hannah scoffed, unable to stop herself, taking a casual step forward just as Rory moved more to his left. "Are you serious right now? How would we be unstoppable?" She paused, shaking her head. "Are you talking about Herrick?" She laughed for real then. "Do you honestly think the elves aren't about to destroy that entire army? You have nothing."

"The elves don't have a chance against us, Hannah," Malbrek insisted. "They won't risk killing any of them because they won't risk you."

Hannah giggled, taking another step forward, closer to Malbrek than before as Rory shifted even more to his left, standing near the corner now. "I don't know where you've been getting your information, Malbrek, but you really need a different spy." She shook her head. "Even now, the Elven army marches. The army will be destroyed in days."

"They cannot destroy so many fledglings. The elves will die."

Hannah cocked her head, watching how Malbrek's hand had moved away from Kira's face, seeming to forget the baby as he spoke. "The elves are not alone," she told him. "And Herrick and his army will be nothing but bones. It's unavoidable."

"No," Malbrek insisted. "They would not risk losing you."

"Uh, I'm barely a factor in this decision at all," she said.

Malbrek glanced at Rory, who stood off to his other side now, waiting for an opening. "You are the Tallerin's lady. They would never risk losing you."

Hannah scoffed, another laugh bursting out of her. "Wow. Just wow. You are ... so way off."

Malbrek sensed that she was telling the truth and sat up, adjusting the baby in his arms, face suspicious. "No," he repeated. "You're all here, like he promised. Now I will destroy both of them, and we will rule the Vanya!"

Hannah showed her teeth in a grimace. "I used to think you were so smart, Malbrek, but I was so wrong. Whoever he is, he fed you a line." She looked over at Rory, then back at Malbrek. "So who's your completely uninformed spy?"

"Nicolo," Klauden said from behind Rory's back.

Hannah frowned. "Nicolo? But..." She laughed again. "Oh. He's been telling you about his visions, huh?"

Malbrek raised an eyebrow. "How do you know Nicolo?" he asked.

"He likes to tell me about prophecies," Hannah said. "I love ignoring him."

"You've spoken to him? You've been to Castle van Reegan?" He looked at her face again, expression confused. "How?"

"No?" she replied. "I've never been to Castle van Reegan." She paused, both she and Klauden filling in the gaps. "He's been playing you for a fool this whole time," she said. "You think he's still at home?" At Malbrek's growing fury, she added, "He's in Firene. With the elves." She paused, then added casually, "And the Sarkoza."

"No," Malbrek grated. "The Sarkoza is ... elsewhere."

"Yeah," Hannah said. "He is elsewhere ... in Firene. With the elves. Making an alliance for a House." She snorted. "He'll destroy the army in an afternoon." She glared at him. "You've got nothing."

Malbrek looked down at the baby in his arms. "Oh, I still have something," he sneered. His hand moved, and Rory leaped forward, throwing himself on Malbrek. Hannah flung her dagger at the magician at the same moment, her weapon imbedding itself in the back of the chair beside Malbrek's face, some of his hair caught by the blade. He slid the chair backward so he was out of Rory's reach and stood abruptly, yanking the baby out of the blanket and holding her out to one side by one chubby leg. Kira woke and started wailing, fists flailing as she dangled from Malbrek's grip.

Suddenly, magic flew out of Klauden, a web of power soaking them all, flooding the dampening field and bouncing out from it.

Everyone froze in place, unable to move, Klauden's spell affecting everything touched by Malbrek's magic. Klauden had managed to corrupt the original spell, shifting its purpose to paralyze them in place. But he couldn't break it and cast more spells. Not yet.

Hannah was frozen, hand holding a second dagger, ready to throw. Rory stood a few feet away, body poised for action, one hand reaching for Malbrek while the other pointed at Kira. Klauden stood perfectly still, head down and hands folded in front of him, mind concentrating fiercely as he sought a flaw in the magic.

Malbrek was leaning back, in the process of falling into the chair he had scooted behind him, hand gripping Kira's ankle. The baby hung upside down, black curls frozen around her round head, eyes open and blazing. Malbrek's eyes moved too, scanning the room, trying to see what had caught all of them.

Hannah could feel the spell ebbing, could sense the power reaching the end of its ability, her fingers twitching slightly, when she heard the front door of her suite open up. There were a few soft footsteps on the stone floor of the front room, then her father appeared in the doorway, looking around the room with cool purple eyes.

"Well, this is a long-expected family reunion," he commented. He looked at Malbrek with a frown. "Kindly unhand my grandchild. That is not how you hold a baby." He stepped forward easily, unaffected by the magic in the room, a red pendant around his neck glowing brightly. He took Kira from Malbrek, hands easily uncurling Malbrek's grip on the baby's ankle. Kira immediately began to wail as Magnus touched her, and the old vampire shushed her gently, bending to grab the discarded blanket from the floor. He walked toward the table along the wall and laid the fussing child on it, his back to the room as he wrapped her up again. "There, there, sweetling," he soothed in a voice Hannah never thought to hear from her father.

The spell continued to fade, Hannah able to move her arms, but Rory was faster, wrapping an arm around Malbrek's neck with stunning speed and spinning so the magician's back was pinned to Rory's chest, the elf's arm across his neck and his other hand pinning Malbrek's arm to his side. Malbrek grunted but wasn't capable of freeing himself without magical aid.

"Father?" Hannah said, cautiously stepping toward the table and her daughter.

Magnus van Kreeosk scooped his granddaughter off the table with practiced ease and turned to face his daughter. "Now, sweetling," he addressed the baby, "it's time to meet your mother." He turned the baby in Hannah's direction. She barely spared a glance for her father, holding out both arms to take her daughter. Magnus lifted the baby up so she could see Hannah's face, a hand on each side of the blanket. Hannah took her slowly, carefully adjusting to the warm bundle as she brought her close. Kira's eyes were wide as she stared at her mother, her body still as Hannah tucked her into one arm and studied her daughter's face.

"Hi," Hannah said softly, awareness of everything else fading away in wonder, "I'm your mom." Her daughter stared up at her, big eyes huge in her pale face, purple just like her grandfather. Then she gurgled, eyes scrunching up as her mouth opened in a small circle. She gurgled again, this time more forcefully, and milky blood spilled out of her mouth and ran down her chin. She coughed, made a face, then let out a relieved sound, eyes closing and face settling into a more comfortable position. Hannah grinned, let out a small laugh, and looked at the table searching for a cloth. Her father handed her one, and she easily wiped the baby's chin clear.

"She drinks blood, then?" Hannah asked.

Her father nodded. "Sometimes." He looked across the room to where Rory still held Malbrek in his grip. Klauden had moved to stand in front of the magician, hands roving over his clothing, removing small trinkets and setting them on the footstool beside them. Hannah saw a small statue of a horse, a length of silver that could be a bracelet, and a tiny blue gemstone. "She also drinks milk on occasion." Rory's gaze flickered to the bundle in Hannah's arms for a moment, then forced his attention back to Malbrek. "Her mortal heritage, no doubt."

Klauden finished disarming the magician, stepping back and nodding deferentially to her father as he approached. "My Lord," Klauden said quietly, staring at the floor at Magnus's feet.

"Dear boy," Magnus said, tapping Klauden on the shoulder, a gesture allowing him to speak. Her father shook his head slowly, purple gaze taking in everyone in the room. Malbrek twisted a little in Rory's arms, and the elf steadied him, tightening the grip across the magician's throat. Malbrek was a fledgling, blessed with speed and strength beyond a mortal, but Rory was a newer fledgling, still stronger in his blood. Malbrek couldn't break his grip.

Hannah secured Kira in her arms and looked up, her attention expanding to include the rest of the room again.

"They are here to seize the castle, my Lord," Malbrek managed to hiss through Rory's hold on his throat. "They wish to steal your legacy." His eyes jerked to the baby in Hannah's arms. "I was protecting your interests!"

Magnus smiled, and Hannah shivered. That was never a good expression on her father's face. She may not recognize this gentle grandfather who had handed her the baby, but she knew that look, knew what came after it. Malbrek wouldn't leave this room alive. "Of course, dear Malbrek. Of course," he said in a soft voice. He gestured to Rory. "You may release him, Revanik." Rory didn't let go, frowning at the foreign name.

Hannah's mouth fell open, and she felt her shock echoed in Klauden, the vampire turning to face her father with a new expression. She knew the word meant a low-ranking outsider who married into a prominent family, like a second child from a Third Family married to a First Son from another House. There had never been a Revanik in House van Kreeosk; Hannah had always been surrounded by high-ranking pureblooded families. Even the van Joosens, Third Family in this castle, outranked First families in other Houses.

Magnus had just acknowledged Rory as Hannah's husband, a lower-ranked outsider, but her husband all the same, father of her First Daughter. She nodded at Rory, confused joy filling her as she stared at her father. The elf frowned but slowly released the magician, his arm sliding back and his hand releasing Malbrek's hand. Malbrek huffed, stepping away from Rory and standing to the side, careful to keep all of the people in the room in front of him. Klauden's hands were held in front of his chest, ready but non-threatening. Rory took a step back, eyes on Malbrek as he stepped slowly to Hannah. She nodded in reassurance, and he tore his gaze away from Malbrek to look down at his daughter.

Hannah lifted her up. "This is your father," she said, handing her to the elf who took her as if she were made of glass. Hannah stepped in front of him, giving him time to focus on Kira without worrying about Malbrek. "What now?" she asked.

"Indeed," Magnus said. "What now?" He turned to his magician. "You say they are here to seize my castle," he said. "Where is your proof?"

Malbrek scowled. "Their presence is not proof enough? They came here to steal your heir, my Lord."

"Perhaps they came to meet their child," Magnus suggested.

"Then why not use the front door?" Malbrek sneered. "They sneak in like thieves!"

"Perhaps because they do not know who can be trusted," Magnus said. "Perhaps they have been mistreated by certain personages in this castle."

Malbrek narrowed his eyes at his lord. "I have only ever protected your interests, my lord." He glared at Hannah, spearing her with years of resentment. "Lady Kreeosk can't be trusted. She's a disgrace."

"She is still my daughter," Magnus replied coolly. "I am well aware of what she is."

Hannah searched her father's face. Did he know about her mother, then, about her grandmother and the wolves? What else did he know?

"You will let her destroy you!" Malbrek insisted. "Destroy this House!"

"I fear the only one trying to destroy this House is you, dear Malbrek. Did you really believe I didn't notice your little games with Anna?" He sighed. "You used to be so much smarter. The years have cost you your edge."

Something in Malbrek's pocket flared red through the fabric of his shirt, and Hannah felt the magic-dampening spell in the room vanish, the wall between her and her magic disappearing. Malbrek cast at once, in his anger, sending a volley of flame at Magnus. Before Hannah could react, Klauden had cast a counterspell, ice coating the magician and dousing the flames before they could reach her father. Rory ducked behind Hannah, taking a knee to shield Kira with his body. Hannah released a wave of force in Malbrek's direction, her spell hitting the magician and knocking him over. At the same time, an echo of the blow thrummed in her chest.

The bond, she thought. *Its runs through Herrick and back into me.* She stared at Malbrek.

<*Can I kill him?*> She sent the thought to Klauden, who was already casting another spell to hold Malbrek in place, and she caught his quick reply.

<*Probably?*> It was not as certain as she wished, but Malbrek was spinning, ducking Klauden's spell and tucking himself behind the rocking chair.

Better make this fast, then, she thought. <*If I try to die, come find me,*> she ordered Klauden. Then she concentrated, the magic manifesting without the words she had memorized once upon a time, three other copies of herself appearing to fill the room. All four of them ran at Malbrek, two from each side of the chair.

The magician didn't know which was the real Hannah, so he attacked one of the two coming from his right side, away from where Magnus still stood. Hannah had taken the outside path, closest to the wall, and Malbrek's blow caused the Hannah beside her to disappear, shattering into shards of spent magic on the floor. He wasn't fast enough to get to her as well. Then she was behind him, a dagger pressed to his throat.

She had a moment of hesitation, of indecision, but then she remembered everything that had happened to her as a result of this man, and she dragged the blade across his neck with a savage jerk, nearly decapitating him in a wave of blood. His body stiffened against hers in surprise, then he slid slowly to the ground. The necklace he wore snapped tight, tangling in the remains of his neck, and the pendant lit up with a spell, the contingency designed to kill the one who attacked him, but Klauden was already speaking, dispelling the magic before it could affect her. Hannah stood there for a moment, one arm drenched in Malbrek's blood, letting the wave of pain flood over her own neck.

She dropped her dagger, both hands going to her neck to stem the phantom flow, then she was on her knees behind his body. She fell to the floor, head landing on the soft red carpet of her old bedroom, Malbrek's warm blood pooling around her face, lapping against her cheek, then everything was wet darkness.

XXXVI

"Hannah." The voice was more real than she expected, a sound heard with her ears instead of in her mind. It was her father's voice. Someone was lifting her body, setting her down gently in what felt like a chair. A cloth wiped at her cheek; another brushed along her arm. "Daughter," he said, and Hannah forced herself to open her eyes, body drained but still very much alive.

She was sitting in the rocking chair, her body slumped against the back. Klauden knelt beside her, wiping Malbrek's blood from her skin. Her father was on the other side, face intent on hers. Rory stood directly in front of her, Kira cradled in his arms. She tried to sit up, strength rallying. Klauden was holding her hand, his power flowing into her, and she sat up straighter, head clearing.

Glancing behind her, she saw Malbrek's body still crumpled on the floor. He was dead. She was alive. Curious, she reached out along the bond to where Herrick should be, wondering how she would find the elf. Pain greeted her, and fury, and she quickly backed away from the connection.

"I'm alive," she croaked. She cleared her throat, reassuring herself that her neck was fine, her body intact. "I'm fine," she said.

Klauden shook his head slowly. "You are not fine," he said quietly.

"But that was better," she told him, looking at him hopefully. "So much better than the fledgling by the lake," she reminded him. She looked down at herself. "Look at me! I'm still me!" She searched his face. "Maybe... Maybe I can live if they all die," she suggested.

Klauden continued to shake his head. "You barely survived Malbrek's death, a man connected to you through the body of a fledgling who, right now, is experiencing keen suffering. Herrick only lives because of you right

242

now." He let go of her hand, getting to his feet and walking away from her. "This is a connection twice removed!" He paced, then turned back to face her. "This is most definitely not good news, chaivin."

"You speak of the army massing near Lake Versin," Magnus said quietly. Hannah gave her father a sharp look. "I may be far away, Daughter. I am not ignorant." He frowned at Klauden. "The bonds remain, I presume?" He sighed. "You do manage to get into the worst kinds of trouble, Daughter."

Klauden nodded in agreement, giving Hannah a *See?* gesture. "I've been seeking a spell to break them," he admitted.

"And found nothing?" Magnus asked, face surprised. "Surely such spells exist in the world."

Klauden frowned. "We have an artifact that will sever all her ties to magic," he offered, "but it's a permanent solution. If she uses it, she wouldn't be able to remove it without the possibility of dying."

Magnus speared Klauden with a glance. "You would cut off your kevnisha for good before using the Book of Samander?" he asked harshly. "I thought better of you and your regard for my daughter."

Klauden's face collapsed under the judgement from Magnus. His emotions spiraled into a fury of guilt and humiliation, and Hannah looked at him, speaking slowly. "Klauden, you said the Book didn't have a spell that would work." She tried not to be surprised that her father knew of the Book already. Magnus van Kreeosk seemed to know everything.

"I said that I couldn't do it, chaivin. Not that it couldn't be done." His shoulders slumped, defeated in every way. The disappointment he expected from her was devastating, but the added disdain of her father was too much, to have let down both of them when it really mattered. His failure also meant that he would lose Hannah in the end; Klauden knew that without kevna, she would have no reason to stay by his side.

"Couldn't do what?" Hannah whispered, aware of the maelstrom raging inside of him, though he still stood firm, head bowed in defeat, even regret.

Klauden looked up, and Hannah felt his love, his deep desperation to save her. He looked at the judgment on her father's face, then he stared at the floor instead. "The Book has a spell," he whispered. "A spell that would bind you to me exclusively, breaking all ties to anyone else." He looked up, seeing Rory holding the baby. "Everyone else."

Hannah nodded slowly, taking in what he said. She would be free of her connection to the fledglings, but it would also break her bond to Rory and possibly her daughter. It would amplify the kevna between her and Klauden, washing away any connections she had built of her own will.

"You would live," he said quietly. "And you would be mine." He laughed, the sound bitter and awful. "But you would not be yourself any longer."

She stared at him, recalling a conversation from years before when she had discovered her grandmother's secret and left the castle. Klauden had offered then to control her mind, to hide the secret for her, to keep her safe from prying minds in the castle. She had refused, horrified by the idea that her mind wouldn't be her own.

Later, in Severin, when she'd been in Solyn's body and newly turned, he had offered a similar thing, but only to control her bloodlust until she learned how. She had accepted then, but only because it was temporary, and she didn't want to kill anyone accidentally. She knew that if she had stayed in Solyn's body, Klauden would have released her when she asked him to.

Now he could save her life using the same thing, but he wouldn't. Couldn't. Because he knew how much her independence meant to her. Klauden was staring at her, willing her to understand. *<I would rather lose you forever to a life without magic than change you into someone you are not.>*

Hannah stood on wobbly legs, crossing the floor awkwardly to grab Klauden in a hug. She didn't care that her father was there. She didn't care that Rory stood there holding her daughter. She just needed to comfort her kevnisha because he was falling apart.

"Revanik," Magnus said, jerking his head at Rory, "come with me." Her father led Rory and Kira out of the room, then spoke in a soft voice. Hannah didn't hear the rest, her attention on Klauden, soothing him, comforting him.

XXXVII

<I failed you.> Klauden's voice murmured in her head, lost and drenched in grief. *<I will not do this to save you.>*

<I understand,> Hannah told him. *<Believe me, I understand, and I love you for it.>*

He looked at her, broken features searching her expression. "You do not love me," he whispered. "I was never the one for you."

"You were," Hannah said quietly, "and you are." She put a hand to his chest, feeling their connection. "But not the way you want."

He nodded, his normally bright eyes dark blue. "I know." He put his head down. "I always knew it would come to this." His next thought was a quiet whisper in her mind: *<I always knew you would break my heart.>*

Hannah reached out and pulled him into a hug. There was nothing to say.

Klauden pulled away, sinking to his knees with his head down. *<I deserve it.>*

<You deserve so much more than this,> she insisted, giving him space.

<I should have known the baby was here,> he said. *<Maybe part of me did know. And I ignored it.>*

<Why would you do that?> She kept a neutral tone.

He looked up at her, meeting her eyes fully. "Because I knew I would lose you the moment you had a reason to leave." He looked around the room, taking in the baby furniture, eyes skidding over Malbrek's body behind the rocking chair. "You were never going to stay with me. I was a fool to let myself believe you would."

<I...>

"I know you tried," he said, still using words instead of their connection. "And I'm glad you gave me the chance, but now I wonder if I was better off before. Better off not knowing."

"Do you wish that?" she asked.

He sighed. "No." His shoulders heaved, and he climbed to his feet, pushing her out of his mind. "Don't mind me, chaivin," he said. "In a few days, you will put on that ring, and you'll never have to feel me again." He left the room, leaving Hannah alone in her old bedroom.

She stood slowly, distracting herself from Klauden's pain by taking in the new furniture, wondering what her daughter's room would eventually look like, wherever she ended up living. Hannah glanced down at the magician's body on the floor and smiled. She had dreamed of Malbrek's death many times. Satisfaction filled her, but it was fleeting. There were too many other things to consider to really appreciate the moment.

She stepped through the doorway into the front room, not surprised to see that the area where she used to keep her clothes was gone, replaced by a comfortable chair and footstool with a small table nearby. She wondered idly what had been done with all of her things.

"Packed away, Daughter," Magnus replied, reminding her that she was in her father's castle again, and she needed to guard her thoughts. Kevna was strong, but her father was stronger, or perhaps he was just that good at reading her face. Magnus glanced down to examine her old red boots. "Though I am glad you recovered your shoes."

Hannah looked down at the shoes she had found in Klauden's rooms, then up at her father. "What?"

Magnus shook his head. "I didn't expect you to notice, Daughter." He glanced at Klauden. "I thought you might, but then again," he titled his head to the side, "clearly you have been under some pressure."

Klauden looked down at the boots, his eyes widening in understanding. "You put a spell on the boots," he marveled. Hannah stared at them, not seeing the magic with her own eyes but only through Klauden's perception. So that was how her father seemed to know everything. "How did you know she would find them?"

"I know my daughter," Magnus said simply. "I knew you'd come back to get the books. I assumed she'd find them in your room."

"You let us get away," Hannah said. "But why?"

Her father shrugged, an odd motion on the old vampire. "I knew you'd be back as soon as you found out about the baby." He paused, then added, "Nicolo certainly took his time getting to the point."

"Nicolo?" Hannah asked, walking to stand near Rory and Kira. The baby was asleep in his arms, a small bundle of satisfied sounds. Rory gently handed her to Hannah, careful not to wake her. Hannah sat in the chair, adjusting the baby against her side, soaking in the feeling before looking up at her father. "Explain," she demanded.

"Giving orders in this House?" her father asked, raising an eyebrow.

"Giving orders in my room," she replied, fully meeting his gaze, every inch his daughter. "Explain."

A slow approving smile crossed his face. "Very well." He looked at Rory and Klauden in turn, rolling his eyes. "You did not make any of this easy, Daughter." He turned to Klauden. "How much have you figured out?"

Klauden frowned, his eyes scanning the room as he organized his thoughts. "You sent Nicolo with Milo to the elves. *You* want a new House allied with the elves." When Magnus nodded, he added, "And you must've known what Malbrek was up to, so you used us to get rid of him."

Magnus nodded again.

"And the baby..." Klauden's voice trailed off, uncertain of where to go next.

"The baby was a surprise," Magnus admitted. "One that I intended to use to my benefit." Hannah held her daughter tight, body tensing in preparation. Rory stepped closer to where she sat, putting his body between them and her father.

"And then?" Klauden asked, sensing a shift in the conversation's direction.

"And then she was born," Magnus snapped, but then his face grew softer, eyes warmer, "and apparently, I am a fool for daughters."

"So you sent Nicolo to Firene but had him lie to Malbrek the whole time," Hannah mused. "What did you have him lie to us about?"

Her father looked offended. "Nicolo never lies."

Hannah raised an eyebrow. "Uh, I'm pretty sure he told Malbrek a ton of stuff that wasn't true."

"Yet," Malbrek finished for her. "It's not true yet." He smiled, showing his teeth. "One of the fortunate things about being a seer is that time is relative. Everything he said will be true at some point. Maybe in the past. Maybe in the future."

Hannah frowned, disliking the idea. Nicolo had said a lot of things predicting her fate, none of which she enjoyed. An idea struck her, and she gave her father a scathing look. "I was fine, far away from all of this, settled in Solyn's body," she said. "I would never have come back here if Solyn hadn't woken up." She glanced at Rory.

"The old man in your forge," Rory said quietly, his mind following her thoughts. "The one who cast something and woke her up."

Magnus smiled slowly, eyes widening as he raised his shoulder in a slow shrug. "Maybe you needed a push to make things happen a bit sooner."

"That was Nicolo?" she asked. Her father smiled again, nodding in confirmation. "So this is all your doing," she mused. "What's your endgame?"

"Yes, what happens now?" Rory asked carefully. "What do you want?"

The old vampire pursed his lips. "I already have what I want." He gestured to the door, all business again. "You are free to go."

Hannah gave her father a suspicious look. "All of us?"

Magnus nodded again. "As you wish." He looked at the doorway to her bedroom. "Though I do recommend packing a bag for the child first, and you should probably leave the way you came in. I'd rather avoid causing a stir if possible."

"But ... you named her the heir..." Hannah stumbled.

"I named an heir," he corrected. "I didn't name *her* an heir."

Hannah stared at him. "But...?"

"Livenna," he replied. "Venna, I should say now." He looked at Hannah. "Things have changed since you left."

"Clearly," she replied. "What about Livenna?"

"She has married Vailen van Joosen," her father said, "and they are now First Family in this castle. Their daughter has been named my heir apparent, First Daughter of Venna van Kreeosk. Our family name lives on." Hannah understood. Though most of the time the wife took the name of her husband's family, this shift allowed her father to make Vailen part of his family, justifying the rank elevation to First Family through his wife's bloodline instead.

"And my daughter?" she asked quietly.

"Still my granddaughter," he replied, "but not in name."

"And me?" she asked, heart speeding up as she waited for his reply. She had never spoken so frankly with her father.

Magnus looked at Rory, nodding slowly. "You are still my First Daughter," he said, "and he your Revanik, but such titles remain among us in this room." He looked at Klauden. "Though I imagine your mother will also know." He sighed. "You may see her if you wish, but do not let the others see you."

Klauden was staring at him, his eyes wide in surprise. "My lord," he breathed.

"Yes, yes," Magnus said, "you are eternally grateful." He sighed. "Happily, you and your mother are not fools and can be relied upon." He gestured with his head to the secret door. "I imagine she will be expecting you in your rooms. Go now." Klauden spared a quick glance in Hannah's direction, and she repeated her father's command.

<You know where I will meet you,> she told him. *<Go.>*

Klauden nodded, then left the room quickly. They heard the secret door snick shut.

"Why are you doing this?" Hannah breathed, the words escaping before she could stop them.

"Can you not believe these the actions of a doting father?" Magnus asked.

Hannah narrowed her eyes at him. "Never."

"Have I been such an awful father, then?" he asked, voice softer than Hannah could ever remember it being. "Can you not believe me capable of love?"

"I don't know what to believe," Hannah admitted. "And while it may be love, I have no doubt that there's something else to be gained from this."

"I am permitted to be a foolish father as well as a crafty politician," he said with a more familiar look.

"Of course," Hannah said with a sigh. "So what do you really want from us?"

"You must start House van Sherinak," he commanded, "as soon as possible."

"What?" Hannah looked down at Kira and over to Rory. "I'm hardly in a position to start a new House."

Magnus gave her a look. "I have no doubt you will figure out how to manage it, Daughter. The Sarkoza must leave House van Lartner. He cannot go to an existing House. The balance of power among the Houses will not survive such a blow, Vanguard Code or no." He frowned, then looked at Hannah, voice the firm tone she remembered. "You must see to it that the House is established." He frowned, looking at Rory and back to Hannah again. "It would go a great deal easier for Klauden if he were wed to you, of course, but the alliance is the most important thing."

"Why?" Rory asked, face suspicious as he watched her father. "Why do you need the elves?"

"Because we have grown too many to stay in these mountains," Magnus said simply. "The elves give us a chance to be more involved in the world without being perceived as monsters." He raised an eyebrow. "The elves would not possibly ally with demons," he said with a wicked grin. "And after the elves, the northern cities will be eager to arrange their own treaties. There is a whole world south of the mountains." He glanced at Hannah. "Thank you, Daughter, for reminding me of that."

"You mean to change your image by allying with us," Rory mused. "You could not possibly be murderers, killers of children, if Firene is willing to work with you. The stories must be wrong." He frowned, considering the strategy. "Some will never believe it, even among the elves. They will always suspect you of devilry."

Magnus shrugged. "But you could say such things about any species," he commented. "There are villains among us all. So our diet is specific. We are more than what our body needs, are we not, fledgling?"

Rory raised his eyebrows, mouth twisting. "Some of you are," he admitted. "Sometimes." He glared at Magnus. "There was a time when you tried to have me killed."

Magnus chuckled. "There was a time when I tried to turn you into a fledgling," he corrected. "As was foretold." He shrugged. "We just got the timing wrong."

"Please don't talk about foretold." Hannah sighed. "I'm so tired of hearing about what is meant to be." She looked at her father. "Do you really mean to let us go?"

"I do." Magnus paused, face softening again, and added gently, "Though I do hope you are not leaving forever, Daughter. I have grown fond of the sweetling these past months."

"What?" Hannah asked, her voice higher than she expected. "You actually want me to come visit?"

Magnus nodded, face closing up again. "You could not be seen, of course. Things in this House will shift as necessary." He gave her a gentle look. "But I wouldn't mind a short visit now and then if you would."

"But who else will be in this House, then?" Hannah asked, realizing that the loss of herself and Klauden had weakened her father's influence considerably.

Magnus shrugged, pursing his lips. "Morenna, likely," he said, naming Klauden's younger sister, "and the van Oren boy will carry on Second Family. Rikerin," he added, naming one of Vailen's younger brothers, "and Millani for Third."

"Millani," Hannah echoed, "as in Milo's sister?" She frowned. "Does he know that?"

Magnus sneered. "He's a fool if he doesn't."

Hannah remembered how Millani and Linus looked talking together as they left the War Council. She had a feeling her father might be surprised when it came to the Sarkoza's sister doing his bidding.

"No worries, Daughter," her father said, easily reading her thoughts or maybe just her face. "Not all daughters are as stubborn as you are. Besides, the Sarkoza will be absent for a bit." He gave her a stern look. "Your House needs to be established well before then."

"Where is he going?" Hannah asked.

"Elsewhere," Magnus said cryptically.

Malbrek used the same word, Hannah recalled.

"What are you planning?" she asked, eyes narrowing.

"Not me," Magnus said. "But the universe has a way of making things happen a certain way."

She frowned. "Nicolo." Sighing, she stood up, cradling Kira in her arms. "I'm done listening to this." She gave her father a look, bitterness and anger and a soft upwelling of old love filling her as she saw him. "I wish you luck in your House, Father," she said formally. "I take my leave of you."

Magnus nodded, accepting the words as they were meant. He gestured at her bedroom. "I will wait until you have left to deal with Malbrek," he said. "You are welcome to his trinkets if you wish." Hannah recalled the small pile of magical artifacts Klauden had piled on the footstool. He would be thrilled to have them.

Her father gave her and Rory a stern look. "You should eat before you leave. You both look terrible, and you just got your daughter." He dipped his chin at them and walked to the door. "I will send someone." He walked out of the door without another word.

Hannah looked at Rory. "I guess we can just ... go, then?"

Rory smirked. "I never thought I'd get out of this place so easily." He shook his head. "Your people are really odd, Hannah. Just when I think I understand something, I'm proven completely wrong." He walked toward her old bedroom. "Let's pack a bag. Eat something."

"And after that?" she asked.

He looked at the baby still snuggled against her side. "One thing at a time."

THE MARIN RIVER: GORN

Gorn Haversont told himself he hadn't softened during his time in the Elven city, insisting the dull ache in his lower back couldn't possibly be from sleeping rough two nights in a row on the road from Firene. He definitely hadn't grown accustomed to those soft feather beds. No dwarf could lose his edge in so short a time.

He had just slept on a rock or something.

He stretched his back again, stepping gingerly to where Lira stood chatting with Caganasti, both elves looking way too refreshed for sleeping on the hard ground.

"Everything okay, Gorn?" Lira asked, noticing his awkward gait.

"Fine," he told her. "What's going on?"

She nodded in the direction of the Sarkoza, the dignitary deep in conversation with Linus and Saria, clearly saying something they didn't enjoy. "He wants us to go on. Alone."

Gorn frowned, looking past Lira to the lines of Elven tents and soldiers behind them, scanning to the river before them. "And why would we leave the fighters behind?"

"Because he thinks he can just tell them to go away," Lira said, voice showing how much faith she had in that plan.

"The Sarkoza has many abilities we do not possess," Caganasti said neutrally. "Perhaps it is best if a small contingent goes on ahead. The army will still be there to fight if we need them."

Gorn frowned at the wizard. He knew that Lira trusted Caga, and his time spent with her over the last years had taught him to trust her instinct, but this seemed risky. "What kind of abilities?" he asked.

"The kind that can make the army disperse if all goes well," Caganasti told him but said no more.

"And wee Hannah?"

"Klauden says there's a way to break the bonds, but they need a few more days," Caganasti said. "If we travel ahead, we can give them that time."

"You think we should do this," Lira said, looking at Caga. "There's something you aren't telling us."

"There are a great many things I do not tell you, my dear," Caganasti said, but his voice was charming, the tone teasing. "You will just have to trust me on this."

"I trust my axe," Gorn said, hand closing on the handle that jutted above his shoulder, "and I trust her." He jerked his head in Lira's direction. "I trust you to get me good ale," he told Caganasti. "What do you think?" he asked Lira.

The elf gave the magic user a searching look, sighing deeply. She rolled her eyes. "I think it looks like we're going ahead alone," she said.

"Not alone," Caganasti said. "The Sarkoza will come with us and, likely, Linus too."

"Not Saria?" Lira asked, glancing over to look at the Warmaster.

Caganasti shook his head. "She will stay with Jasper and the army here, waiting for the sign."

"Sign?"

"That it's all over or that the army is coming." The magician shrugged. "Either way, I'm sure she has a plan."

XXXVIII

When they stepped through the hidden door out of the lower tunnels, the sun was high in the sky. Rory carried a new leather bag over his shoulder, one hand resting on his weapon as they exited, eyes quickly scanning for possible threats. Hannah followed, carrying Kira in a sling secured around her waist and shoulders. The baby was asleep, face cuddled against Hannah's chest, her body a small bundle of warmth reminding Hannah of her new life with each step. Klauden was last through the door, and he turned to make sure it shut tight behind them, the wooden slats fading to gray as he cast a small spell, making this side of the door harder to spot from a distance.

Hannah and Rory turned to watch him work, and she noticed that Klauden wore a different robe. He must've changed when he went to see his mother, the difference too subtle to see in the dark tunnels using nightvision. In the midday sun, the change was striking, his new robe a fine red fabric embroidered with delicate black whorls. The vampire was always handsome, but the clothing framed his shoulders, the color complementing his pale skin, his blonde hair. Hannah sucked in a quick breath at the sight, and her desire swept over Rory as well, the elf's face reddening as he stared at the vampire. Rory took in a ragged breath, then forced himself to look away, taking a few steps down the path.

Klauden noticed their stares and frowned. "What?"

"You look great," Hannah told him. "Your mom gave you that?"

Klauden looked down, as if remembering his new clothing. "Oh, yes." He squinted at Hannah, soaking in her appreciation. "You like?"

Hannah narrowed her eyes at him. "You know I do," she snapped, turning to follow Rory. "What's the occasion?"

Klauden shrugged, following her. "Can my mother not give me a gift?"

Hannah bit back a sharp reply, trying not to direct her frustration at kevna in his direction. "How is she?" she asked instead. Hannah had always liked Klauden's mother.

"Surprisingly well," he said. He shook his head. "So much has happened," he mused. "I never thought to see such changes."

Hannah looked down at where Kira snuggled against her chest. "Nor I," she agreed. Rory turned back to check that Hannah and Klauden still followed as they made their way along the path, following the natural rock depression around several corners. They were nearly back to the camp where they had found the wolves before anyone spoke again.

"What now?" Rory asked, turning to look at them.

Hannah looked down to Kira, who was just starting to stir. She nodded at Rory, who slid the bag around so he could reach inside, pulling out a small glass bottle with pink-tinged milk inside. He handed it to Hannah with a warm smile, his fingers touching hers as he let it go, and she tugged the small cloth covering out a little bit, setting the bottle above Kira as the baby sucked the cloth into her mouth, the liquid seeping through. Hannah found a conveniently flat rock and sat down, balancing the bottle so Kira could continue to drink. She watched her daughter eat for a moment, caught up in the novelty, the idea that she had a daughter at all. The bottle was half-empty before she looked up.

Klauden and Rory were staring at her, both of their faces deep in thought. Hannah knew she should have been listening, should have heard the swirl of their thoughts, but instead, she was focused on Kira. Kevna was still present, but Hannah hadn't noticed.

"So." It was Rory who spoke, her husband looking from her to Klauden and back again.

Klauden nodded. "Where do you intend to go from here?" he asked quietly.

Hannah looked at Rory. "We need to sleep," she said, feeling the ache of exhaustion in her body now that the nervous excitement of going home had passed. They had been awake since the day before. "We still have three days," she added. "We can teleport there, to Lake Versin, right?" she asked Klauden.

"I can get us nearby," he said.

Hannah nodded, then looked at Rory, her hands tightening around Kira. "I don't think…"

Rory pursed his lips, looking at their daughter. "A battle is no place for a baby," he agreed. "I will keep her safe." He gave Hannah a hard look. "But you need to stay alive."

Hannah couldn't read his thoughts, kevna blocking her side of their fledgling bond, but she didn't need telepathy to hear his unspoken command: *Come back to me. To us.*

"I will," she promised. "I will use the ring, and then the Sarkoza can do what must be done." She frowned at Rory. "Will you go to Firene, then?"

Rory shrugged. "I can head that way. I think my daughter and I may enjoy some time in the wilds," he offered. "Let's see what she thinks of camping."

"Where will you find milk?" Hannah asked. "And blood?" She thought of the second bottle in the bag, wondering where they would find more to fill them when they were empty, the enormity of her new responsibility overwhelming.

Rory raised an eyebrow, his face calm. "The same place I will find my own meal, Hannah," he said, reminding her that he was also a fledgling, perfectly capable of taking care of himself. He gave a disarming smile. "Besides, I hear the ladies can't resist a man with a baby."

Hannah frowned at him, shaking her head in mock disapproval. "Please don't use our child as a prop."

"Our child will need to drink," Rory replied, and Hannah relented.

"I trust you to keep both of you safe on the journey," she said quietly, heart swelling as she looked at him, her elf who had so quickly jumped in to join her on this new adventure. *He could have left*, she thought. *He could be free of all of this, but he chose to stay here with me. I'm so incredibly lucky.* Rory seemed to sense the bent of her thoughts and gave her a warm smile. She returned it, appreciation filling her. He nodded slowly at her, eyes meeting hers in a perfect understanding that didn't require kevna.

Hannah glanced down at Kira, the baby slowing but not yet finished with the bottle, then turned to Klauden. The look on his face broke her heart, the vampire staring at her with longing. She could feel his anguish as he watched the easy way she talked with Rory, the two of them connected in a way that would never be broken. *<A connection,>* he reminded himself harshly, *<that she wants, that she chose. I will never have that with her.>*

He thought of Solyn and the baby and knew that there was a chance for such camaraderie between them when they discussed their child, but the possibility wasn't enough to soothe the pain of the current moment. Klauden noticed that Hannah was watching him, and his face closed, his emotions pulling back behind a curtain, the vampire trying to make it easier for her.

"Three days," he said, and the words hurt as he imagined what those days would be like, him aching for Hannah while she bonded with her baby and her elf. He looked away. "I should leave now, meet the elves on the way, join the Sarkoza."

Hannah wanted to object, kevna demanding that she cling to Klauden in the time remaining, needing to ease the pain she had caused him, but she said nothing. Nothing she could say would help.

After a long moment, Hannah suggested, "You should rest."

"I can rest later," he insisted.

"Klauden," she said sharply, drawing his face to hers, "we are near the wolves. We can camp here for one night. We can leave tomorrow."

Klauden wanted to refuse, but something in her voice stopped him, the vampire suddenly as bound by kevna as she was to please his kevnisha.

XXXIX

Colby was pleased to see them when they strolled into the camp a little bit later, cooing over Kira like a proud uncle, though he regarded Klauden with a certain amount of suspicion. After a moment of careful consideration, Hannah and Rory let him hold their daughter, the baby awake and staring at the big man with her eyes wide in fascination. Her chubby hands found the necklace around his neck, and she promptly jammed it into her mouth, baby gums drooling all over the metal.

Hannah tried to stop her, tug the necklace free, but Colby only laughed, letting her suck on the pendant as she liked. "She's a fierce wee one," he declared. "Definitely worthy of the pack." He looked at Hannah. "Like her mother."

Hannah flushed, embarrassed by the uncalled-for praise. "I'm so thankful for your help," she repeated, though part of her wondered what cost she would eventually pay for this community, knowing that being part of the pack was a benefit at the moment, but that there may come a time when they needed her help on something. She hoped she would be able to give it when they asked.

"It's nothing," he insisted. "Anything for family." Clearly, Colby had held Kerrin in high regard to feel so indebted to his descendants. The big man gave Rory a neutral look. "And friend of family, I suppose," he added. His expression as he turned to Klauden was considerably cooler. "And I imagine allies are always a good thing."

Hannah had introduced the vampire as a friend, a title that granted him admission to the camp but definitely not the warmth afforded Hannah.

"It's everything," Hannah insisted, gesturing at Kira. "You made this possible."

Colby laughed, glancing from Kira's gently pointed ears to Rory. "Not quite how this works."

Hannah grinned, narrowing her eyes at the jab. "You know what I meant." She sighed, suddenly wistful. "I wish everything in my life was so simple."

Colby sensed her sadness, tearing his attention from Kira to squint at Hannah. "More trouble, vampire sister?"

Hannah chuckled, the sound bursting out of her. She could still feel Klauden's gloomy acceptance, but the vampire sat on the edge of the campsite, facing away from them to stare into the surrounding trees. "Always," she admitted.

"Care to tell us about it?" Colby pressed. "Maybe it is another simple thing."

Hannah smiled, wishing he could help. She looked at Rory, who was watching her carefully. He gave her a small nod, shrugging, as if asking what she had to lose. "Not unless breaking bonds is a simple thing," she said with a sigh. "And it seems like it's not."

Colby's open, friendly face had grown serious at her words. "What kind of bonds?" he asked quietly, pausing as he bounced Kira on his knee. The baby looked at his face, a small line growing between her eyes as she wondered why he had stopped.

"Magical bonds," Hannah told him. "Vampire bonds."

Colby frowned. "We have such a thing. But it's dangerous." He bit his lip. "It is not something to be taken lightly."

"What do you mean?" Hannah asked as she turned to him, something like hope blazing in her chest. "Can you break bonds?"

"We are pack," Colby said, as if that explained everything. "We are bound." His face fell. "But sometimes, there are those who cannot remain pack." Kira fidgeted on his knee, making small grunting noises. Colby seemed to remember that she was there and started to slowly bounce her again. "There is an unbinding ritual," he told her.

"How does it work?" she asked, realizing that both Rory and Klauden were staring at the big man, faces guarded, but she could feel the wild hope in Klauden.

"Magic, vampire sister," he told her. "Dangerous magic."

"Tell us," Klauden asked, the vampire standing up before the leader. "Please tell us."

XL

B astan, Colby's second, explained the ritual to them in great detail. If a pack member committed an unforgivable transgression against the pack, the person would be unbound, each tie connecting them to the others neatly severed. It was a long, painful process, one that they rarely risked using. The unbound person suffered the most, but those they cut ties with also felt some pain, usually dependent on the closeness of the connection. In some cases, the unbound former pack member died, unable to bear the pain of separation.

The ritual could only be completed during the full moon, which was in two nights' time, the day before they were to meet the army near Lake Versin. They would be short on time, teleporting to the elves right before they would engage.

"But what if it doesn't work?" Klauden asked Hannah, the four of them huddled off to the side of the campsite. Rory held a sleeping Kira, watching the discussion but not saying anything, listening to both sides.

"Then it doesn't work," Hannah said. "I use the ring. I lose all magic forever, but I'm not connected to the fledglings anymore. Milo can do his thing with the army."

"But this is dangerous, chaivin." Klauden's mind was working quickly, comparing this new knowledge to what he already knew of binding magic.

She nodded. "I know that." She sighed. "Everything is dangerous, Klauden." She looked at him, wanting him to understand how much this possibility meant to her, knowing he could feel it, but that he didn't really comprehend it. "This could work!"

"And what if it works?" he asked, expression that of the patient scholar she knew so well. "What if it severs all connections you have?"

"You mean kevna," she said.

"And your bond with him," Klauden added, looking at Rory.

Hannah shrugged. "Then I lose my connections with you. Both of you." She was surprised to find that the words hurt as she said them, and she paused, wondering why she was sad at the possibility of losing kevna. She rallied, focusing on the positive instead. "But I keep my magic."

She had grown to appreciate her magic in the last day, especially when it came to cleaning Kira. She hadn't realized just how messy babies could be. She was loving it, enjoying every new experience with her daughter, but the sheer amount of liquids that came out of the baby were mind boggling. Without her magic to clean everything, Hannah would have to move next to a stream and never stop washing and drying stained fabric. "I'd like to keep my magic," she whispered.

"Is magic worth risking your life?" Klauden asked, voice quiet.

"A chance to break my bonds to the fledglings—and nothing else—is worth the risk," she told him. She stared at him, kevna letting him feel her determination, her need to try this. "You wouldn't use the Book of Samander," she reminded him, "because you wanted me to remain who I am. This is another chance to stay myself." She sighed, suddenly deciding what she really wanted. "If I must break the bonds, I will only sever the ones to fledglings," she promised both of them. "I will leave the rest as is."

What? Part of her was shocked at the words. *Why wouldn't I break free of kevna if I could?* The rest of her couldn't forget the look on Klauden's face, a look she knew she would have at the idea of losing him forever if she gave herself time to really think about it.

She bit her lip, glancing at Rory, but the elf only dipped his head in understanding, yet more evidence of the truth in his promise to her this time. *When you can, for as long as you can, choose to be with me.* He would support her no matter what she chose to do.

She reached out, taking Klauden's hand in hers, trying to reassure him. "I know you're afraid for me," she told him, "but I have to do this."

"I know," he said finally, looking down. "You have always been stronger than I am."

She cupped his chin, lifting his face to meet hers. "No," she told him. "If this goes badly, I will need your strength to bring me back." She leaned forward, placing a soft kiss on his forehead. "I still need you."

Klauden didn't reply, but she heard the words in his mind as he looked at Rory sitting with Kira, words as damning as any prophecy Nicolo could share.

<For now.>

XLI

Moonrise found Hannah standing in the center of a roughly drawn circle in the center of a copse of trees. Klauden held her left hand, the vampire on one knee at her side. Rory held her right hand, the elf kneeling on her other side. Both looked up at her expectantly, waiting.

Colby had told them that the pack member normally stood in the center, held in place by stronger members of the pack.

"Would you tie them up?" Hannah had asked.

Colby nodded. "No one willingly severs ties to the pack. It's an awful business."

"Should I be standing for it, then? Wouldn't it be easier sitting down?"

Colby had frowned at her, face sympathetic. "You will not be able to sit, vampire sister."

She looked forward to where the leader stood just beyond the circle, Kira happily tucked in one arm, the baby watching her in the circle, then shifting to stare at the big man who held her. Hannah smiled, glad to see how well her daughter had taken to the wolf leader, but a small part of her wondered if Kira simply adored everyone she met. She knew the thought wasn't true immediately—Kira loved being held by Hannah and Rory, but she was distant with Klauden, small face closing up when he came too near. She didn't go so far as to cry in his presence, but she definitely didn't enjoy him like her parents and Colby.

The big wolf nodded at her now, eyes taking in the height of the moon. Bastan, his second, stood just inside the circle behind Hannah. She thought he might have given some kind of signal because both Rory and Klauden tightened their grip on her hands. Hannah dipped her chin, letting him know that she was ready.

She was expecting to feel the magic, thinking it would be something similar to what she and Klauden could harness. Instead, a sudden vacuum enveloped her, emptying the circle of all power. She looked down to make sure Klauden was still there since he had disappeared entirely from her mind. The vampire knelt where he was, his eyes wide as he gripped her hand even tighter. She gave him a tight smile, returning the grip, then spared a glance at Rory. The elf was frowning, but his hand was steady on hers. At her look, he gave a quick squeeze of reassurance, then looked behind her at Bastan.

"Can you feel that?" she whispered.

Klauden nodded slowly. "There is nothing," he said quietly. "All magic has vanished from this circle." Rory looked up at her, gave a quick jerk of his chin, reassuring her, then looked back at Bastan.

Hannah took a deep breath, though she didn't have to. Her body didn't need more air, but she wanted the calming effect she remembered from being in Solyn's body.

I can do this, she told herself. She waited a moment for Klauden's reply, but there was only silence, as everything magical had been erased from her. The feeling was almost familiar now after the creature on the beach and the ring Rory had given her. She wondered how this ritual would break ties if she couldn't even see them.

As she had the thought, a small tendril became visible to her eyes, a thin silver thread attached to her chest and disappearing beyond the edge of the circle. She squinted at that one, wondering if it connected her to a fledgling, and suddenly she could see another one, then another. A small group of threads ran from her chest beyond the circle, most of them going in the same direction. She tried counting, but lost it as they seemed to double, then triple. She stared down at her chest, forgetting the hands holding hers.

This is so weird, she thought. No more threads appeared for a moment and she looked up. *Is that it?* A burning sensation had her look down again at another thread, this one much thicker, but somehow warped as she studied it, the cord mottled in color and sparking unevenly in places. She frowned at it, then there was another burn, this one sharper and longer. The new cord was the same thickness but bright silver and shining. It left her chest and ended in Rory's, the elf seeming oblivious to the connection, face darting between the werewolf behind her and Hannah.

"Are you seeing this?" she whispered, staring at her shared fledgling bond with Rory. "It's amazing." Rory squeezed her hand again, one quick jolt as he reacted to her words, but he didn't seem to notice the silver cord connecting them together. She looked back at the other cord, the one fizzling on and off.

"So that's Herrick," she said, shuddering at the idea of that being attached to her body. "And when Malbrek died, it broke somehow." She looked at Klauden, remembering his reaction in her old bedroom. "You were so right. I should be dead by now. That is really bad." She nodded at Colby. "So is this—"

Her words broke off as shooting pain enveloped her entire body. She would've fallen, but Klauden and Rory each grabbed an arm at the elbow and held her steady. Klauden shot an angry glance at Bastan but said nothing. Hannah opened her eyes, wondering what she would see, expecting her body to be gone somehow, but instead she squinted against the brightness of the glow, trying to make sense of the shapes now surrounding her body.

Her chest still had the tiny silver tendrils, the mottled cord, and the shiny connection to Rory. Nothing had changed there. What had appeared was the web made of light that surrounded her and Klauden, both of them encased in brilliance. Hannah could see where he held her hand, but in the bright light, his hand was actually inside of hers, his body sinking into her. Hannah reeled, the connection too much to stand.

"Klauden," she grunted, shaking her hand. "Let go of me."

The vampire obeyed, pulling his hand away—and to Hannah's eyes, out of her—but she could see the hurt on her face as he glanced at Rory, the elf still holding her hand and arm.

The light faded, but not enough. "Take a step back," she told him. "Just one."

Klauden stood and stepped back, watching her carefully. The light faded, but didn't disappear, the web around her shrinking to encase her skin. The part closest to Klauden formed into a hollow tube between them, expanding again when it reached him to cover his body. "One more step back," she ordered, watching the tube narrow as he moved, the light dimming even more. She could see the other cords again, their light no longer blinded by what must be kevna.

This explains so much, she thought, *like why it's impossible to ignore him when he's touching me. I knew the magic was strong, but I didn't think it worked like this.*

"Alright," she said roughly. "Can you see it?"

"I can see it," Bastan marveled. "Never have I seen such a thing."

"I believe you," Hannah told him. "Now what?"

"Cut them," he said simply.

"What?" she asked, looking down at the cords running out of her body. "How?"

"Sever the ties," he told her. "Break them. One by one." There was a pause, then he added, "I'd start with an easier one, the thinnest thread."

Hannah frowned. "Can I use a blade?"

"Not unless you wish to die," Bastan said. "They are magical ties. You must use your mind. You must choose to sever the connections."

"I get it. So that's why it's torture," she commented, reaching for her chest with her free hand and searching through the mass of threads to find a thin one. The person has to choose to break the connections. She wondered what happened if they weren't willing and decided she didn't want to know. She wanted to break free. "Here goes," she said, then stared hard at the cord, concentrating on it.

Her mind whisked away from the scene in the circle, following the thread across the mountains and over the river, slowing as she reached a rough campground. The cord ended in another body, a young man with dark hair who sat before a fire, face contemplative. He looked up at her, sensing her approach. Hannah looked down, seeing a ghostly outline of her body standing beside him by the fire.

"You," he said, and Hannah didn't know if he spoke aloud or not. "And yet not you," he added, staring at her for a long moment.

"Me," she replied. "Not her."

He nodded, understanding what she meant, that she was not Anna. "Are you here to end this?" he asked, his face calm as he studied her.

"I suppose so," she said. "Do you wish to be free?"

He considered, then nodded slowly. "Will I die?"

"I don't know," she told him. "Are you willing to try?"

He glanced around, seeing things that Hannah could only guess at, other bodies nearby, the quiet rumble of men talking in different languages. "I don't want to do this," he said finally, and she could feel his reluctance to join in the battle against the elves. "I don't want to die now, but I don't want to be a pawn. Set me free."

Hannah nodded, then thought about releasing him, picturing the cord between them cut with a sharp blade, there one moment and gone the next. There was a gasp as the cord vanished. Hannah caught a glimpse of his face, peaceful as he fell forward, body thumping next to the fire. She didn't think he was dead, just dazed, but the pain in her chest jerked her back into her body before she could tell for sure.

"Ow," she groaned, splaying her hand against her chest as the pain faded.

"Chaivin?" Klauden asked, poised to take a step toward her.

"I'm okay," she assured him, holding her hand out, palm facing him. "Stay over there." She glanced down at Rory, the elf's face determined as he held her up. She took a deep breath, nodded, and began to search for another thread. "I can do this."

The next fledgling wasn't as calm when contemplating his possible death, and the echoing pain in her chest was fierce. Hannah would've fallen to her knees, but Rory held her up, keeping her steady. The next two were calmer, the pain less, but after a dozen cords, sweat was pouring down Hannah's back, her muscles aching from the strain. The more reluctant the fledgling was to sever the connection, the more it hurt her, and Hannah's perception receded, shrinking to the next thread, the next cut, the next burst of agony in her bones.

Near the end, she found a familiar face at the end of one of the threads. Fergus was not the awkward young man she remembered, the fledgling grown strong with her bond and the blood. She'd wondered if she would find him still alive, hoping for Elsbeth's sake that he had escaped.

A longer look showed her that Fergus was not with the others, Rory's second from Severin standing under the stars on what looked like the deck of a ship. A familiar blonde approached, her voice quiet through the bond as she asked if he was alright.

"Is this it?" His voice was sad but resigned. "I had hoped for more time."

"I don't have to break the bond," she told him. "If you aren't with the army, you are safe. I can leave you be."

"But we'd still be connected."

"Yes. Do you want to be free?"

He looked at Elsbeth, mouth moving and words coming out, their meaning lost in the distant connection. "I wish to stay with her," he told Hannah.

"There's a chance—"

"Yes, of course," he snapped. "There's always a chance. Let me have mine."

"Very well." Hannah cut the cord, watching as his body fell forward into Elsbeth's familiar arms. *<Good luck,>* she thought, but she didn't know if he heard her.

She returned to the circle and the clearing, hands beginning to shake a little as she followed the next thread. Hannah wondered idly if she normally gained some of her strength from magic. Without any magic in the circle, she was relying on her physical and mental power instead. Her body was aching, muscles stiff with exertion as she reached for the next fledgling.

Finally, the little threads were gone, and Hannah took a long shaky breath. "I need," she tried, body exhausted. "I need—"

"She needs to feed," Klauden said, gesturing with his chin at Rory. "Help restore her strength," he ordered.

Rory stood slowly, clearly stiff from holding her upright in such an awkward position. He reached out his wrist to Hannah's face without hesitation, not caring who was watching. The wolves knew what they were, knew what they needed to survive.

"Hannah," he said quietly, pressing the inside of his wrist to Hannah's mouth, "drink."

"I'm fine," she slurred, taking a drunken step to the side, nearly falling over.

Rory caught her easily, wrapping his arms around her back and lifting her so her mouth rested against his neck. "Drink," he whispered against her hair. "Do it."

Hannah wanted to resist, to insist that she would be fine in a moment, but her body was singing from exertion. If she was going to finish this and cut the bond to Herrick, she needed more energy. She let her fangs sink into Rory's neck, relishing the blood and power flooding into her. There was nothing sexy about the feeling; this was about energy and survival, not the desire that she normally associated with such intimacy. She released him a few moments later, leaning back and letting her body adjust to the new blood. She couldn't afford to take too much and let herself get bloodstupid.

Enough, she thought, pushing Rory to arm's length. He studied her face, then nodded, stepping around to stand behind her, body holding hers upright, arms wrapped around her waist and hands tight on her hips, leaving her arms free. Klauden was watching the elf over her shoulder, the two of them having a wordless discussion that she couldn't see, couldn't hear, and she wondered at being outside and separate from the two men in her life.

I don't want to lose them, she thought clearly. *Either of them.*

She looked down at her chest; two cords remained: one snaking around to connect to Rory behind her, the other heading off into the night. She nodded, gritting her teeth as she concentrated on the cord connected to Herrick, letting herself be tugged along the battered magical bond.

The elf sat alone in a tent, seemingly waiting for her. <*I knew you would come,*> he thought, and she knew he spoke in her mind.

Even with Malbrek dead, she could feel the strength of the connection between them. This would be no quick flick of a metaphysical blade and a pain in her chest. This would be ... complicated. She stood across from the elf, taking in his pale face, the dark circles under his eyes, the new scar on his neck. She stared at it, the skin ragged and barely mended at the edges. She remembered dragging her blade across Kelvin Malbrek's neck, feeling the agony in her throat, sure she had spilled her lifeblood down her shirt. But she had woken unharmed. Herrick was not so lucky, his body bearing the physical wound.

"You've come to finish me."

Hannah nodded, disliking how much of the elf she could feel—his ambition, his rage, his self-righteous fury flooding into Hannah, making her want to set him free.

"This should never have happened," she told him, readying her mental blade, knowing that cutting this cord would be awful in different ways. She struck quickly, not letting herself worry too much, closing her eyes as her entire body lit up in agony. Herrick screamed, both out loud and in her mind, then she was nothing, floating in darkness.

XLII

"Hannah!" The voice was loud but close to her head, Rory shaking her as she slumped in the circle of his arms. Klauden's voice joined the shouting, the vampire standing in front of her again, blinding her with that light, his hands reaching to cup her cheeks as he looked at her face. The world blurred into darkness again, both voices fading.

Klauden couldn't use kevna to bring her back, so he did the only thing he could think of in the moment, leaning down to kiss her hard, mouth claiming hers. At the same moment, Rory leaned down and bit her neck fiercely, making it hurt but not sucking hard, using his teeth to mark her, both men fighting to bring her back with the shock of lust and pain.

Hannah rallied, her body stiffening in Rory's arms as her eyes fluttered open. She lifted a weak hand to touch Klauden's cheek, the other falling on Rory's head where he leaned against her neck. Both men released her, Klauden staring into her face, thinking frantic thoughts that she couldn't hear. Rory kissed her neck gently over the place he had bitten, raising his head to stare over her shoulder at Klauden.

His face must've asked the question because Klauden's eyes darted in that direction, and he nodded quickly. "She's back." He searched Hannah's face as she blinked a few times, still dazzled by the light.

"I'm back," she mumbled, closing her eyes but keeping her feet. "Klauden, step back. It's too much."

He moved back, but she saw hurt flash on his face as he did, again glancing at Rory. She grabbed his finger, not wanting him to think she didn't want him. "It's everywhere," she tried to explain, "and I can't see anything else around it. If you move away, I can do what I need to do to finish this."

Finish this, Hannah thought, opening her eyes to look around the circle, finding Colby standing where she had left him, still holding Kira, the baby's wide eyes watching the trio in the circle. Hannah wondered if she could see the remaining cords.

"It's done," she said, leaning back against Rory's chest. "They're gone."

There was a pause, a polite cough, then Bastan said, "They are not all gone."

Hannah's chest tightened. She looked down at the cord binding her to Rory, at the web joining her to Klauden. "But..." she began, then found her voice. "The ties to the fledglings are gone," she told them. "Herrick is gone." She stepped away from Rory, anger giving her strength, and turned to face Bastan. "The ritual is over."

"The ritual is over when all bonds are severed," Bastan said. "You did not say you wanted to keep some of yours."

"I didn't know I wanted to keep them," she admitted. "But I'm sure now." She glanced at Rory and over her shoulder at Klauden. The vampire had stepped closer to her but stayed a step away, not wanting to overwhelm her with whatever she could see. "It's over."

Bastan lifted his hands, sadly shaking his head. "The ritual is over when every bond is cut," he said. "I cannot stop it."

"Then I will," Hannah said. She grabbed Rory's hand and reached behind her to grab Klauden's hand, intending to march all of them out of the circle. The pain was agonizing, every muscle in her body lanced with agony, and she screamed, unable to stop it. Her body jerked with pain, but Rory and Klauden gripped her hands tighter, neither one letting go.

She looked up when she could, the pain fading after a moment. She saw Rory, his face set, supporting her in whatever she chose to do. She could break their bond, and he would forgive her. But she didn't want to let him go.

Turning to Klauden, she bit her lip, seeing the vampire without the influence of kevna. She could see their connection, and she could break it if she wanted, could cut through each one of those strands binding them in a web. It would hurt, but not as much as trying to walk out of this circle with those ties in place.

This is what you wanted, she told herself. *A way to be free of him. I know.*

She gave him a sad smile, for all the pain she'd caused in his life. *I could set him free,* she told herself. *He should be free.*

His words from the beach echoed back to her: *Even if you get what you want, if your elf takes you back, and you leave with him, abandoning me with Solyn to make our own way in the world, I will never be free of you. And I don't want to be. Ever.*

I don't want to do this, she realized. *I don't want to sever my bonds with either of them.* Hannah's heart shifted, or perhaps she at last understood it, seeing the truth in herself. She nodded, the decision already made.

I will not do this.

Gritting her teeth, she took another step closer to the edge of the circle. The pain doubled, muscles rigid in agony, but somehow, she took the next step, and the one after that. She would make it, she told herself, not knowing if the screams were out loud or in her head anymore. She had to make it.

But her strength was fading, the boost from Rory's blood already gone, her body sagging forward, slowly falling. *I'm not going to make it.*

Then Rory was standing behind her, one leg pushing hers forward. Klauden stood behind her other side, his leg pushing hers, and the web spilled over all of them. The pain eased for a brief, glorious moment, and both Rory and Klauden cried out, the agony hitting them both instead of her. They shuffled forward once more, all three of them screaming, then they were out of the circle, all of them tumbling to the ground in a boneless heap.

XLIII

"That was…" Hannah's words trailed off. She looked down at Kira instead, her daughter asleep in her arms, warm bundle reassuring against her chest. Hannah's body still ached from the strain of the ritual, but being with Kira was restorative in other ways.

"Foolish," Klauden finished for her, the vampire sitting on her right side, occasionally looking up at where the moon had started to set.

"Successful," Hannah told him. "I'm no longer bound to the fledglings or to Herrick. I'm free."

"Are you?" Klauden asked, and Hannah felt the questions in him, his desire to know why she would choose to stay bound to him when she could have been truly free.

Hannah looked at Rory, the elf sitting on her left side and contemplating the fire before them. He hadn't said much since they woke from the ritual, lost in his own thoughts. She glanced down at Kira, then back at Klauden. "I am as I choose to be," she told him. "And I shall remain myself. This has been a huge success," she repeated.

"Yes," Rory said quietly, "a success." He narrowed his eyes at Hannah. "But he's right. It was foolish."

"I couldn't lose you," she said, looking at them both in quick succession.

"We almost lost you," Rory said. "It was a foolish risk." He sighed. "I know why you did it, but it could have killed you."

"But it worked," she said, nudging him with an elbow.

"I'm thrilled that it worked," Rory said honestly. "But I'm not thrilled that you chose to do it at all." He looked at Kira. "Will you be so careless with your life when you face Herrick? She needs a mother, Hannah."

275

Guilt sliced through Hannah, followed by a flash of annoyance. "You all need me," she said firmly, "and I need you. Would you expect me not to fight for us?" She marveled at how easily the shift had happened, her acceptance of her connections to both of them.

Rory sighed, then a soft smile crossed his face, his worry for her passing into grudging admiration. "Never," he said. "But I need you to think of yourself, Hannah. I need you alive much more than I need a bond to you."

Hannah groaned. "I don't know if I could have broken the bonds with you," she told him honestly. "Even if I wanted to." She looked down at Kira again. "It took all of my strength just to stop it."

"If you want to, you can do whatever you want," Klauden said in a weary voice. "Nothing ever stops you, chaivin."

"Would you have done it?" she asked him. "Broken the bond with me if you had the chance?" Klauden looked away, but she knew the truth. "Right," she said, adjusting Kira in her arms, "you would've done the same thing." She smiled at Kira. "And don't guilt me because of the baby. You're a father now too."

Klauden frowned at the mention of Solyn, his face growing distant as he reached out to check on his fledgling. Hannah sensed that all was well in Firene, Solyn spending time with Millani and Eriken, though both still treated her like an underling. Hannah wondered if such things would change over time in the new House. She hoped so. Solyn deserved to be well treated for once in her life.

"It's time," Klauden said softly, glancing once more at the moon. He got to his feet in a flurry of robes, giving her and Rory some time alone.

Hannah nodded, briefly squeezing Kira before setting her down on the blanket. The baby stirred but didn't wake, her face settling back into sleep. Hannah looked from her daughter to Rory. "You stay safe," she told him. "I need both of you in my life."

"I know," Rory said, reaching out to touch her face gently. "But I'm more worried about you."

"I won't do anything foolish," Hannah promised. "I will make sure Herrick is dead, and that's it."

Rory nodded, knowing that she had to go but still hating it. "I expect you to come back to me." He paused, then added, "For as long as you can."

He looked over at where Klauden stood, knowing that, at some point, Hannah would have to marry the vampire.

"Will you stay here, then?" she asked, looking across the fire to where the wolves hunkered down in their own conversation.

"Colby asked me to stay for a time, just until this business is settled with the army," Rory said. "I don't think he wants Kira to leave yet."

"Make sure that man doesn't steal our baby," Hannah teased.

"Of course," Rory said. "He wouldn't stand a chance." He grinned. "I'm glad she will have people in her life to help her," he said quietly. "She will never be alone."

Hannah knew his meaning. Her and Rory's lives had never been particularly quiet, danger seeming to find them everywhere. If something happened to them, Kira would still be taken care of. It was reassuring.

"I will find you after," Hannah said, getting up on her knees and leaning forward to give Rory a hug goodbye. His mouth found hers for a soft kiss, a promise that Hannah returned. She leaned down to kiss Kira on the forehead and stood up. Rory lifted Kira gently and got to his feet, following her to where Klauden stood.

"Be well," Rory said to Klauden, raising his free hand to his forehead, then to his lips.

"She will come back to you," Klauden promised, reaching out to take Hannah's hand. "I swear it."

XLIV

The magic deposited them on a road near the north side of the Chripsen Forest. Hannah landed solidly, finally adjusting to the way the spell worked. She didn't let go of Klauden's hand right away, though, taking a moment to look around while enjoying the feel of him close to her. To her left, the dirt road wound close to the edge of the trees. She looked at Klauden, trying to imagine him in this very spot a few months before, at the start of his journey to find her in Severin.

He tipped his head in the direction of the forest. "Lake Versin is that way, but Caganasti says they've made a small camp just to the east."

"So close? Won't the fledglings attack?"

Klauden shook his head. "Apparently, the bulk of the army is back near Firene, across the river, ready to stop them if they make it that far."

"So why are we so close to them? And what is Caganasti doing in the no-man's-land between two armies?"

"Only a small group is nearby." Klauden frowned. "Apparently, the Sarkoza plans to use his Voice to dispel them all."

Hannah's eyes widened. "Can he really do that?"

"His power is very strong," Klauden speculated. "I would not be shocked to see him command armies."

"But he doesn't need to command all of them," Hannah told him. "Some of them wanted no part of this fight. They left when I broke the connection." She paused. "Or they died."

Klauden threw her a sharp look. "Died?"

"I don't think they did," Hannah said quickly. "I know Herrick didn't. But the others?"

"The goblins will scatter when the leaders cease to lead." Klauden looked around at the trees surrounding them now. "Though I wouldn't want to live around here for the foreseeable future. The goblins will spread everywhere, and they, too, need to eat."

Hannah bit her lip. "Klauden, what did my father mean when he said that Milo would be elsewhere?" Klauden frowned, recalling that both Malbrek and Magnus had used the word. "Will he die?"

Klauden shook his head. "I don't think so. It's a very specific thing to say, as if they didn't know what happens to him, only that he isn't here."

"If something happens," she said suddenly, "and I'm not—"

Klauden stopped her, stepping close to lay a gentle finger across her lips. "No," he said quietly. "None of that."

Hannah sighed, reaching up to take his finger into her hand. "But this could go badly," she began.

"No," Klauden repeated, lifting his hand back to her mouth.

She spoke around him. "I know I never think about the future, but now—"

Klauden slid his hand to her cheek, leaned forward, and kissed her, silencing her words with his mouth. Hannah let herself be kissed, wondering if she should feel guilty since she had promised to return to Rory, but then she remembered the elf's face, his words as they pledged their intentions. He would understand. Hell, he probably could feel some of it. She returned the kiss, letting herself fall into Klauden, the magic covering them both.

Eventually, he pulled away, eyes darkening as he recalled their exposed position with an army nearby. Hannah left her hands on his shoulders, looking at him, feeling the same pull. "This doesn't change anything," she said quietly. "I'm still going back when this is over."

Klauden nodded. "I know." His fingers trailed in her hair, twisting a curl around and around. He looked up at her, face serious. "But you will come back when we marry."

"I will," she promised, face heating in guilt. "But it's in name only, Klauden," she reminded him. "I can't..." She struggled to find the words. "It's not fair to either of you."

"None of this is about fairness," he told her, letting his hands return to his sides.

She grabbed his hand, tugging him back to her. "But I mean it—if something happens to me, I need—"

"Chaivin!" he said in a voice louder than she had expected. "I have pulled you back from the edge of death more than once. I'm fairly confident I can get you through a simple battle."

Hannah laughed, unable to stop herself. "A simple battle?" she repeated. "You've changed so much, Klauden."

He sighed, rolling his eyes. "Let's go find them and see what the Sarkoza has planned."

"We can scout, at least," she suggested. "We're so close." She chuckled. "Sure would be nice if I had a connection to one of them," she commented. "I'd know when they plan to move."

Klauden looked skyward. "Not long now," he said, judging the height of the moon and the hours left before dawn. "Caganasti has been scrying most of the day. I assure you, he knows their plans."

They set off to the east, following the edge of the forest and moving away from where the army should be camped. "So who's with Caganasti, then?" Hannah asked. "Just the Sarkoza alone?"

"Apparently, Linus is with them," Klauden said, shaking his head.

"Where is Jasper?"

"Back with the bulk of the army beyond the river. Saria is there with him."

Hannah nodded. "So just the three of them?" she asked. "It's good that it's a small group, but they don't have any real fighters."

"Caganasti is a master wizard," he commented, raising an eyebrow.

"Well, yeah," she agreed. "But he's not a fighter." Her tone made her pause, realizing the subtext.

"You don't think me a fighter, chaivin?" Klauden asked, reaching out a hand to hold hers as they covered a particularly treacherous pile of tree limbs.

Hannah scoffed. "You're definitely useful in a fight, Klauden. Don't get me wrong—but there is something to be said for a solid fighter at your back."

"You speak of your elf, no doubt."

"I've been in lots of fights, Klauden," she said. "Magic is great—when it works. But if they get close, I don't care what kind of fireball spell you cast. It still won't stop a well-aimed sword."

"You just faced a dangerous ritual so you could keep your magic, chaivin," Klauden observed. "You think your powers useless?"

Hannah shook her head. "No, but I prefer the reliability of a good blade," she admitted.

"Then you will be relieved to know that they are not alone and defenseless with only a master wizard and the Sarkoza," he said, sarcasm thick in his voice. "Two fighters are with them, at Saria's insistence, of course."

"Good," Hannah said. "Not that I doubt Caganasti's ability to throw spells or the Sarkoza's Voice."

"Except ... you doubt both, chaivin," Klauden pointed out, glancing at her. "You think your presence will be enough to turn the tide of battle?"

Hannah frowned, aware of how egotistical she sounded. "If I were still connected to them, I could be useful," she said finally. "But as I am?" She shrugged. "I guess I'm just here to help."

"That's all any of us can do," Klauden agreed.

They walked in silence for a time, vampire speed allowing them to cover way more ground than a normal human. Even Klauden moved with a certain grace, though it would never match the way Rory now moved as a fledgling. Hannah imagined a time someday when the two of them could practice together. She wondered if she could still take him down and smiled at the thought. Klauden must've caught the image because he glanced at her. Hannah expected his face to be sad, but instead, there was a new acceptance there, an understanding.

They were still holding hands when they approached the small campground a few hours later, the sun just beginning to peek over the horizon. Hannah yawned, body adjusting to the daylight, promising herself that she would sleep when all of this was over. Perhaps for a solid two days.

Klauden grinned at her, stifling a yawn of his own as they walked out of the trees into the small clearing. The fire was low, but Hannah recognized the seated form of Caganasti from behind, the elf's topknot a stark outline against the soft red glow. He didn't turn as they approached. Linus was sitting near the fire, a steaming mug in one hand, eyes still heavy with sleep. Milo was on his back, still on his blanket but clearly awake and ready for the day. He seemed to be studying the last of the stars.

The other two people in the camp were a surprise, and Hannah's face lit up with a broad grin. "Lira!" she shouted, letting go of Klauden's hand and leaping over to the elf. She was not surprised to see the stocky dwarf sitting beside the gorgeous blonde.

"Wee Hannah!" Gorn exclaimed. "They said you'd be coming."

"What are you doing here?" Hannah asked, her heart glad to see her old companions.

Gorn gestured at the others. "They needed someone to look after them while they did their thing," the dwarf said, his voice low. "Damn mages think they're invincible."

Lira frowned, but she didn't contradict him. "I am glad to see you well, Hannah," she said. She glanced behind Hannah to where Klauden stood, already in conversation with Caganasti. "And *this* must be the famous Klauden," Lira added, sizing up the vampire with keen eyes. After a moment, she nodded. "I get it," she told Hannah.

"Get what?" Hannah asked, but Lira only rolled her eyes.

"Did you manage to break your connection to the army?" Lira asked instead, and Hannah stared at her.

"How do you know about that?" she asked.

Lira gestured in Caganasti's direction. "Caga is an old friend," she said. "He tells me things."

There was something in her voice that made Hannah think there was more there than just friendship, and Gorn met Hannah's gaze, eyes widening meaningfully. Hannah smiled, happy for the elf. She knew that Lira had loved Rory for a time, but she also knew that their friendship was deep, forged over a century of companionship, nothing more.

"Does he now?" Hannah asked, raising an eyebrow.

Lira scoffed, tearing her gaze from the tattooed elf. "It's not like that," she insisted. "We're friends."

Hannah nodded slowly, not believing her for a second. "Of course," she said. "He's super friendly."

Gorn chuckled. "It's good to see you so well, wee one," he said, reaching out to tug her into a hug. "We thought we'd lost you."

"I think I lost myself," she said, leaning into the hair that met his beard.

The dwarf pushed her away to arm's length. "And now?"

"And now ... it's better," she said. She glanced behind her to where Klauden stood next to Caganasti, Milo joining their conversation from where he lay on his back.

Gorn looked from the vampire to her and back again. "So, where is Rory?" he asked casually.

"Safe," Hannah said immediately. "He has our daughter," she added with a smile.

The dwarf's face lit up. "A daughter!" he exclaimed, nudging her in the ribs. "Well done, lassie!" he turned to Lira. "Did you know about this?" he asked.

Lira shook her head, her face pleased but speculative. "You and Rory have a daughter?" she asked. "Do his brothers know?"

Hannah shrugged. "I honestly don't know. I just found out, then we left right away. Maybe someone told them?"

"Someone told us what?" Linus asked, the tall elf walking over still holding his mug, the contents no longer steaming in the morning air. "I heard my brother's name." He looked around, then at Hannah. "Where is Rory?"

"He's fine," Hannah assured him. "He's staying away from the fighting."

Linus raised an eyebrow. "Can I ask why my brother, the former Warmaster, is not here to face an entire army?"

Hannah smirked at him. "Because your brother is currently taking care of our daughter," she said. "Congratulations! You're an uncle."

Linus glanced behind him to where Klauden stood. "But Solyn is still in Firene," he said, confused.

"Not Solyn," Hannah said. "Me, apparently."

Linus raised an eyebrow, but then understanding flooded his face. "When you weren't in your body," he mused. He looked at her, smirking as he added in a low voice, "But you told them that you'd only been with Rory in the other body. Did I misunderstand some crucial rule? I thought it was important that you hadn't been with my brother."

Hannah bit her lip, remembering the awkward war council discussion about her purity. "It can be important," she said, "where I came from. But in this new House, I think some of those rules will change."

"Already changed, you mean," he said. "What does this mean for your alliance with van Sherinak?"

"Nothing has changed," she said. "I will marry him and legitimize the House."

"But a child with the Tallerin..."

"*A* Tallerin," Hannah corrected. "Rory no longer wants part of that, if he ever did."

"But a Tallerin does not always get to decide his fate," Linus said. Hannah wondered how much he referred to himself, recalling the way he and Millani looked at one another.

"Maybe that's something else that should change," she commented.

Linus agreed. "When this is over, we have a lot of things to discuss, Sister mine."

Hannah smiled at the title, recalling how he had used a version of it during the war council. "I'll be glad to," she said, "after I return to Rory, and we decide what we plan to do."

Linus smiled, eyes approving. "My brother is a lucky man," he said finally. He glanced back at Klauden once more, shaking his head. "And hopefully better at navigating complicated situations than in his youth."

Hannah caught Lira's eye. Both she and the elf stared at Linus, their faces showing support for the absent Tallerin. "Rory will be fine," Hannah said finally. "I'm more concerned about what we are doing here. What's the plan?"

XLV

"I just need to be close enough for them to hear me," the Sarkoza said. "I can help with that," Caganasti offered. "I can amplify your voice so they all hear." The elf frowned. "But we will all be in range of your voice," he added. "What will it do to us?"

The Sarkoza shook his head, dismissing the threat. "Nothing," he told them. "You think I cannot control those affected?"

"I think you have an insane amount of power with that gift," Caganasti said quietly. "A gift that some would see as a threat."

Linus frowned, squinting at the vampire, his mind sifting through possibilities, but he said nothing, the normally jovial elf quiet as they stood on a small bluff overlooking Lake Versin. The army spread out beneath them, mostly goblins now, but a handful of fledglings still lingered.

One had stood guard on this bluff, but his body rested in a crumpled pile a few feet away, an arrow through the heart from Lira's bow knocking him down, Klauden's magic keeping him silent so he couldn't sound any alarm before Gorn approached and lopped off his head. Hannah felt nothing at his death, though she shivered, unable to stop it.

One fledgling was no match for this group of warriors, but in one-on-one combat, if it came to that, some of their people might be in danger. Hannah had studied Linus, the sword on his hip seeming more decorative than anything else. Clearly, that brother had gotten different gifts.

The Sarkoza looked at Caganasti and nodded. He was ready. Caganasti began to cast, a simple enough spell, and Hannah stepped back, away from Milo. The others did the same, not wanting to be in front of that Voice. They knew what he could do in theory, that he was persuasive, but they had never seen it used. Hannah wondered if part of them didn't believe it could be done at all.

"Listen," the Sarkoza whispered, his voice echoing to the army below. Hannah felt herself stop, body pausing to pay attention to the sound of his voice. She knew it was happening, but she still couldn't stop herself. Klauden was behind her then, his hand on her shoulder, and she felt part of herself break free from Milo's power, kevna keeping her and Klauden separate from the spell.

"Depart this place," the Sarkoza suggested. Hannah's foot lifted, her body wanting to obey, but she forced it back down with kevna's help. She could feel Klauden start to move away from her, but then he flexed his hand on her shoulder, the touch bringing him back.

Linus backed up immediately, Lira and Gorn following for a few steps, but then they shook their heads, pausing as they stared at the Sarkoza's back. Caganasti didn't move, seemingly immune to that silky whisper.

"Go home if you can, or someplace that seems fine to you," the Sarkoza suggested. Part of Hannah sighed, wanting to obey but unable to since she didn't know where her home was anymore. She leaned into Klauden's hand on her shoulder, reaching back with her other hand to twine her fingers with his. The goblins below had started to move, some running, some taking awkward steps. Voices began yelling, obviously not as affected by the words, ordering them back in place.

"You do not have to stay here," the Sarkoza told them. "You are free." He paused, then added, "The elves are not your enemy." He looked over his shoulder at Linus, who seemed to remember himself and nodded. "Your enemy is Herculindarus Canadys," he said softly, the name sliding off his lips. "When Herrick is dead, you can be free."

There was a low shout from below as bodies swarmed around a small white tent. Metal clanged as goblins began to fight one another, then a larger scuffle erupted in front of the tent. Hannah's keen eyes made out the distant form of the Elven former healer, body thin and waif-like as he swung his sword wildly. A blonde man jumped on him from behind, and Herrick disappeared under a pile of bodies. Hannah waited to feel something, anything, as her former fledgling died, but there was nothing. His was a distant end, another dead fledgling in the world.

After a moment, the crowd near his body began to slowly disperse, goblins heading this way and that, a handful of men trailing into the woods to the south and east of the lake. They had abandoned most of their belongings, tents and campfires and racks of food and weapons left where they were. They waited for a time, making sure that no one remained clustered in groups, then Caganasti stopped his spell. The Sarkoza turned to face them.

Hannah heard Linus inhale a sharp breath, the repercussions of such power finally sinking in. "Do you understand what just happened?" the Sarkoza asked, still using the power of his voice. Hannah stood still, protected with Klauden by kevna, but she saw Linus, Lira, and Gorn nod slowly. "You see what I can do."

The Sarkoza glanced at Caganasti, and the elf agreed reluctantly, rolling his eyes, clearly agreeing with something half-heartedly. Milo turned back to the group. "When they ask what happened here, you will say only that I am persuasive, and that you'd rather not speak of it again." He waited for them to nod slowly. "You saw a brilliant battle. Master van Sherinak is a powerful magician. I am a formidable foe. There is nothing more to be said." They nodded again, faces blank. "The army is gone. Someone will need to come and clear this up."

Linus nodded slowly, his face vacant as he stood under the Sarkoza's power. "I will send them."

"You will tell no one my true power," the Sarkoza said, voice firm and clear. Lira and Gorn nodded slowly, faces empty of personality.

The Sarkoza turned to face Hannah and Klauden, eyebrow raised as he considered them. "You seem immune," he commented. "Interesting."

"We will tell no one," Klauden said, his voice firm as he stood behind Hannah, a hand gripping hers. She caught the thoughts from his mind. In a fight like this, against just Milo and Caganasti, Klauden thought she and he might have a chance. But if he decided to turn the others against them, it would end badly for them. It was very important not to upset the Sarkoza, Hannah decided. She blinked, eyes wide, agreeing with Klauden.

Milo turned to look at Caganasti. "I expected you were immune," he said. "But did you know about them?"

Caganasti shook his head. "I did not. But I'm not shocked. Kevna is powerful." He paused, then added, "But not as powerful as the forces of destiny around them both."

Milo sighed, shaking his head. "I tire of everyone talking about destiny," he griped, and Hannah couldn't help but smile. She knew exactly what he meant.

"Now go, return to the others," the Sarkoza said dismissively. "We will catch up."

Hannah gave Lira, Gorn, and Linus a nervous glance as they turned obediently and walked away.

<What about all those goblins and fledglings?> She sent the thought to Klauden, unwilling to speak in front of Milo yet.

<That's why they have fighters with them,> Klauden snapped. *<They should be fine. I would think you'd be more worried about us poor, helpless magic users.>*

<I'm more worried about what happens when Milo decides he doesn't want an alliance anymore,> she told him. *<If we weren't together and touching right now, could he influence us like that? Could he make us think whatever he wanted?>*

<I don't know,> Klauden replied, his thoughts speculative in her mind. *<Perhaps this is why he travels "elsewhere" in the near future.>*

Hannah frowned. *<Should we tell him?>*

<No! Didn't you hear? The man is tired of hearing about his destiny.>

XLVI

Hannah stood under the tapestry in the war room in Firene, Kira smiling in her arms as she held the baby facing the bright colors of the weaving, bouncing her slowly the way she liked. They had been back in Firene for two days, mostly in Rory's old rooms and down on the beach, but they both knew this meeting was coming. They had spent a few weeks with the wolves, then another few weeks on the road as they slowly made their way back to the Elven city. Figuring out their new dynamic had been interesting, both of them still feeling their way in the relationship while they suffered from the normal sleep deprivation a child brings. Kira was a good baby, easily satisfied and generally content, but they still slept in small shifts, building a new normal for their family.

Now Rory sat on the table's edge, his long legs swinging back and forth as they waited for the others to arrive, mouth opening in a big yawn as he cracked his neck and gave her a soft smile. Hannah had seen Klauden for a little bit the day before, the two contemplating possible paths forward for the new House. Milo had grown insistent, wanting to know when and where they planned to marry. Hannah remembered what he had done with the army, and she didn't want to upset the Sarkoza.

Linus had called this meeting to settle the matter. Rory's brother walked in next, smiling at his niece, offering a small wave. The baby giggled, but she wasn't inclined to leave Hannah's arms.

A moment later, Klauden came in, followed by Solyn, her rounded belly pushing out beyond her breasts now. The fledgling sat gratefully, heaving a sigh as her body sank into the chair. Klauden leaned against the table, lips pursed, but he didn't sit. His mind whirled with ideas, considering each quickly before discarding it. He glanced at Solyn, wondering—not for the first time—how she would react when he and Hannah finally went through with it and married. She seemed to be fine with the idea, accepting her role as fledgling rather than wife or mate, but he had learned that women could change rapidly, especially pregnant women. He didn't love Solyn the way he loved Hannah, but he cared for her, and he wanted her to be satisfied with him. He glanced over at Hannah, who seemed to have figured out how to be a family with her elf, and she smiled at him, knowing his mind. They nodded at one another, not speaking yet, waiting for the last member of the meeting to arrive.

Milo entered a few moments later, taking a seat at the table. The vampire still looked as nondescript as ever, the kind of face to easily disappear in a crowd, but Hannah had begun to wonder how much of his appearance was by design, carefully crafted to keep others comfortable around him, especially those who knew about his gift. Hannah forced herself to smile at him, wary as she would be around a dangerous animal, one who could turn on her at any moment. She liked Milo, but she would never really trust him again, not after what he had done with the others on the cliff.

Her and Klauden's mind remained their own, but Linus, Lira, and Gorn were unable to talk about what they had seen. Their reluctance had sparked many rumors—mostly focused on how the new alliance with the House was a stroke of military genius, and the leader of that House, Klauden van Sherinak, was a force to be reckoned with.

Hannah sighed, looking down at Kira, who gurgled happily. She wanted to leave Firene and the new House and all of these responsibilities and expectations, to relax with Rory somewhere safe and quiet with their daughter.

Linus acknowledged everyone in the room, sitting down a few seats away from Rory. The elf spun on the table, tucking his legs up so he faced his brother but clearly not bothering with a chair. Hannah turned away from the tapestry, not sitting down either, continuing to bounce Kira as she stood.

"So," Linus began, "we have a minor situation."

"Hardly minor," Milo said, giving Klauden and Hannah a pointed look, clearly unhappy. "We have waited long enough. It is time."

"I know," Hannah said, glancing at Rory, who in turn looked at Klauden. The vampire sighed, then sat beside Solyn, hand taking hers in what seemed an unconscious gesture. "What would you have us do?" Hannah asked. "How do we proceed?"

Linus cleared his throat. "Would you bear with me for a moment while I make a suggestion?"

Everyone turned, their faces expectant.

Linus looked at Klauden. "You need Hannah and her family name in order to gain the support of the other Houses." When Klauden nodded, he added, "But you plan to live with your fledgling. According to your customs, she cannot be your wife. Is that correct?"

Klauden frowned, then nodded his head. For everything that might change at Castle van Kreeosk, Klauden wasn't foolish enough to start a new House with a fledgling bride and be taken seriously by the other Houses. He would need a proper wife from a First Family, like Hannah.

He glanced at Hannah, watching her face as she realized that this marriage might be as much of a burden to him as it was to her.

<Klauden, do you want to marry me?>

<We already agreed, chaivin. It's part of the Elven alliance.>

<I know all that,> she told him, *<but I'm asking you—do you want to marry me?>*

There was a long moment before he replied, his voice quiet in her head. *<I have wanted to marry you for as long as I can remember,>* he admitted. *<You've always been part of any future I imagine.>* He glanced over at Rory. *<And I'm happy for you, truly I am. I just want to have you in my life in whatever way works for you.>*

Hannah bit her lip, struck by the similarity to Rory's words, overwhelmed with gratitude. *Who am I to be so lucky? I have the most understanding men in my life.* Her eyes filled with tears, and she looked away, focusing on Kira as she sniffed, reining in her emotions.

Regaining control, she looked at Klauden, then at Solyn. *<If you want to be with Solyn, you should be with her,>* she told Klauden. *<We can figure something else out.>*

She heard Klauden's soft chuckle in her mind. *<I'd rather not work something else out with the Sarkoza.>*

She grinned at him. *<We can totally take him.>*

<*Maybe,*> Klauden agreed. <*But let's not tempt fate. Marry me.*>

Hannah relented, knowing she would. <*I will.*>

Linus was watching their faces, clearly suspecting that something was going on between them, but only a moment had passed. "That is correct," Klauden said out loud.

Linus nodded, then turned to Rory, the elf sitting on the table, hands on his knees as he watched his brother. "And you," Linus said, "don't wish to stay here and rule Firene."

Rory's shoulders jerked at the words, but Hannah could see the truth in the way Rory turned to look at her and Kira. He looked beyond them at the tapestry on the wall, the scene an Elven victory, then back at his brother, shaking his head. Hannah understood. She did have some love for her people, though not nearly as much as Rory had for his, but that sense of loyalty was nothing compared to the way she felt looking at her daughter. "No, Brother," he said, "I do not wish to rule here."

"So we must find a way to make you unsuitable," Linus mused. "Well, more unsuitable," he added, turning back to where Hannah stood. "And we need to solidify the alliance between Firene and House van Sherinak with some kind of public display." He looked at all of them. "A situation indeed," he said, but he was smiling in a way that said he'd already seen the whole picture. "A lord in need of a proper lady, and another lord in need of an improper one." Linus pursed his lips. "Have you heard of peace-weavers, Sister mine?"

Hannah considered. She had read something of the practice long ago in the library beneath the castle. "You mean women married to secure alliances?" she asked. "Doesn't that usually end in bloodshed?"

"Sometimes." Linus shrugged. "Other times, it's settled old debts and forged peace."

Hannah had a sneaking suspicion of where this was headed. "And why would you mention peace-weavers?"

"An alliance between Firene and the newest House of the Vanya would be a great honor," Linus said. "Such a union would certainly promise to bring peace between our people." He looked to Rory again. "And you, Brother, could certainly not rule Firene without an elven Consort at your side. But the people would never believe that you didn't intend to return one day to rule. Not unless you had married an outsider."

"Wait," Hannah stopped him. "Are you suggesting I marry *both* Klauden and Rory?"

Linus nodded. "Exactly."

"But how?"

"You're already pledged to Rory, his Consort in every way. He just needs to claim you publicly, and there will be nothing anyone can do about it. And with a child, it's very clear that this isn't a temporary arrangement." He turned to Klauden. "And you need an alliance with Firene. How better to establish a connection than to wed the Tallerin's Consort? It would have to be a very elaborate state ceremony with elements of both your customs and ours. Such things happened often enough throughout history. Men often have multiple wives. This is no different."

"But..." Hannah stuttered, trying to find the words, any words. "But..." She took a breath, swallowed hard, and opened her mouth again. "But where would I live?"

Linus shrugged. "Where you like," he said. "After Rory claims you and Klauden marries you, you can go anywhere you want, though I imagine you will stay with my brother, and I don't think he will want to stay long in Firene. People will understand at first. Love and passion and desire and all that. Stay too long, though, and the people may turn on you. As for Klauden, you will have a wife, so none will pursue you for state connections, and you will be free to live with your fledgling in peace."

Hannah looked from Klauden to Rory. "But I thought you had rules about bigamy," she said, remembering her conversation with Rory.

"I said we had rules about whom I was allowed to marry," Rory said, a grin spreading across his face. "I'm definitely not allowed to marry a vampire from the Vanya if I plan to claim the throne here."

Hannah looked at the Sarkoza. "What about you? You wanted the House to break some traditions, but this is more than a small departure."

Milo frowned, thinking it over. "It makes sense," he said at last. "It will explain why you're not living with Klauden at the new House. You will be busy with Firenian obligations." He nodded, looking at Klauden. "And there is something to be said for Klauden van Sherinak, valiant warrior who claimed the Tallerin's Consort for his own."

Hannah snorted. "Hardly. We've been betrothed since we were children. It's not like he stole me away or something."

Milo raised an eyebrow. "No one will remember that by the time I'm done," he said, and though he meant it as a joke, Hannah felt the hair on her arms rise, knowing he could do what he said.

Instead, she smirked, relying on her normal charming behavior. "So I'm to be a stolen bride, then." She shrugged her shoulders, then said to Rory, "You okay with this?" Rory rolled his eyes, but said nothing, nodding at her in agreement. "Whatever gets the other Houses to fall in line works for me." She paused, then asked what she really wanted to know. "What do you *actually* expect of me in this?" She looked at Milo boldly.

"I expect you to marry Master van Sherinak," Milo said pleasantly.

"And where would you expect me to live? In the House?"

Milo frowned. "Only on occasion," he said, glancing over at Solyn's belly. "Especially to claim his child as the heir."

Solyn's mouth twisted for a second at his words, the expression gone before anyone but Hannah could see it, but she felt the fledgling's burst of anger at the idea. <*Your child is your own,*> she thought, hoping it was loud enough for Solyn to hear. <*This is just politics.*>

Solyn's eyes narrowed, but she slowly dipped her head, acknowledging Hannah's words.

"I will not *live* there," Hannah said firmly. She looked at Linus. "Nor will I live here." Finally, she turned to Rory. This was something they had discussed a little bit. "We're going to find a place near Telran," she said, "not in the city itself, but nearby. Close enough that it's not the other side of the continent," she said, smiling at Klauden, who returned the grin, "but far enough away that we should be mostly left alone."

Linus accepted what she said and looked at Milo. The Sarkoza gave Hannah a long look, glanced at Klauden, scowled, then nodded in agreement.

"Very well," he said, looking at Hannah. "A peace-weaver it is."

XLVII

Hannah stood in front of the full-length mirror, staring at the simple white dress she wore. The sleeves were long, the tops tapering to a point that looped around her middle fingers. The top of the dress was fitted around her waist but loose around her hips, falling in a graceful arc to the floor. Hannah slid one foot forward, her bare toes peeking out from beneath the hem. She frowned, hand going to her hair, red curls wild around her face and around her shoulders. She gathered it up, wondering if she should pull it back. She rarely did anything besides running a brush through her hair in the morning and evening, the curls going this way and that as they chose.

She hadn't worn her hair in a braid since childhood, free hair the mark of a woman among her people, but she wasn't with her people now. Many of the elves braided their hair. She recalled Rory's hair in a similar fashion when she'd first arrived in Firene, her elf falling back into the customs of his people when among them.

Her fingers began to work, quickening the rhythm as she moved, remembering how it felt. The curls fought her a little bit as she reached the back of her head, and she made a face, untwisting it to start over again.

"Need a hand?"

Hannah turned, glad to see Lira behind her, the elf gorgeous as ever in a light blue dress, a small belt around her waist, her arms bare. She had never seen Lira in a dress or without weapons. Her hair was the same though, bound in a perfect braid ending at her waist.

Hannah sighed. "I can't get it to twist right. The curls fight me."

Lira smiled, picking up the brush from the small table and running it quickly through Hannah's hair. Hannah smiled at her in the mirror, glad to have someone with her. The silver hairbrush glinted in the afternoon sunlight coming through the window, and Hannah thought of her mother. The brush and mirror set were the only things she had left of Alin van Kreeosk. Hannah wondered what her mother would say about everything. Would she approve of Rory? Yes, Hannah decided, she would've liked him. And she would've adored Kira, sucked into the baby's orbit just like Magnus. Hannah's parents hadn't been particularly close or loving to one another, as evidenced by the existence of Hannah's half-sisters, but they both loved their daughter in their own way.

Lira finished the braid, tying it with a small piece of white ribbon. She looked at Hannah's reflection, giving a small frown.

"What?" Hannah asked.

"You need a few more things," Lira said, tilting her head. "Something old?"

Hannah shrugged. "I can wear my boots," she suggested.

"Please don't," Lira snapped, face thoughtful. "Wait a moment." She left the room, and Hannah fidgeted in front of the mirror, tucking stray wisps behind her ears. Lira returned with a small gold necklace and a blue piece of lace.

Hannah looked at her. "What's that?"

Lira gestured for her to turn around and face the mirror again, then stood behind her and slid the necklace over her head, tugging her braid over it and putting both hands on her shoulders as she nodded. The gold chain had a small red pendant on it. Hannah picked it up to examine it closer.

"This is really beautiful," she said.

"Thank you," Lira said. "It's very old, and it's definitely mine, so call it *borrowed*."

Hannah recalled the old rhyme for weddings. She thought of the rest of the list. She touched the dress. "This is new, so that's done." Frowning, she added, "I don't have anything blue."

Lira held up the scrap of blue lace, her eyes mischievous.

Hannah raised an eyebrow. "Do I just hold it?"

Lira smirked. "No, you tie it around your thigh."

Hannah chuckled. "What? Why?"

"For Rory to find later tonight," Lira said coyly. "Don't worry—he'll know what to do with it." She helped Hannah hold up the skirt of the dress and secure the blue lace around her thigh, then frowned at her bare feet. "Where are your shoes?" She went over to the bureau against the wall, shuffling through the bottom shelf for a moment. She returned with a pair of thin slippers that tied around her feet with long ribbons. Hannah started tying them, but Lira snorted, shooed her away, and laced the ribbons up and down her calves, securing the slippers in place.

Hannah stood up, surprised by how sturdy the shoes felt. She could definitely move in them. She looked at Lira. "Thank you."

"You are very welcome," Lira said, giving her a onceover. "You nervous?"

Hannah shrugged. "Should I be? It's just a small ceremony."

Lira shook her head. "It's Rory, so I think you're crazy, but I'm sure you'll both be fine."

"Have you seen him?" Hannah asked, wondering what Rory was doing at this moment.

Lira snorted. "Linus and Jasper are with him," she said. "He's fine."

"And Kira?" she asked. He had left with their daughter when he urged her into the room that morning, insisting that she use the time alone to rest and get ready.

"Surrounded by adoring fans, as always," Lira said. "She cannot get enough of Gorn." She smiled. "I don't think his beard will ever be the same. She's been chewing on it."

"Oh no!" Hannah said, thinking of her baby. "I can go get her."

Lira grabbed her shoulder. "Not now. Today, you're getting married."

"But—"

"Relax," Lira insisted. "She's fine. She's spending the night with me, Gorn, Linus, and Caga."

Hannah narrowed her eyes at Lira. "Caga? Since when does he enjoy babies?"

"Since he enjoys spending time with his friends," Lira replied primly, "some of whom he hasn't seen in many years."

Hannah wanted to probe deeper, but the door opened, and two servants came in. One began tidying the room, picking up the minor mess Hannah had made, but the other bowed to them both. "It is time, my lady," he said. Hannah nodded, looking at Lira.

"I'm ready."

The servant led them down the long hall and down several staircases to the lower level. They headed toward the center of the palace, to the grand ballroom that Hannah had only glimpsed through an open door a few times. As they drew nearer, Hannah leaned back to whisper to Lira. "I thought this was a small ceremony," she said.

"Your definition of small needs work," Lira said, then they entered the ballroom. Hannah paused, suddenly feeling like she had returned to Castle van Kreeosk and was attending one of her father's parties. The room was filled with elves in all manner of fancy dress, some in simple understated finery like Lira, some in elaborate displays of wealth and culture. Hannah was glad that Lira had helped her with her hair—no one in the room had unbound hair except the children, a few girls who lingered in fancy clothes near parents. She gave Lira a desperate look. If this was a small ceremony, then what kind of gala would her wedding to Klauden be like?

Thinking of the vampire, she found him standing near the front of the room. He wore his best red robes, the color bright and impressive amid the elves' finery. Solyn stood on his arm, the fledgling glorious in a dark blue dress that highlighted her curves. Milo and Millani stood near them, the twins more obviously related as they wore matching black and white. Eriken and Nicolo stood behind them, the seer wearing robes like Klauden's but in a dark green.

Hannah scanned the room, looking for Kira and finding her in Gorn's arms, the baby held up against one shoulder but resting against a white cloth. Gorn may adore Kira, but he wouldn't risk his fine black vest to the perils of baby drool. He winked as Hannah caught his eye. She smiled back, nearly overwhelmed by all of the people in the room, most of them strangers. Lira stood beside her, subtly guiding her down the middle of the crowd, people stepping aside as they made their way up to the dais at the front of the room. Some of the faces were friendly, but some were definitely not happy, judgement and suspicion clear as they watched her pass.

When the last person moved aside, she saw that the dais held three men. Jasper stood at the center, facing the room, the prince wearing a fine shirt and dark pants, the symbol of his office obvious on the medallion resting on his chest. Standing to his right was Linus, the elf handsome with his hair tied back to reveal sharp cheekbones. He was smiling broadly, looking back and forth from her to where Rory stood, her bridegroom on the bottom step of the dais, closest to her. He wore a white shirt over black pants, a wide black belt on his hips, but he carried none of his usual weapons. His hair was braided, silver hoops at the tops of both ears glinting in the light of the setting sun.

She thought of all the different ways she had seen Rory in the nearly two years she had known him, wild and carefree on the road near Talperin, serious when he questioned her near Kalford, gentle as he kissed her, passionate as he made love to her, accepting as he held his hand to hers, and now the man she wanted, standing in front of his people and claiming her as his own.

Love for him welled inside her, followed by a wave of desire as she stared at him. He really was handsome, and when he smiled at her, his eyes had the same wild ferocity that she had first fallen in love with back in the cave during the storm on the road outside Talperin.

She made it to the front of the dais, and Rory held out his hand, helping her step up, then turning to face her so they could see each other as well as Jasper and Linus. Lira stepped up on Jasper's other side, standing behind Hannah to mirror Linus.

"<Good people of Firene,>" Jasper said, his voice easily filling the room though he didn't shout, "<we are here to mark a joyous moment in the life of our Tallerin.>" He spoke in Elven, but Hannah followed along easily enough. Jasper looked at Rory. "<Rorinvalranus Tallerin, you wish to claim this woman as your Consort?>"

"<I do,>" Rory said, his face glowing as he looked at her.

"<Where is the symbol of your promise?>"

Linus handed something to Rory, placing it gently in his palm. Rory smiled and held out a small gold ring, the band smooth and unmarked. Hannah smiled back. It wasn't the ornate Elven ring he had given her back in Severin when she had been in Solyn's body. It wasn't the silver ring from Klauden that she had worn since leaving home. It was a simple ring, a new ring, unmarked by any culture or history, a symbol of their new freedom to choose their fate.

He slid it gently onto the fourth finger of her right hand, the customary place for Elven rings.

"<Hannah van Kreeosk,>" Jasper said, turning to her, "<do you accept Rorinvalranus as your Tallerin, to be his Consort from this point forward?>"

"<I do,>" Hannah said, smiling broadly.

"<Where is the symbol of your acceptance?>"

Lira stepped forward and handed a larger gold ring to Hannah. She slid it onto Rory's finger, the band resting snugly against the joint.

"<Who will speak for this man?>" Jasper asked, and Hannah raised an eyebrow, unsure of Jasper's meaning.

Linus spoke immediately. "<I will.>"

"<You will swear that this pledge is true and that this joining is one of love?>" Jasper asked.

"<I do so swear,>" Linus said solemnly, then smiled as he added, "<My brother is completely crazy for this woman.>"

"<That will do,>" Jasper said, narrowing his eyes at his brother. He turned to Hannah. "<Who will speak for this woman?>" Hannah froze, unsure who would speak for her.

"<I will,>" Lira said, and Hannah gave her a grateful smile.

"<You will swear that this pledge is true and that this joining is one of love?>" Jasper repeated.

"<I do so swear,>" Lira said formally. "<This is a love match.>"

Jasper nodded. "<And so, it has been both decreed and vouchsafed.>" He looked out at the room. "<Does anyone here have any reason why these two should not be joined?>"

Hannah froze. She had seen the Valrina in the crowd, the blonde elf gorgeous in a peach dress, her eyes glaring daggers as Hannah passed her. The moment stretched out, but no one spoke. Jasper nodded.

"<So it may be,>" he said. "<Join hands,>" he ordered. Rory took Hannah's hands in both of his, a soft smile on his face. "<Seal the joining with a kiss.>"

The smile on Rory's face grew as he leaned in, his lips warm and inviting as they met hers. She melted into the kiss, forgetting everyone else for a brief moment. The world shrank to the feeling of his touch, her body rising to meet him, her skin tingling in excitement. He released her slowly, and a low cheer went up in the room. Rory turned to face the room, lifting their joined hands above their heads in a small fist pump, and the crowd cheered again.

The next hours passed in a blur for Hannah. She was introduced to dozens of people whose names she almost immediately forgot, the slippery Elven syllables sliding out of her memory. There was an elaborate party with dancing, and Rory moved her around the dance floor with a precision that she hadn't expected but should have. Of course a soldier with the fighting skills he possessed would be a skilled dancer, and the fledgling blood had only made him smoother in his movements.

There was a dinner where people demanded Hannah's attention, but she spent most of it staring at Rory, her mind repeating the same words: *I'm married to Rory. I'm Hannah Tallerin for good now.*

As the party wound down, Rory took her hand and led her to where Kira still clung to Gorn's beard. After an awkward conversation where Lira and Gorn basically ordered the new couple away, they promised to return Kira in the morning.

"Go have a wedding night!" Gorn insisted. "Wee Kira and I will be fine company for one another tonight."

"Thank you," Hannah told him, and Rory gave the dwarf a meaningful nod.

"So," Rory said, "you ready to get out of here?"

Hannah smiled slowly at him, belly warming at the idea of being alone with him for a few uninterrupted hours. "Yes, please."

They were near the door when Hannah saw Klauden. She had been forcibly ignoring the vampire all night, not sure how to act around him while she married someone else. He had given her space and freedom, present enough to be polite but staying far enough away. She paused, wondering what to say, but Klauden only smiled at her.

< Go. >

< I— >

< Go, chaivin. We will have our time later. >

Hannah nodded and followed Rory out of the room, chest suddenly nervous at the idea that she would have to do this all over again in a few days but with a different man. She focused on the handsome elf at her side, the man she had chosen, and her heart warmed. Pushing Klauden out of her mind, she bit her lip and smiled at her husband.

He led her down the hall, both of them pausing to duck into an alcove while some partygoers passed loudly in the hallway. Rory pulled her close to his chest, her back to him, clearly done entertaining well-wishers with more congratulations. Hannah reached her arms up and around his neck, pulling him closer, face finding his in the dim light, tugging him close for a deep kiss. His hands slid over her shoulders and down her arms, ending with her hands where he twined his fingers with hers, their new rings clicking gently together.

They broke the kiss after a long moment, looking at one another eagerly. He gestured with his head, and she nodded. They left the alcove, hurrying through the thankfully empty halls to Rory's rooms.

He turned around as they reached his suite. Using his foot to push the door in, he leaned down and grabbed Hannah, tossing her over his shoulder and carrying her into the room. Hannah squealed with laughter at the unexpected brute move, then he was kicking the door shut behind them, carrying her through the front room with its chairs and small dining table to the bedroom, where he gently laid her down on the bed.

"It's tradition to carry your bride over the threshold of your new house," he said, "but I thought this would have to do for now." He grinned at her. "When we get our own house, I'll do it again."

"I look forward to it," Hannah told him. "But maybe a bit more gently since we'll have Kira with us."

Rory nodded, looking down at her. "It's still sometimes unreal to me," he said quietly, "that we're a family."

"And now we're officially married," Hannah said. "I never thought..."

Rory grinned. "I know." He crawled on the bed beside her, pillowing his head on his arms, turning to look at her. "You remember that night in Kalford?"

She turned to lay on her side, head propped up on her hand as she looked at him. "Of course," she told him. "I could never forget that night."

He smiled. "You were so innocent," he said. "So naive. But I wanted you anyway."

"Am I so much older now?" she asked. He chuckled, and she added, "And I wasn't young or innocent then, either." She frowned. "Maybe naive."

He rolled onto his side, reaching out a hand to touch her face. "You were the most beautiful creature I'd ever seen," he said softly. "I had to have you, no matter what it meant."

"I know what you mean," she breathed. "But remember, I also wanted to bite you the entire time." She glanced down at his scarred neck. "You know what I mean now."

He shook his head. "I'm amazed at your restraint."

She scoffed. "Restraint is not something I really have, Rory."

He nodded, accepting her words. There was a pause, then he said, "And now you don't have to restrain yourself."

Hannah bit her lip, her fangs growing in her mouth at the sound of his voice. "Neither do you," she whispered.

"Is this what it's like, then?" he asked, his finger tracing her jawline and settling on her mouth, the tip slipping between her lips to slide up one of her fangs.

"Is this what what's like?" she asked, closing her eyes as a shiver ran through her.

Rory refused to shift topics. "Is this what it's like between a fledgling and a Maker?"

Hannah's eyes flew open. "I—I don't—" Was he really asking her about sex with Klauden right now?

His hand left her mouth to cup her cheek. "Relax, Hannah. I'm only asking the question." He frowned. "I don't need the blow by blow, but I do need some idea of what to expect."

Hannah sat up. Though they had been together for over a month now, they hadn't done more than kiss, each distracted by Kira and travel and everything else. The logistics of vampire sex weren't something she expected to discuss, but she realized that she should have. Rory was a careful lover, considerate and slow, and he would ask what she wanted, letting her explain herself as the words came to her. She studied his neck again, realizing that she couldn't see the silver necklace he usually wore, the one with Klauden's ring on it.

"Where's the ring?" she asked, changing the subject as she leaned down to touch his skin, sliding her hands around the back of his neck.

Rory leaned into her touch. "I gave it back to Klauden," he said softly. He gave her a long look. "I didn't think he'd want to see ... tonight."

Hannah nodded, understanding what he meant. Kevna pulsed and she knew that Klauden would feel tonight whether she wanted him to or not. She refused to reach out to him, feeling like that was going too far. Two people were plenty for a marriage bed.

"Hannah…" Rory sat up, grinning down at her. "You're still adorable beyond words."

Hannah smiled at him. "You're the most handsome man I've ever seen," she said honestly. "I never tire of looking at you."

Rory grinned, then reached out a hand to her as he stood up. Hannah took it and followed. "Where are we going?"

Rory led her out of the bedroom and back to the front room. "Sit with me," Rory said, pulling out a chair from the dining table for her to sit. "We should talk."

"We can't talk in bed?" she asked, taking a seat.

Rory shook his head. "We can, but I keep thinking about other things, and if I don't say this now, I won't say it at all."

He pulled out a chair and slid into it, hand reaching out to take hers. She stared at him. "You want to talk about vampire sex at the table?" she asked.

Rory snorted. "Sure," he said with a wink, "but I need to ask you something else first."

Hannah narrowed her eyes. "What?"

Rory took a deep breath, then looked her in the eye. "Hannah, do you want more children with me?"

"Uhh…" The sound came out of Hannah as she stared back at him. She hadn't really thought about it, so focused on Kira and the army that there wasn't room for anything else. Thinking about what she hoped was in store this night, she realized that she should have thought about this. She recalled Klauden asking her a similar question on the cliff, and she had the same answer. "No," she said quietly. "Not now, anyway." She frowned. "Maybe in the future, but for now, I'd like to spend time with just you and Kira."

Rory nodded. "That's what I thought too." He stood and walked over to a shelf on the wall. He pulled down a small tin, then gathered a teapot and two mugs, bringing them to the table and setting them down carefully.

"What's this?" Hannah asked. "Midnight tea time?"

"This is special tea," Rory said, looking at her expectantly, "or it will be if you do the spell."

Hannah's eyes widened as she recalled the tea Klauden made for them while they were on the *Volant*, the spell to prevent pregnancy. She stared at him. "You talked to Klauden about this?"

Rory shrugged, then nodded. "I had to." He paused, looking at her. "We were together one time, Hannah, and you had a baby." He paused again, then added, "You were with him twice, and Solyn got pregnant." Hannah had an idea of what it cost him to say that, but he went on, "I think it's safe to say that you're fairly fertile. And if you don't want more children right now, then we should drink this."

Hannah watched him fill the teapot with water from the pitcher on the table. He looked at her. "Some heat?"

Hannah leaned in, pushing the magic into the water, heating it to a boil in a few seconds. She could feel echo of Klauden as she did it, her magic tied to his now, and she pulled away, knowing that he probably knew what she was doing. Rory added the tea to the water and sat back, gesturing for her to continue. Hannah concentrated again, letting Klauden's magic flow through her, the spell taking hold.

She poured the tea into the mugs, sliding one over to Rory. "So," she said, taking a small sip and feeling the tea settle her churning stomach, "what do you want to know?"

Rory took a sip of his tea, gathering his thoughts. "Well, I imagine the general idea is the same," he began.

Hannah nodded. "It is," she told him, "but the blood just makes it ... more."

"So there's biting," Rory said, and she could see him trying to separate this discussion about abstract vampire relationships from the very real experiences she now shared with Klauden.

She took another sip. "Do you really want to talk about this?"

Rory shook his head. "Absolutely not," he said, "but we need to." He looked away, sipping his tea, then put the mug down with a sigh. "Look, I know what I'm in here. You feel him. He feels you. I can feel him through you. I know how good it can feel because you remember how good it felt." He frowned, taking another sip. "It's very strange to know how Klauden can make your body feel, Hannah."

"I'm sorry, Rory," Hannah said. "I—"

"No!" he said, grabbing her hand. "That's not what I mean. Not at all." He frowned, finding words. "I understand your connection with him ... as much as I can anyway." He looked up, thinking. "I just need to know if we will be the same or something else."

"We will not be the same," Hannah said. "Not really." She tilted her head, remembering how she had tried to explain this to Klauden and failed. "It's about desire," she said, echoing her words to the vampire.

Rory took another sip, gesturing for her to go on.

"When I'm with you, it's about wanting you and wanting more, and the moment between the desire and the fulfillment." She paused, looking down, then back at him. "You satisfy me because you pay attention to what I want."

"And him?" Rory prompted gently, needing her to say this.

"He satisfies me because he's in my head," she admitted. "He knows what I want because he can hear me, feel me." She cocked her head. "What's it like for you with the fledgling bond? I can't feel it around kevna, but I remember from Herrick."

Rory shrugged. "I can sense your emotions," he said, "and I get a general idea of what you think about something." He chuckled. "Though I could probably tell that from your face, Hannah."

She smirked at him, finishing her tea. "Anything else?"

He frowned. "I can sense your pain," he said quietly. "On the beach," he added, "I knew you were hurt by something."

"Did you hurt your foot somehow?" she asked, remembering how she had felt something in her foot but had thought it a result of the sting from the Manawyrm.

He snorted. "I stepped on a sharp shell," he admitted, "and I tripped."

Hannah nodded. "I felt that, but only because kevna was fading with the magic." She looked at Rory as he finished the last of his tea, needing to know the answer to her next question. "Rory, can you hear my thoughts?"

He frowned, then shook his head. "Not like that. I get a sense of how you're feeling, but it's nothing specific." He narrowed his eyes. "You can actually talk to Klauden in your head, can't you?"

She nodded.

"I thought so." He sighed. "That would make for an amazingly close connection," he said.

"Yes."

He pursed his lips, looking at her. "Hannah, I still have Caga's ring, the one that blocks magic."

Hannah looked up at him. "Oh?"

"Do you want to wear it tonight?" He walked over to the shelf, lifted a small velvet pouch, and tipped it, the metal ring landing on his palm. He set it gently on the table.

Hannah stared at him, thoughts racing. If she wore the ring, it would cut her off from all magic, leaving her alone with Rory. Klauden would still feel her, but she wouldn't feel him. She narrowed her eyes at Rory. "Are you asking for me or for yourself?"

"What do you mean?"

She smirked. "I know you can probably feel what I feel when I think of him. Do you want me to wear it so you stop lusting after him?"

Rory grinned. "He is a handsome bastard," he admitted. "But I ask for you. I'm fine either way. I can concentrate when it matters."

Hannah pursed her lips. It would be a welcome relief to be alone with just Rory. She thought of her wedding to Klauden in a few days. Rory would feel that too, whatever happened that night. "Do you want to wear it when I marry him?" she asked, voice serious. The ring would cut him off as her fledgling, leaving him unable to feel her at all.

Rory considered, and it was a mark of just how much he had grown that he could look at her. "Maybe," he said. "Maybe not." He leaned in, taking both of her hands. "I know what I signed up for in this, Hannah. I will take you as I find you, when I can, for as long as I can. I know you have other connections." He sighed, shaking his head. "I know you love him. Hell, part of me loves him, and that's just weird."

"Because he's a man?"

He gave her a thoroughly rakish smile, a look that sent desire spiraling through her. "No. Because he's so different from anything I am. He's calm, reserved, studious, thoughtful." He looked at Hannah. "I'm none of those things. I will never be those things." He sighed. "You definitely don't have a type, Hannah, that's for sure."

"He's what I expected my whole life," Hannah admitted. "He's what I thought I wanted." She looked at Rory. "And then I met you, and I realized that I wanted something else, that I could have something more." She bit her lip. "I'm so grateful to know you, Rory, to have you in my life in any way at all."

His eyes reddened with the sheen of tears, and he leaned down to kiss her gently. "I'm with you, Hannah, all the way. Whatever happens, happens."

"I love you, Rory," she said as tears welled in her eyes. She reached out and grabbed the ring from the table, sliding it onto the finger of her left hand, feeling the hollow space where her magic had been.

She was alone with Rory, just the two of them.

"I love you, Hannah Tallerin," he replied. "Will you have me?"

"Always," she said, tugging him closer and covering his mouth in a kiss that quickly grew passionate. He lifted her from the chair easily, swinging her sideways to sit on the table, feet dangling on either side of his hips as he pressed himself to her.

"I love kissing you," she moaned against his mouth. Reaching up, he pulled the tie from her hair, fingers slowly undoing the braid, sliding her curls free. He looked at her, eyes darkening with wicked intentions as his hands went to the belt at his waist and quickly unbuckled it, the leather falling to the floor at his feet. He reached up to tug on the back of his shirt, sliding it up and over his head, tossing it on the table behind her. She ran both hands along his arms, relishing in the sight of so much bare skin. She touched the bumpy scars on his shoulder, remembering them from the first night in Kalford. A morningstar, he had said. Her hands trailed down his toned chest, sliding gently over the new scars from the tent in Salva, when Anna and Herrick had nearly killed him. He leaned forward, leaving soft kisses along her jaw, moving down to her neck. His hands traced her sides down to the outside of her legs, finding her feet and the slippers still tied around her calves.

He let out a soft sound, then pulled away to lift one foot. Resting it against his chest, he slowly unwrapped the ribbon that Lira had tied around her leg, the silky material sliding off in a flutter as he let the slipper fall to the ground. He slid both hands along her calf, causing a small shiver. He kissed the top of her foot, then replaced it with the other shoe, removing the ties in the same slow manner. When she was barefoot, he ran his hands up the outside of her legs, pausing when he found the strip of lace tied around her thigh.

"What is this?" he muttered, leaning down to look more closely, pushing the skirt up over her legs as he did so, revealing the blue lace.

"Something blue?" she offered, her voice husky.

"Nice," he said softly. "But I see something red." His head disappeared beneath the bottom of the dress, and Hannah gasped, legs wrapping around him as she lay back on the table. Pleasure flooded her, and she called out his name, then he was lifting her off the table, her legs hooked around his waist. He lifted the dress over her head, abandoning it on the floor of the front room, carrying her into the bedroom wearing only the blue strip of lace.

Laying her gently on the bed, he looked her over, taking in a naked body he had only seen once before, eyes lingering on the massive scar in the center of her chest. She let herself be looked at, biting her lower lip in eager excitement. "You like what you see?" she asked, voice still husky with pleasure.

He nodded, a few strands of his hair free from the braid. "Very much, Hannah." He knelt on the bed, crawling up her body, and she held him close, kissing him hard, mouth nipping at his lower lip and drawing blood as her fingers worked his hair free. He gasped, then returned the bite on her tongue. She rolled over, resting her body atop his while she enjoyed the kiss and the ecstasy of the blood, but then she turned, sliding off his pants and getting reacquainted with the parts of him she hadn't seen since she inhabited Solyn's body.

When he finally pushed her aside and rolled on top of her, hips between her legs as he filled her, Hannah was delirious with pleasure, and sinking her fangs into his neck was the most natural thing in the world.

XLVIII

Hannah was in bed, her head resting on Rory's bare chest, feeling the slow beat of his heart as he lay beneath her, his hand idly rubbing up and down her back. She sighed, closing her eyes and enjoying the peaceful moment. She knew it wouldn't last long.

The sun was rising, and Kira would wake soon. Hannah bit her lip, knowing that Kira wasn't what made her heart beat faster or her stomach tighten with nerves.

Today was her wedding to Klauden. Soon, Hannah would leave Rory's rooms, leave her prince and her daughter behind to participate in what everyone agreed was an elaborate political affair. Having seen what the elves considered a small ceremony, Hannah was not looking forward to it. She didn't dread marrying Klauden—she had promised she would—and she loved him. But the idea of being paraded about like a trophy stung her pride.

"Hey," Rory said, noticing her scowl, "what's wrong?"

"Other than everything?" she snapped.

Rory chuckled, hand moving to turn her face gently back to his. His eyes were serious as he looked at her. "Talk to me," he said quietly.

Hannah frowned, not knowing where to begin. Rory waited, letting her find her way to the words. "I just … can't really believe this is happening today."

Rory nodded, expression urging her to continue.

"I want to stay here with you," she said quickly. "I don't want to face everything that's beyond that door."

Her husband leaned down and gave her a soft kiss, his hands gently holding her face. "Beyond that door, Hannah, is whatever you want it to be."

"It's going to be a nightmare," she grumbled.

"You think marriage to Klauden will be a nightmare?"

She noticed that Rory had said "marriage" and not "wedding." Frowning, she wondered what the distinction meant to him. "No! Not that." She pulled away, sitting up and letting the blanket fall to her waist. "I just hate these huge fancy events."

"You didn't always hate them," Rory commented, no doubt thinking of the stories she had told him about her father's parties. "You know what to do."

Hannah sighed. "I do, but when I do, when I return to Lady van Kreeosk," she sneered her old title, "it makes me uncomfortable, like an old dress I've outgrown."

Rory smiled, understanding the feeling. "I know what you mean. Coming back here isn't the easiest thing for me either." He sat up, hands reaching for hers. "People will stare, but today, they will all envy you."

Hannah scoffed. "Envy me? Why?"

"You're marrying the handsome vampire prince from the Vanya, Hannah," Rory said. "The savior of Firene!" He laughed, eyebrows raising as he poked her with one of her hands.

Hannah giggled, letting him push her back down into the bed, pressing himself on top of her. They kissed, long and slow, still marveling in the newness of their rekindled physical relationship. After a long moment, she pulled away, face serious as she looked up at him.

"I'm marrying Klauden today," she said. "I will be expected to spend the night with him."

Rory nodded, leaning down to give her a quick kiss. "I know that," he said. "We already discussed this. I will have Kira. She will be fine. We will see you tomorrow."

Hannah reached out and touched his face, her hand sliding up the length of his ears, pushing his long dark hair flat against his head. "And you?" she asked. "Will you be fine?"

Rory bit his lip. "I will be here, Hannah," he said finally. He cocked his head, his hand tracing her jawline. "Look, am I thrilled to think about him kissing you today? Not particularly." His body moved closer to her, hips sliding between her legs.

"Do I want to imagine him here with you?" he asked, sheathing himself. "No." He began to move slowly, watching her face as she let out a low moan.

"Do I want to think of you making that sound with him?" He slid his hands over her skin, causing her skin to prickle with delight and desire as he moved his hips slowly. "No." He leaned down, tracing kisses on her neck.

"Do I want to think of your body with his, his touch on your skin?" He pressed himself into her again. "No." He leaned down to claim her mouth with a passionate kiss, body moving faster, harder against her. He pulled back, looking down at her.

"But I know what is between us," he said, body still moving, "and I know what is between you and him." He leaned down, kissing her again, teeth sliding along her delicate skin.

"I will take you as I find you, where I find you," he promised, "and I will be here when you return. Always." He bit her, and they lost themselves in the moment, both stifling their cries so they didn't wake Kira who slept in a crib across the room.

Later, Rory collapsed on top of her. Catching his breath, he lifted himself on his elbow to peer down at her, face speculative. "What is this really about, Hannah? I know you will occasionally have sex with Klauden. I knew that when I decided to fight for you. You feeling guilty for the inevitable?"

Hannah looked up at him, liking this new honesty between them but still feeling her chest heat at the frank discussion. "How can you forgive me?" she whispered.

"Forgive you for what? For kevna? There's nothing to forgive."

"Do you remember the night he made me his fledgling?" she asked, voice soft. Rory nodded, eyes softening. "You told me then that if something ever happened with Klauden, you would still love me, but you wouldn't be able to forgive me." She looked away, then back at him. "And you left me in Severin. And denied me when I got to Firene." She sighed. "Why would you forgive me now? Accept this now?"

Rory nodded. "That's a fair question." He let his hand drift over her chest, fingers sliding over the bumps of scar tissue, his touch raising goosebumps when he reached her non-scarred flesh. He sighed, gathering his thoughts. "Do you believe me when I say I love you?" he asked.

Hannah nodded. "I never doubted your love. Just your commitment." She frowned. "You do seem to run away when things get hard." She glanced across the room to where Kira still slept, a tiny miracle for which Hannah thanked the gods. She didn't want to have this conversation while feeding the baby. "Though you haven't done that since we found out about Kira." She thought, remembering him on the beach when he found her practicing. "Or since the morning on the beach." She stared at him. "Why are you still here?"

"I didn't understand," he said softly, tracing her scar again. "I thought I did, but I didn't. Not until I let myself feel the bond with you—in the dream."

"The dream where you told me we were through?" she asked, eyebrows raising in surprise.

"That was when I really started to understand what kevna meant," he told her. "And I get it." He frowned, shrugging. "Is part of me still jealous? Sure." He paused. "But I wouldn't take it away from you, either of you. He saved your life, Hannah, over and over. He's the reason you're here with me now. I can't begrudge him some time with you. Of course I understand him loving you."

"So what you feel is more magic? A result of the fledgling bond?" Hannah asked, disliking the idea. It was too close to her suspicion of kevna.

"Maybe," Rory said, "but I doubt it. I loved you long before Salva, and I didn't acknowledge the fledgling bond until long after that night."

"Do you think it's kevna though, bleeding through me into you?"

Rory shrugged. "Maybe," he admitted. "I'm not the magic expert here. I know how I feel, though, and I swear to you, Hannah, I will be here for you. Always."

"Do... Do you want the ring tonight?" she asked quietly. "It will keep you from feeling ... whatever happens."

Rory frowned, then shook his head. "No." He gave a slow, wicked grin. "Hell, maybe there's a small part of me that honestly wonders what it's like to bed him." He raised an eyebrow. "Have you thought about giving it to him?"

"Klauden? Why?"

"He's only been with you and Solyn, right?" When Hannah nodded, he continued, "So it's always been magic and bonds. He doesn't know what it's like to just be with someone without all the fuss." Hannah started laughing, unable to stop herself. Rory looked at her. "What? I'm just looking out for the guy."

"But if Klauden wears the ring, you won't know what he feels," Hannah said, her wicked smile matching his own.

"I didn't say I want to know what he feels," Rory said, leaning down to kiss her again. "I said I want to know what he feels like."

Hannah giggled, losing herself in the kiss. When Kira woke a few moments later, they both got up to start the day, working together to build their new life.

XLIX

Hannah stood in front of the same full-length mirror, but this time she wore an elaborate red dress, the bodice tight-fitting to flaunt her small curves, the long line of her shoulders and neck exposed. It had been a long time since she had worn such a dress, but she still remembered how it felt, the soft fabric delicious against her skin. Though off the shoulder, the dress had long sleeves that covered part of her hands, the seamstress cleverly hiding the sigil burned into Hannah's palm. Better not remind the elves of the kind of creatures they are inviting into their city, Millani had said when the dressmaker fitted the fabric around Hannah's small frame. The vampire had been eager to help design Hannah's look for the ceremony, but she wasn't exactly friendly. Hannah wondered if she would've been the same way had she only lived in her father's castle as a Second Daughter, then been brought to Firene to sway the elves into an alliance.

Looking over her shoulder to where the vampire stood, Hannah took in the beautiful woman, her long hair free down her back, her elaborate dress striking in emerald green. Millani may have come to be a pretty distraction for the elves, but there was something more to her stolen moments with Linus now. Hannah knew how charming Rory could be when he wanted to be; she imagined his brother would have similar gifts. Milo may have brought his sister to tempt the elves, but Millani may find herself being tempted instead.

"You look lovely, my lady," Millani said, giving her a cool smile.

Hannah nodded, accepting the compliment. By her old standards, she did look good. Her hair was free, red curls wild around her face and over her shoulders. She frowned, thinking of the old rhyme. The dress was new, but she still needed something old, blue, and borrowed. She glanced at Millani. "Do you know the old rhyme about brides?" she asked. "About what we should have when we get married?"

Millani raised her eyebrows. "Something old, something new, something borrowed, something blue?" she recited. "I know it." She scanned Hannah's appearance. "The dress is new," she said. She nodded, lifting her hand and leaving the room. Hannah smiled, remembering Lira doing the same thing. She looked down at her feet, lifting the skirt of the dress just enough to see the worn toes of her red boots peeking through. No one would see them during the ceremony, and Lira wasn't there to scold her. The boots were definitely old, a reminder of who she had once been, but also a promise of who she now was, a vampire about to get married to her soul mate in a political alliance.

Millani returned a moment later, one hand holding a length of black lace. Hannah's face reddened, lips twisting as she tried not to smile. "What's this?" Hannah asked.

Millani's face blushed, but her voice was steady. "It's my lace, but I understand you're supposed to tie it around your thigh under your dress," the vampire said. "It's called a garter, and Lord van Sherinak is supposed to discover it later."

"You've been talking to Linus," Hannah said, taking the lace from her hand. She held it up. It was finely crafted, the delicate lines showing excellent craftsmanship. "Did you make this?" Hannah asked. "It's amazing work." She would never have noticed such a thing before, but a year spent sharing Solyn's body had taught her to appreciate the time it took to create such things.

Millani smiled shyly, and her face warmed for a moment. "Thank you, my lady."

"You can call me Hannah," Hannah told her. "I may not be coming to live at the House with you all the time, but I will be there—and you can't always defer to me like this."

"But I am only Second Family," Millani objected.

"So what?" Hannah pressed. "House van Sherinak is a new place. We can make our own rules." She paused, then took the chance. "I'd like it if we could be friends, Millani."

The girl's face brightened at Hannah's use of her name. She nodded, eyes lighting up. "I would like that too, my—Hannah." She looked at Hannah. "Do you need any help?"

"I think I've got this," Hannah told her, an idea forming as she recalled Rory's words that morning. "Can you give me a moment alone? I will be out directly."

"Of course," Millani said, leaving the bedroom.

Hannah walked over to the bureau which held her few belongings, eyes settling on the blue velvet bag Rory had given her before she left his rooms that morning. She could feel the circle of the metal ring inside as she pressed the bag against her thigh, wrapping the black lace around it to secure it in place. *There*, she thought, letting the dress fall back into place. *Something blue.*

A few moments later, Hannah and Millani were escorted down the halls of the palace, but instead of going to the ballroom as she expected, the servants led them down a different hallway and outside. A small chariot stood there, a white-and-gold base with a small platform just large enough for one person to stand on. Hannah looked at the servants, then at Millani. "You can't be serious," she said.

Millani gestured to the chariot, helping Hannah step on. The horse pranced a little as she moved but settled immediately when Milo walked out of the palace, his dark pants and green shirt matching his sister's dress. He whispered something to the horse, and the creature stood perfectly, eerily still. Hannah gave him a polite nod, trying not to let her displeasure show on her face. She had agreed to this farce, she reminded herself. She had known it would be showy.

Milo climbed onto the horse's back easily, settling himself in a perfect rider's posture, then tugging on the reins. Hannah gave Millani a reluctant smile as the chariot lurched forward, following Milo's lead through winding streets. He took smaller roads through the city to the eastern wall, then turned to follow the inside of the wall to the main gate from that direction. As they turned onto the main street, small crowds of onlookers had started to form, waving and smiling as they moved past. Hannah did her best to smile and wave as they moved. She understood the symbolism. Milo was bringing her from the eastern gate, from the direction of the Vanya. She wondered how many of these people remembered that she was the Prince's Consort or realized that she had come from Rory's bed that morning. It didn't matter. The drive was for show, the display of control, and it was something Hannah understood. She may be far from home, but she was still her father's daughter.

They passed increasingly large crowds, simple bakers and shop keepers giving way to more lavishly dressed nobles and merchants, then they were going through the main gate into the palace proper, a small throng of people permitted to follow them. They stopped at the steps of the palace, where Klauden stood on the top step, resplendent in red robes, his blonde hair moving in the soft breeze, his high cheekbones and bright eyes making more than one woman in the crowd smile in appreciation. Hannah looked at him, her future husband, and had to smile too. He really was handsome, and her heart swelled to see him there, eyes eagerly watching as Milo helped her from the carriage, her hand in his as they walked up the steps. He handed her over to Klauden with a flourish and a bow, then she and Klauden walked inside, side by side as they followed the main corridor down to the ballroom.

Hannah took a deep breath, trying to settle her nerves before they entered the large room.

<*You look lovely.*> Klauden's voice was soft in her mind, awestruck.

<*So do you,* > she told him, letting him feel the warmth of her pleasure as she looked over at him. They smiled shyly at one another, taking the last few steps down the hallway.

<*Ready for this?*> Klauden gave her a long look.

<*I think so,*> Hannah told him. <*Are you?*>

Klauden's heart warmed, love flooding her entire being. <*I have been ready for this my entire life.*> He took her hand more firmly in his and walked through the double doors, leading her down a center aisle between orderly lines of onlookers and witnesses. Hannah saw her father first, his tall figure impressive on the dais. Hannah had known he would be there to perform the ceremony along with Jasper, but she hadn't seen him since her room in the castle, and she flinched, unable to stop it. Scanning the crowd, her gaze found Klauden's parents, Jorus smiling proudly at his son, Keller nodding at Hannah as she walked by them. Gerter and Isla van Lartner were also present, Hannah recognizing her grandparents with Klauden's help. A few more prominent House leaders were present, most standing near where Milo joined his sister and family, the vampires beautiful and clearly powerful standing near the elves. Hannah marveled at the sight, never thinking she would find so many vampires standing in a room full of elves without feeding. She thought many elves would wake up with mysterious scratches tomorrow, but she knew no one here was foolish enough to actually bite anyone. There were still rules to be followed, especially when forging new alliances.

She scanned the room one more time, eyes finding Rory near the side wall. Her husband was surrounded by Lira, Gorn, Linus, and Caganasti, all of them with perfectly smooth expressions. Even Gorn didn't seem distracted by Kira, the baby turned toward him, face buried in his beard. He gave Hannah a quick wink of support as she caught his eye. She saw Rory but let her gaze skip across his face and away. Just as she had ignored Klauden while marrying Rory, she had promised herself she would do the same today for Klauden, focusing on one man at a time.

Hannah was surprised to see Solyn standing with them and not with the vampires as she had expected. The fledgling's face was calm, and Hannah could sense her through the bond with Klauden. Solyn wasn't upset to see Klauden marry another. She knew he would be living with her in the new House with their child. She smiled at Hannah, the reassurance echoing through her bond with Klauden into Hannah. The fledgling glanced back at Rory and nodded, the implication clear. She would watch out for him while Hannah was gone. He may not be the man Solyn wanted, but he was family now, and Solyn understood what that meant.

They reached the front of the room still holding hands, then stepped onto the dais, facing her father instead of turning as she had done with Rory.

"<Children of the mountains,>" her father began in their language, "<we come to celebrate a destined union between Hannah van Kreeosk and Klauden van Sherinak.>" He glanced at the elf standing beside him, Jasper nodding as he repeated a similar welcome in Elven. "<People of Firene,>" he announced, "<we come to celebrate the momentous joining of Klauden van Sherinak and Hannah van Kreeosk.>" Hannah didn't miss the way the elves listed the man first in all things. For all that her people had restrictive customs, they did not share the gender stereotypes of the elves. The crowd clapped politely, the smattering a far cry from the riotous sound she had heard when she married Rory. This was a much more refined crowd and event. Hannah held herself steady, keeping her back firm and her shoulders straight, hand holding Klauden's tightly.

"<Hannah van Kreeosk,>" her father said, looking at Hannah, "<do you accept Klauden van Sherinak as your lord and husband?>"

"<I do,>" Hannah said, feeling her cheeks start to burn as she recalled doing this a few days before.

"<Do you promise to honor and obey his wishes for as long as you both shall live?>" her father prompted. Hannah smirked, glad no one but her father and Jasper could see her face.

"<I do,>" she said. Klauden chuckled in her mind.

"<Will you swear to bring pride to your House and your people, continuing the bloodline of this family?>"

"<I will,>" Hannah said, and while she had known to expect the question, part of her still hated the lie. She didn't expect to continue Klauden's bloodline—Solyn had already done that. But the ceremony was old, and the promise was routine.

"<Then place your ring as a symbol of your oath,>" Magnus said, handing her an ornate band with swirling designs on it, the same ring her mother had given him when they married, her Family ring. Hannah took it with hands that were surprisingly steady and slid it onto Klauden's left hand as her people's customs decreed. He smiled at her, watching her face as she did it, eyes filling with joy. She smiled softly at him, glad to be covered by his happiness, before turning back to her father.

"<Klauden van Sherinak,>" her father began, "<do you accept Hannah van Kreeosk as your lady and wife?>"

"<I do,>" Klauden said, his voice soft but powerful in the quiet room.

"<Do you promise to honor and obey her wishes for as long as you both shall live?>"

Klauden smirked, giving her a quick look. <*Of course,*> he thought, <*why would anything change?*> He squeezed her hand. "<I do,>" he answered.

"<Will you swear to bring pride to your House and your people, continuing the bloodline of this family?>"

"<I will,>" Klauden said, thinking of the swell of Solyn's belly as he squeezed Hannah's hand again, this time reassuring himself that she was really there, that *this* was really happening.

"<Then place your ring as a symbol of your oath,>" Magnus said. Klauden reached into a pocket of his robe and pulled out a very familiar silver ring, one he had given her long ago.

<*This was always meant for you,*> he told her, waiting for her to move her hand closer, a sign that she accepted his offer. <*Will you have me?*>

<*I will,*> Hannah told him, letting him slide the ring on her fourth finger, this time the gesture meaning so much more.

"<Very well,>" Magnus said. "<I hereby declare these two be joined.>" There was another polite smattering of applause, then Magnus continued, "<Let this match be sealed with a kiss.>"

Klauden bit his lip, eyes slipping for a brief second to glance at Magnus, not thrilled about kissing Hannah in front of her father. Then he seemed to remember himself, recalling that they had just been married, and this was their very first official kiss as a married couple. He reached for Hannah, covering her mouth with his, staking his claim on her as clearly as he could without biting her in front of the whole room. Hannah fell into the kiss, Klauden responding to the pull of her body perfectly, kevna singing over them both. They pulled apart slowly, reluctantly, Hannah's fingertips tingling in anticipation of more kisses like that one.

Her father began speaking again, and Hannah tried to pay attention. "We are overjoyed to learn that the van Sherinaks plan to start a new House, one allied with the elves of Firene!"

Magnus nodded to Jasper, who dipped his head in appreciation. "<We are thrilled to share this auspicious occasion with our new kin,>" Jasper announced, speaking in Elven again. "<May the union of House van Sherinak and our Tallerin's Consort be a symbol of our people's newfound alliance!>" He reached out to grab Hannah and Klauden's joined hands, lifting them up in a small cheer, the same gesture Rory had made at the end of their ceremony. The elves exploded into cheers and whistles, a sign that the official business was over.

This party seemed to last longer than her last wedding, Hannah slipping back into her old behavior like a favorite shirt, smiling prettily on Klauden's arm, saying what the other House leaders wanted to hear, accepting many toasts of honor for her new family name and her new House. The dinner was short, a brief affair of thin soup in a nod to their new allies' delicate dietary needs, and soon, Hannah found herself dancing with Klauden to a slow song she hadn't heard since leaving home.

Klauden led her across the room easily, and Hannah remembered dancing with him in the inn in Severin the night the army attacked. He had been so careful then, not wanting to smother her with their new bond, accepting that she had chosen another, yet still willing to risk his life to protect her. Her hand slid over his shoulder, remembering the blade that had been aimed at her head, Klauden intercepting the blow to take the hit on his shoulder instead. He had teleported them to safety then, and both of them had nearly died from blood loss and injury.

She remembered his face when he first realized that she was alive, that he hadn't killed her in his bloodlust, then the feeling of him kissing her, really kissing her, both of them ecstatic with life and love and joy. And magic. She could feel kevna now, the power swirling between them and around them, making every touch of his hands on her set her skin on fire. He leaned down to kiss her gently, carefully, as they slowly danced, the soft murmur of voices fading to the background. In the moment, there was only Klauden, her betrothed, her mate, her husband.

<*I remember, chaivin,*> he whispered in her mind. <*I will always remember.*>

She looked up at him, searching his face. His expression was careful, and she could feel him steeling himself, waiting for her to say something that would hurt him.

"We should go," she said quietly, taking his hand and leading him slowly off the floor.

"Where?" he asked, letting himself be led.

"Away from here," she said, smiling politely at a few guests who glanced their way, but making her way to the doors. "Come with me."

Klauden let her lead him outside, easily dismissing those who wanted to share a few words with the happy couple, clearly pleased to be done with such niceties for the evening. Hannah recalled Rory's eagerness as they left the ballroom, and she smiled, then forced herself to push the elf out of her mind.

One person per wedding, she told herself. *Get it together.* She looked at Klauden, leading him down the hall to the stairs. The vampire was following her, face carefully blank. They made it to the second landing when Klauden paused, looking down the hall to the rooms he shared with Solyn.

<*No,*> Hannah told him. <*Come with me.*>

Klauden narrowed his eyes at her. <*You don't have to do this,*> he responded in her mind. <*I know you wish to be with him.*>

<*Not tonight,*> Hannah insisted. She used his hand to pull him close to her, pressing her body against his as she tugged his head down to hers for a kiss that was not gentle. <*Tonight, I am yours,*> she told Klauden, <*and you are mine.*>

"Are you sure?" Klauden whispered against her lips, body hard against hers, but his mind still clinging to some semblance of rational thought. "You don't have to," he repeated.

"I want to," she replied, looking at his face, into his eyes, letting the truth show on her face. "I want you."

Klauden nodded slowly, then raised an eyebrow. "Where?" He wouldn't bring her back to his rooms, and he wouldn't go to Rory's rooms.

"My rooms, silly," Hannah said, leading him up another flight of stairs and down the hall to her suite.

Klauden followed her in slowly, mind recalling the last time he had been in those rooms. "I was so wrong," he said, thinking of her in the tub, standing naked in front of the mirror.

"You were," she said, "and you weren't." She walked to the bedroom, lingering in the doorway, waiting for him to follow her.

Klauden took a few steps, then paused. "What about Rory?"

"What about him?" Hannah kept her voice neutral, pushing away thoughts of her other husband. Rory wasn't here now. Tonight ... was about Klauden.

"I thought..." His voice trailed off.

"You thought what? That I would marry you, then leave you alone on our wedding night?" She frowned at him. "You really do think I'm a heartless jerk, don't you?"

He shook his head, taking the last few steps to stand before her. "Not heartless," he said, "just sometimes thoughtless. If anything, you have too much heart."

"You have my heart," she told him, "and my soul. Always."

"But?" Klauden prompted, waiting for the part where she confessed, *yet again,* that she chose Rory, as if he didn't already know he wasn't the partner she needed in life.

"But nothing," she said this time, surprising him. "That's it."

"So," he began, reaching out a hand to touch her hair, twisting a curl around one of his fingers, then holding up his hand with the new wedding ring on it, "does this mean I can kiss you again?"

"You can do a lot more than kiss me, Klauden van Sherinak," Hannah promised him. "You're my husband now."

A slow smile crossed Klauden's face as he reached for her, sliding his hands across her bare shoulders and up her neck. "You aren't going to lecture me about normal sex? Tell me how I don't know what I'm doing?" he asked, leaning down to trace a soft line of kisses along her throat, working his way up to find her mouth, kissing her furiously.

"I never said you didn't know what you were doing, but it is funny you should mention normal sex." Hannah laughed, stepping back into the room and leading him to the bed. "I have something for you."

"What?" he asked, eyebrow raising.

"You'll have to find it." Her lips curved into a wicked smile as she sat on the edge of the bed.

Klauden eyed her dress. "I can't imagine you'd be able to hide anything in that dress," he said, "definitely not the top."

Hannah raised an eyebrow at him, knowing that he could glean the knowledge from her mind, but he held back, wanting to maintain the mystery for as long as he could.

"So it must be under here," Klauden said, kneeling before where she sat on the bed, scooting in so his body pressed between her legs.

"Maybe," Hannah said.

Klauden reached down, hands finding her old boots. He lifted the dress up a little, glancing down at her feet. He smiled. "Certainly Millani didn't know you wore those."

Hannah shook her head and shrugged. "I needed something old," Hannah admitted.

Klauden nodded, hand sliding slowly up the back of her calf. "Let me think." He nodded at the dress. "Something new," he said. "Something borrowed?" he asked. "Something blue?"

Hannah smiled, biting her lower lip. He returned the look, desire rising in him as he leaned forward, both hands sliding up her calves, lingering on the back of her knees before slipping up to her thighs. His fingers found the velvet bag and the lace, and he frowned, leaning down to explore. He pushed the skirt up, folding it to reveal her bare thighs and the black lace.

"Take it," Hannah urged. "It's yours if you want it."

Klauden grinned, pushing her back on the bed. "I want it," he said quietly, then bent to place a delicate kiss on her thigh. Hannah shivered, catching the direction of his thoughts. She moved to sit up, to have him open the bag, but he ignored her, sliding her back on the bed once more. "In a moment, chaivin," he told her, mouth moving up the soft sensitive skin of her thigh. "I have always wanted to do this in a proper bed."

Hannah recalled the last time he had dragged her leg over his shoulder, both of them on the cliff outside the castle. They had made love several times on the way to Firene but never in a proper bed, always frantic couplings against rock walls or in the hold of the *Volant*. Her objections died on her lips as he moved closer, and she dissolved into pleasure. When he bit her, his desire bled into her, both of them vibrating with ecstasy.

"Now," Klauden said a while later, face resting on her thigh, hair pressed against his head, "what is this you've got for me?" He untied the black lace slowly, fingers tracing the outline against her skin, then picked up the velvet pouch. "Blue," he breathed, "and borrowed?"

"It's the ring," Hannah told him. "The one from Caga."

Klauden froze, sitting up to look at her. "You wish to wear the ring with me as you did with him?" He wasn't sure how he felt about that. He understood why she had worn it, and it had kept her alone from him and his thoughts. But he had still felt his side of their connection, still felt everything she did that night and the days after.

Hannah shook her head. "No. It's for you."

"Why would I wear it?" he asked. She would still feel him and, through her bond, so would Rory. Her elf would have the same night he had endured, but he wouldn't have Solyn distracting him. He thought of Kira and wondered if the solace of a child was enough. He would know soon enough.

Hannah sat up, leaning close to him, watching the thoughts on his face but trying not to hear them in his mind. She touched him, bringing him back to her. "Because," she said, her fingers tracing his jawline, sliding into his mouth to trace his fangs, "you don't know what it's like without the magic."

"And why would I want to know that?" Klauden focused on the sensation of her touch, his desire building into passion.

Hannah shrugged, pulling away. "Curiosity?" she offered. She leaned down and kissed his chin, moving her mouth slowly, knowing how much he wanted her to kiss him but holding back, mouth just out of reach. "I know what you want right now, and I can give it all to you, and you know the same thing about me." She nodded at the bag in his hand. "That will cut you off from magic, from kevna, from me. You won't be able to read my mind or emotions. You will have to rely on my body to let you know what I want. It will be ... different."

"This is about desire," Klauden breathed, thinking about what it would be like to kiss Hannah without feeling her thoughts around him, to focus on the feel of her lips on his, the softness of her skin, the taste of her blood. "About wanting and waiting." He echoed her words back to her.

"Exactly," she said, "but only if you want it." She paused. "I understand if you don't. Without kevna, you might not feel..."

"Chaivin," he whispered, his fingers tightly holding the bag.

"Yes?"

"I already told you: I know how I feel. I've always known it."

"But you can't be sure," she said, not wanting to start the same argument again but unwilling to let the point go. "It's always been kevna for you."

He caught her hand, forcing her to look at him. "I'm sure," he said. "I went to the beach and touched the creature."

"You did what?" she asked, pausing in her slow torture of his face to look at him. "When?"

"That night on the beach. After you left, I went back." He sighed. "You were so insistent that I had to know. I already knew, but I did it anyway." He looked at her, eyes softening. "It was always you, and it will always be you."

Hannah nodded, her eyes burning as she looked at him—her friend, her mate, her husband. "I do love you," she whispered.

"I know," Klauden replied. He looked down at the bag. "You think I should do this?"

Hannah looked at him. "That's your choice," she said. "I just thought I would let you make it."

"Is it so different, then?" he asked.

Hannah frowned. "Yes. And no."

"Is it better?"

Hannah shook her head. "No. It's just different." She sighed. "If you want to find out, put it on. If not, that's fine too."

"But I won't be able to feel what you want. How can I tell if what I do is good?"

She smirked at him. "Pay attention. Watch. Listen. You're pretty smart. I'm sure you can figure it out."

Klauden frowned, his lips pursed as he considered the possibilities. Finally, he nodded, tilting the pouch and letting the metal circle fall onto his palm. Klauden's presence retreated from her mind, Solyn disappearing entirely. Hannah focused, searching for him, and Klauden was still there, but he was alone. She could no longer see herself through his eyes. Kevna was still present but thinned out. She became aware of another presence as kevna receded, Rory in his rooms singing softly to Kira. He looked up as she felt him.

<Go.>

The word was clear in her mind, then she was back in the room with Klauden, the vampire staring at her with wide eyes. Hannah remembered Rory's words from that morning. He could understand her love for Klauden, but he didn't need to see it. She focused, building a wall between them, determined not to think of him until the morning.

"How do you feel?" she asked Klauden.

"Empty," he replied, reaching out and touching her hand, awe filling his face. "You feel like skin and softness," he whispered.

"Kiss me," she said.

He leaned forward, mouth moving slowly against hers. Hannah relaxed into him, letting herself focus on her physical body without the overwhelming magic that normally swallowed her senses.

"What do you think?" she asked, speaking against his lips, hands sliding down to rub his shoulders through the robe he still wore.

"I'm not sure," he said, biting his lip. "All I feel is..." He shivered as her fingers slid up into his hair, pressing against his scalp, "everything."

"Focus on that," she said, sitting up to face him, lazily untying the laces of his robe. She pushed it off his shoulders slowly, letting the feel of her fingers against his skin linger, physical desire pulsing in her belly as she touched him. She let him undress her, abandoning her boots on the floor and pulling him into the bed with her, pushing him onto his back and climbing on top of him. She felt a small echo of his pleasure at her touch, but it was quiet, subtle, and Klauden's small gasps and moans were more of an indication of what he enjoyed. Hannah took her time teasing him, letting the desire build and recede in small waves.

"How does it feel?" she asked finally, pressing him inside of her and moving slowly.

"Amazing," he breathed, sitting up and wrapping his arms around her back. "So this is your normal sex, then?"

Hannah nodded, leaning down to kiss him as they moved together.

After a moment, Klauden leaned back, eyes closing in pleasure for a moment before he opened them to watch her. "Interesting," he said, "and different. But not enough." Hannah frowned, but then he leaned up to bite her, and pleasure streaked through her. As her mouth found his neck and bit down, she heard his soft words in her mind.

<Yes, chaivin. This. Always this.>

L

The dawn found Hannah laying on her side, Klauden pressed to her back, one arm tucked under her head, the other wrapped around, holding out her left hand so their rings lined up in the faint sunlight. His other hand wore the metal ring from Caganasti, Klauden still cut off from magic. Hannah looked up and over her shoulder at him, tilting her head toward the magic ring.

"You decide you like a life without magic?" she asked.

Klauden chuckled, his soft breath teasing the back of her neck as he moved his arm and hand, pulling her closer into his embrace. "It definitely has its moments."

She raised an eyebrow, settling into his arms. "Could you do it?" she asked quietly. "Live without magic?"

Klauden took a moment to think, and Hannah marveled that while she could still feel his presence, his essence, she couldn't follow his thoughts. Without his side of the bond, she only had a weakened version of kevna, like looking through a filmy window. "I could," he said finally, "but I wouldn't choose to."

"Why?"

"I'm a wizard, chaivin. Spellcraft is what I know." He kissed the back of her neck. "You have spells, but your essence is more than that. You're a warrior in more ways."

"You are more than your magic, Klauden," she told him.

"I am well aware of that, chaivin." He huffed, lips finding the skin of her neck beneath her hair. Hannah shivered, skin prickling pleasantly at his touch. "I love that I can please you," he said quietly, kissing his way around to her neck.

Hannah turned slightly so she could see him. "Why wouldn't you please me?" As soon as the words left her mouth, she grimaced, knowing that she had told him over and over again just how little he satisfied her. He raised his eyebrows, calling her out. "Fine. I've said that. But that's not what I meant."

"Tell me what you meant, chaivin," he said, hand pulling close to her body, sliding from her waist down the curve of her hip.

Hannah smiled, turning around in his arms so she faced him. She put a hand on his hip, her other hand tracing his jawline. "This was never an issue for us," she said, leaning forward to kiss him softly. "The physical part has always been great."

Klauden grinned. "Even without kevna?"

Hannah rolled her eyes. "Last night was amazing," she told him. "And you know it. Stop fishing for compliments."

He smirked, then his face grew serious. "Would it have been enough for us, you think?" Hannah bit her lip, considering.

"I don't know," she said honestly. "We wouldn't have known otherwise, so maybe."

"Do you think your parents had enough at the beginning?"

Hannah shook her head. "No way. Theirs was never a love match. I think maybe my mother loved him in her own way, and she was definitely hurt when Anna and Livenna were born, but no. It was never like this."

"Very few things in this world are like this, chaivin," he said quietly, moving forward for another soft kiss.

"What about your parents?" she prompted. "Are they content?"

Klauden frowned. "I suppose. My father is, but he needs little more than a book to be satisfied with the day." He sighed. "Just like me. But my mother? She probably wanted more."

Hannah touched his face, thinking of his father. "You're not your father, Klauden," she said. "You need more in your life than a library. You deserve more than that."

He smiled at her, leaning down to kiss her again, slow and long. "Thank you for saying that, chaivin." He paused, leaning his forehead against hers, a hand sliding down her side. "Will you leave soon, then?"

Hannah nodded, knowing that he didn't mean leave the bed or the room. "We're heading to Telran. Probably tomorrow."

"And when will I see you again?" His face was open, his eyes hopeful.

Hannah felt her heart grow heavy, knowing she wouldn't see him again for at least a few months, likely not until Solyn had the baby. "Klauden—"

"Don't," he said quickly, covering her mouth with his. "Be with me now," he whispered against her lips.

"I am," she replied, returning the kiss. Klauden lifted his right hand, the metal ring still on his finger. Hannah reached out to touch it, folding her fingers through his. All sense of magic left her, and suddenly, she was just Hannah, and he was just Klauden, and he moved closer to her, mouth claiming hers as his body moved in her, both of them enjoying the physical connection between them.

Later, she rested on his chest, looking around the room she would soon leave. Her hand was still entwined with his, the magic still absent, and she looked up at his face. "What are you thinking about?" she asked.

He looked down at her. "You."

"What about me?" she prompted.

He grinned. "I know you will leave me soon. I know I will not see you again for some time. And I will look forward to seeing you again." He paused, thoughtful. "But I will not ache for you, pine away while you are gone, chaivin."

Hannah leaned up on one elbow, looking down at him. "Good," she said. "Because when we let go of this," she moved their joined hands, "kevna will come back."

He nodded. "Of course. But I am more than my magic. There is more in my life than just kevna."

Hannah smiled at him. "I'm so glad to hear you say that," she told him. "It makes my heart feel better knowing you will be alright without me."

"I will never be without you," he corrected, no doubt thinking of the bond they would always share, no matter how far apart they were in the world, "but I think I can let you go now if you want me to."

"But who will you be without me?" Hannah asked, knowing she had asked herself the same question after leaving home. If she wasn't First Daughter, betrothed of Klauden van Sherinak, who could she be? She smiled, thinking of how much her life had grown in the last years. *I am a mother. I am a Consort. I am a wife. I am more than my parents' expectations.*

Klauden sighed, chest moving. Hannah watched him, knowing that while she wanted to be with Rory, to live with him and their family, part of her would miss Klauden, would think about this moment in bed with him. Her heart was a complicated place, and she was only beginning to understand it.

Her vampire looked at her, lips sliding into a grin. "I will remain myself, Hannah. Haven't you heard?" He lifted an eyebrow. "I am a very important state official these days, slayer of armies and founder of Houses." He brought their hands to his lips, placing a soft kiss on the back of her hand before sliding his fingers free from hers, pulling the ring off and setting it on the small table beside the bed.

Kevna washed over them both, the magic swelling with pleasure and satisfaction. Hannah welcomed the bond, seeing herself through Klauden's eyes again, and she knew that while her life may never be simple, it would definitely be satisfying.

EPILOGUE

"I'm sorry, but did you just say *twins*?" Hannah asked, staring at Millani with wide eyes.

"Oh yes!" the vampire exclaimed, clapping her hands together in delight. "Two boys!"

Hannah glanced over her shoulder to where Rory stood holding Kira, the baby sitting up on the elf's shoulder, a hand buried in her father's hair to hold her steady. "Did you know about this?" she asked.

Rory shook his head, eyes wide. He nodded his head in Kira's direction. "Our hands are full with just the one," he said with a smile. "I can't imagine having two."

"How is Solyn?" Hannah asked. Klauden had assured Hannah that all was well with Solyn, and Hannah could feel warm satisfaction from the fledgling but nothing more. Klauden had done an excellent job keeping the details from her, only saying that all was well as she and Rory journeyed to the newest castle in the Vanya.

"Very well," Millani insisted. "She's looking forward to seeing you." Millani led them deeper into the new castle, some of the bricks still showing the lines of magic from where Klauden and Nicolo had conjured them. Hannah marveled at the sight, knowing that parts of the castle were still under construction. She had never been in a new building like this—her father's castle was ancient, built several centuries before her birth, and the palace in Firene was over a thousand years old, though she couldn't tell by looking at it. The elves kept everything so clean. Hannah wondered if those buildings had smelled like magic when they were newly constructed too.

She followed Millani to Solyn's chambers, the fledgling sitting comfortably in a rocking chair, a blanket wrapped around her waist and tucked underneath the bundle of one baby who nursed in her arms. Klauden stood by the window, the vampire turning as they entered, his handsome face beaming with pride as he looked from the baby he held to Hannah. He was bursting with joy, eyes filling with tenderness as he looked at Solyn, and Hannah smiled, happy to see him so content.

Klauden moved over to her, holding out the bundle in his arms for her. "May I introduce Jorren van Sherinak?" he said. Hannah took the baby carefully, smiling as she stared at the tiny face of the week-old baby. He squirmed in her grip, opening luminous blue eyes that stared at Hannah for a moment before slipping back into sleep.

She looked at Klauden. "He has your eyes," she said softly.

He glanced to where Solyn sat, blue eyes wide and happy as she looked at them. "He has our eyes."

"Kira," Hannah said, turning to face her daughter and Rory, "would you like to meet your cousin?"

Kira giggled, leaning down to stare at the baby in her mother's arms. "This is Jorren," Hannah introduced. Kira's mouth opened wide as she looked at him, the lock of Rory's hair she still held growing tight as she leaned forward. Rory grabbed her hand, sliding his hair free with a wince, and held her so she could stare at the baby.

After a long moment, Kira looked back up. "Jorn," she said, her newfound ability to talk blending the syllables. "Mine," she declared, a word she had already mastered, then turned away, already bored with the spectacle.

Klauden chuckled, and Hannah returned Jorren to his arms, loving the look on his face as he took his son. Hannah stepped over to where Solyn sat nursing the other baby and looked down at him. "Kellus van Sherinak," Solyn introduced. The baby opened his eyes to look up at Solyn's voice, and Hannah stared into eyes as green as her own. She looked up, seeing Klauden watching her.

<*He has your eyes,*> Klauden said in her mind, and she nodded. They had discussed this possibility, that Klauden's child might have something of her since she had been in Solyn's body when she conceived.

Hannah looked down at the baby. "Hello, Kellus," she said softly. She looked up again, reaching out for Kira. Her daughter looked down at her other cousin, face contemplative. "This is your cousin Kellus," Hannah told her.

"Kels," Kira said formally, looking down at the baby.

Hannah grinned at her daughter, tickling her belly gently. "Are you going to claim him too? Is he yours?"

Kira stopped giggling and looked down at her cousin for a long moment, eyes contemplative, but then she looked back across the room to where Klauden held Jorren. She shook her head, pointing at Klauden. "Jorn mine." She looked down at Kellus. "Kels nice."

A small shiver ran down Hannah's spine at the words, and she met Klauden's gaze across the room, then looked at Rory, who was reaching out to take Kira.

Rory looked at his daughter. "Kira," he said firmly. "No claiming cousins as your personal property." He looked up at Hannah and Klauden, then added quietly, "And you're too young to stake claim on any boys, you hear me?" He speared Klauden with a glare. "I know you like to promise children for marriage when they are born. I expect you to keep my daughter out of any of those plans."

Klauden nodded solemnly, but his thoughts were searching, recalling something Nicolo had said a long time ago, something about a prophecy involving twins and a girl of mixed blood.

<No.> Hannah stopped him. *<I don't want to hear about that,>* she insisted. *<No more prophecies or destinies or ancient magic,>* she told him. *<Just life and the choices we make.>*

Klauden nodded and smiled, looking around at his family, joy filling him and spilling into every person in the room as he let the prophecy go, living in the moment.

<Yes, chaivin. We chose well.>

The End

ABOUT THE AUTHOR

Author of the Klauden's Ring Saga and the Conjuring Fascination series, JM Paquette writes fantasy and paranormal romance novels. When she isn't writing, she can be found teaching English to college students as Dr. Paquette or watching her favorite Russian shifter romance movie, *I Am Dragon*. Her areas of expertise include the history of the English language and the intricacies of grammatical rules, but her favorite class to teach is on *Lord of the Rings*. (If you've ever wondered why English is a crazy language, watch her video series on YouTube under Editor JMPaquette!) She enjoys editing manuscripts for academic and creative writers alike, and she adores tabletop roleplaying (THAC0, anyone?) where her halfling ranger/Twi'lek adept/vampire wizard/[insert race and class here] is often underestimated. You can also find her guest co-hosting the podcast Drinking with Authors—even though she doesn't drink, she loves getting to know fellow authors! Check out JM Paquette at authorjmpaquette.com and 4horsemenpublications.com and as Author JM Paquette on Facebook and Instagram.

Connect with JM:
www.authorJMPaquette.com
www.facebook.com/authorjmpaquette/
Email: authorjmpaquette@gmail.com

OTHER BOOKS BY JM PAQUETTE

Klauden's Ring (Klauden's Ring #1)
Solyn's Body (Klauden's Ring #2)
Hannah's Heart (Klauden's Ring #3)
The InBetween (Klauden's Ring #4)

Call Me Forth (Conjuring Fascination Prequel)
Invite Me In (Conjuring Fascination #1)
Keep Me Close (Conjuring Fascination #2)

Heart of Stone (Rock Star Fairy Tales #1)
One Mummy to Go, Please! (Shawarma Warrior King #1) with
Beau Lake

The General Guide to Worldbuilding

BOOK CLUB QUESTIONS

1. The Klauden's Ring series is filled with destiny, a force that Hannah is determined to fight. How much influence do you think prophecies and so-called destinies have on individuals?

2. Hannah is hellbent on making her own decisions. Do you think she has free will, or are her actions the result of forces beyond her control?

3. Hannah repeats her belief that love induced by magic isn't "real" love because the feelings aren't something she has chosen for herself. Do you think love is a choice? We say people fall in love, like someone falls off a cliff, like gravity—how does that saying reconcile with the idea of love as a conscious decision?

4. Klauden and Hannah discuss the benefits of having magic, and Hannah suggests that being a wizard or spellcaster is a good thing, but it's not as strong in a fight as a warrior with a sword. Do you agree with her? Why or why not?

5. Hannah spends a lot of time fighting to remain herself, staying true to the person she wants to be, and even undergoes a dangerous ritual to keep her magic. What would you endure to retain your skill set?

6. In the end, Hannah chooses not to break her bonds with either Klauden or Rory. What do you make of her decision to accept kevna and all that comes with it? Would you accept a bond like that with someone? Why or why not?

7. Magnus van Kreeosk takes a surprising turn in this book, choosing to support his daughter and granddaughter and even

acknowledge Rory as his son-in-law. Why do you think he changed from the man Hannah expected to meet at the castle? What kind of future do you predict for their relationship?

8. Milo van Reegan, the Sarkoza, is able to control people with the power of his voice. How would you deal with a vampire who has such a power?

9. Lira and Gorn return in this book. What do you make of their friendship and their positions in Hannah and Rory's lives? (Are you rooting for Lira and Caga to get together? Why or why not?)

10. You know the choice that Hannah makes, but what would you have done in her place? Team Rory or Team Klauden or Team Both?

11. (Spoilers) Millani van Reegan and Linus Tallerin seem to have a connection. What do you think will happen with this unlikely couple? (Stay tuned for their story!)

Discover more at
4HorsemenPublications.com

10% off using HORSEMEN10